To my perfect wife! Thank
this possible.
　　xxx [signature]

THE RISK OF BEING CERTAIN

Jonathan Small

The characters and events portrayed in this book are fictitious. Any similarity to real persons, living or dead, is coincidental and not intended by the author.

No part of this book may be reproduced, or stored in a retrieval system, or transmitted in any form or by any means, electronic, mechanical, photocopying, recording, or otherwise, without express written permission of the author.

Copyright © 2022 Jonathan Small

All rights reserved.

ISBN: 979-8-8335-2767-2
Imprint: Independently Published

To Shisha

1

Maybe it was just economics at play here…

Like some sort of twisted game of supply and demand. Neanderthals with no imagination and far too much testosterone than was good for them. Creating demand and manipulating the market to the extent that this sort of aberration came into existence.

What *was it*?! Was this a human being?

Stephen felt himself staring. Then, awkwardly, wondering whether or not she had even noticed…

'Are you okay, Steve?'

'Oh. Yes, sorry, just lost in thought. I've a lot going on at work at the moment, just zoned out there for a bit.'

She *did* notice.

But did he care?

Not really, but he decided that he ought to at least pretend to pay some attention. She looked a bit put out. He found himself wondering how long she would be able to sustain the thought.

'You were talking about how terrible it is that your brand of self-tan is out of stock on Amazon?'

'Yeah, exactly, it's just not *fair*! I now have to go to the pharmacy to get it, and it costs 79p more for a smaller bottle, I mean, how ridiculous? It's not just the cost, it's like living in the Stone Age or something. Having to go to a high street shop in 2019 to get simple supplies?! Now I know how *old* people must have felt before the internet, they must have all been bloody miserable. All the time!'

'Yes, I'm sure they were.'

Was she *serious*?

This is why he didn't make a habit of going out on dates anymore. At least, that's what he told himself, in order to avoid reflecting on the genuine reasons. It sounded plausible enough to justify his lack of effort, on the basis that all the intelligent and interesting people had clearly got lucky at school or university, and there was nobody left.

Of course, this was utter nonsense, and he would never even dream of doling out that excuse to another human being when asked the question. But then, it had always been easier to for him to lie to himself than it had been to lie to others.

It had been about half an hour, and they'd gone from discussing how the rain ruins hairstyles, to the great Amazon spray-tan controversy of the 21st century. He wondered what was next?

It's not that he didn't *want* to try and stop his mind drifting, he just lacked the energy necessary to snap out of it.

This was Kenny's fault. That obsequious little turd of an intern of his had set this date up. Presumably in an attempt to butter him up. Well, it had backfired. Stephen found himself musing over the idea of exacting some sort of hideous revenge, when he realised that his date had clearly picked up his lingering state of distraction.

'What'd you say you did for a living, Cindy? Kenny told me you run your own Company?'

'Yeah, I'm in marketing.'

'Marketing?'

'Yeah, I'm sort of famous actually. I'm an influencer on Instagram.'

In that moment, it occurred to Stephen that Kenny may not have arranged this date for the purpose of buttering him up. The little bugger must have known about this woman all along. He was probably sitting in the office at that precise moment, having a quiet chuckle to himself over a cup of coffee. To be fair, it was a well-orchestrated ruse, but Stephen only had himself to blame, because when Kenneth had dangled the bait in front of him the previous day, he'd missed the opportunity to join the relevant dots.

The intern had shown Stephen a photograph of the subject, and told him, in fairly vague terms, that she was an entrepreneur.

He should have realised at that point, that it was seldom the case that people who looked like Cindy ran their own businesses. At least not *traditional* businesses.

Of course this was a ridiculously old fashioned and prejudiced assumption. But Stephen was the type of individual who tended towards generalisations of this nature. As far as he was concerned, young, pretty women didn't occupy themselves with difficult or challenging careers, not necessarily because they lacked the intellect, but because their looks made it unnecessary.

Hiding from the world had made him a bit naïve, especially when it came to women. But since he never really spent time with people who challenged his views, he neatly avoided the exercise of re-evaluating them. He actually liked women, but he couldn't figure them out, so he protected himself by treating them with a cold detachment that made him come across as a misogynist.

Cindy looked like one of those models from the front of a women's magazine. The ones their readers all wanted to look like; but never could. Blonde hair, blue eyes, and a body so perfect it looked like it was sculpted. In fact, Stephen surmised that were she to find her way on to one of those covers, she wouldn't even need any airbrushing. They could take a photo of her with a old phone camera, and just blow it up for the magazine.

And yet there he was, sitting and complaining to himself about being on a coffee date with her. Maybe *he* was the one with the issues? Maybe his boss, Jim, was right? Maybe he needed a holiday?

'What do you do, Steve?'

He'd wondered how long it was going to take for that subject to come up. He wasn't sure how he was going to explain it though.

'I'm in sales.'

That was technically true, he thought to himself. A stock broker *is*, essentially, in sales.

'Oooh that's sooooooo cool! What do you sell? I hope it's something awesome like phones or cars? I mean, it's still cool if it's boring stuff like hardware or kitchens. But if it's something *cool*, I can definitely offer my services to promote your products.'

This was going to be tougher than he thought.

'Actually, Cindy, I work on the stock market, so I'm more of a market trader really.'

'Oh, so like, you sell stuff at a market, like groceries and stuff? Is there money in that?'

'Loads. If you sell the right stuff in the right area.'

Maybe out of sheer boredom, but more likely out of misplaced frustration and a streak of childish malice, he decided to get creative. It wasn't as if he planned on ever seeing this woman again, he may as well have some fun.

'Cool, so you have money then Steve? I mean, not that it's the most important thing, but you know, just *wondering*.'

'Naa, I got robbed by Somali pirates last summer and they took all my savings. I was taking the ferry to the Isle of Wight on holiday, and got kidnapped. I was taking all my cash to the island so I could set up a market stall there for the tourist season.'

'Oh you poor *thing*! That's just *awful*, how did you escape?'

He wondered if she was actually curious, or if she was just trying to be polite and tactful.

'I ended up jumping out and swimming to shore. I'm a really strong swimmer. I suppose the adrenalin got me through the cold, it was quite an ordeal.'

'Oh wow, that's incredible!'

Silence descended… it worked… maybe he'd manage an early escape now.

'Steve… I want to hear *all* about your story, it sounds fascinating!'

He hadn't expected that response. Although he was just insightful enough to realise that he'd asked for it. Karma clearly wasn't *just* a bitch… she was vacuous bottle blonde covered in self-tan… On reflection, it stood to reason.

'Thanks, Cindy. It's really kind of you to take an interest, but it's quite a long story and I need to get going.'

'I understand Steve, let's set up another coffee date… maybe *dinner*?'

***

Stephen's little coffee date with Cindy had been relatively early. It was a Monday morning. The one day in the week when Stephen went into the office later than usual; so he figured he may as well use the time semi-productively. It was efficient. It also gave him an excuse, and an incentive to keep the date short. He was back in the office by half past ten.

'Kenny! You little shit! Get in here!'

'Morning boss, how was the coffee date with Cindy?'

'You bloody-well *know* how the date went, you prat! Was that your idea of a practical joke?'

'Come on boss, I just thought you could do with a bit of fun. I mean, did you *see* her? She's hotter than the end of a blowtorch!'

'Kenny, unfortunately I also have a sense of hearing. She had an IQ in single bloody digits, and she was about as deep as a saucer.'

'Boss, you're uptight. You need a break.'

'I need more intelligent staff, Ken.'

'No doubt boss, but seriously; Jim asked me to try get you to take some leave.'

'What were you doing talking to *my* boss, Kenneth?'

'It was just in passing really, it's no secret that you haven't taken leave in three years.'

He was right. Stephen didn't actually consider Kenneth to be a bad kid. He reminded him of himself when he was fourteen years younger. Full of hope, and going through life with blinkers on, jumping from one assignment to the next, trying to find an edge, make a name, get a permanent position so he could get in on the game and make some money.

Not much had changed for him in that respect. Maybe that's why he was so exhausted? Maybe that's why he tried so hard to push Kenny? Maybe the youngster was like some sort of reflection of a younger Stephen West?

Would the older version of the man be able to teach him the *real* lessons he needed to learn about this particular rat race? Before he woke up at thirty eight. Alone. Obsessed with climbing the greasy pole.

The problem was, try as he might, he couldn't really bring himself to actually be hard on his bright young intern. He liked him too much, and he indulged him as much as he indulged himself.

Stephen wasn't even remotely interested in taking a break. He was willing to concede that he needed to find a way to recharge, because he was exhausted. Jim was probably right; but going on holiday would be like admitting defeat. It would show weakness, or perhaps even laziness.

If he worked just a *bit* harder, that promotion to the board was likely to come through in time for Christmas. *That* would be a fantastic Christmas gift worth celebrating.

'Whatever Ken, just do me a favour, don't set me up on any more bloody dates. *Ever*!'

'Affirmative, boss.'

'Do you know what's in my diary for today?'

'You have a meeting with the legal team now at eleven, and then you're playing golf with Mr Roberts down in Surrey this afternoon.'

'The legal team?'

'I don't know the whole story boss, but apparently they need to speak with you urgently about something.'

He hated being summoned by the lawyers. He was convinced that they always treated everyone as if they were children, regardless of the fact that, as far as he could tell, very few of them had the faintest idea about the real mechanics of what he and his colleagues did. They also treated traders like criminals, and asked impertinent rhetorical questions whenever any transactions were even *slightly* adventurous or risky.

'Well you'd better sharpen your pencil Ken, because they're likely to rattle off all sorts of compliance bullshit that we'll have to pretend to take seriously.'

'I won't be there, boss.'

'What do you mean?'

'Apparently they want to see you alone.'

'That sounds bloody ominous. Well, at least I'm getting out of the office later, even if it's only to play golf. It almost makes up for it.'

'Indeed boss. Want me to come caddy for you?'

'Trying to get out of the office as well, *are we*?'

'Come on boss, the fresh air is likely to be good for me. Maybe if I'd gotten more fresh air in the first place, I wouldn't have been daft enough to set you up on that ghastly date. The air conditioned environment I live in here at the office isn't doing me any good, it's melting my brain.'

'Fair enough, I suppose you haven't much brain to spare. We'll get a cart and you can drive me round. What time do we tee off?'

'Just after lunch boss, I'll arrange the kit. Thanks for letting me come along.'

'Don't say I never treat you well, Ken!'

'I spose you're going to tell me that when you were my age, your boss made you lick his boots clean, and carry the clubs around instead of driving.'

'*Something* like that!'

'Well, I'm glad you're so evolved then boss!'

'Pull your tongue out of my arse you little shite, and get the stuff ready. I don't know how long the lawyers plan on detaining me, and we can't afford to be late.'

'On it!'

'Oh, and do me a favour. I haven't had the chance to look at the paper this morning. Find me a copy, and ask Mary to get hold of the tech people. I can't log onto my personal trading account for some odd reason. They're usually good at fixing that sort of thing.'

'Will do.'

***

Stephen drifted into the large boardroom that had been allocated for his morning meeting with the lawyers. He had no intention of being early, so when he arrived at the precise time scheduled for the start of the engagement, the other participants were already ensconced in their heavy leather chairs at the other side of the vast mahogany table.

The lawyers always chose to use a boardroom which was capable of seating at least three times as many people as were due to be present at their meetings; and always sat alongside one another, facing their counterparts in what looked conspicuously like some sort of judicial panel.

He wasn't sure whether this was a conscious and deliberately contrived practice, designed to intimidate; or whether it was simply a force of habit, bred into them by constantly having to sit in front of judges and adjudicators. It was probably a little of both.

There were three of them, two of whom he recognised. Lawyers always seemed to travel in packs though, so he wasn't surprised by their number. He assumed that the third one was the latest shark to be introduced into the company pool.

The legal team at the company seemed to grow and proliferate like nettles in spring. If you looked away for longer than a few minutes, by the time you looked back, there would be another one popping their spiky head up and daring you to object. Perhaps the board of directors felt that the more of them they had on the payroll, the safer the company was going to be - like some some sort of insurance policy. Maybe they were right? But Stephen thought it was a bit of a waste of resources.

'Good morning, Stephen. I'm sure you've met my colleague, Sarah Greystone. This is William Morris, from Glinbrook LLC, the company's solicitors.'

'Yes, we're acquainted. Good morning Sarah. Pleased to meet you Mr Morris.'

'I'm recording this meeting. I take it you don't object to that.'

'Well, Delores, I don't expect that it would make any difference if I did, so…'

'Quite.'

'What have I allegedly done, or *not done*, this time?'

'Have you looked at your personal brokerage account this morning, Stephen.'

'Actually, it's funny you should mention that. I've been struggling with some technical issues on it. For some reason, I can't access my profile, and I'm very irritated, because I made some rather large trades last week and I need access to it.'

'Your account has been frozen.'

'Excuse me?!'

'You heard me Stephen, don't make me repeat myself.'

'Who froze it?!'

'The Financial Conduct Authority.'

'Why?!'

'You're being investigated for insider trading.'

'Bullshit!'

'I'm putting that response down to frustration, Stephen. I remind you that although this meeting is privileged, it *is* still being recorded. The privilege, in this instance, vests with the company, so we're obliged to point out that whatever you say to us will be reported to the board of directors. In the circumstances, we suggest that you also appoint the services of your own solicitor; sooner rather than later.'

'I've done nothing wrong, Delores, this is a stitch up. If I'd been trading unlawfully, I'd be stinking rich by now, and I probably wouldn't be working anymore.'

'Stephen, don't play games with us. Contrary to what you may believe, we're on your side. As of this morning, you *are* a lot richer, and you know that.'

'I'm not following you.'

'You're a trader Stephen, you will have read the morning Financial Times.'

'Actually, I haven't, yet.'

'Excuse me?'

'Delores, we don't all sleep with a copy of the Financial Times under our pillows. I've been tied up this morning.'

'Well, assuming you're telling me the truth, you need to know that as of this morning, the share price of Ringmire Pharmaceuticals PLC fell through the floor.'

'Jesus!'

'Again… you're being recorded, Stephen.'

'But the results of the application aren't due to come out until tomorrow…'

'What application?'

'It's a long story…'

'It had better be a very good one, Stephen. Because the FCA knows you took a massive short position on the stock last week, and the knock that Ringmire's taken in the market is so significant that it seems nigh on impossible for you not to have had insider knowledge.'

'Well, I didn't. And they can't bloody prove that I did!'

'It's not that simple, Stephen.'

'Mr Morris is right. You can't just ignore this and pretend that it'll go away.'

'It's never that simple with you people, is it?'

'What are you trying to imply?'

'With respect, Delores, you lawyers and your cohorts at the FCA ooze around the city in your expensive suits, patronising the people who actually understand the financial markets, and then try and destroy anyone who is intelligent enough to make some real money.'

'Well, you certainly know all about using the pejorative prefix of *"with respect"*, you clearly aren't that different from *"us lawyers"*.'

'You know what I mean…'

'Stephen, we aren't the ones out to get you here, we didn't make the allegation. We're the ones who have to safeguard the interests of the company. I'd have thought that that would be abundantly clear to somebody as intelligent and resourceful as you. But let me spell it out for you, in case it remains unclear.'

'Go ahead.'

'You are a senior trader at this company, so whatever you do, even if it's for your *personal* account, reflects on us. Fortunately, your little windfall didn't involve any stock that we had a position on, and we know that you cleared the trade with compliance before you did it, so as to give them the opportunity to check for conflicts of interest. That's all very well and good, but the fact of the matter remains: you took a significant position on a very insignificant stock, and made an absolute killing in the process. You don't need to be a lawyer to understand that it looks suspicious, do you?'

'So it's now illegal to make money by trading intelligently, is it?'

'It's illegal to trade with insider knowledge, and coincidences of this nature are so statistically improbable, that they have to be investigated. Don't pretend not to understand, it's unbecoming of somebody in your position.'

'It's unbecoming of the FCA to harass people and freeze their personal trading accounts.'

'It's their *job*!'

'They're arseholes.'

'That may be the case, Stephen, but it's irrelevant. So stop behaving like a little child.'

She stared across the table coldly, and let the admonition hang in the air. Stephen realised that he was taking his frustration out on her, and that this wouldn't help matters; but he hadn't really had the time to think through the situation with sufficient clarity to enable him to be dispassionate about it.

'So what do you want from me then? I suppose you want to hear my side of the story?'

The room went quiet for long enough that he started to feel a little awkward. William Morris broke the silence.

'Actually, Stephen, I don't think that would be wise.'

'Sorry, what?'

'William's right. Stephen, you'll need to secure the services of your own solicitor. What you say may give rise to a conflict of interest between yourself and the company, so it's best for all concerned that we do this strictly by the book.'

'Then why on earth did you call me into this meeting in the first place?'

'To inform you that you're being placed on gardening leave until the investigation has run its course. We can't have one of our senior staff members trading on behalf of our clients whilst under investigation.'

'That's outrageous!'

'It's standard procedure. One more thing; you understand that you're not allowed to discuss the specific details of the case with anyone, even internally.'

'Yes, I get it.'

2

Stephen left the boardroom feeling numb. He picked up a copy of the Financial Times on the way back to his office, and once he got there, he asked his personal assistant, Mary, to hold his calls. He closed his door and began the process of piecing together what had happened.

After about half an hour he heard a knock at the door. It was Kenny.

'What's happened, boss? You look a bit shaken.'

'I'm in a bit of shit, Ken.'

'What have you done?'

'Can't really talk about it, but I took a gamble on my personal account and shorted a stock last week. Turns out my hunch was right, and I've made a small fortune.'

'So, you should be celebrating!'

'It's not that simple. I made so much money on the trade, that the authorities think I was up to no good.'

'They think you had inside knowledge, boss?'

'Yip.'

'But obviously you didn't, *did* you?'

'Course I didn't.'

'Well then, it'll all work itself out, won't it.'

'It's tricky Ken, I've just read the newspapers. The reason I made the gamble is actually not related to why it paid off, which is more than a little unfortunate, when it comes to trying to demonstrate that I didn't have any knowledge.'

'Boss, I understand I really ought to know this stuff by now, but I don't *really* get the practicalities of short trading. We covered the theory briefly at uni, but I obviously wasn't paying too much attention. Can you explain it to me?'

'It's actually quite simple Ken. Do you honestly not know how it works?'

'I sort of do. But it's not exactly like I get to see it in practice.'

'I suppose you're right. It just looks complicated from afar, and they tend not to teach you too much about it at university. It's also frowned upon in some circles, because it's always been associated with all sorts dodgy conduct.'

'So how does it really work then, boss?'

'Right. So as you know, most of the time, we buy stock with the calculated hope that it will improve in value, either over the long or the short term. It's pretty much what we do, day in and day out, and if we're clever, our calculations are likely to be more or less accurate, so we make money for our clients over the chosen period of any given investment.'

'Yes, I suppose that that is a fair simplification, boss.'

'As you also know, the time period and the spread of stock is important, because most stock tends to fluctuate in value over time. What we generally aim to do, is ensure that in spite of the fluctuations, there is a decent upward trend over the timeframe we've specified with our clients. As far as spread is concerned, we hope that what we gain on the swings is more than we lose on the roundabouts. If we judge this correctly, our clients will make significant gains, despite losses in certain specific stock. The strong ones ought to make up for the weak, and so on and so forth.'

'Yeah, so far, that's pretty standard, boss.'

'But what if you think you know a stock is going to take a nosedive in value, and you want to make money off of the downturn?'

'This is where I get a bit lost, boss. I know I should really understand this by now, but I honestly still battle to imagine how you could *make* money off of a stock with a rapidly diminishing value.'

'There's a very interesting mechanic which is perfectly legal, but largely misunderstood. Also, it's highly risky, so I suppose that the authorities don't really mind if there are those of us brave or stupid enough to try and exploit it. Let's say you think a stock is going to take a bit of a knock for various reasons. You're actually allowed to *borrow* it against some form of collateral, and sell it off, as long as you return it on a specified future date.'

'How do you *borrow* shares, boss? They aren't exactly physical.'

'Well, it's all a little abstract really. But you can, as long as you have sufficient equity to cover the value. That is to say, the assets you put up as collateral obviously need to match or exceed the value of the shares being borrowed.'

'Okay.'

'So let's say you borrow one hundred shares, valued at ten pounds a share. You agree to return the shares, *not the value of the shares*, just the shares by no later than a certain time on a specified date; the timeframe is often flexible though, and would depend on a number of variables. Sometimes there isn't a specific time constraint, but the lender can usually 'recall' the shares - which is to say: request their immediate return - at any time. If this request precedes the expiry of a set term, the lender may incur a penalty though.'

'Right.'

'So after you've *borrowed* the shares, you sell them on to a third party for the prevailing market value. Let's say, for the sake of our example, it's £1000.00 at the time of the transaction.'

'Okay, so now you have £1000.00 in your brokerage account, but you owe it to the party you've borrowed the shares from?'

'No… you weren't listening, you owe them *100 shares* - value has nothing to do with it, yet.'

'Okay.'

'So, just before you're due to return the shares, something happens in the market, and the value of the shares drops significantly, let's say it's pretty drastic, and they are now only worth £7.00 a share.'

'Doesn't sound too drastic, that?'

'It is when you're doing it at any reasonable scale, young man!'

'Ah, I see.'

'So in our little scenario, we would have to buy the shares in the market at £7.00 apiece, and return them. The profit we would make would be the difference between what we sold them for, and what we paid to get them back. So we would have made £300.00 in a few days, off of a £1000.00 investment. Obviously, in the real world, there would be securities lending and brokerage fees payable on the transaction, but let's put those aside for the sake of argument.'

'Shit…'

'So you see how significant that would be at a serious scale.'

'Wow!'

'Of course, the risk is that they *don't* devalue. If they actually *appreciate* in value, even by a small amount, you'll be seriously out of pocket - especially if you do it on a large scale. In that scenario, the party on the receiving end of the transaction will be no worse off. That's why they don't mind lending out the shares in the first place. The deck is usually stacked in their favour, because most decent stocks tend to appreciate in value in the ordinary course of events. Betting *with* the market is usually safer in the long term.'

'So you did this at scale recently, and won?'

'Massively!'

'But if it's legal, then what's the problem?'

'The problem is that I took a *significant* position on it. To give you a vague idea without getting into any inappropriate detail: I put up seventy five percent of my portfolio as collateral for the transaction; and I've been playing the game for a while, so the portfolio isn't exactly peanuts. The FCA assumes that I must have had insider knowledge, because putting up that kind of collateral would be almost insane if I didn't.'

'So, sorry if this sounds impertinent boss, but if you *didn't* have knowledge, why take such a massive risk?'

'I can't really tell you that Ken, I didn't have insider knowledge, but I was damned sure of my position. Once it all comes out in the wash, I'll take you through it and explain my reasoning, but I've been advised by the lawyers to stay quiet on the details; and the less you know, the better.'

'I take it I'm not going golfing with you and Jim then? I suppose you'll need to speak to him about it in private.'

'Yeah, sorry, I'll make it up to you. I promise.'

***

At the start of the day, Stephen was actually looking forward to his game of golf. He didn't ever really enjoy the game itself; he didn't see the point of chasing a small round object around a series of oddly shaped gardens, and he resented the fact that his colleagues and higher-ups seemed to expect participation as part of the job. But today, somewhat uncharacteristically, he was looking forward to the fresh country air, and the opportunity to get some time alone with Jim.

That was, until he'd been confronted by Delores Macintyre and her cohorts.

Jim wasn't only his boss. He was a mentor, and something of a surrogate father figure. It wasn't that Stephen didn't have a father of his own. It was just that he didn't get along particularly well with his own father. Jim had stepped in to fill that gap for Stephen, and although it was difficult for him to admit it, he relied more heavily on this relationship than he ought to have done.

Jim obviously knew what had happened, and the thought of disappointing the old man hurt. It hurt more than a little, because in some strange way that he hadn't really taken the time to consider properly, Jim was closer to him than anybody else.

'You're a damn fine trader, Stephen.'

'Thanks Jim. But I sense you're going to qualify that statement.'

'Well, clearly you're bright enough to know when I'm priming you for something.'

'I should hope so.'

'That stunt you pulled with Ringmire was seriously stupid, son. It wasn't like you.'

'*That stunt* just made me a fortune, Jim. Also, I didn't have any bloody insider knowledge, I promise you. I'd done some research on an unrelated piece of information about the company, and it was just a coincidence that the bottom fell out.'

'Save the details of your thinking behind the trade for the lawyers, I don't want to know, and I probably *shouldn't know,* either.'

'But you believe me, don't you?'

'I *do* believe you Stephen. Because I know you aren't actually daft enough to get mixed up in that sort of nonsense on purpose. But…'

'But what?'

'Come on, my lad. I know the basics; the lawyers have already shared them with the board. You put up three quarters of your personal portfolio as security for that trade. Not only does that make you look as guilty as sin, it's horrendously reckless.'

'So? It was *my* money Jim, I wasn't doing it with clients' funds. Besides, I couldn't do anything like that with clients' funds. Even if I wanted to. You know I would have to put in an investment research report to the board, so it's not as if I'm a risk to the company or its clients.'

'Stop being so obtuse Stephen, of course you're a bloody risk to the company. We can't have our investors finding out that our senior traders are being investigated by the FCA! It would land us in all manner of shite.'

'I didn't think of that, sorry Jim.'

'It's more than that though, Stephen. I need to know *Why*?'

'Why what?'

'Why gamble away almost all of the money you've amassed over the better part of the last two decades on a single short trade. If you *aren't* guilty of insider trading, you're clearly unbalanced.'

'I was bored…'

'Not good enough. There's another reason, and I need to know; because your future at the company depends on it!'

'You can't be serious?!'

'Stephen, your strange motivations aside; what you did wasn't only reckless, it was also done behind our backs. You never shared your insight on the stock you traded with anyone else at the company. I know you put the trade through compliance in accordance with the rules, but that's just ticking boxes for the sake of good form, it's not being a team player.'

'So my personal trades all have to be discussed with the "*team*" then?'

'It's more complicated than that, and you know it! I understand that we don't have a position on Ringmire stock, but you know that Smith is busy doing research on taking positions in various pharmaceutical stocks at the moment. You didn't bother to share your insights with him. Assuming you acted without inside knowledge, we could *also* have taken a stab at the stock and made some money if the two of you worked hastily on a proposal together. But you didn't bother.'

'Smith's a wanker!'

'I know that. I can't stand him *either*, but he's part of the team, so we have to suck it up and work with the bastard. Your loyalty to the company has been brought into question, and *I'm* the poor sod on the board who has to stand up and plead your case.'

'I never asked you to do that, Jim.'

'Well, I have. So stop being so bloody ungrateful, and tell me what's going on in that complicated head of yours.'

'Okay fine! You want to know? Here it bloody-well is! I'm sick and tired of grovelling at the feet of people who aren't as clever as I am. Half of the people above me in the food chain have less than half of my ability, but they all went to fancy independent schools, and have Oxbridge degrees, so they have a leg up.'

'Is that what you think? Seriously?'

'It's true, Jim.'

'No. It's not!'

'…'

'The name of the company is Ashden, Cole & Roberts, right?'

'Yes.'

'Arthur Ashden, Anne Cole and James Roberts. Not *one* of the three of us came from independent schools and fancy universities. Did you know that?'

'I…'

'You don't even know who you work for, *do you?*'

'I just assumed…'

'You have a bloody great chip on your shoulder, because you think you come from an underprivileged background. You don't. Your dear old dad was a banker. I'll grant you, that he was the first generation in your family to come out of pretty bad circumstances, and I'll even concede that he may have struggled a little bit because of that fact; but that's no reason for you to be bitter about your lot in life. *My* dad was a postman, and I went through school and university on scholarships. Arthur and Anne's stories aren't remarkably different from mine.'

'But…'

'But why don't we only hire and promote graduates from impoverished backgrounds, and shitty little colleges?'

Stephen went quiet. He didn't quite know how to respond to that point.

'Because we have to be commercially realistic, and recognise the fact that clever graduates from fancy private schools and universities get along well with our clients, and have had the benefit of superlative education, which taught them to think critically, and relate very well to other wealthy people. Not everyone brought up with a silver spoon in their mouths is famously intelligent, but by the same token, the reverse is *also* true. The cream always rises to the top in time, which is exactly where you're headed, if you get your head out of your arse, and learn a little humility.'

Stephen was a lot of things. Humble wasn't one of them; and although he wasn't especially self-aware, he knew it. It was part of the reason his relationship with his father was in tatters, and part of the reason didn't easily make new friends. He was generally well liked by his colleagues, but that was because he didn't spend too much time with them outside of work.

'Sorry Jim, I just grew up in the shadow of people who always seemed to have it easier than we did. By *we*, I mean my family. My parents broke themselves to make sure we had opportunities that others just had automatically.'

'You *think* they had them automatically… and I'm sure some of them *did*. That's the way generational wealth works, my lad. *Your* kids will have those advantages, if you ever stop mucking about and have kids one day.'

'*You* don't have kids, Jim.'

'That's not for want of trying, son. We wanted kids desperately, but we weren't able to have any.'

'I'm not sure I want kids.'

'That's okay too; but if you *do* end up having kids, they won't experience the feeling you're describing, because you're already a very wealthy individual. I know you don't get along with your father, but he set you up for the life you have, and you should be inordinately grateful for that. Don't piss it all away, because you feel like you've been dealt a poor hand.'

'Don't get me wrong Jim, I'm very happy with what I've managed to achieve in life.'

'That's all very well and good son, but are you happy in general? Not just with what you've achieved. That's *pride*, it isn't *happiness*.'

'Yeah… of course I'm happy, Jim. I make six figures, and I'm only thirty eight years old; I have an intellectually challenging and rewarding job; and I'm not tied down by anything. I also have young Kenny setting me up on dates with gorgeous, impressionable girls.'

Jim let out a massive sigh and shook his head.

'Do you actually *believe* the shite you talk young man? Or are you just so tired that you're running on autopilot? I mean, did you just memorise that crap, or what?'

'Jim, what are you getting at? I'm successful, in objective terms. What else *is* there, really?'

'Christ son, being successful in objective terms is by no means the route to happiness. Earning five grand a year more than the minimum wage, and living in a flat with running water is successful in *"objective terms"*! Sometimes I wonder how bright you really are.'

'Well, to be honest Jim, I never actually gave it much thought. Life sort of just happens, and you get on with it, don't you?'

'You do. To start with, Steve; then you grow a brain and start using it to reflect and look for meaning. Thing is; if you aren't really happy, and you don't *know* yourself well enough to gain a realistic insight into what you picture for your future, you could end up burning out by forty and going insane. We don't sell fucking apples and oranges, my boy. The job's not soft. You know that.'

'Again, Jim, I feel like I'm at a disadvantage, because I haven't really considered it.'

'You *are* at a disadvantage Stephen, because you're too focussed on making money and climbing the ladder. Those aren't sustainable long-term objectives.'

'They *aren't*?'

'Money is secondary young man; it's a means to an end. The moment it becomes the end itself, you have a problem, because then what you *have* will never be enough.'

'So? I'm still battling to see your point here Jim.'

'The point is this, Stephen: once (and only *if*) you manage to clear your name with the FCA, and do the appropriate amount of grovelling with the board, I want to recommend you for the promotion that you've been so keen on getting. But before I *do*, my partners and I need to make sure you have the right picture of where you're headed, so that you don't burn out in five years, and go and open a bloody surf shop on a beach in Tahiti.'

'Seriously?'

'It's not selfless, my boy. We aren't investing in you if you aren't in it for the right reasons; because it has a singular effect on your future in the business. Just like *you* don't make a habit of buying rubbish stocks for your clients; *we* don't promote without being absolutely sure about it.'

'Okay, I understand, but…'

'You don't understand, Stephen. But that's okay, it's to be expected. All you need to understand for now, is the fact that you're not indispensable. You're a clever bastard, there's no doubt about that, but there are plenty of young men and women in the industry who are just as clever as you. A certain IQ is a prerequisite for the sort of job we do, but it isn't what we look for anymore; it doesn't make you special. It *used to*. But not anymore. It's like an airbag in a car. Once upon a time, only a handful of cars had airbags. Nowadays, it's almost impossible to find one that *doesn't*. So when you look for a new car, you don't really even need to specify it on the list of things you're after.'

'So what *are* you looking for then?'

'Self-awareness.'

'Seriously?'

'Yes. It's becoming more and more apparent that our business is about *people*; not only figures. In any event, computers handle the real number crunching. We need our decision-makers to understand human behaviour, and they can't start to even contemplate the behaviour of others, unless they have a deep and abiding understanding of themselves.'

'Okay Jim, I'm not going to lie to you, I'm a bit nonplussed. What do you want me to do to satisfy your criteria?'

'Two things: *First*: you're already on gardening leave, so you have some time off to reflect on your recent conduct; Second: I've convinced the company to pay for you to go and see a psychologist. To be fair, it's not like therapy, she's an 'Executive Coach'. A seriously good one. She *is* a psychologist, but she specialises in helping over-achieving little sods like you *"find"* themselves, in a way that determines whether or not they'll manage in their chosen career in the long-term.'

'Come on Jim! Really?'

'You sound shocked. Good! but you haven't run off yet, so I take it you're up for it. Now let's finish our game.'

They finished their game in relative silence. Jim had said what he wanted to say, and wasn't intent on spending any more time being diverted from his game. Stephen had a lot to say, but he decided that it was best not to push his luck.

Since neither of them had any intention of engaging in any post-game smalltalk, they skipped the customary nineteenth hole, and returned to the city. Stephen had considered going back up to his office, but he suspected that Kenny would be there, and he didn't feel like any more human interaction. So he got off the lift at the ground floor and headed straight home without collecting his laptop.

***

He woke up early the following morning and got ready for his day in his usual fashion: by having a hot shower and a shave, brushing his teeth, and taking a double espresso like a shot of tequila. He had it down to a fine art, so the whole exercise never took longer than about twenty minutes.

It was only about halfway through his train ride to the office that he realised that he shouldn't actually have been going into the office. Surely they wouldn't have barred his access to the building though? He needed to have a word with Mary, regarding the rearrangement of his diary, and it was probably necessary to fetch his laptop.

He wasn't too sure whether or not Mary even knew he'd been sent off on leave, because hadn't had the time to speak with her before he left. There was no use in calling her now though, he'd just pop into the office and chat with her in person. He also remembered that he'd have to speak to Jim about arranging a first meeting with the psychologist, and he needed to find out if he was still allowed to communicate with Mary and Kenny whilst he was on leave.

***

'Mary, a word, please.'

He wondered whether or not she already knew the whole story? Of course she would. Jim's personal assistant would know, so all the personal assistants in the building probably knew by now. In any event, he noticed that she was a bit distracted, so she obviously knew *something*.

'Morning, Stephen. I've taken the liberty of making an appointment for you to see doctor Cumberland-Smith this evening, I hope that's okay.'

'Do I have some illness that I don't know about, Mary?'

'Stephen, are we going to pretend that you don't know what's going on here? I know you don't have much proper human interaction, and I do *so* enjoy our little games, but I've been instructed to stop enabling you.'

'By *whom*?!'

'Come on Stephen, you may be my direct boss, but we both work for higher powers, in reality.'

This is what he got for allowing his PA to run his life. In reality, she was in charge of him, and Jim's PA was in charge of *him*. It was almost comical, but that didn't make it any less true. All the big boys and girls out in the giant playground of the corporate world, employed surrogate mothers to keep them from falling off the jungle gyms. Mary was his one, and if he was being honest, he didn't think he could live without her.

'Okay boss! so what time is the appointment?'

'I've made it for three, so you can go straight home afterwards.'

'Very funny, Mary… you know I don't like going home for anything other than sleep.'

'I'm not laughing. Actually, I *am*, it's a three hour consultation. What fun! Anyway, you'd better get used to being at home, technically you shouldn't even be here *now*.'

Well, she evidently knew the whole story then.

'Three sodding *hours*?!'

'Indeed. I hear she's the best, but even the *best* is going to have to take some time to decode what goes on in that complicated head of yours, Stephen.'

'Thanks for the compliment Mary, I'll remember that at bonus time.'

'All great people are complicated, Mr West!'

'Nice save.'

'By the way, I've made your intern aware of the fact that you'll be taking some time off. It didn't seem to come as much of a surprise to him. He'll be temporarily re-assigned, but I've been instructed to ensure that he's available if you need him for anything, as long as it has nothing to do with work. Jim seems to think that you're good for one another, so he's encouraging the little bond you're fostering there. Personally, I think it's cute.'

'I don't see what's 'cute' about it, M. But okay. The poor little sod's likely to end up with one of the new associates, his life will become considerably harder.'

'Then he'll learn to appreciate you when you're back. Assuming you aren't disbarred or incarcerated.'

'Thanks for the vote of confidence there. You clearly know what's going on then?'

Mary laughed and shook her head.

'Of course I do, Stephen. But I also know you'll be fine. I was just kidding about the disbarment and incarceration stuff.'

'Thanks Mary, please look out for Ken while I'm away though, he's not a bad kid.'

'You know, Stephen, you're nowhere near as much of a prick as you would like everyone to believe you are. I suppose it's why I put up with you.'

Stephen smiled. He was grateful for his relationship with Mary. It was probably one of the most functional ones he had.

'So not because of my dazzling charm and good looks then?'

'No, I'm afraid not. You're not even remotely my type.'

'What *is* your type? You know pretty much everything about *me*, but I know sod all about *you*. Sorry. Maybe I am a bit of an arse. We've been working together for over three years now, and I haven't taken any time to get to know you better.'

'That's not because you're a arse Stephen. It's because I don't tend to discuss my personal life with anyone around here. If you *must* know, I'm not into men. Keep quiet about it though, because I don't need a building full of overgrown adolescents giving me hungry looks all day. Being mildly attractive is bad enough, being known to be a lesbian will make it positively *intolerable*.'

'Shit. I get it. Your secret's safe with me, M.'

'*See*. You're not so bad *after all*!'

'Maybe I just value my life.'

'I'm glad you're beginning to understand the power-balance in this relationship, Mr West.'

'I've understood it since day one. By the way; do you know anything about this executive coach I'm going to be seeing?'

'All I know is that she's hardcore. The company's spared no expense on this one. I'm told that she charges £1000.00 an hour; which is roughly ten times the average cost of going to a normal psychologist.'

'That's *insane*! They must be serious about this then. I don't know whether to be flattered or terrified.'

'By the look of her profile pic, she's about fifty five, and a bit of a dragon. She's actually quite hot, in a scary sort of way. Like a very expensive dominatrix.'

'It keeps getting better. Now I *am* a little terrified.'

Mary stopped and looked at him thoughtfully.

'Do you like your job, Stephen?'

'Not you *too*! You've been talking to Jim, haven't you? I feel like I'm being placed under a massive bloody microscope.'

'Sorry, this stuff with the executive coaching and psychology just has me thinking about what makes everyone tick.'

'I *do* like my job, in point of fact. I'd be a strange kind of masochist if I didn't, considering how long I spend doing it every day.'

'You just strike me as more of a creative type than most of the people around here.'

'That's a pretty unique insight, M. I'm definitely more creative than a lot of people here, but I didn't think anybody noticed. Besides, I think you need to be little creative to stand out in this sort of job.'

'Isn't that just what landed you in hot water? Being a bit creative?'

'Yeah, I suppose you could say that. But to be fair, what landed me in the current situation was more a combination of creativity and arrogance. That sort of thing works well for musicians and artists, but eventually leads to the downfall of finance professionals.'

'So it's one or the other then?'

'No, not really, it's the arrogance that's the problem.'

'So creativity is still okay?'

'Yes. But even then, it depends on your definition of creativity. Good traders, like good lawyers and accountants, need to be *just* creative enough to find elegant solutions to complicated problems, but *not* creative enough to devise solutions or models that are reckless or illegal. It's difficult to find the balance sometimes, but that's the art of good business.'

'You make it sound like a giant risky board-game.'

'Yeah, that's unfortunately how I see it, most of the time.'

3

Stephen left the office once it became clear to him that there was nothing there for him to do. He no longer had a reason to speak with Jim, and he got the feeling that his boss would be irritated by the fact that he was there in the first place.

He managed to get a referral to a solicitor from Oliver Short, one of his old university mates, and set up an appointment with him for the following day; but once this little task was complete, he found himself at a loose end. He walked around aimlessly until midday, and then tried to spend as much time as possible over lunch at a nearby restaurant.

He could only stretch his meal for just over an hour, and after his second coffee, he was bored stiff. So he headed towards his destination, which was on Sloane Street in Knightsbridge. He took the tube, which killed almost another half an hour, but when he arrived at Knightsbridge station he realised that the Doctor's offices were in throwing distance, so he had to find another way of amusing himself for at least another hour and a quarter.

He found a small bookshop, and browsed away the time in that half-hearted and distracted way people do when they aren't actually looking for anything in particular; but eventually, he gave up and headed to the Doctor's offices early.

***

'You're a little early Mr West. Doctor Cumberland-Smith will see you as soon as she's ready. Please take a seat in the meantime.'

'Thank you. I'm sorry, I didn't catch your name.'

'It's Susan.'

'Ah, Susan. I assume it's just through that door behind you?'

'That's right, Mr West.'

'Thanks Susan, please call me Stephen.'

'Very well, Mr West.'

Stephen felt himself blushing. Susan, the young receptionist, was incredibly cute.

She looked like one of those sexy librarians that seem to exist only in fantasy... and in some of those pornographic films from the late nineties that took themselves seriously enough to pretend that they actually had plots. Maybe there *were* gorgeous young librarians out there somewhere, although Stephen had never seen any. Not even at university - where you would expect that the odds would be at their most favourable, given the supply of young pretty woman in need of regular part-time work.

Susan was about five foot three, had short, styled, auburn hair, and deliberately noticeable glasses. The type that are worn as much for their utility as for the statement they make. They had bold, black rectangular frames that provided a provocative contrast to her hazel eyes. She was wearing a matching black skirt-suit with what looked like a very expensive white shirt underneath. The shirt gaped at the top just enough to ignite some curiosity, but not enough to be remotely indiscreet or inappropriate.

Stephen realised he was staring, and hastily averted his gaze to study the artwork on the wall behind her.

He wondered whether or not she may have actually been flirting with him. She was smiling at him in a way that he considered to be playful, but he wasn't sure that he was picking up the right signal. He could have sworn that he saw her wink at him when she addressed him as '*Mr West*'; following his request that she call him Stephen.

He decided that he must have been kidding himself. She was probably just being friendly. He was terrible at reading signals, and at dealing with women in general. Why did they always have to make their conduct so cryptic? If he was being honest with himself, he actually didn't know where to start, when it came to the process of figuring out how to deal with a member of the opposite sex.

Although he'd been on a handful of first (and sometimes second) dates over the past five or six years, he hadn't actually managed to get to a *third date* since he was in his early thirties. Even *then*, he'd never really found himself in any sort of long-term relationship. He'd had a few flings in his twenties - but nothing remotely serious.

As far as he was aware, he'd never really been *flirted with*. He wouldn't know what to look for. She was probably just being friendly. It was obviously her job to be polite with the doctor's clients, and he didn't want to make an arse of himself by trying to initiate conversation with her. She'd probably think he was some kind of creep if he did.

So he settled down on the large Chesterfield in the waiting area, and read the latest financial news on his phone. In between articles, he did take the time to glance around, if only to try and get the odd surreptitious look at Susan.

The waiting area was magnificently appointed. It was like an interesting cross between a modern art gallery, and an old cigar lounge. An odd combination, to be sure. But it worked.

It was a small square room with dark oak flooring and golden yellow walls. You came in on the left hand side, through a solid oak door with brass handles, and could see its twin was in the same location at the opposite end of the room.

To the right of the entrance, facing reception was the oxblood Chesterfield in which Stephen was enveloped, and a small, mahogany coffee table - placed just far enough in front of it to make reaching for a drink possible, but slightly uncomfortable. In the centre of this table was a large onyx bust, which seemed to be some sort of abstract expressionist take on the Roman two-faced god, Janus.

Beneath the table, was a very large, dark-red Baluch rug, which was as well worn as the sofa. But similarly, in a way that made it feel opulent and permanent, rather than tatty.

There was a large standing lamp in the corner, between the sofa and the wall on the right, and further down that wall, adjacent to the coffee table, hung an abstract charcoal sketch of a woman's face which was deliberately incomplete.

Instead of sitting at a raised reception counter - Susan sat in a high-backed, leather executive's chair, behind a large mahogany desk with a black leather inlay. On her left, placed at a careful angle facing her, was a massive Apple monitor. It was clearly one of those monitors which housed the actual computer inside it, because there was only a solitary cable running down off the back of the desk and neatly behind the modesty panel. Her peripherals were wireless, and almost invisible.

The desk was a classic piece of antique furniture, made at a time when there wasn't a need for those little cable holes you find in more modern office surfaces. Having the cable run down the back was a small price to pay for getting to use something so beautiful and timeless.

Behind the desk was a large piece of splatter art, which took the form of a bright green butterfly on a large, square, unframed white canvass. It was an impressive piece of work, and Stephen was specifically impressed by the fact that it was all done in one colour.

It was very difficult to create depth and contrast in a work like that using only one colour. Art was his only significant interest outside of financial markets, and he had a very good eye for such things. Abstract expressionism wasn't his favourite style - but he didn't dislike it, and he found that splatter art often worked very well to brighten up a room. This piece certainly did.

After about a quarter of an hour, Susan showed him into her employer's office.

Dr Bridgette Cumberland-Smith stood up from behind her own large antique desk to greet him.

Her office was decorated in exactly the same style as the reception area, and Stephen immediately registered the fact that the Doctor had extraordinary taste, and no shortage of resources.

She looked exactly as he'd imagined from Mary's passing description of her.

Although she was definitely in her early fifties, she had the body of someone at least ten years younger. In fact, she looked stronger and fitter than most people did in their early thirties. She had long, straight, raven-black hair, piercing green eyes, and very sharp features. She had the same sort of glasses as Susan, and was wearing a charcoal pinstriped pencil skirt, with a white silk blouse.

Now he knew what she looked like, but he still had no idea what to expect.

***

'Hello Mr West. I gather you know my name, but I can tell you're not too sure how familiar to be with me.'

Stephen was a little off balance. He wanted to reply, but something was restraining him. She obviously sensed this, because she continued before he could.

'I don't actually *care* what you call me, although I prefer something at least related in some way to my first name. I draw the line at hypocorisms, unless I'm sleeping with the client in question.'

'Ummm. Hello, doctor.'

'Doctor isn't my first name Stephen, it's a title. But I'm flattered that you're so uncomfortable that you can't bring yourself to call me *Bridgette*. I've just learnt more about you in the last twenty seconds than I did from your file. Thanks!'

Stephen felt like he was eleven years old again, and standing in the headmaster's office. Mary was right though; she *was* fairly attractive.

'Please take a seat.'

'Thanks, *Bridgette*.'

At least she was smiling now. Maybe things would improve.

'Have you ever been to see a psychologist before, Stephen?'

'No.'

'Terrific. That'll make this a lot easier. Although I *am* a psychologist, I'm not really seeing you in the capacity of a counsellor, which is the capacity most people tend to associate with psychologists.'

'I understand.'

'I'm seeing you in *two* capacities: one, as an executive coach, and two: as an assessor. It's *my* job to get to know you, and give you some personal guidance, whilst simultaneously setting you some tasks and assessing your suitability for a very demanding and high-stress professional position. I am *not* here to listen to you pour out all of your daddy issues, *nor* am I here to hold your hand and give you cuddles when you're sad. We *may* touch on the daddy issues briefly, but only insofar as they're relevant to any specific professional insecurities you may have.'

'Alright.'

'Good. Now that we seem to be on the same page regarding the extent of my mandate, we can get on with the messy business of examining all of your dirty little secrets, and determining whether or not you have what it takes to be one of the *chosen few*.'

'Umm, where would you like to start?'

'Your personal records were sent to me by the company after you signed the relevant consent, so I have a basic idea of your background.'

'Fair enough. I'm not sure how much detail there is in those files, so let me know what gaps you need me to fill.'

'I've read all the boring stuff, so I know where you went to school, what your parents did for a living, how you did at university, and all the usual background stuff. Nothing special there. I note that you weren't ever caught stealing, abusing small animals, or stabbing any other children at school, so I think it's safe to assume that you don't have any serious personality disorders. At least not the kind which would likely have an adverse effect on your ability to function in corporate life.'

'Personality disorders?'

'Yes. These sort of things usually manifest themselves at a young age, and very few children are emotionally intelligent enough to keep them hidden. By the look of your IQ scores, you're intellectually gifted, but from what I can gather so far, you aren't very emotionally intelligent. Certainly not emotionally intelligent enough to hide a personality disorder with any degree of efficiency.'

Stephen felt numb. This woman was like something out of a movie… was she *insane*?

'You look pale, Stephen. Would you like a glass of water? You've already had too much coffee today. I can tell by the way your leg is shaking. Nice colourful socks, by the way.'

'No, I'm fine… thanks.'

'Suit yourself. Just to be clear, I know you're an incredibly intelligent individual, but there's a lot more to intelligence than you've considered.'

'Okay.'

'I have a fairly decent grasp of your history, and Jim gave me a detailed assessment of his *own*. Mostly regarding your professional accomplishments, but a few personal observations found their way into his summary.'

'Jim's been *assessing* me?'

'Come now Stephen, do you think he's an *idiot*? He wouldn't waste my time and the company's resources on this little exercise without first doing his own homework on you, *would he*?'

'No, I suppose that was a stupid question.'

'It was. But never mind, we're *all* allowed a little stupidity every now and then.'

'… I'll try to up my game, Bridgette. I'm just a little perturbed at the moment, as you may imagine.'

'Yes. I see that. Jim tells me that you're a bit unbalanced, but that he thinks it's just because you're insecure and you battle with women. In his view, if you manage to settle down and get over your perceived sexual inadequacies, you'll become a nicer person.'

'I don't have any *"perceived sexual inadequacies"*! Thank you *very* much, Bridgette!'

'It's quite natural for very bright young over-achievers like yourself Stephen, you needn't worry about it, that's one of the things I'm here to help you with. Jim says you've been a bit reckless lately, and have managed to submerge yourself in some rather hot water with the Financial Conduct Authority. He thinks that if you were in a proper relationship, and engaging in more frequent intercourse, you wouldn't have behaved as rashly as you did.'

'I don't see what that has to do with anything, Bridgette.'

'Stephen, I'm sorry I have to be blunt about these things. You need to see me as a sort of cleaner. I need to clear out all the excrement before I can get to work. We don't have the luxury of time here, so I have to come at the mess with a high pressure hose. I can't cart it away lethargically, like a dung beetle.'

'But..'

'Think of this session like receiving the first anaesthetic injection at the dentists office. It hurts like hell, but then the area goes numb, and the procedure ends up being less unpleasant than you expect.'

'Don't I at least get to explain *my* side of the story here, Bridgette?'

'Not really Stephen, that's what *counselling* is for, and as I already clarified; I'm not seeing you in that capacity.'

***

'I know I said that I'd been through your background information already, but I'd like to confirm a few things just to make sure the information I have is accurate.'

'Alright. What would you like to know?'

'You're a Lancastrian I see. Your father is in banking, and your mother's a teacher. You attended Lancaster Royal Grammar School as an adolescent, and then moved on to Lancaster University, where you did an undergraduate degree in Economics. You then moved on to complete your Masters' in Finance at Imperial College's Business School.'

'Yes.'

'That's not an unimpressive CV. Each of those institutions are highly regarded, and I have it on good authority that the MSc in Finance from Imperial is among the most sought after qualifications in your industry.'

'I've heard that.'

'It's also apparently among the most *expensive* courses on the market. I have a client who is trying to get his daughter in there for the next academic year.'

'I suppose you could say that. Although it was almost twenty thousand pounds cheaper than the Oxford equivalent at the time. My student loan didn't stretch far enough for *that*.'

'Hmm, yes. You're clearly bitter about that. Do you think that the Oxford course was *superior*?'

'It doesn't matter what *I* think. Does it?'

'That's the *only* thing that matters, actually.'

'Well, to be brutally honest, I would have loved to accept the position that was offered to me at Oxford. But my father didn't have sufficient security to cover the additional loan.'

'Ah. So you blame *him* for that?'

'You mean, do I blame him for not being ambitious enough, and making more of himself?'

'You could put it like that.'

'No. Not really. My father isn't stupid or idle, and to be fair, he actually did remarkably well considering that *his* father lived on benefits, and his mother abandoned them when he was about three years old. I must sound like a seriously ungrateful swine.'

'You do.'

'I'm not ungrateful, I'm just irritated that even though both of my parents worked hard in decent jobs, I didn't have some of the opportunities that many of my peers seemed to have.'

'How many of your university friends went up to Oxford or Cambridge?'

'That's not the point. I was clever enough to go, and I really wanted to.'

'That *is* the point, Stephen. Do you think that the Oxbridge crowd are more intelligent or capable than any of your friends from university?'

'No, certainly not.'

'So then your argument is pure nonsense. *Isn't it?*'

'Is it? I knew I was as clever as the Oxbridge elite, I just wanted the opportunity to prove it.'

'You *have* proved it. To everyone other than yourself!'

'They still dominate my industry, and it bothers me.'

'No they don't, Stephen. You and I both have a firm enough grasp of statistics to understand, almost intuitively, that that cannot be mathematically possible. You only see Oxbridge graduates above you in the corporate hierarchy, because you're actively looking for them. If you constantly search for red cars on the road, eventually you'll assume that red cars are more common than everything else.'

'I just get the impression that they receive favourable treatment because of where they studied, and you can't tell me *that* doesn't happen.'

'It does, some of the time. But these things eventually re-arrange themselves. Those with the intestinal fortitude, the intellect and the requisite ambition find their way to where they ought to be in the so called "pecking order". Your boss certainly did. I know for a *fact* that he never had any hand-ups or special treatment as he rose to where he is today.'

'It doesn't seem fair, that's all.'

'Fairness has very little to do with it, Stephen. It's your perception that makes it appear unfair, and you don't really have a balanced view of it, because you haven't grown past your bitterness at not being able to get the thing that you wanted. Like a little child in a playground who throws a tantrum when he can't have the specific toy he wants, notwithstanding the fact that he has absolutely no idea whether or not it's any better than the one he has.'

'I think it's a bit more complicated than that.'

'No. You want to believe that it is, because it would validate your childish perspective. You need to grow up, Stephen.'

He went silent and stared petulantly across the desk at her. He was sick of being patronised, although he knew his position on this issue was slightly irrational, but he couldn't help it. At least, he didn't think he could.

'I know this is difficult, but humour me a little here, will you?'

'Okay.'

'What's the very first thing you wanted to be when you were a child? You know, the seemingly unrealistic things that children want to be before they start to gain a better understanding of the world. What was that for you?'

'Seriously?'

'Yes. As I said, humour me!'

'I wanted to be a fighter pilot.'

'That sounds fairly typical, it's usually something like that. But then it changes at least once. Usually in early adolescence, when you understand the world a bit better, but before you end up making a more concrete decision on a career path in your late teens.'

'So?'

'During this period, how many different things did you want to be before you decided to go into finance?'

'Just one.'

'And?'

'I wanted to be an architect.'

'I see. I assume you had a talent for drawing and design.'

'Yes. I think I was reasonably talented.'

'So what made you move in a different direction?'

'I don't really know, to be honest. Life just took me in a different direction.'

Bridgette smiled and made a brief note before continuing.

'It was a pretty drastic departure, don't you think?'

'I suppose. But I could have ended up doing one of a handful of things, even something silly, like art.'

'Would that really have been so *'silly'*?'

'Come on Bridgette, being an *artist* isn't exactly a realistic career choice.'

'Yet there are many artists in the world?'

'It's not very stable though, *is it*?'

'It's like anything Stephen, it depends what you do with it. You went into finance, because although you probably have a fairly vivid imagination, you couldn't bring yourself to use it when you chose to do something you thought would make you better off than your father. That way, you could prove to him that you were special.'

'Is that what you think?'

'It is. You've also followed a fairly predictable pattern by choosing a career that is, in some way, related to what your father did. He was in banking, so you found something which you knew he would be capable of relating to, but which would end up far exceeding his station. Many of the ambitious children of court clerks or policemen become solicitors; those whose parents are nurses become doctors; and those whose parents are bookkeepers become chartered accountants.'

'Maybe that *does* happen, but that's certainly not what happened with me. Besides, art was a hobby for me. Turning a hobby into a job tends to destroy the happiness you derive from the hobby doesn't it?'

'Sometimes. It depends on your definition of the term 'hobby' really. Do you still derive pleasure from your art?'

'I don't know. I haven't drawn or painted anything in years.'

'So you've abandoned it then?'

'No, I just haven't had time. I've been meaning to start up again.'

'Alright.'

She made some more notes and offered Stephen another drink. He ordered a still water even though he wanted a coffee. The quip she'd made about him having had too much coffee earlier was still on his mind, and he didn't want her to assume that he was ordering coffee to prove some sort of point.

***

'Now let's talk about your perceived sexual inadequacies, *shall we*?'

'How do you know Jim's right about my supposed *'difficulty with women'*, Bridgette?'

'Because Jim's a very astute individual, and because I tested his theory when you came in.'

'What do you mean?'

'Did you ask my receptionist to call you *Stephen* when you got here?'

'I *did*. How did you know? Do you have cameras out there?'

'No. I *assumed* you would.'

'Why?'

'Because she's a pretty little thing, and you were probably trying to come across as charming. But, if I had to guess, you didn't go any further than that. She even provoked you to do so, by playfully refusing to accede to your request. You just accepted it, and probably buried yourself in your phone. I doubt that you tried to initiate any conversation, and I'd be willing to bet a large sum that you didn't try to get her number. If I'm correct, you just sat there like a twelve-year-old at his first dance, hoping that a girl would agree to dance with him, in spite of the fact that he had no intention of asking one to do so.'

'How do you *know* this.'

'Because I've been reading men like you for the better part of the last three decades, and I'm exceedingly *good* at it. I instructed Susan to respond to you that way if you asked the question.'

'Okay, but how do you go from there, to *"perceived sexual inadequacies"*?'

'That wasn't the end of the experiment. When you walked into this office, I deliberately knocked you off balance by dropping the subject of sex into the conversation before you'd even had the chance to sit down. You took the bait, went weak at the knees, and nearly fell over yourself.'

'I *did*?'

'You know you did Stephen, I asked you to call me by my first name, and you fumbled so hard that you ended up calling me by my title. If you think about it, you wouldn't have done that if I was a man. You're a highly successful individual, and although Jim has told me that you're tolerantly tactful and deferent to your seniors at work, you aren't scared or intimidated by any *man*. Jim also told me that, and it stands to reason, because you would never have gotten as far as you have, if it weren't the case.'

'So?'

'So, most successful, good-looking, and superficially charming single men of your age are hunters. They view almost *all* women as prey, and they aren't scared to try their luck with *any* of us. A normal man in your position would have used the fifteen minutes you waited outside to chat Susan up mercilessly, and when he picked up my quip about sleeping with clients, he would have immediately registered it as an invitation to do business. He would, if *anything*, have been thrust directly into his comfort zone.'

'Bridgette. I'm just polite and tactful, I can assure you that I have no problems with women.'

'Stephen, you're in denial, and I don't have the time to indulge you on this issue. You're either struggling with some inadequacy issues, which I can fix, or you're too soft for your profession and won't last another year in it. Although it may seem terribly unfair, you work in an industry that requires you to be an alpha. You need *real* confidence, because at your level, you can't fake it. I'm not asking you to be a sex-crazed lunatic with more testosterone than brains, I'm asking you to throw out the baggage that's preventing you from being comfortable in your own skin.'

'Okay, so let's assume you're *right*. Which I'm not conceding, by the way. But for the sake of *argument*: how do you propose I go about *'fixing'* the alleged difficulty.'

'Simple. You can start by going out and having some non-commercial sex!'

'What do you mean by, '*non-commercial*'?'

'Not *paid for*, Stephen. I thought you worked in the city? Surely you're well acquainted with the concept of *commercial* sex.'

'Not really Bridgette, I don't go in for that sort of thing, as you may have guessed.'

'Well Stephen, let me warn you. If you don't sort out your problem with women soon, you're headed straight for the sex supermarket. You'll put off proper dating until eventually you lose whatever confidence you have in that area of your life, and you'll end up paying for sex because it'll just be easier. Whilst I have no moral qualms about things like that; I frankly think it should be legalised and regulated; it isn't a substitute for a proper relationship, and it'll end up doing you more harm than good, in the long-run.'

'Okay. But it isn't just that *easy*. Although you refer to it as "*non-commercial*", you *do* make it sound like going to the store and picking up a bag of groceries.'

'That's your problem Stephen, you've built up the perception that it's difficult. It really *isn't*, not with *your* resources. You're well off, good looking, and under the surface, you probably aren't really a bad guy.'

'I acted like a total arsehole on my last date!'

'I'm sure you did. Insecurity turns many decent people into unmitigated tools. But now that you're aware of the danger, you can work on it.'

'I still don't concede that I have a problem.'

'We'll get there, but in the meantime, I have some assignments for you to undertake. They may sound ridiculous, but they're necessary. You need to follow my instructions to the letter, *understood*?'

'Understood.'

'I want you to start a diary. Not an appointment diary, more like a "*journal*". You'll record nearly every single thing you do for the next few months. Jim's told me that you won't be working for at least a month, so you'll have the time. It doesn't have to be daily, but it must at least be weekly, and it must include all of your social interactions.'

'Okay.'

'I want the diary to be detailed and personal. I don't really intend on looking at it *myself*, unless I suspect you aren't doing it properly, or aren't actively invested in this process. If I *do* look at it, rest assured that I will do so in my capacity as a clinical psychologist, so its contents will remain strictly confidential, and won't feature in my report to your employer.'

'Fair enough.'

'Then, I want you to go and seek out some old friends from school or university, and try to involve yourself in some of the activities that you were interested in before you started working. We'll resume our conversation in a week's time, and I expect you to have made some progress by then.'

'Got it. Anything *else*?'

'Not for now. Susan will arrange a time for our next consultation. I know I scheduled three hours for this consultation, but I had no intention of sitting with you for three hours this evening. I wanted the time booked out in your diary so that you wouldn't go back to the office and forget what we've just spoken about. I want you to take a walk, or even just go home.'

'Apparently I'm not allowed back at the office anyway.'

'Oh yes, well that's perfect then. A bit of forced leave will do you good.'

4

Stephen left Bridgette's offices feeling a little dazed. It had been a long and tiring day.

Most people in his situation would have been inordinately grateful for the opportunity to have some time away from work. But not Stephen. He used work as a means to hide from the world, and, most often, from himself. He felt strangely exposed when left to his own devices, without the distraction and comfort of a routine that kept him in a constant state of pre-occupation.

Fortunately, he was so tired that sleep wouldn't be a problem. The problem would be figuring out what to do with himself once he woke up.

***

The following morning, he surfaced considerably later than usual, and discovered that Mary had sent him a little care package. She'd had his local supermarket deliver what looked like two week's worth of food. She really was the most amazing person in his life. He didn't know what he would do without her.

Previously, this sort of realisation would have made him feel grateful for having her around. Now it just made him feel a little embarrassed, because he was far too old to have somebody else managing his life for him, and buying him groceries. Had he really become that useless?

He'd never really done any proper grocery shopping for himself, because he tended to eat all of his meals at or around the office. As a consequence, he didn't know how to cook anything other than fried eggs on toast.

He noticed that Mary had included eggs and bacon in the shopping basket, but apart from those items, and the obligatory milk and bread, there was nothing else that seemed remotely normal. No pies, no crisps, no ice cream, and no frozen pizza.

In his search for the aforesaid items, he came across at least three kilograms of chicken breast, rice, broccoli, plain oatmeal, berries, kale, beansprouts and even egg whites in a carton. Who the hell bought egg whites like that? In fact, there were even half a dozen pre-packaged *"fit meals"*, which all looked to be some sort of combination of chicken, rice and green vegetables.

By the looks of the contents of the shop, you'd be forgiven for assuming that he was one of those bodybuilder types with a body-fat percentage in the single digits. He wasn't. Although, somewhat *unfairly*, he was in reasonably good shape for his age. He didn't look like a bodybuilder, but he could easily have passed for some type of athlete; perhaps a tall footballer, or a tennis player.

He went to gym a few times a week, because it helped him to clear his head. But he was never particularly serious about exercise. He spent most of his time on the rowing machine, or doing sprint training on the spinning bikes. Every now and then, he would do some resistance training, but it tended to bore him, so he never committed to any long-term programmes.

He resolved to get used to the chicken and cruciferous vegetable *"fit meals"*, because they looked easy to prepare. Starting from scratch with just the raw materials would be a lot more challenging.

Perhaps Mary was conspiring with Bridgette to get him to go out more often and meet people, or maybe she just thought he was getting fat.

Either way, he was going to play along, and complete Bridgette's little tasks. He'd worked too damn hard to drop the ball now, and he wanted to get that promotion… even if it meant jumping through some hoops.

He didn't really know where to start, apart from getting a notebook for the silly journal, and perhaps going to the gym. If he was going to be living on chicken and broccoli for the foreseeable future, he reasoned that he may as well put fuel to good use.

It wasn't as if he'd elect to play golf without the motive of using it as some sort of networking exercise; and it didn't seem as if Jim was in the mood to drag him around. To be fair, he was sort of *persona non grata*, so Jim couldn't exactly take him around with clients.

If Bridgette was serious about him taking up old university hobbies, she'd have to accept that that would involve him playing some computer games. In truth - much like most young men of his generation, Stephen had spent the bulk of his time at university playing computer games. At least that's what he did in between getting drunk with his mates, and trying to attend lectures.

In addition to this, he decided that he'd have to make some sort of attempt to find a '*date*'. He couldn't endure the thought of Bridgette looking at him with a smug expression during their next consultation, and shaking her head because he hadn't made any effort to prove that he wasn't suffering from '*perceived sexual inadequacies*'.

He resolved go on one of those fancy dating sites… the ones with the clever algorithms. He predicted that the good doctor would be satisfied if he'd managed to go on a date or two before their next scheduled consultation.

Speaking of dates, he'd arranged to meet up with his old friend Charles that evening. He was pleasantly surprised that when he sent him a text message, he not only got an instant reply, but a suggestion that they meet that evening at a place in Stephen's neighbourhood. By looking at Charles' social media profile, he could ascertain that his old mate appeared to be doing well.

They hadn't seen one another in about six years. Whenever he heard the stupid expression, '*time flies*', he cringed a little, but he was forced to admit that there was some truth in it.

They were best mates at university. It felt odd noting in the ridiculous journal that they '*were*' best friends - but he felt that this was probably the most appropriate way in which to record the nature of their relationship, given that they hadn't seen one another for so long.

Apart from Charles and Oliver, Stephen didn't really have other close friends. He'd sort of stayed in touch with a few mates from university on social media, but only tended to see them at weddings, and the odd funeral. He was friendly with some of his work colleagues, but he wouldn't have exactly called them *friends*. It was a bit sad really.

Maybe Charles still *was* his best mate? Though he didn't expect that he was still *Charles'* best mate. He assumed that Charlie had a host of other friends. From what he could gather, they guy still lived like a student.

Stephen still couldn't believe that his friend didn't end up becoming an actuary. It always seemed a bit odd to him that the man turned his part time job as a computer game tester into a full-on career. His parents must have been a bit put out. To be fair though, it looked as if he'd become quite important in the gaming world. He *designed* games now, he was no longer just testing them.

Actually, there was every possibility that he made considerably more money than an actuary now, so as far as Stephen was concerned, it couldn't have been too silly a career decision. It looked as though he still lived with that group of creative types, and he was evidently still played in a band.

Stephen was forced to admit to himself that he was a little envious of Charles Taylor, but he knew enough about himself to understand that he couldn't stomach living the sort of Bohemian lifestyle he assumed his friend had continued living.

By the looks of his social media feed, he had *two* girlfriends! That *knew* about each other! In fact, by the looks of it, they were *also* sleeping together. Maybe Bridgette was right… maybe he *did* have perceived sexual inadequacies, because he didn't think he could manage that sort of thing. Most of his colleagues at work would consider that arrangement to be better than driving around in a Ferrari and dating a bikini-model, but it freaked Stephen out a bit.

***

He couldn't believe he had to go and consult with a solicitor. It all seemed so ridiculously unfair.

He was willing to concede that Jim may have been right about the chip on his shoulder. But he still felt that the odds were firmly stacked against him.

The system never did him any favours.

The way he saw it, those with the generational wealth and the social capital that almost always accompanied it, seemed to lead a charmed existence, sheltered from the travails of ordinary life.

The fact that his life was so far from being ordinary in any remotely realistic sense, didn't seem to occur to him. As with his ridiculous theory that pretty young girls weren't ever independently successful or hard working, Stephen's unrealistic view of the wealthier members of society demonstrated a breathtaking lack of ability to contextualise the world around him; at least from a social perspective.

Whilst it was true that he had a particularly high IQ, he had the emotional intelligence of a grizzly bear.

As far as he was concerned - when the rich made money, they never got blamed for making it unlawfully, even if they were dodgy. As soon as someone like *him* made a legitimate windfall, the vultures homed in. It was like they were determined to keep him in his place.

"No, Mr West, we don't care how clever you are! You aren't welcome in our club, because you weren't born into it."

Sometimes he felt like he'd shown up at a society wedding in short trousers and sandals, wearing an old T-shirt. He managed to learn how to speak without his northern accent, but the bastards still seemed to know that he wasn't one of *them*.

His father always told him that life was unfair; and when he was growing up, Stephen just thought he was a pessimistic old sod. Perhaps he was right though.

That said, he was grateful that he had the resources to employ a well-respected legal representative, and because he *knew* that he hadn't actually done anything illegal or unethical, he was certain that he could overcome this little difficulty with the Financial Conduct Authority.

Apparently this Ian Wright was a seriously good solicitor. His jaw-dropping hourly rates had the singularly strange effect of being simultaneously horrifying and comforting.

The firm's offices were situated on St. Paul's Churchyard, between Godliman Street and Dean's Court. Basically, as close to the Cathedral as it was possible to get without actually being inside it.

Their proximity to the London Stock Exchange certainly wasn't coincidental. Wright and his partner evidently thought it expedient not to make their clients wander too far from their places of work in order to consult. Given that their specialty was commercial malfeasance, most of these clients would inevitably work within comfortable walking distance of the seat of the stock exchange at 10 Paternoster Square.

The offices of Ashden, Cole & Roberts certainly were.

***

'Good morning, sir. Welcome to Wright & Hill. Do you have an appointment?'

'Yes, good morning, I'm here to see Mr Wright. I'm Stephen West.'

'Ah yes, Mr West, take a seat. Mr Wright will be with you in a moment. Can I offer you something to drink?'

'No, thank you, I'll just wait.'

'Very well sir, I'll tell him you're here.'

The offices of Wright & Hill were typically those of a law firm. Their design philosophy seemed to be the opposite of the one which was habitually adopted by accounting firms. It was as if they deliberately set out to spend as much money as they possibly could. Presumably in an effort to reassure their clients that they were successful.

The dark blue carpet was so thick, it was like walking around on stack of blankets, and there was so much brass and polished wood around, that you'd be forgiven for thinking you were in an antique store. Clearly Wright and his partner were a bit old fashioned. Or at least, that's what they wanted their clients to believe.

Stephen was shown through to a capacious boardroom that was even more luxurious than the reception area, and was offered something to drink. He got the impression that he could have ordered anything he wanted, but he settled for a coffee and a glass of water.

***

'Mr West?'

'Yes, please call me Stephen. I take it you're Mr Wright.'

'Yes, it's Ian.'

'Hi Ian, pleased to meet you. You've come highly recommended.'

'Ah, yes, I see you were referred by Oliver Short. He worked with me briefly many years ago, and we've stayed in touch. How do *you* know Ollie?'

'We were at University together. I must admit, I haven't seen him for years though. You know how it is.'

'Yes. Time really does have an uncanny knack of escaping us as we grow older.'

'It certainly does.'

Oliver Short was one of Stephen's two closest friends from university. He was a highly successful corporate lawyer, so as soon as Stephen found himself needing representation, he gave him a call; even though he knew that his friend didn't do this sort of work. Oliver had referred him on to Ian.

'Well, to business. I know it must be singularly unpleasant to have to come and consult with someone in my line of work, but I promise to try and keep it as painless as possible. Given my specialisation, I assume that you're a trader, and I assume that you've found yourself in a bit of a sticky situation with the ladies and gentlemen over at the FCA.'

'Yes, that's essentially the situation. Perhaps I should have sent you a short note explaining the position before we met, but to be honest, I'm not really sure about the correct protocol in these circumstances.'

'No, that wasn't necessary. I'll ask you to tell me the story from the beginning, and please bear with me if I interrupt you from time to time with various questions. I'll also take notes while you talk. You mustn't assume that I'm not listening when I do this. I've learnt to listen and write simultaneously, and I'm tolerably good at it. I'll stop you from time to time if I need to though.'

'Great, thanks Ian.'

'So, let's get started. I assume the trade under scrutiny was for your personal account, or you wouldn't necessarily be here. I see from your intake documentation that you work for Ashden, Cole & Roberts.'

'Yes, that's right.'

'Before you continue; although I assume you understand the nature of privilege, it behoves me to reassure you that anything you say to me shall remain strictly confidential.'

'Thank you.'

'Go ahead then Stephen, what happened?'

'I've been working as a trader for just over fifteen years. As you may imagine, I've grown a fairly healthy personal portfolio, albeit that I started out from scratch. I don't own property, or any significant physical assets other than a couple of modestly valued works of art; so almost all of my disposable resources are used to trade. I'd like to think I'm reasonably good at what I do, and I've managed to amass a portfolio valued at just north of one and a half million pounds.'

'You've certainly done better than most professionals at your age.'

'Thanks. I'd like to think so.'

'Alright, so you obviously trade quite actively for your own account then.'

It was a statement, not a question. Stephen got the impression that Ian knew the industry well and probably had some sort of trading qualification himself.

'Indeed. I also have a proclivity to take risks. I'm not sure *why*, because I've worked hard for what I've made, but I like to play the game.'

'Fair enough. That's probably how you've been able to grow your asset base so rapidly.'

'Yes, that's a pretty accurate assessment.'

'So about two weeks ago, I was reading a newspaper, and there was an odd little story amongst the more innocuous columns at the back, about a relatively obscure researcher who got escorted out of his place of employment by security the day before. It made news, because apparently, he made a bit of a scene, and interrupted a live news broadcast which was being filmed near to the entrance of the building he'd come out of. The presenter evidently had a bit of a laugh over it, and one of the journalists who were hanging around at the time, decided to find out what was going on.'

'I'm intrigued Stephen, this sounds like it's going to be interesting.'

'Well, it certainly interested *me*, because I recognised the company, and I remembered hearing about the chap who'd been escorted out of the building; a fellow by the name of Greenberg.'

'Go on.'

'The company he was being flung out of was Ringmire Pharmaceuticals PLC. It's a relatively small drug company with a few big products, but nothing commercially serious. They do relatively well, because listed drug companies tend to do well as a matter of course. But they aren't one of the really big players in the industry. Ashden, Cole & Roberts don't trade any of their shares, even though we do like to buy into pharmaceuticals from time to time. Ringmire floats beneath our radar.'

'Okay, so how did you know about them?'

'My father is a diabetic. Years of poor eating habits brought on type two diabetes when he was in his early fifties. About a year and a half ago, Greenberg gave an interview on Sky news, claiming that Ringmire were testing this new miracle drug called *Davaproxin*, which is supposed to "*cure*" diabetes.'

'Wow, that sounds like a pretty serious claim.'

'Yes, too good to be true, really, and the company was a little bit embarrassed by the interview, because they hadn't given him permission to do it. They wanted to downplay the claim, because the drug was only in the very early stages of development. So, almost immediately, they put out a press statement clarifying the fact that although they had high hopes for the drug, they weren't claiming it to be as miraculous as Greenberg had indicated.'

'I see.'

'I remember having a stand up row with my father about it at the time. I was visiting my parents when the story came out, and he was convinced that Greenberg's claims were genuine. I showed him the Company's follow-up press release after it was published, but he'd got it into his head that *Davaproxin* was going to change his life. This was odd actually, because the old man is hopelessly pessimistic about most things. But I suppose that the notion of being able to resume his bad habits without consequence was a dream he wanted to hang on to.'

'Ah, so I assume there was some difficulty with the drug?'

'Well, that's the thing. As you may gather, once this sort of medication has been tested internally, it has to pass muster with the MHRA before it can be licensed for sale and distribution in the UK; and the whole process takes ages. In fact, *Davaproxin* turns out to have reached the stage of MHRA scrutiny far sooner than most drugs which are projected to be licensed with the sort of schedule under which it would end up being classified.'

'How do you know that?'

'When I read the article and recognised Greenberg, I went and did a little digging. To be honest, I assumed that the *Davaproxin* thing had turned out to be a bust, and I rather churlishly wanted to be able to point that fact out to my father. I'm not proud to admit it, but it's the truth.'

'We all have our little foibles, Stephen.'

'Quite.'

'I gather you turned up some interesting information.'

'Indeed. I learnt that *Davaproxin* had, according to Greenberg, been an unmitigated success in internal trials. So confident was he and his team of researchers, that they submitted it for MHRA scrutiny far earlier than they would ordinarily have done with such a drug. I can imagine that he wouldn't have had to cajole the directors of the company too much to get approval for an early submission, because he was the expert at the company, and it would please the major shareholders no end to be able to release a potentially groundbreaking product onto the market *sooner* rather than *later*.'

'Okay, I think I can see where this is going.'

'As it turns out, the details of clinical trials are available to the public through the Health Research Authority on their website, and I found out that an interim MHRA report on the drug would be released this week. In fact, today.'

'And?'

'I'll get to that, because it becomes more interesting than you may expect. When I looked into Greenberg, I found all sorts of interesting news items dating back at least ten years. He seems to be a bit of a maverick, and although he's been credited with some impressive research, he's known for making claims about his work which often exaggerate its true significance.'

'I see.'

'His stunt on Sky news was not the first time he'd gone public with all sorts of wild claims about a drug he was involved with. The company put up with him, because his claims would often cause the value of their shares to go up in the short term, and by the time the truth came out after years of delayed study results, nobody would really care or remember.'

'Right. So you suspected that the reason he'd been sacked from Ringmire, was that they'd found some difficulties with *Davaproxin*, and they were serious enough that the company could no longer tolerate his behaviour. In the circumstances, you expected the interim MHRA report to be unfavourable enough to cause a significant drop in the value of Ringmire's shares.'

'Precisely.'

'Okay. But there must be something more to it than that? Because surely the drop in value wouldn't be too significant based on an interim report? and surely you wouldn't have taken a very large position on the stock based on something that flimsy?'

'Well, it's complicated.'

'It seldom *isn't*.'

'The drop in value turned out to be *very* significant, and I'm afraid your estimation of my rationality is a bit too generous.'

'So what you're saying is that you *did* take a large position on the stock, purely on the basis of your speculation regarding the interim MHRA report?'

'Yes.'

'Okay, but then what about the report, and its effect on the share price? I'm assuming you short traded the stock?'

'Yes. So, based on my admittedly flimsy speculation regarding Greenberg, I put up just over seventy five percent of my equity as collateral on the trade, and I'm due to return the shares tomorrow.'

'*How much?!*'

'Approximately one point two million pounds.'

'Sorry, that's rendered me a bit lost for words.'

'Yes, me too, as it transpires.'

'So how much will it now cost you to buy back the shares you borrowed?'

'Last time I checked, which was just before our meeting started: Two hundred and seventy six thousand pounds. I expect it'll drop slightly more before the close of business. I plan on finding a way to buy the borrowed shares, and return them this afternoon, so I need you to write to the FCA and request that they allow me access to the account for that specific purpose.'

'That's quite a significant spot of good fortune.'

'Yes. I'm as surprised as anyone, to be perfectly honest.'

'If my quick mental arithmetic is accurate, that's almost an eighty percent decline in the share price. That's *insane*!'

'That's the problem. I've just made almost a million pounds off of this shorting of stock, in less than a week.'

'But. How?'

'It's a little disconcerting. It turns out that I was right about *Davaproxin*. The interim report is far from favourable, but that has absolutely nothing to do with the catastrophic drop in the share price.'

'I shouldn't have thought so.'

'It turns out that Greenberg has been fiddling the test results and internal reports on almost every single drug that the company has released since he started working there, over two decades ago.'

'What? How did it come out?'

'He wasn't sacked over *Davaproxin*. He was sacked over an internal audit done by a new research scientist that they'd brought in to test some of his work. The board were starting to worry about his process after he sought approval to have *Davaproxin* released for early scrutiny. They went ahead and released it anyway, because they didn't anticipate any major fallout from a negative interim report, and they wanted to keep him onside whilst they were auditing his research behind his back.'

'Okay, but still, surely it was all a secret?'

'It *was*. Until Monday morning, when a whilstle-blower's account of the situation found it's way on to the front pages of nearly every bloody newspaper in the country. The MHRA has suspended the licenses on almost every one of Ringmire's products pending further investigation, and the share price is sliding down the hill faster than a bowling ball covered in motor oil.'

'A whistleblower?'

'Yes. It turns out that a number of junior research assistants were complicit, and were being forced to sign non-disclosure agreements before being paid off and quietly let go. One of them decided to blow the whistle, because he suspected that the company would use them as scapegoats if anything ever came out.'

'Oh my god!'

'Yes, it's a monumental cock up.'

'I suppose that *is* the technical term for it.'

'So you see, Ian, that is how I came to be in so much trouble with the FCA. On reflection, and although I remain bitter and indignant about it, I suppose I can't really blame them.'

'Yes, quite.'

Just then, Ian's receptionist came in with the coffee and water he'd ordered, together with tea for Ian, and a plate of biscuits.

Ian took the tray from her and served Stephen himself. He was grateful for the brief lull in the conversation, and took some time before continuing. Ian could evidently sense his client's need for a break, so he let the silence hang until Stephen broke it.

'Do you think we could buy those shares back whilst I still have the chance?'

'Yes, that shouldn't be a problem, because you *are* innocent until proven guilty, and if you aren't allowed to buy back the shares and return them before the deadline, you'll be severely prejudiced. I don't think we'll have too much resistance, as long as you agree to keep the balance of the funds realised from the initial sale in escrow, pending the outcome of their investigation.'

'I have no difficulty with that.'

'In fact, I would assume that the circumstances will, in any event, trigger a securities recall, if only for the restitution of voting rights. I understand that recalling for voting purposes isn't all that common nowadays, but in these circumstances, it would definitely be prudent of the lender to recall the shares.'

'That's a very good point actually, I hadn't considered that.'

'If there's a recall, the FCA would have to allow the relevant transactions.'

'Fair enough. But what do you think about my prospects in general?'

Ian went quiet. He was clearly thinking about the situation. He looked down at his notes and made some additional ones before answering.

'I think they're reasonable. But I also think we have a lot of work to do. We can't ignore this and pretend it will work itself out, because the circumstances surrounding the situation are far too volatile. It's also likely to be reported in the media, so we need to make sure that every aspect of your defence is handled with care and discretion.'

'Thanks Ian, I feel a little bit better having explained the situation to you. But to be honest, I'm not sure I actually understand how this scenario all works from a legal point of view. I know I'm not a lawyer, but I did take a course in commercial law, and I understand the basics. Surely the FCA have to prove that I've been guilty of insider dealing, and that I've acted with intent? That's presumably a fairly difficult burden to discharge?'

'Yes. But it isn't that simple, really.'

'It never is, is it?'

'No, not really, Stephen. The thing is, that whilst they *can* charge you criminally, which *would* invoke a particularly onerous burden of proof; they aren't restricted to that particular course of action. Under the current legal framework, they can approach it from a civil-law perspective, and seek a purely administrative sanction.'

'Okay?'

'So, whilst this wouldn't necessarily *reverse* the onus of proof; their burden would be significantly lessened. They would only need to demonstrate your guilt on a balance of probabilities, and the sanction would still be relatively severe. At the very least, you could be ordered to return the proceeds realised from the sale, fined, and even disbarred.'

'But still, how do I prove a negative here, Ian?'

'We don't run about trying to prove negatives, Stephen. We produce as much evidence as we can, so that we find ourselves in a position to swing the probabilities in your favour, should the matter ever get to the point of a trial.'

'Shit.'

'You see, they already have what we call a *'prima facie* case'. Because, on the face of it, it really looks as if you had insider knowledge, and that your conduct amounted to what is defined in the relevant legislation as a *'misuse'* of that information. So we can't simply sit on our hands, and force them to prove it. We have to prepare a proper case in defence of your position, even though there are currently no formal charges or complaints pending .'

'I feel a little bit sick.'

'Sorry Stephen, I know this must be a terrible situation to find yourself in, but I'm here to fight for you. I aim to provide the FCA with sufficient evidence to exculpate you during the investigative phase of the process, so that we don't end up having to argue the matter at a trial, or even a disciplinary hearing. I can't guarantee that this will work, but you have the full weight of the firm behind you on it.'

'Thanks Ian, I appreciate that.'

'You're welcome Stephen, I'll make the relevant arrangements for the return of the borrowed shares, and I'll be in contact with you throughout the process. I'll apply my mind to the next steps, and let you know what I need from you; but at the very least, I'll need a printout of your recent trading history, going back about three years. I expect that it'll be necessary for you to depose to an affidavit in respect of what you've just outlined for me, but obviously I'll want some more specific details from you on certain aspects. I'll send you a brief memo during the course of the week, outlining my views on a sensible course of action, and asking some detailed questions.'

'Okay, I understand.'

'I want you to get some rest, try not to think about it, and remember not to discuss the case with anyone.'

'Thanks.'

***

Stephen left the offices of Wright & Hill feeling considerably worse than he had when he went in. What he'd convinced himself was a relatively minor difficulty, was now something more significant.

It's not that anything had changed over the past hour, but sitting with Ian, and being confronted with the harsh reality of his situation had more of a sobering effect on him than he'd expected it would.

It's never pleasant being accused of misconduct, but when the scope and nature of the complaint against you involves something which could very well lead to a criminal prosecution, regardless of how remote the possibility, it's likely to make you feel a little queasy. This is exactly how Stephen felt as he crossed the street into the grounds surrounding the Cathedral. In fact, he felt as if he would fall over if he didn't find somewhere to sit down. So he ambled over to the steps on the western portico of the Cathedral and took a seat.

All things considered, it wasn't a bad place to stop and reflect. He was sitting on part of one of the most impressive shrines to human endeavour the city had to offer. The monument, along with most of the other impressive edifices dotted around the capital, had a strange way of humbling those who took the time to appreciate their significance.

Looking around him, he couldn't help wondering how much toil and frustration the builders and architects went through during the process of constructing the grand building. It was certainly likely to have been a lot more difficult than what he was going through at that moment. But these things were all relative.

Although he wasn't especially prone to self-doubt, and seldom engaged in any form of self-recrimination, Stephen started to reflect on his situation without the self-indulgent filter he was used to applying whenever he'd done something foolish or reckless.

What the hell was he thinking with that trade?

It seemed to make sense at the time. In fact, looked at logically, his reasoning behind taking the ridiculously large position he took on the shares was fairly straightforward. He didn't expect the drop in the value of the shares to be too extreme, and wanted to use the scale to make it worthwhile.

But still, what if the *Davaproxin* assessments were *positive*, and the share value went *up*? That's when the scale creates havoc on the other edge of the proverbial 'sword'. His thinking had been too rigid and mechanical. This realisation scared him more than the thought of the possible repercussions of the investigation he was now under. He'd been so arrogant that he hadn't even stopped for an instant to consider that he may actually have been wrong. *That* was stupid... and dangerous.

He hadn't told Jim the real reason why he didn't share his information with Smith and the rest of the team. It had nothing to do with his aversion to Smith, and everything to do with his aversion to being second-guessed.

Jim was right, he definitely had some soul searching to do. He also had to try and get rid of the chip on his shoulder. It had transformed from being something which propelled and motivated him, into something which was now holding him back.

Maybe he *was* just running around on autopilot.

5

It had been ages since Stephen had been out socialising. He spent a fair deal of time attending office functions that were supposed to be 'social', but that sort of thing never truly is.

Fortunately, Charles had chosen the venue for their little catchup, because Stephen wouldn't have had the first idea where to go, even though he'd been living in Shoreditch for the past five years. He'd chosen a popular "*Speak Easy*" in the area. A trendy retrospective take on the old illicit watering holes which proliferated in the United States during the initial prohibition era of the twenties and early thirties. These sorts of places were now considered *de rigueur* in London, specifically amongst the younger crowd.

Stephen didn't follow trends, but he had to admit that the concept was actually quite interesting, and once he found his way into the establishment he was blown away by the attention to detail. He'd never really considered the term 'retro-chic' to be a realistic description of anything. Invariably there would be too much '*retro*', and not enough '*chic*'. But this place set the standard - it was exactly enough of both, and it was impressive.

The main bar had what looked like a solid oak countertop, dimly lit by hanging brass dome lights. Behind it were alcoves cut into the raw brickwork and bordered with clean, bold retro picture frames. These alcoves housed bottles of expensive spirits that became elements of the 'pictures', which appeared inside the frames. It was clever and stylish; as were all of the eclectic design choices in the place - from aged brass tabletops, to the button backed sofas adorned with colourful cushions. It shouldn't have worked. But somehow it did.

It came as no surprise to Stephen that this place was known to his mate Charlie. It was totally his sort of vibe.

He immediately noticed him when he scanned the room. He was leaning against the side of the bar with a whisky in front of him, and a contented smile on his face.

Same old Charlie, completely at peace with himself and with the world around him. If he could have bottled and sold his unique brand of uninhibited self-confidence, he'd be a billionaire by now. He still sported long curly black hair, and wore clothes that looked like they came straight out of some indy film, set in the late seventies. Stephen didn't know how he did it, but somehow he made it look modern and cutting edge. Charlie was a force of nature!

'Charles!'

'Stevie! How you doing mate?'

'I'm good thanks. You?'

'Can't complain. A bit busy, but at least it's keeping me out of the pubs.'

'You look well though. Clearly being busy suits you.'

'Thanks Steve. Yeah, as I say, I haven't any complaints.'

He shrugged and smiled. He was clearly in a good place. Meeting up with him after all this time was strangely comfortable. It felt as if there's been absolutely no break.

'So what are *you* up to these days, Steve?'

'Mainly work, to be honest, but I'm off for a bit, so I'm looking forward to getting some *personal-time* in. I need to pick up a hobby or something.'

'Glad to hear it! Too much work is definitely unhealthy!'

'I suppose it is.'

'I'm not one to talk though. I've been working like a maniac for the past few months. Deadline looming.'

'Not so chilled in the game design world then, Charlie?'

Hi friend burst out laughing and almost chocked on his drink in the process.

'No mate, we don't work in garages and sheds any more. It's bigger than the global film industry! So the pressure to stay competitive is pretty constant.'

'I suppose that was inevitable. I suppose it's all very corporate now hey?'

'Painfully.'

'That's the price of progress Charlie.'

'Yeah. It sort of crept up on me. My parents thought that video game design was a copout when I didn't pursue a career as a bloody actuary, but I probably work much harder than an actuary now.'

'You probably *do*. But you probably also *earn* a lot more.'

'I hope so. I actually showed my Dad my payslip the last time he tried to give me a speech about wasting my education. He almost had a *heart attack*.'

'Good for you Charlie!'

'It felt a bit dirty, to be honest Steve. I don't give a toss what I make. But I did it to get the miserable old bugger off my back. I suppose I also wanted to show off a bit. I still feel awkward about it.'

'I wouldn't. Besides, it worked, didn't it?'

'Yeah, but it opened another can of worms. Because now my mother wants to know why I haven't bought a house, and settled down with what she calls *"a nice girl"*.'

'Shame on you Charles, how disappointing for her.'

'I haven't really got the heart to tell her that I date two *naughty girls,* who are covered in tattoos, and probably like one another more than they like *me.*'

'I think not being able to tell your mother about that sort of thing is a small price to pay for getting to do it, mate. I can't imagine you have many complaints in *that* department, either.'

'No, I certainly don't take my situation for granted, Stevie. What about *you*? How's the love life?'

'*Non-existent,* mate. Same old cliché: too focussed on work, and too out of practice to muster the enthusiasm to give it a bash.'

'Fuck sakes, Stephen! *Really*?!'

'Don't *you* start too, Charlie boy. I've been getting an earful about it from a psychologist that my boss has hired to *assess* me.'

'Assess you for *what*? To see whether or not you've lost your *balls*?'

'Pretty much. He won't push through my promotion until he's satisfied that I'm happy, and that I've '*found myself*'; or some such bullshit.'

'Wise man, your boss. He can't have you going through a meltdown when you're forty, because you're miserable and unanchored.'

'Whose bloody side are *you* on, Charles.'

'I choose *life,* mate. I may be overworked a lot of the time, but I'm as happy as a pig in the proverbial.'

'I'm sure you are.'

'Before you say it; it's not because I'm having threesomes a few times a week. That *helps,* to be sure, but it's because I love most of the work I do, and when I'm not struggling with the odd deadline, I take the time to do the non-work related things that make me happy.'

'You make it sound so easy. Maybe we're just wired differently.'

'It *is* easy, you just have to live on your own terms, instead of the terms you *think* you should be living on.'

'What do you mean?'

'When I left university, I decided to do exactly what I wanted to do. I disappointed my parents by not going into the career that my qualification suggested I should have gone into. I didn't do it because I just wanted to be bloody-minded and act out; I did it because I knew it was right for me, and I had no intention of sacrificing my future happiness on the altar of parental expectation.'

'I suppose that makes sense.'

'It did to me at the time, and it still *does*. Once I'd got a taste for that sort of departure from the norm, I made a few *other* seemingly eccentric life-choices. I decided to move in with a group of mates, because I found the idea of living alone boring. Then I chose to date two open-minded women instead of following the life textbook and settling for marriage and kids. I found that that sort of lifestyle suited my personality better.'

'Fair enough. You were lucky you knew what you wanted in life.'

'I didn't. I still don't. I knew what I wanted to do for a living, but I didn't really have any long term goals. I don't really have any of those yet, either. But I haven't met anyone my age who *does*, so I'm not to stressed about that.'

'You seem to know yourself pretty well though, Charlie.'

'Yeah, I am fortunate in that particular respect.'

'I thought I had it all figured out. But I'm not so sure anymore. I like my job most of the time, and I like making money, but it's been pointed out to me recently that earning money isn't a good enough long term goal.'

'Do you agree that it isn't Steve?'

'No. Not really Charlie. I still think it's a fair aspiration. I suppose you agree with the argument to the contrary?'

'I don't know, to be honest. I never thought in terms of money. I also like having it, but it's not what drives me. I know it's what drives most people, but I've never taken the time to consider the implications.'

'I might be a little obsessed with money. Maybe it's unhealthy, but at least it's uncomplicated.'

Stephen had never been particularly good at self-reflection, probably because he'd never bothered trying. Ever since he was a child, he'd concentrated on overcoming obstacles and solving problems; but he didn't spend any time analysing his own motivations. He didn't ever consider why it was that he'd identified a particular obstacle to overcome or problem to solve, he simply forged ahead and spent his energy on the process of achieving the goal. The reason behind wanting to achieve it never seemed important to him.

'So what does the psych want you to do?'

'She wanted me to contact my old university mates; which is why I've reconnected with you. Sorry mate, it wasn't my initiative.'

'Hey, I've also been a rubbish friend, so I can't blame you there.'

'She want's me to do some of the things I used to enjoy doing back then; and she wants me to have sex.'

'Sounds like a smart doctor to me, mate!'

'That's just because her agenda suits your proclivities.'

Charles almost choked on his drink again.

'Are you saying that enjoying yourself and having sex doesn't suit you, Steve?'

'No. You know what I mean.'

'I honestly don't, mate.'

Stephen was forced to laugh. When he went back over what he'd said in his head, he had to concede that it sounded as ridiculous to him as it must have sounded to his mate.

'Okay Charlie, you've got me there.'

'It makes sense. Your psychologist is trying to take you back to the last time you were likely to be really happy, which, for most people, was at university.'

'They were good times, I'll give you that.'

'Course they were. Maybe if you relive them a bit, you can figure out what you lost from those days.'

'I don't think I'm unhappy though. Just busy, and maybe a little too involved with work some of the time.'

'Your problem is that your work has made you one-dimensional. That sort of thing even happens in *my* industry. Any job that forces you to pull big hours can do that.'

'Christ Charles, you make it sound like I've developed a disability or something. What makes you think there's something wrong with me?'

'Steve, you're not *here* mate.'

'What do you mean?'

'You're physically in the space you're occupying, but your mind is elsewhere. You aren't present.'

'Since when did you become a psychic?'

'It's not rocket science. I know you well enough to tell.'

'Really?'

'Yip. To be fair, you'd also probably be able to tell if *I* wasn't present.'

Stephen paused. He *was* elsewhere, but he put that down to being preoccupied with the FCA investigation that was hanging over his head, and the suspension from work.

'To tell you the truth Charlie, I'm in a bit of shit at the moment, so my mind *is* wandering a bit. Sorry.'

'How deep is the shit?'

'I'm not too sure actually, but it's damned unpleasant.'

Charlie though about what Stephen had told him for a few moments before continuing.

'Forget about it. There's probably sod all you can do to fix it right now, so save the energy. You need to start doing something other than work to keep your mind occupied.'

'Yeah, I've been working eighty hour weeks for years now, it's no wonder I haven't been doing anything else.'

'Or any *one* else, clearly. You can't live like that for very long mate, and your boss knows it, because he was probably the same as you when he was your age.'

'You should meet my boss. I think he was born in a suit and tie. That's why his sudden concern for my state of mind is so weird.'

'You'd be surprised how little you know about the people you work with, mate. Most people hide from themselves at work, so they end up hiding from everyone else too. Most people aren't really suited to what they do, so they have to take on a different persona at work. You don't actually get to know them unless you make the kind of effort that seems inappropriate.'

'You're probably right. I only just found out this week that my personal assistant is a lesbian, and is choosing to hide it from everyone at the office because she's scared that she'll be leered at constantly by all the childish men in the bloody building.'

'Yip, sounds pretty standard. So you see, your boss is probably a decent chap. He just has to be a different person at work; which is okay up to a point, but if you wear the disguise for long enough, you become the other person. He knows that, so he's trying to save you from falling down the rabbit-hole.'

'I enjoy my job though.'

'Okay, I can accept that. But you can't let it define you completely. I'm being a bit of bloody hypocrite saying that, because I do it myself. But I'm trying to change.'

'Seriously?'

'Yeah. Seriously. I know you don't play games anymore Steve, so you may not know this; but I'm pretty famous now in the gaming world. It's hard for something like that not to go to your head. It's also easy to let yourself be defined by how other's perceive you.'

'That's interesting. I don't tend to think about that sort of thing.'

'Have you never wondered what you'd do if you weren't a trader?'

'No.'

'Would you still do it if you were wealthy enough not to have to work?'

'What's wealthy enough?'

'You're a numbers guy Steve, you must have a figure.'

'Okay, I follow you. I don't know actually, I haven't given it any thought. Would you do your job for free? Assuming you didn't need an income.'

'Yeah. Probably.'

'I wouldn't know what to do with myself, to be honest.'

'That's why you need to go through this process mate. Your boss has gifted you with a rare opportunity. Use it! You had loads of interests and hobbies at university. Please tell me that you haven't given up drawing? You were a seriously talented artist.'

Stephen looked at Charles sheepishly.

'Ummm.'

'You're a twat!'

'Yes. That seems to be the prevailing opinion. I just thought that since it was never realistically going to pay the bills, it wasn't worth pursuing.'

'Right. Like playing video games was never going to pay *my* bills. Twat! Anyway, nobody's asking you to run off and paint pictures for a living. You just need something other than work to occupy yourself and keep you balanced.'

'Okay, okay, I'll go get some art supplies. Anything else, uncle Charlie?'

'What else did you do back then?'

'Same as you, mate. Played computer games, Dungeons & Dragons, and got drunk with my mates. Nothing earth shatteringly unique and special.'

'Well, getting drunk probably isn't something you should turn into a hobby, unless you're planning on starting a craft brewery in your spare room. But in addition to pulling out the pencil case; play some games, join a D&D group, and try to meet someone.'

'Know any good dating sites?'

'Not really, no. I've never found the need.'

'Smug bastard. Next round's on you!'

***

Stephen woke up late on Wednesday morning.

After his customary morning espresso, he began to mull over what Charles had said the previous evening about finding some hobbies to engage in. Although, trying to work out what to do with himself was exacerbating the dull headache that had taken hold of him almost as soon as he'd surfaced. He couldn't remember the last time he'd drank that many cocktails.

He felt like a spider whose web had been covered in an oily substance. No matter how hard he tried to find his grip, he seemed to keep slipping.

It started to dawn on him that this was evidently why he'd been avoiding taking leave. Maybe he was subconsciously aware of the fact that he'd forgotten how to amuse himself outside of work.

After leaving university, he actively avoided his old pastimes, because they'd seemed so childish.

How was he supposed to take himself seriously as a business person if he spent his weekends playing computer games, or pretending to be one of the members of the fellowship of the ring?

He was irritated with himself. Why couldn't he have had more mature hobbies? Like *golf*, or *fly fishing*?

He didn't suspect that he could ever make himself enjoy golf, so that had to be crossed off the list immediately. But he hadn't tried fly fishing. Maybe that would end up being his 'thing'. It appeared to be a relatively peaceful and civilised exercise, and it was certainly popular with some members of the posh whiskey-drinking crowd at the office.

But first… the date thing!

He wished Charles had been more helpful. He knew all he needed to do was run a basic web search - but how would he know which site to *pick*? It probably wouldn't be a good idea to have multiple accounts, that could lead to all sorts of confusion. What if he got it wrong, and ended up buying a foreign bride by mistake? This was stressful.

He decided to call Mary… *she'd* know what to do.

'Morning M, how are things at the office without me? Keeping *busy*?'

'Morning Stephen. I thought it would take at least a few more days before you contacted me.'

'You should be flattered M, it's because I miss you.'

'Don't talk shite, it's because you've had me tying your shoelaces for so long that you've forgotten how to do them *yourself*. Do you need to find out how to cook one of the fit meals I sent you? I thought the instructions were pretty clear. Oh, hold on. A *'microwave safe'* dish is pretty much anything that isn't metal, Stephen.'

'Very funny, Mary. Thanks for the tasteless food, by the way.'

'Can't have you putting on too much weight Stephen, Jim told me that the good doctor has prescribed some *dating* for you.'

'My god. What ever happened to *"client confidentiality"*?'

'To be fair, I think Jim guessed it. Because he told her that you battle with women, which he learned from *me* in the first place. But thanks for the confirmation.'

'*Bloody hell* Mary, what makes you think I have problems with women?'

'Apart from Cindy, when was the last time you went on a date, Mr West?'

'You know about Cindy?'

'Of course I know about Cindy, Stephen. Kenneth told me. Stop avoiding the question.'

'I don't remember.'

'Me neither; and I've been working for you for over three years. If that's not a problem, then what is it? Do you prefer men?'

'No! Of course not!'

'Don't sound so indignant Stephen, remember, I'm not heterosexual.'

'Sorry, I'm just a little uptight, because the *'doctor'* thinks I have *'perceived sexual inadequacy issues'*.'

'Who doesn't?'

'What do mean?'

'We all have some sexual inadequacy issues, Stephen. That's normal. You just have to crack on and get past it. It's why they invented beer.'

'Actually, that's the reason for the call. Do you know any good dating sites?'

'No. I've been dating the same person for ten years now. We met at a friend's party.'

'Bugger!'

'I'm a touch busy, but I can have Kenny research some for you, if you'd like.'

'No! Not *Kenny*! leave that little sod out of it. He was responsible for hooking me up with Cindy. I'll have to brave the internet on my own.'

'May the force be with you, Stephen. I'm sure you'll come right, so to speak.'

'Thanks M, hold thumbs for me!'

After hanging up, Stephen felt a little embarrassed that his first instinct was to call Mary in order to help him navigate the task of trying to find a dating site. He was starting to realise just how absurd his reliance on his personal assistant had become.

He resolved to try and sort his love life out without any more assistance. At least, without any more '*non-digital*' assistance. He opened his laptop and ran a search.

Dating site reviews UK

… … … … … … … … …

The first thing that popped up was a list of the top ten review sites, not the top ten dating sites, as he'd expected.

Although it was more or less what he was looking for, he was still a bit taken aback by just how many websites were dedicated to reviewing *other* websites. He thought there
would be the odd digital GQ article, and some similar pieces from other popular magazines. He didn't expect to find more than a dozen whole sites

dedicated to the exercise. He was clearly a bit behind the times.

He went with to the first review site, and ended up having to create an account before continuing. This was irritating, but he was just savvy enough to understand that all the others would likely have the same requirement. The word "free" was clearly a bit of a misnomer, but he accepted that allowing the site to send him rubbish emails from time to time was a small price to pay for the useful information promised.

Almost immediately though, he realised that the reviews weren't even remotely detailed. Some had short write-ups, but it was really nothing more than an elaborate 'top-ten' list.

He wasn't about to sign up to another similar review site, so he decided to investigate the actual dating site with the highest score.

EDgE

It had 10/10 - but it didn't seem to have any reviews or write-ups. He'd have to just go to and see what it looked like.

… … … …

'Home'

… … … …

The world is changing… so is dating!

EDgE is a specialist site… it's authentic… it's serious… it's for people who know exactly what they want, and aren't afraid to take it - this site is for people who don't want their time wasted. It was created <u>by</u> the best… <u>for</u> the best.

Our process is proprietary, it's only available to members, and only after upfront payment and vetting - we wouldn't presume to waste your time with silly questions… So don't waste ours - sign up and experience the real thing!

'Pricing'

£360.00 up-front and £100.00 a month thereafter.

He nearly fell off his chair, they obviously weren't joking when they said it was *"serious"*. He decided to look at some of the other sites, they couldn't all be that expensive.

… … … …

The review site didn't end up making much of a difference. All of the dating sites listed in the top ten appeared to be identical, and the reviews looked like they were all just slightly reworded copies of the same thing.

Although, it *was* nice of them to separate the *'serious relationship'* sites from the *'casual hookup'* sites. Maybe he was a bit old fashioned, but that seemed a bit much. Once he'd moved through the top ten, things did start to get a bit more interesting though.

Eventually he landed up at *"Top 10 infidelity sites 2019"*, and decided that he'd had enough.

Maybe it was worth giving *'EDgE'* a go? Maybe he could even get Jim to expense it? Seeing that he was evidently so keen on Stephen exploring his dating options.

It must have received full marks for a reason. The next highest on the list only got eight out of ten.

***

CONGRATULATIONS MR WEST!

Your deposit has been received and your receipt has been emailed to you…

We have also emailed you your unique access code, and a link to confirm your email address - please follow the link and sign in with the details provided in the email.

Once you have confirmed your email, we will assist you with setting up your account and preparing the necessary personality profiling assessments.

Before you leave this page, we suggest that you follow the link below to acquaint yourself with our current special offers - as an introductory gift, we have included a discount voucher for 30% off of our unique shop items… this is our way of expressing our appreciation for your business, and introducing you to the world of specialised dating.

Although this seemed somewhat elaborate, Stephen was impressed. EDgE certainly seemed to be a professional outfit, and he was curious to see what sort of items were being sold at the online shop. He didn't think dating sites sold anything other than their main service.

EDgE SHOP

……………

Welcome to the EDgE Online Shop - this bespoke platform is only available to our members - please enter your login details below.

Login SUCCESSFUL

… … … … … … … …

Hello Mr West - click the button below to enter the SHOP.

… … … … … … … …

EDgE SHOP - DARE TO BE SPECIAL - DARE TO BE YOU!
For Her
For Him
Date Packs
Special offers
Shipping Details
FAQ
Help?

Stephen's headache was starting to get worse. Exploring the shop wasn't likely to help matters, but his curiosity compelled him to keep going. He decided to have a look at the special offers.

Special Offers

Our unique 'date packs' are the flagship offerings here at EDgE - As far as we're concerned, if you're going to have an evening of fun, you may as well do it the right way - the EDgE way!

We currently have all four of these packs on Special Offer - if you're new to EDgE, your promotion voucher will be applied to the already reduced price of these packs, making the saving simply... irresistible!

In case you were wondering... We don't reveal the contents of the packs at point of sale... because the mystery is part of the fun - we don't do things in half-measure - so you can rest assured that whatever we have included will be top drawer, and well worth the outlay.

He'd heard of these 'date pack' things... Kenny got one a while back, and it sounded interesting. It was for a *'fun night in'*, apparently.

Stephen remembered him saying that it had fluffy handcuffs, chocolate body paint, expensive vodka and some foreplay card game thing. A bit kinky, but a great idea actually. Obviously not a *'first date'* sort of thing - the kind of thing you do once you're ready to be a bit more intimate. He had no doubt that *EDgE* would do them properly.

Although, he assumed they'd be relatively expensive. He remembered Ken saying that his one cost him about £40, which seemed a bit ridiculous for some bits of plastic, chocolates, and a small bottle of craft vodka.

... ...

The Bronze Edition - standard price £290.00 - now only £260.00 The Silver Edition - standard price £350.00 - now only £300.00The Gold Edition - standard price £420.00 - now only £350.00The Platinum Edition - standard price £870.00 - now only £600.00

His assumption had been accurate. What on earth could they *have* in those things?! He couldn't imagine it was just a set of fluffy handcuffs and some expensive plonk... if it was, it would have to be a bottle of Dom Pérignon, gold plated cuffs covered in mink, and hand made imported chocolate... and that would just be for the *'Bronze Edition'*.

He contemplated buying one just to find out what it contained, but he stopped himself and decided to wait until he actually managed to find a date before indulging in any ludicrously expensive *'date packs'*.

He closed the online shop and decided to keep going with the site registration. They'd doubtless require him to create a personal profile, and although he didn't exactly feel like working his way through that sort of process, he had nothing better to do.

THANK YOU FOR CONFIRMING YOUR EMAIL ADDRESS!

… … … … … … … …

Your account has been successfully activated and you may now proceed to create your personal profile.

Please take the time to complete the relevant forms.

The blocks marked with a red star are 'required fields' and have to be filled out, whilst the other blocks are optional.

… … … … … … … …

We encourage our users to use the opportunity to complete all fields though, because the more data we have, the more likely we are to be able to find suitable matches from our database.

You will note that the forms include a section marked 'personal information', and a section marked 'personality assessment'. The first of these sections should take no longer than five minutes to complete, and the second, no longer than two hours.

All information gathered by our system in this process is kept strictly confidential, and only released to possible matches with specific permission, on a match by match basis…

No longer than *two hours*?! What had he gotten himself into? He was too far along to stop, so he took some headache tablets and cracked on. At least Bridgette couldn't accuse him of slacking off on the dating exercise.

… … … … … … … …

Please take note that we do not allow our clients to upload photographs to their own profiles, given the potential for misrepresentation. After having completed the relevant forms, we shall contact you and arrange to send a professional photographer to your place of business or residence in order that appropriate photographs can be taken for your profile. In this manner we can present you at your best, and vouch for the authenticity of the material - you will appreciate that this is for the benefit of all concerned parties.

Insofar as the two personal references are concerned, we ask simply that they do not include family members.

… … … … … … … …

Personal references?! He supposed he'd have to use Jim and Mary. At least they both knew what he was up to, so it wouldn't be *overly* embarrassing… Still a *bit* embarrassing, but this dating thing was Jim's idea in the first place, and Mary may as well have been his mother, so…

… … … … … … … …

We have emailed you a booking form, to assist with arranging a one-on-one vetting consultation with one of our client advisors, who will pay you a short visit at your place of residence. These appointments are usually very brief, and seldom take longer than twenty minutes.

Stephen started to understand why it was that this dating site was so expensive. They certainly expended a lot of time and effort getting their members '*set up*'. He realised that he'd have to clean the flat before having them around, so he arranged the consultation for the following week. He also realised that he'd better get hold of Jim and Mary to tell each of them to expect a call from EDgE, in case they thought it was some sort of scam.

'Hi Mary, me again.'

'Miss me *already*, Stephen? Getting withdrawals from office life?'

'No, nothing like that. I just wanted to give you a heads-up. I signed on to this ridiculously expensive dating site, and they needed me to provide references. I've given them your and Jim's details, so expect a call from them, and try to be *nice*.'

'I'm touched that you listed me as a reference, Stephen; and when am I ever not "*nice*"?'

'Thanks M. I appreciate the help!'

'Of course, Stephen. Enjoy the rest of your day. Go do something fun!'

'I'll try, thanks!'

Jim was probably going to laugh at him, but he'd have to suck it up. At least his headache was starting to abate.

'James Roberts' office, you're speaking to Denise. How may I assist you?'

'Hi Denise, it's Stephen here. Is Jim available by any chance? I didn't want to call on his mobile, in case he was in a meeting.'

'Morning Mr West, you've actually caught him in between meetings. I'll get him on the line for you, shall I?'

'Thanks, Denise.'

'Stephen. Good to hear from you lad, how's the leave?'

'It's not too bad actually.'

'You don't sound too bloody enthusiastic about it.'

'It *is* 'gardening leave', Jim. It's not like I chose to take the time off.'

'Yes. Quite. But never mind, try to make the best of it. What can I do for you?'

'I need a small favour.'

'Name it.'

'As per the good doctor's unequivocal orders, I'm trying to find a date; and to that end…'

'I'm married Stephen, and I don't go in for that sort of thing.'

'Gimme a chance Jim, I was trying to get to the point.'

'Sorry, you just make it so easy sometimes.'

'The long and the short of it, is that I've managed to sign up to one of these fancy dating sites, and they need *non-family* references. Since you've worked me so bloody hard over the last few years, I've hardly any mates left, so I've listed you and Mary as references.'

'What a bloody indictment. I *told* you you needed to get a life, son.'

'Please take their call, and be nice. Also, I'd thank you to refrain from telling them what you told Bridgette.'

'Oh. You *know* about that? Sorry my boy; I just had to give her all of the salient facts, as I saw them.'

'You can make up for it by allowing me to expense the dating site. It cost me an arm and a leg.'

'Haven't you heard?'

'Heard what?'

'You've just made a fortune, you're a bloody millionaire Stephen. Pay for your own dating sites!'

'It was worth a try.'

'No it wasn't. Grow up. Then maybe you'll actually make some poor bird a half-decent boyfriend. Don't think I'm not aware of the fact that you even had that lovely personal assistant of yours buying your fucking groceries, my lad.'

'I didn't ask her to do that.'

'Maybe not… but the fact that she did it anyway tells me more about *your* failings as a functional human being than it tells me about her mommy complex.'

'I take your point.'

Stephen felt more than a little guilty that he'd asked Jim to expense the dating site. The old man was right - he *did* need to grow up. It was absurd that he was still reflexively relying on Jim and Mary to take care of him.

He spent the rest of the day nursing his hangover, and turned in early.

6

Stephen woke up on Thursday morning feeling somewhat better than he had the day before, but he still didn't really know what to do with himself. After engaging in the painfully awkward exercise of writing in that journal that Bridgette had insisted he keep, Stephen found himself bored and fidgety.

He'd managed to make himself some eggs on toast, after which, he showered and sat down to read some news on his tablet. The first thing that loaded was another story about Ringmire PLC. So he closed the news app and tossed the tablet down onto the sofa alongside him. He didn't need to read anything else about the embattled pharmaceutical company. He'd only just managed to shake his headache from earlier. He didn't need to induce another one.

Fortunately, Ian had managed to arrange for him to purchase and return the borrowed shares, so as far as Stephen was concerned, the state of the company was now irrelevant.

He needed some fresh air. Perhaps it was worth trying out the *fly fishing* thing? Perhaps he ought to go and buy some kit so that he could give it a go. He knew Jim was into it, and he could probably have borrowed some equipment from *him* before splashing out on his own, but he wasn't inclined to ask any more favours.

After staring at the wall for about ten minutes, he couldn't come up with any better ideas, so he looked up the closest fishing shop, and went to investigate their wares.

When he got there, he realised that it was evidently a 'high-end' shop, because it was beautifully appointed. It had dark green walls, adorned with a number large wooden plaques holding mounted fish, and sporting elaborate brass plates describing the details of the trophies.

There was far more space than necessary between the various equipment displays, which, together with the dim lighting, and the smell of leather and cork, gave the place a curious sense of opulence. Clearly, the proprietors weren't particularly concerned about paying for more than double the floorspace they actually needed.

Of course, as is so often the case with these things - the customers don't necessarily make this connection. On the contrary, most of them would be likely to feel inordinately comfortable in the space. As a consequence, they would be likely to spend more time browsing and, by implication, more money.

Stephen made the connection immediately, because he was wired that way. Although he wouldn't admit it, he was obsessed with money - most specifically, the relationship between cost and value.

Perhaps it was a result of growing up with a fastidious father figure, or perhaps it was just a symptom of his antipathy for the more privileged classes - but either way, Stephen was acutely aware of the fact that price and value were not necessarily synonymous concepts. He used to cringe whenever somebody told him that something was 'worth' a specific amount, just because that was the price they'd paid for it.

During his post graduate degree, one of his economics professors had explained that the value of something was determined solely by the price that somebody was willing to pay for it, at the moment at which the seller decided to sell it. This had stuck with Stephen, and ever since, he couldn't help but consider it, whenever he decided to purchase anything more expensive than a half-decent bottle of wine.

But… because things are never really that simple, Stephen's overweening sense of pride often overruled his reluctance to waste money. It was for this reason that he wore ludicrously expensive clothes and shoes to work, used vastly overpriced golf clubs (in spite of the fact that he didn't even like the game), and ate at obnoxiously expensive restaurants whenever he was entertaining a colleague or a client.

He justified the expense by telling himself that it was the cost of doing business, but it still stung him a little every time, and would leave him feeling slightly guilty for days.

Interestingly, his attitude was completely different when it came to artwork and interior decoration. His love of art and aesthetics trumped his sense of value when it came to these things, and he never gave purchasing a good piece of furniture, a handwoven rug, or a beautiful piece of art a second thought.

The fly fishing was going to be just like the golf. He knew it was a rich man's game, and he refused to let the other participants know that he wasn't part of the club.

Of course, the helpful gentleman at the fishing store seemed to be aware of this. He'd evidently developed a very keen sense for wealthy-looking city types who clearly didn't have the first clue about what they were looking at, but were invested in the idea of getting into the game, or '*sport*' as the proponents of the pastime adamantly describe it.

After he'd ambled aimlessly around the fishing-rod displays for a few minutes, he was politely interrupted by a very articulate and well-presented individual in an open-necked white shirt, grey trousers and a light Harris Tweed sport coat.

The scene played out like it usually does; the subtext being so thinly veiled, that it may as well have been expressed openly.

'Good morning Sir, is there anything I can assist you with today?'

'Yes, actually. I'm interested in some fly fishing kit, but I'm not too sure where to start.'

As he said it, Stephen felt like kicking himself. He knew this would make him a target for an unscrupulous sales-person. It was now too late to change tac though, so he'd have to go with it, and see where it led.

Of course, the shop assistant was more than happy to oblige. He paused for few moments, looked his customer up and down one last time, and beamed amiably.

'Oh… so you're completely new to the sport then?'

What he meant was: '*Marvellous… I hope the Omega you're wearing is genuine.*'

What Stephen heard was: '*Ha, hello weakling! Welcome to my domain! Thank you for giving me the opportunity to demonstrate how much more powerful I am, and how insignificant you are in my pond. Perhaps you haven't noticed, this is a very exclusive shop, you probably can't afford our equipment.*'

'Yes, I'm thinking of giving it a bash, I expect I'll pick it up pretty quickly, so I need some decent equipment. I don't want anything that I'll end up having to replace in a few weeks' time.'

('*I see your chips, and I raise you. You may be a big fish in your little pond, but I'm a bigger fish than you in real life. You sell fishing rods for a living, and I'm a big shot in the city with a swanky office, and a large wallet. So even though you're supposedly the alpha here, I can probably afford better kit than you.*')

'Certainly sir, I can tell that you're the sort of chap who doesn't do things in half-measure…'

('*Oh how wonderful. So you're a rich wanker, and you think that your money will make you look important to us shop assistants. It'll be a pleasure to empty your pockets. Indeed, I'm sure it'll make both of us feel infinitely better about this little interaction.*')

'I'm glad we appear to be on the same page.'

('*That's right my lad! I'm more than capable of keeping up with the rich fishing crowd, so wake up and pay attention.*')

'We certainly are, Sir.'

('*Alright you obnoxious bastard, get ready for a world class fleecing!*')

Stephen learnt, much to his annoyance, that once he started plumbing the depths of the deceptively sparse fishing shop, there was almost no end to the amount of equipment needed for the seemingly simple exercise of catching a relatively small fish.

Clearly, he'd chosen a ridiculously expensive establishment, because even the cheapest rods, (which were sold separately to the reels), were just over two hundred pounds apiece. Given his earlier exchange with the shop assistant, he wasn't about to go for something at the bottom of the range, so he settled for something which cost around £700.00. Even *that* seemed to make the shop assistant sneer a little, so he chose a particularly expensive reel, and what seemed like half a ton of *'essential'* paraphernalia to make up for it.

He ended up dropping over £1000.00 on the whole exercise, and left feeling like a bit of an idiot. He was now committed to the fishing thing though, because he wasn't about to allow himself to let all of that exorbitantly priced equipment go to waste.

The following day, he sent Jim a message, and was pleased to note that the old man was thrilled about his new-found enthusiasm for *'the sport'*. Jim suggested that they go out that Saturday for a fishing lesson. Apparently he'd been itching to get down to Hampshire, and fish on *"the River Test"*.

Stephen was keen to get out of the flat, and was equally interested in the idea of putting his new fishing gear to some sort of productive use. So he didn't need much encouragement to agree, even though Jim insisted on picking him up well before dawn.

He spent most of Friday engaged in the less than exhilarating exercises of reorganising his cupboards, and tidying his flat. The boredom of being at a loose end was starting to weigh heavily on him.

***

Stephen woke up in the usual panicked and confused way you do when your alarm yanks you out of a deep sleep, like some sort of sadistic drill sergeant with a penchant for unnecessary cruelty.

If he could have mustered the energy to swear out loud he would have done so, but he was fully occupied with the task of getting hold of the phone next to his bed, so that he could stop the noise.

As is often the case with modern phone alarms, they get progressively louder over time, so as to make absolutely sure that you can't sleep through them. Because it had taken some time to drag him from his slumber, this evil thing was now approaching the decibel level of a smoke alarm. The curious thing about really loud alarms, is that they're often so piercing that they tend to stun you, rather than spur you into any sort of coherent action.

After fumbling around in the dark for what felt like minutes rather than seconds, Stephen managed to stop the cacophony and turn on his bedside light, hoping that this would help him to keep his eyes open.

It was 4:00 in the morning. On a Saturday. Now that he was semi-conscious, he wondered what on earth was going through his head when he agreed to go out fishing with Jim this early. He stumbled into the bathroom for a quick shower to wake him up a bit more, and then hastily got dressed.

Fortunately he'd prepared all of the fishing gear the previous evening, and placed it strategically by the door. It almost took up the whole passage though, and he barely managed to avoid tripping when he went to open the door for Jim.

'Morning Stephen. You look awful.'

'It's bloody four in the morning Jim… I'm surprised I'm even able to stand up.'

'You youngsters are useless when it comes to getting up in the morning. I've been up since just after three.'

'That's not the morning, Jim. It's the middle of the sodding night.'

'Well, if you want to catch fish, you need to get out early my lad. I want us to be in Hampshire before six, so let's crack on. I have some coffee in a thermos flask in the car.'

'Sounds marvellous!'

After loading Jim's Range Rover with all of the gear, they headed out of the city. Jim didn't seem overly concerned with speed limits, so they were making good time on the journey, and after having found his way through a cup of strong black coffee, Stephen felt more human.

'So Jim, I'm not moaning, I'm genuinely curious. Why do we need to fish so early?'

'Because it's summer, and the fish tend to be a bit more active in the early hours.'

'Ah. So we want them to be active then?'

'Well, obviously we want them to be active, son. If they aren't active, they won't be running about looking for a spot of breakfast will they?'

'Ah, yes, okay. That makes sense.'

'You genuinely have no bloody idea about fishing, do you?'

'Afraid not.'

'What *do* you know about, apart from work?'

'Art, Art history, and … well, that's about it really.'

'You're pulling my leg, aren't you?'

'No, I'm not. My mate Charles says that work has made me 'one dimensional'. I suppose he's right.'

'Well, it's a good job I've got you seeing Bridgette then.'

'You think she'll help me 'find myself' then, Jim?'

'I think she'll make you uncomfortable enough to push you into the sort of corner that'll force a bit of self-reflection. I suppose that could be classified as help. She certainly helped *me*.'

'So you saw her in that capacity as well then?'

'Yeah, that's how I know she has the goods. I think she also did some work with your other boss, Anne Cole, but Anne keeps pretty much to herself, so we've never really discussed it.'

'Shit… so I'm not the only one with issues?'

'Everyone has issues Stephen, you aren't as unique as you'd like to think you are, my lad.'

'I suppose not, I just haven't really thought about it.'

'That *is* something fairly unique about you Stephen. You're oblivious to the rest of the world. Like one of those old people who drive around town, concentrating so hard on the road in front of them, that they never look in their bloody mirrors, or check their blind spots.'

'That's an interesting way to put it.'

'It has the same consequences. It can lead to accidents. Like the one you've just had with the FCA.'

'Don't remind me!'

'I'm sure you'll come out of it alright, but use it as a lesson.'

'Yeah, I will do.'

The rest of the journey was relatively quiet. Not awkwardly so. Both Jim and Stephen had said what was on their minds, and were content to sit in silence until they reached their destination.

***

When they arrived at the river, they made their way over to the stretch of water that had been allocated to them for the morning. Jim explained that when you fish on a river, you're allocated a permit to fish on a particular 'beat', which comprises both banks on a stretch of water. He indicated that they normally ran about a mile per beat in the area they would be fishing, and most landowners only allowed about three to four permits per beat at a time - so it wouldn't become overcrowded.

It turned out that they were the only ones fishing on their allocated beat that morning, and Stephen was more than a little relieved about that.

Once they'd unloaded the necessary equipment, they headed down the side of a short, but steep embankment, to a spot Jim had carefully selected.

Stephen didn't realise that they'd actually be standing in the water, but he was wearing a pair of Wellington boots, so he'd be fine as long as they stayed in shallow water. Jim was wearing full waders, and although Stephen had also brought this particular item of kit along, he considered them unnecessary, because he didn't intend on making his way out into the murky depths. Jim agreed that it would be unnecessary and cautioned him about going out too far into the water.

After getting acquainted with the basics of tying flies on, creating the whipping motion used to let the line out, and casting, Stephen was left pretty much to his own devices. Although from time to time, Jim would come closer to see how he was doing and give him various pointers.

'Ideally, you should be learning to fish in a lake, son. But I prefer river fishing, and as long as you concentrate and do as I've told you, you'll be fine. River fishing tends to be a more lively affair most of the time.'

'Okay, thanks Jim. Is there anything specific I should be concentrating on?'

'That godawful casting motion you're using! You can't get proper momentum unless you develop a smooth motion my boy, it's all about rhythm and timing. It's like golf… and sex!'

'Right…'

'If your performance in bed is anything like your casting, perhaps you should just join a monastery and give up trying to find a girlfriend.'

'Thanks, Jim. Very funny.'

'I think it's hilarious actually. Seeing you so far out of your element. It's good for you, being a little humbled every now and then.'

'I should think I've been humbled enough in the last week.'

'Naa, you could still do with a few truckloads of humility, my lad. But don't worry, you'll get the hang of the fishing, it's not difficult once you're used to it.'

'I hope not. I'd like to catch something.'

'Well, if you keep casting like that, the only thing you're likely to catch is a cold. You need to create a larger arc behind you. Remember, you can only get the line out as far as you need in front of you, if you give yourself enough room by letting the line get far enough out behind you.'

'Yes, I understand the physics Jim, it's just that every time I try to get the line to go out far enough behind me, I end up getting it caught in the bloody foliage on the embankment.'

'Alright, I understand that, then use your brain and move further out into the water in order to give yourself more room. It's relatively shallow for quite a bit.'

'Ah. Okay, that makes sense.'

After moving a bit further out into the water, Stephen started to get a better handle on the casting motion. Eventually he became quite confident, and was starting to enjoy himself - although he still hadn't managed to catch anything. He noticed that Jim had gone in all the way up to his knees, and was starting to get some bites. So he decided to go back to the car and put on his waders. That way, he'd be able to get out to Jim's depth, and give himself a better chance at hooking something.

Although he obviously didn't have a mirror, he knew he must have looked ridiculous in waders. He always thought they looked fairly ludicrous. Even when worn by those archetypical Scottish fishermen used in whiskey adverts on TV and in magazines. They always looked like ill-fitting dungarees, attached incongruously to overly large wellington boots. This was, of course, exactly what they were. They never looked too offensive in the water, but that's because you only ever tended to see their occupants from the waist up.

As far as Stephen was aware, they didn't produce tailored ones. Because of this, they evidently made them in such a manner as to cater for as many body types as possible - giving each set enough room to fit the largest person they could imagine having a particular shoe size. Their efforts weren't likely to work out very well for corpulent anglers with small feet, but they were just as bad for tall thin people like Stephen, who wore size twelves.

He looked like an enormous clown.

Nevertheless, he was glad that he'd managed to get them on, and he felt emboldened by the freedom they afforded him. He could now venture much farther out into the water, without having to worry about getting wet. It was a good feeling. Similar to the one you feel when you use goggles to see underwater for the first time. You feel like your eyes should be burning. But they don't.

Jim warned him not to stray too far, because he wasn't sure where the channels were; but Stephen didn't pay any attention whatsoever to the old man's admonition. He was enamoured with the idea of being able to wade out into deeper water with impunity. In fact, he suspected that the further he went, the better chance he'd have at landing a larger fish. Indeed, every single ocean documentary he'd ever seen, had taught him that the deeper the water, the bigger the fish.

Still a little wounded from Jim's comments regarding his sexual prowess, or more specifically, his alleged lack thereof; Stephen felt that he had a point to prove. The fact that he hadn't even managed to hook anything as big as a tadpole didn't discourage him, and he managed to convince himself that catching the biggest fish of the day would somehow make up for a lack of numbers. So he waded out farther with each cast, until he found himself almost up to his elbows.

Although the waders were so big that he could have gone all the way up to his chest without getting wet, he realised that he wouldn't be able to cast particularly well with his arms so close to the water, and the flow of the river was becoming progressively harder to withstand. So he turned around to make for shallower waters.

That's when he slipped.

The grips on the soles of rubber boots are fairly effective most of the time. Even under water. But there's not much they can do to deal with large, smooth, algae covered surfaces that are almost perfectly round in shape. When you add a relatively strong current into the mix, they're no more effective than a pair of brogues.

As he was turning around, Stephen miscalculated the effect that the current was having on his freedom of movement, and lost his footing.

Whilst waders are an exceedingly useful piece of equipment in the ordinary course of events, they're not particularly useful when they start to fill up with water. Also, they don't fill up gradually, so as to afford their imperilled wearer an opportunity to extricate themselves from the situation before it becomes overwhelming. They take on water like a stone-laden plastic bag being tossed into a swimming pool.

Almost as soon as he'd realised what had happened, Stephen found himself struggling to keep his head above water. In his panic, he'd dropped his overpriced fishing rod, and was almost involuntarily screaming for help. The current was pulling him swiftly down-river, and his waders were dragging him under as they took on more water. He was flailing his arms, and trying to stop himself from being dragged away.

Fortunately, Jim heard his cries for help, and came running along the bank to tell him what to do.

'Stop being a silly bastard! You aren't going to win a fight with the current.'

'I'm bloody drowning here, Jim!'

'No you're not. Don't overreact. Let the waders fill up.'

'You what?!'

'Just listen to me! Let the waders fill up completely, and they'll stop dragging you under!'

'Seriously?!'

'Trust me. Just do it. Then try to float on your back and let the current take you downstream. You'll eventually find your way to a shallower part of the river.'

'Okay.'

Stephen did as he was told, and it worked.

Jim was right about letting the waders fill up. Once they were completely submerged, they became almost weightless, and he was able to float on his back until he was pulled to shallower water. He managed to crawl out onto the embankment, remove the waders, and empty them out. Although he could have put them back on at that point, he decided that he would rather make his way back to the car without doing so. Fortunately, he'd listened to Jim and brought a spare set of clothes with him.

When he got there, he found Jim waiting for him. The old man was laughing so hard, he could barely breath. Stephen wasn't sure whether it was because of what had happened, or because of the fact that he was ambling along barefooted in a pair of wet red underpants, but he assumed it was a bit of both.

'Nice knickers, son. I didn't know you went in for provocative colours.'

'Very droll, Jim.'

'I should take a picture for Mary.'

'I'm not going to hear the end of this, am I?'

'No. Not really.'

'You were the one who brought me river fishing on my first bloody outing, Jim.'

'Yes. But *you* were the one who didn't bloody-well listen when I told you not to go in so deep!'

'Ah… well I suppose there *is* that.'

'Pity about the rod though, that was a nice piece of kit.'

'It certainly wasn't cheap, Jim.'

'No, I can't imagine it was.'

'Bloody silly design, those waders! I mean, surely they should be made in such a way as to stop them filling up with water.'

'Ah, yes. About that… didn't you get a belt with them?'

'No.'

'That's strange, especially considering that they sold you every other piece of fishing equipment known to man. Wader belts are designed to stop them filling up, and most of them come together nowadays.'

'Clearly mine didn't. Pretty fundamental oversight, that. Although it could have been deliberate. I certainly wouldn't put it past the snotty bugger who sold me the things.'

'No son, I think you're overreacting. Not even *you* could manage to piss someone off that effectively in such a short period of time.'

'Well, I'm certainly not going back there anytime soon.'

'That's a pity. I'm sure they'd enjoy hearing about the incident. Maybe they'd give you a complimentary belt, and a discount on a new rod.'

'I somehow doubt that, Jim. They'd be more likely to try and sell me a set of water wings.'

Jim doubled over with laughter again.

'You aren't giving up are you?'

'No. I'm done for today though. Perhaps next time we can go to a lake or something?'

'Of course! Let me get another hour of fishing in; then I'll treat you to lunch and a quiet scotch. It certainly looks like you could do with one.'

'Sounds marvellous.'

7

After having a good lunch and a stiff drink, Stephen was feeling considerably better. Although he didn't want to give up on the fishing just yet, he realised that it was a lot like golf, and it didn't really excite him. He was willing to give it a fair chance, but he wasn't convinced that the hobby would stick.

Normally, this sort of realisation wouldn't phase him. But he was becoming a lot more conscious of the fact that his life was more or less devoid of fulfilling pursuits outside of work, and he was intelligent enough to understand that this wasn't a good thing. Appreciating art, and reading the odd book on art history wasn't really a pastime. In fact, now that he'd been away from the office for almost a week, the apparent emptiness of his existence was starting to depress him.

He didn't even have a pet at home for company, and although he wasn't overly worried about being alone, he realised that he wasn't actually a loner by nature. Whilst it was true that he'd lived on his own for almost two decades, he'd only really slept alone, because he'd spent the rest of the time around people at work. He got along tolerably well with most of his colleagues, even though they weren't close friends, and he'd become rather close to Mary, Jim, and even Kenny. The problem was that even these three had been kept at what could only be described as a 'safe' professional distance.

For the first time in his life, he'd actually stopped to evaluate his personal situation, and he didn't like what he saw. Evidently Jim had seen it, and the old man was right. Something needed to change.

Shortly after he got home, he decided to send Charles a message.

'Hi Charlie. It was great seeing you again this week. What are you up to tomorrow? Have any specific plans?'

'Steve! I'm a bit tied up to be honest. My company's been taking part in a massive games convention this weekend. I do have some VIP passes for tomorrow though. If you're free, come join me - should be fun! You can meet some people and check out the new games.'

He was a bit out of touch with the gaming scene, but he certainly wasn't enamoured with the idea of spending Sunday alone, so he was grateful for the invitation.

'Cool, thanks mate - just tell me where and when - I'll be there.'

'Sweet - details to follow! Oh... by the way - I've also invited Ollie and Karen - sure you haven't seen them in ages.'

He was right, Stephen and Oliver had also been very close at University, but they hadn't seen one another since Ollie and Karen's wedding, which was about six years ago. Although Stephen had actually spoken to him earlier in the week, when he was looking for a lawyer, they hadn't arranged to meet up.

Ollie was a corporate lawyer, and Karen worked fairly high up in the banking world. They were both at University with Stephen and Charles. As far as he knew, they had two children now, and lived out in Surrey. He felt a little guilty that he hadn't even met the children, or seen the couple in such a long time.

***

The gaming convention was a far cry from the nerdy gatherings he'd attended in his late teens and early twenties.

Their proponents always asserted that they were 'conventions', but he recalled that they were more like small flea markets, set up in whatever shabby little halls could be rented by the organisers for as little money as possible. Even in the early 2000's when electronic gaming was growing steadily, there was still very little industry involvement, so there was no real budget to speak of, and attendance was measured in the hundreds.

This was, to those gatherings, what a local soapbox race is to Formula One.

Evidently, the game companies were now running the show, because it looked like they'd spent the GDP of a small country on this event. When Charles had sent Stephen a pdf map of the layout the previous evening, he hadn't even bothered to open it, because he assumed that he'd find his way around without any difficulty. He was now inordinately grateful for the map.

After making his way through the turnstiles and setting a course for Charles' base of operations, he bumped into Oliver, who also seemed to be following a map on his phone.

'Ollie?!'

'Steeeeve! How you doing mate? Haven't seen you in bloody *years*! Now I've spoken to you, and bumped into you in the same week. It's about time!'

'I'm well thanks, Ol. It's been *way* too long! I think the last time I saw you was at your wedding… speaking of which, how are Karen and the kids?'

'All good thanks mate. Thankfully we've managed to foist the kids off on their grandparents today. They aren't old enough yet to appreciate this sort of convention. Karen's just grabbing coffee; she'll be with us in a few minutes, if you don't mind hanging around. We can then go find Charles together. Maybe we can drag him away and all grab some lunch together.'

'Splendid!'

'Oh, by the way, how did you get on with the solicitor I referred you to? Have you seen him yet?'

'Yeah, thanks for the referral. I have seen Ian, he seems to know what he's doing. He's also a nice chap.'

'He's a rockstar, Steve. A bit pricey, but well worth it.'

'Yeah, I like him.'

'You okay Steve? I know I didn't ask you when we chatted on the phone briefly, but is everything alright?'

'Yeah, just a bit of a misunderstanding with the FCA.'

'They can be right bastards, that lot. Anyway, I won't pry. It's between you and Ian now, but if you ever need anyone to talk to, I'm here.'

'Thanks Ol, I really appreciate that.'

'Anyway, enough about business. When was the last time you came to one of these conventions?'

'It must have easily been fifteen years ago now.'

'A lot has changed since then.'

'You're not kidding. This is seriously huge.'

'Yeah. It's interesting actually. I went to the first one of these particular conventions in 2008. It was held in an old brewery. I looked up the statistics for interest sake the other day, and apparently their turnout was around four thousand people back then.'

'That's bigger than anything I ever went to, mate.'

'Yeah, well apparently they now get over twenty times that number.'

'I can readily believe that. Things definitely *have* changed.'

'So, what've you been up to Steve? Still working in the city?'

'Yeah, same place, same gig.'

'You must be climbing the ranks quite nicely by now?'

'Funny you should say that. I'm busy trying to secure a promotion at the moment.'

'Nice, I'm sure you'll get it.'

'How about you? Still at the old firm? *Partnership* on the horizon?'

'Partnership in the rear-view mirror, mate.'

'Oh? how do you mean *'rear-view mirror'*?'

'I made partner two years ago, and then quit last month. I'm done!'

'Wow! What prompted *that*?'

'To be honest mate, I thought my life would improve once I made partner. It just got *worse*.'

'How so?'

'You fool yourself into believing that when you get more senior, you get to take your foot off the gas a bit, but it turns out that that's simply not the case.'

'Really?'

'The demands of the job increase as you rise in the ranks. Selling time's a mug's game, because the more senior you get, the higher your billables are, so you're expected to maximise your billing potential, and pull even *bigger* hours to keep the overheads covered. It's basically like an airline: the first class passengers pay for the fuel; the rest of them make the *profit*. The ones paying for the fuel can't afford to drop the ball, or the plane will crash.'

'I never thought of it that way.'

'Yeah, it's an interesting industry. I used to love the work, but the higher up the food chain you get, the more nasty it gets. You get tired of the fact that nobody ever comes to see you when things are going *right*, and you end up getting owned by your clients, which is particularly shitty, because most of them are overgrown narcissistic children. When you're junior, your boss has to account to the clients. Only when you're the boss, do you realise the full implications of that responsibility.'

'You must get well remunerated though?'

'It's blood money, Steve; and the blood is *yours*. When you're younger all you can see is the gleaming pay package on the horizon. When you reach the horizon, you realise that you actually have to keep *working* for that paycheque, and the only thing to look forward to is retirement. You're looking down the barrel of another quarter of a century of fifteen hour work days, wiping the arses and cleaning up the mess left by clients who have less than half your brains and ten times your money. I'm not *that* much of a masochist, frankly.'

'Shit Ol, you make a fairly compelling argument.'

'Steve. I've spent my entire adult life formulating good arguments.'

'I guess so. I tend to focus on the money thing a bit too much.'

'That's one of the hazards of *your* chosen profession mate. You live around figures all day, so they're bound to carry more significant meaning to you.'

'People keep telling me that the money is secondary, but I battle to get my head around that, to be honest.'

'Nobody has *everything* figured out, Steve. I just know about human nature. When you wade through the fucking sewers of high society like I've had to do for the last fifteen years, you learn all sorts of things about life. Most of which you'd rather forget.'

'So what do you plan to do for a living?'

'No bloody clue. Luckily Karen can keep us going until I find something that'll make me happy. She actually makes more money than I *ever* did. I'm scared as all hell to be honest, but I know I made the right decision.'

'It certainly *sounds* like you did.'

'Speaking of Karen. Here she comes, let's go find Charles.'

'Hi Karen, good to see you!'

'Hi Steve! Ollie told me you'd be joining us today. I'm so glad we could meet up again, we can't keep going years without seeing one another.'

'You're absolutely right, Karen.'

Karen looked across at her husband and smiled wryly. She'd picked up on the fact that Stephen was more than a little preoccupied. He wasn't even looking at her when they greeted one another. He was fixated on the young woman standing next to her, in a way that was unsettlingly obvious.

'Oh, sorry, where are my manners. Steve, I don't know if you ever met my little sister, *Alexa*?'

Stephen's world had stopped. It was like everything had suddenly slowed down to the extent that he couldn't perceive any external motion. He could feel his heart beating in his ears and his throat went dry. After an uncomfortably long pause, he managed to regain some semblance of consciousness and found the first response that popped into his head.

'No.'

Karen's sister was short, petite and extremely attractive. She had long black hair, piercing grey eyes, and a pale complexion. She carried herself with the poise of a ballet dancer, and had the demeanour of someone who was completely at ease with the world around her. She'd noticed him staring, but instead of averting her gaze, she looked directly back at him and smiled playfully. He nearly fell over.

'Well then. Alexa, this is Stephen. Stephen, meet Alexa.'

'Nice to meet you, Alexa.'

'Nice to meet you Stephen. How do you know these two?'

'Oh, we were all at university together.'

'Ah, cool, I'm surprised we haven't met one another yet.'

'Me too.'

'Allie, we have to get going, I told Charlie you wanted to meet him, and he said he'd only be at the company stand until eleven thirty.'

'Right. Sorry K, I'm sure I'll see you around during the course of the morning, Steve.'

'Yeah, I'm sure we'll bump into one another at some stage.'

Stephen didn't want her to leave, but he'd also run out of things to say, so he just stood there grinning like an idiot. Luckily, Oliver broke the awkward silence for him.

'Love, I also agreed to meet up with Charles a little later. I want to do some catching up with Steve before I do though, I'll let you know where we are once we've decided on a course.'

'Perfect, I'm sure we'll find one another. Lovely seeing you, Steve!'

'Same *here*. See you later though!'

***

'Oliver. Now that we've parted company with the ladies…'

'Yes Stephen?'

'You didn't tell me that your sister-in-law is the most beautiful woman this side of the equator!'

'She's my *sister-in-law,* Steve. What would you have liked me to *do*? Put up a banner? Or started a bloody text-group entitled: '*Which of my grubby mates would like to try and get their hands on my screamingly attractive sister-in-law*?' Fuck off!'

'But seriously, is she *single*?'

'I think so.'

'Fuck…'

'I thought that was the answer you were looking for?'

'Yes… and no…'

'Explain.'

'It's obviously great that she's single. But it means that I have no excuse for not asking her out.'

'Why the hell would you want an excuse?'

'It's complicated. I'm out of practice. I'll probably cock it up.'

'Stop being such a coward Stephen. Ask her out. So *what* if she says no? She probably *will*, you're not her type. But hey, maybe she'll give you a shot. Karen really likes you, so that'll stand you in good stead.'

'What do you mean, I'm not her *type*?'

'She actively dislikes bankers, lawyers, accountants and those who work in the corporate world. She's into creative types, and she's heavily involved with gaming. That's one of the reasons we're here. She's always wanted to meet Charles.'

'Oh for Christ's sake. Her and every other pretty girl in the greater metropolitan area! What am I missing here? Girls used to like *rugby players*.'

'I don't think she's standing in line to join Charlie's little harem Steve, she's definitely not *that* type. She just loves games, and she was interested to find out that we were mates with a relatively famous game designer.'

'Still, that jammy bastard is so charming, it wouldn't surprise me if she became instantly enamoured of him.'

'Tell you what. Since you're such a nice chap, I'll help you out a little with Alexa. Don't tell her what you do for a living. She isn't likely to ask, because she says that doesn't put much value in what people *do*. Apparently, throwing around job titles is considered pretty naff in modern circles. I'll tell Karen to avoid bringing up your job in conversation. Then, after she's gotten to know you, she probably won't judge you as harshly for being a '*city boy*'.'

'Thanks... I think.'

'Oh, and by the way, a lot of pretty girls are into gamers now, mate. It's not like the old days, we've turned the table on the jocks. It's taken hundreds of years, but we're now in the golden age. '*Esport*' is the new thing.'

'What's '*Esport*'?'

'Stephen. Do you live under a rock?'

'Yeah. It appears so.'

'Some games are now played and watched like traditional sports. You know, like cricket, and rugby, and tennis.'

'You're kidding.'

'No. It's massive Steve. There are teams, with coaches and managers, and even sponsors.'

'Seriously?'

'Absolutely. I'm not overly interested in the Esports leagues, but I'd far rather watch Esport than most other sports, to be perfectly honest.'

'I think I'd prefer playing the games myself.'

'Yeah, but if you think about it, there isn't much difference between watching a traditional sport, or a computer game. They're both games, in reality.'

'I suppose that's one way of looking at it.'

'It's certainly worth checking it out.'

'I'm busy kicking myself for giving up the computer games now.'

'Playing computer games is in your blood, mate. Start up again and get into it. There's no stigma attached to gaming now. Not like there used to be.'

'Do *you* play anything?'

'Absolutely. I play '*The Other Planet*'. You should give it a shot, it's an MMORPG.'

'What's an MMORPG?'

'Massively Multiplayer Online Role Playing Game. Bit of a tongue twister, *I know*. But it's where the biggest part of the gaming world has been going for a while now. They're the most immersive type of games, because they don't really have to have linear story progressions, and they never really finish.'

'Huh. So sort of like an endless roleplaying game then?'

'Pretty much, yeah. That's where it came from. You have a character, and you level up and get gear, and go on quests; some of which are part of a story line, and some of which are just there to add depth. It's seriously cool. I know you were into roleplaying back in the day, so it would be right up your alley. *The Other Planet* is a pretty awesome concept, actually. It has all the typical fantasy races, like elves and dwarfs and orcs and things, but it's set in space, on an alien planet. Sort of a mashup between traditional fantasy and sci-fi. Weird, but cool; they did it really well.'

'Sounds fantastic. I'll give it a bash. I assume it's PC based though?'

'Yeah. Don't you have a PC?'

'Naa. I just use laptops. I've been thinking of getting a console.'

'Don't be a twat. Build a PC, like we used to do; I'll help.'

'Awesome!'

'Go and look around the various game exhibits and see if you can find any other gaming stuff you're interested in. There are often pretty good deals on peripherals at these conventions. We can meet up later for lunch. I need to go and find Karen; she's probably still with Charles and his two girlfriends. I can't have her getting caught up in his web *either*.'

'Don't joke. That guy is a force of nature!'

For the first time in as long as he could remember, Stephen was actually excited about something. Getting back into gaming was a far more interesting proposition than messing about with fishing. In fact, he felt like a kid at Christmas, walking around the various gaming exhibits and taking in the surroundings. He was genuinely looking forward to building a computer and playing games with Oliver.

Although he felt slightly guilty about being so enthusiastic about playing computer games, he remembered that Bridgette had told him to do some of the things he did at University, and he reasoned that, technically, what he was doing was simply following her instructions. She probably didn't think it would be computer games… but then again, she was highly perceptive.

The fact that games were now evidently more mainstream than they were when he was growing up did make him feel slightly better about the whole business.

By the looks of things, the gaming crowd were no longer just a bunch of freaks who lived in dark basements, eating crisps and wearing sweatpants. He was sure that there were still a lot of those types of gamers out there, but at least there was some diversity now. He still couldn't believe that more girls were into gaming now too though. It was weird.

***

After about half an hour of browsing the various stalls, he felt a light tap on the shoulder.

'Hi again Stephen.'

It was Oliver's sister-in-law. She was standing with an odd-looking little chap, who was wearing a baseball cap, an ill fitting Star Wars T-shirt, and faded black jeans. He must have been around thirty years old. The T-shirt was clearly older.

'Ah, Alexa. Enjoying the convention so far?'

'Very much so! Sorry, Stephen, this is my friend Dave. Dave, this is Stephen, he's a friend of my sister's from university. Dave and I play together.'

'Hi Dave! So you're *also* into gaming?'

Stephen realised how stupid the question was as soon as he posed it, but he hadn't had time to think of anything better, and he didn't want to be rude and ignore the chap.

'Absolutely mate! You?'

'For sure!'

'What do you play?'

'Umm'

He hadn't planned how he was going to deal with this sort of encounter. He was desperate to impress Alexa, but he was so preoccupied with this particular goal, that he hadn't even stopped to think about how he was going to achieve it. He felt like he was fumbling around in the dark. Fortunately, he remembered the name of the game that Ollie had been talking about earlier.

'The Other Planet!'

'Wicked! that's what *we* play!'

He felt slightly ill. His little fib was about to backfire horribly.

'So, are you in a guild Steve?'

He didn't have the faintest idea what a 'guild' was, but he assumed it was a group that did quests together, or something like that.

'Yeah, I'm in an awesome guild.'

'Well, *we're* recruiting at the moment. So if you fancy a change, let us know. I'll send you my handle. What's your number?'

Somewhat reluctantly, Stephen gave his enthusiastic new acquaintance his telephone number, and made a mental note to get hold of the game as a matter of urgency.

'So… are you enjoying the last expansion?'

He was hoping that once he'd given over his contact details, they'd be able to change the subject, but Dave was evidently pleased to have found another fan of the game, and it didn't seem as if he was ever going to let up. Stephen needed some sort of an exit strategy.

'Yeah. I'm really into it.'

'Me too. They moan a lot on the forums; but you know how it is, forums have basically become a platform for whinging about stuff.'

'For sure.'

'So what do you do in the *real world*, Steve?'

This was not the exit he was hoping for. Clearly, Dave wasn't as averse to throwing around job titles as Alexa allegedly was. It looked like Oliver's plan for him to keep quiet about his job was about to fly out of the window. He panicked.

'I'm a graphic designer.'

As he said it, he realised it was a grave error, but there was nothing he could do to take it back without sounding like a complete and utter nutcase. To make matters worse, Alexa's eyes lit up as soon as she heard it.

'Oooh, that is so cool Steve. I thought all my sister's friends were boring bankers, and lawyers, and city types! I'll have to have a word with her about hiding you away from me.'

Although he wasn't particularly good at reading people, he suspected Alexa was now flirting with him, and he knew that there was now no way he was going to come clean about what he actually did for a living. There was something about this woman that made him lose all reason. It scared him a little.

'Well, I think we need to get to know one another a bit better. But Charlie's asked me to meet up, so I'd better go and find him. I'm having lunch with Ollie and your sister though, I hope you'll join us.'

'Sound's good Steve, we'll see you then. I'll pop Karen a text to find out where you'll be going.'

'Great!'

Stephen was impressed with his response. He'd managed to sound a lot cooler and more confident than he was feeling. But he realised that lunch would be a tricky affair, unless he managed to enlist Oliver's help up front.

So he decided to send him a message.

'Ol… I've fucked it up… like I said I would… need help - where ARE you?'

'Rofl… I'm at the Razer exhibit by entrance 3… I'm sure you'll be fine - see you in a bit.'

'Promise not to laugh too hard…'

'No fucking way… I get the feeling this is going to be hilarious.'

Stephen considered feigning injury and running away to regroup, but he was far too interested in seeing Alexa again, so he went to find Oliver.

'What've you done Stephen?'

'I sort of told your sister-in-law, and her nosy mate, Dave, that I'm a hardcore gamer.'

'So? She probably won't figure out that you're not. Not *immediately*, anyway…'

'It's a bit more tricky than that…'

'How so?'

'I told her that I played that *The Other Planet* thing you're into. Turns out; so does she, and so does bloody *Detective Dave!*'

'Ah, I probably should have mentioned that. She's a big *'Planet'* player.'

'Yes well, I've also told her that I'm in a hardcore 'guild'. Whatever that is?!'

'Nice one!'

'It gets considerably worse.'

'Surely not?'

'Turns out, her curious cohort was *very* interested in what I did for a living.'

'Oh shit, you didn't confess to being a stockbroker did you?'

'No. Although I sort of wish I *had*…'

'So…?'

'I just lied like an idiot, and told her that I was a bloody *graphic designer*!'

'You're kidding?'

'No.'

'To be fair, that was an inspired choice. She's fascinated by graphic design.'

'Yes. I realise that now, because she's suddenly quite interested in getting to know me better!'

'Well, good work then!'

'For *fuck* sakes, Oliver. I don't need to tell *you* the implications of lying, do I? You're the sodding lawyer!'

'*Ex* lawyer…'

'Ex or not; *you* know as well as *I* do that lying is bloody stupid, because you can't control the ripple effect. Lies always come out, and when they do, the liar looks like what he *is*… a fucking *halfwit*.'

'Fair point, but it's still funny.'

'You have to help me, mate. I need to find a way out of the corner I've put myself in here. I like this sister-in-law of yours, there's something special about her, I can tell.'

'She's a pain in the arse, Steve. She's interesting alright, I'll give you that. But she isn't half difficult. I suppose the smart ones are always a bit tricky to deal with.'

'Ollie, you're making me like her even more. I've always been more attracted to the clever ones. Please help me.'

'Okay, but you have to let me tell Karen. We'll need her *buy-in* on this.'

'*Anything*! Oh, and by the way, I bloody-well invited her to lunch with us too. I couldn't help myself.'

'This is going to be an interesting lunch!'

***

Oliver gave Karen a call, and arranged for her to find Alexa, so that they could make lunch plans. They ended up leaving the convention building, and finding a small pub down the road that had an open table.

Stephen was pleased to note that Dave wasn't joining them. He didn't need the nosy little bugger digging any more holes for him fall into. Although, almost as soon as they sat down, he realised that the hole he'd dug for *himself* was bad enough.

'So Stephen, what made you go into graphic design?'

'Well, I always had a thing for art growing up. I spose it just captured my imagination.'

'That's so awesome, I know the feeling.'

'So what do *you* do for a living, Alexa?'

'Oh, I bake cakes! Not as creative as graphic design, but I've managed to start making some fairly attractive wedding cakes. Hopefully one day they'll be good enough to get me recognised.'

'She's being overly modest Stephen. I know I'm her sister, and I'm a bit biased, but her work is amazing!'

'I'm sure you're right Karen. I can't imagine how difficult it must be making something that looks good and can *also* be eaten. It's definitely an art… I battle to make myself egg on toast, to be honest.'

Stephen paused and reflected. That was probably the first honest thing he'd said to her.

'Well, you should come visit my bakery sometime. I'll show you what goes into it.'

'I would absolutely *love* that!'

He wasn't sure whether or not that sounded a bit too enthusiastic. Although at this point, he couldn't really help himself.

'Super!'

'I don't spose you get out to the country much Stephen, do you still live in that apartment in Shoreditch?'

'Yeah, I'm still there Karen.'

'Alexa's bakery is down in Surrey.'

'Oh wow, where exactly?'

'I'm in Shere. I'm very lucky, it's such a special little place.'

He'd heard of Shere, although he'd never been. He vaguely remembered one of his colleagues talking about going there. It was one of those really picturesque places that they used in movies from time to time.

'Yeah, I've heard it's lovely.'

'You should go and see the bakery, and have lunch or something.'

'That sounds like a great idea, Karen. As long as Alexa can spare the time. I wouldn't want to put her out at all.'

'Of course not Stephen. Happy to have you any time. I'll send you my number, and we can make an arrangement. I'll get your details from Karen.'

'Wonderful - I'm on a bit of extended leave at the moment, so my diary's open.'

'I'll bet you're getting a lot of gaming in, then - done anything special in-game recently?'

'Nothing *overly* significant, you know, just the usual.'

'I feel out of the loop Sis, you know I don't play these games. Let's talk about something else. I can see Stephen is eager to elaborate, but I suspect you'll have plenty of time to chat when he comes to see you.'

'Sorry Karen. I just get carried away when it comes to the game… and we *are* at the convention.'

Stephen made a mental note to send Karen flowers the following week, and a large box of expensive chocolates.

'Speaking of *games*. Look who's come to join us love! Hey Charlie, glad you could get away from the madness for a bit. I don't think Stephen's met Jen and Amy. Ladies, this is Stephen. I think you've already met Karen's sister, Alexa.'

'Yeah, we have indeed. Nice to meet you, Stephen.'

'Hi…'

Charlie hadn't been joking about his two girlfriends. They didn't exactly strike him as the '*take home to mum*' type. Jen had dyed purple hair, done up in pig-tails; a nose ring; jet black nail-polish; and matching lipstick. She was very attractive, and she actually had a rather posh accent; but he could see how Charlie's mum may form a negative impression of her.

Amy was a tall blonde, with striking blue eyes. She appeared a bit more conventional, until you looked down and saw that she had a massive tattoo of a spider on the left side of her neck. She was wearing a tight leather corset and a mini-skirt; an ensemble that made her look exactly like the sort of woman who either dated the lead singer of a metal band, or was herself the lead singer of such a band.

'Hope you're all enjoying the festivities. We've had a seriously good turn out this year.'

'It's amazing Charlie, thanks for the invite. I haven't been to one of these things in *years..*'

'A bit different to the ones we went to back at University, hey Steve?'

'And how! I didn't realise how the industry's changed.'

'So you didn't come last year Steve?'

'No, sadly not Alexa, I was away on business.'

'That's a pity - it was also a really good one.'

'Still, I suppose you don't need to come to these things to get wind of the new developments in *The Other Planet*, since you're mates with the lead designer. I'm so jealous.'

Stephen didn't actually know that it was one of Charlie's games. He realised that although this was pretty cool, Charlie could give away the fact that he wasn't a gamer.

'Oh I'm sure Steve's not interested in…Ouch!'

'Sorry Charlie, I must have slipped there. Didn't mean to stand on your foot. I try not to bug Charlie too much about the game. I know he has all sorts of confidentiality restraints in his contract with the company. So it would be sort of unfair for me to pester him. Besides, they're pretty good with their announcements. Isn't that *right* Charles?'

Stephen shot his mate a pleading glance. Thankfully, the ever perceptive Charles Taylor immediately picked up what was happening, and played along like a seasoned actor.

'Yeah, we *are* pretty good that way. Steve's right!'

8

Fortunately, the lunch was fairly uneventful following the initial exchanges, and Stephen managed to avoid making a fool of himself. Jen and Amy ended up taking Alexa and her mate Dave to meet some of the professional gamers that Charles' company sponsored, and Karen was interrupted by an urgent work call that she decided to take in the car.

So Stephen and Ollie ended up staying at the pub and having a few drinks with Charles.

'Right, *you two*. Now that I have you alone, I'm begging you: help me learn about this game! I'm going to be meeting up with Alexa sometime in the next two weeks or so, and she thinks I'm an expert.'

'I don't have the time mate, sorry.'

'*You do,* Oliver! I know you're not working. I need a bloody '*crash-course*'!'

'You need a lot more than that. But alright, I'll train you up. It might be fun.'

'You're not off the hook, Charles. I may also call on you for some tips.'

'Much good they'll do you. I'm hopeless at that game.'

'But you *designed* the thing?!'

'Doesn't mean I'm any good at playing it. Think of it this way Steve: your clients make lots of money, but they don't know how to invest it. That's why you do it for them.'

'Interesting point Charles, but surely you know something about the game I can use to my advantage?'

'Yeah, okay. Choose a character that does ranged damage. You know, one that casts spells or shoots arrows, or any other damage from a distance. I always force my team to make ranged characters more powerful. Don't quote me on that, I'll deny it if you do, but it's true.'

'If you'd have told me back at university, that one day I'd be getting Ollie to teach me how to play a computer game that you developed, so that I could impress a girl, I would have laughed in your face and told you that you were a raving lunatic.'

'It's a strange new world, mate. Let's face it, our old dreams are coming *true*. Don't complain, just go with it.'

'I don't have much of a choice now. *Do I?*'

'Well, technically speaking, you *do*. You can ditch the notion of hooking up with Ollie's lovely sister-in-law, and go feel sorry for yourself in your fancy loft apartment; or you can play an awesome computer game, and give yourself a shot at some happiness. I've said it before, and I'll say it again: choose *life*.'

'You're right. I get it, it just seems so strange. I've spent the better part of my adult life trying so hard to be more of an adult; playing games feels a bit counter-productive.'

'Everyone plays games, Stephen. What makes golf, tennis and fishing any more "*adult*" than computer games? It's a perception that's created by older generations who are too scared to admit that they don't understand how the technology works, so they brand it as "*childish*", just so that they can feel better about their ignorance.'

'Charlie's right mate. It's the responsibility of *our* generation to break away from that mode of thinking. If we don't, our kids will end up guilt-ridden for enjoying games, and go through life resenting the fact that they had to '*grow up*'. You probably have the same sort of resentment, you just haven't thought about it for long enough to figure it out.'

'Do you honestly believe that, Ollie?'

'I do. I'm not suggesting that it holds a monopoly on things to resent about growing up, but it's not like tax or interest rates; it's something you have control over. Karen figured out ages ago that the only thing that helped me to recharge and take my mind off work, was playing games. So *she* was the one who encouraged me to get back into gaming. I felt the same about it as you do, at the time. But I soon discovered two things: One: she was right; and two: our mate Charles is a talented little sod. That game is awesome!'

'You're making me blush, Ol!'

'No, it's true Charlie boy, *The Other Planet* is epic!'

'I suppose it would be rude not to give it a go then!'

'Yeah, I'd be offended if you didn't. I'll get you a free copy, and a six month subscription. By the way, serious games come with subscriptions now. It helps us keep them updated.'

'It helps you earn more than a bloody surgeon mate. Let's cut the bullshit, shall we?'

'Fair point. Still, like you said Ol, I'm a gaming *genius*!'

'I wouldn't go *that* far. But I'll admit you earn your keep.'

'Whilst I have you lot giving me all sorts of sage advice, how the bloody hell am I going to get past this nonsense about being a graphic designer?'

'The truth will set you free, Stephen. I don't see how you can get away with that one. Just *tell* her.'

'Yeah, Charles is right Steve. I can't see a way out of that one. You're just going to have to do it slowly and carefully. You'll have to pick your moment and hope for the best.'

'Fuck...'

***

Stephen woke up on Monday feeling a bit better than he had the day before. It had been exactly a week since he'd had his world turned upside down. He was adjusting, albeit gradually, to the fact that he had nowhere to go when he got up in the morning, and it wasn't bothering him nearly as much as it did at the commencement of his exile from the office. He was also getting used to writing in the journal. He didn't want Bridgette to catch him slacking off on it, and although it remained a fairly awkward exercise, he was finding it less offensive than he had at inception.

He was actually surfacing a bit later than usual, and even taking the time to make himself cooked breakfasts. He'd learnt how to knock up bacon and eggs quite efficiently, but he realised that it was probably a good idea to start opting for a healthier alternative, so he added fruit and oats to his new shopping list.

He'd never made a shopping list before, because he'd never really bothered keeping anything in the house other than the odd frozen pizza, or leftover sushi from one of those late night sushi specials which started when most normal people were already in bed.

He wasn't about to ask Mary for any more assistance with groceries. Not just because he knew that Jim would find out, but because he was starting to evaluate his conduct more critically, and he realised that getting Mary to help with that sort of thing was almost as bad as having her pick out his wardrobe. Jim was right, he needed to grow up.

After making himself breakfast, he decided to browse social media. He was still avoiding the news, and he wanted to see whether or not he could find Alexa on one of the platforms. It occurred to him that social media stalking was probably a bit creepy, but he couldn't help himself.

Alexa had already sent him a friend request, which immediately put him in a good mood, until he realised that his own social media profile was singularly boring. He didn't have any fun photographs or updates. He never had any pictures of himself with friends, and every picture he'd uploaded in the past few years had been some boring landscape of a golf course, or the view from a hotel room that he'd snapped whilst attending the odd work excursion, or out of town conference.

There was nothing really objectionable, like stupid drunken photos, or selfies; but it looked as if his profile could have been one of those fake ones generated by computer software. The last time he'd updated it, he'd posted a photograph of his overpriced fishing equipment, and before that, it had been a over a year since his last post. He made a mental note to try and make the profile look a little more exciting when he got a chance.

Alexa's social media profile wasn't much more interesting. Most of it was taken up with pictures of her bakery, her cakes, the pretty little village in which she lived, and her two cats. Nevertheless, it was still a more comprehensive window into her life than was Stephen's. She didn't seem to have many pictures with other men, which was encouraging; and it seemed like she spent a fair amount of time with Karen, which was also a good thing as far as Stephen was concerned. He liked Karen, and he knew she liked him. So she'd be a strong ally.

In fact, Karen was a lot like Stephen in many ways. She also worked in finance; and as far as he knew, she had similar qualifications to him. They'd always had a healthy mutual respect.

Alexa was thirty four. Younger than Stephen, but certainly not enough to make them incompatible in any way. She clearly ran her own cake-making business as she'd said, and the photographs of the cakes she made evidenced the fact that she was seriously talented.

Stephen found himself wondering why it was that someone like her wasn't already married. On the face of it, she was, to his mind, absolutely perfect. Maybe Ollie was right, maybe she *was* intolerably difficult? Either way, that wasn't going to stop him trying to get a date with her.

He considered doing a little more digging, but if he asked Ollie anything, he was likely to get laughed at; and if he contacted Karen, she'd think he was pathetic.

She'd also run straight along and report it to Alexa. In Stephen's experience, sisters were like that. His Mum had two sisters, and the three of them spent almost all of their free time inveigled in one another's lives. He had a brother who lived up north, but they hardly ever spoke. It wasn't that they had a terrible relationship, they simply didn't have much to say to one another, so neither of them bothered.

After re-examining his own social media profile, he found himself wishing he had some interesting tattoos, and a motorbike. Most girls he knew when he was growing up *said* they weren't interested in that sort of thing, but it seemed to him that nearly all of them *were*.

Whilst he was busy on the internet, he decided to book those appointments with the people at EDgE. He was seeing Bridgette again the following day, and he couldn't very well tell her that he was delaying the process of trying to find a date, on the basis that he was holding out hope for something to happen with Alexa. It was true that she'd sort of invited him to her bakery, but he wasn't sure whether or not that would actually happen, much less whether or not it would constitute a real 'date'. For all he knew, she could simply want another computer gaming friend, like Dave.

He remembered that his intern was coming over at lunch time with some documents for him to sign. They needed the originals back immediately, and Jim didn't want Stephen anywhere near the office, so he decided to send Kenneth.

Stephen did a quick search for a decent looking pizza place that was open early and did lunchtime deliveries. He'd never ordered any food for home during the day, so he had no idea as to whether or not his usual place did lunch. He missed Kenny, and he knew that the youngster would appreciate a free lunch. It would also give him the opportunity to find out what was going on at the office.

After lunch, he'd attempt to get hold of that game, and order some computer parts. If Alexa did contact him and try to set something up, there was no way that he'd put off seeing her for longer than a few more days; so he'd have to get going with '*The Other Planet*' as a matter of priority, or face the possibility of looking like an idiot when she discovered he hadn't got a clue what it was about.

***

Karen had promised to send Alexa Stephen's number the day before, but she'd forgotten, so Alexa gave her a call.

'Hi Sis, what's up?'

'I called to remind you to send me Steve's number.'

'Ahhh yeah, I forgot, sorry. You fancy him, don't you?'

'I'm not sure really, he's a bit awkward. Seems nice, although…'

'Although what?'

'I looked at his social media profiles this morning. It's pretty boring. Doesn't look like he gets up to much.'

'You can't have it all ways Allie. Remember that last chap you went out with?'

'How can I bloody-well *forget*?!'

'He got up to all sorts of things, if I recall correctly.'

'I take your point. But I mean, this guy looks like he hangs out at golf courses and random scenic hotels. Bit odd. More like an *accountant* than a *graphic designer*. In fact, his last post was a picture of bloody *fishing equipment*. You have to admit that that's seriously boring, K!'

'You're pre-judging the poor guy. Besides, what do *you* get up to these days? Apart from work? You haven't dated anyone since you started the bakery three years ago.'

'I suppose that's true. But how well do you know him? He's an old mate of Ol's, *right*?'

'Yeah, as I told you before, we were at uni together. He was pretty close to Ollie, but you know how it is, life sort of drags us off in different directions. I don't know exactly what he's like now, but he was pretty normal in his early twenties.'

'So basically, you're saying that he's not likely to be a weird stalker. It doesn't look like he's been dating anyone in a while. In fact, I can't see any evidence that he ever *has*.'

'I don't know, to be honest. He had a few girlfriends back in the day, nothing serious as far as I know, but it's not like he's a thirty nine year old virgin living with his mum. I think he's done quite well for himself, *actually*. He lives alone in one of those flash loft apartments in London.'

'Oh god, he's not one of those superficial man-children from a rich family, who got bought the place as a graduation present by *"daddy"*, is he?'

'No. Ol says he comes from a pretty normal family, I think I remember him saying that his dad was a banker, and his mum was a teacher or something. The dad did fairly well, but didn't shoot the lights out.'

'Good! Remember that ghastly chap I dated briefly when I was in my early twenties? The one whose parents bought him a sports car and a Rolex for his twenty first birthday?'

'Oh yeah, he made me want to vomit! No, Stephen isn't one of those, I can confirm that.'

'Phew. Okay, I'll arrange to meet up with him. You sure he's not a weirdo?'

'No, he's not a weirdo. I think he works too hard, like *someone else* I know, but other than that, there's not much to tell, *really*. You'll have to figure it out for yourself.'

'That's fair. But for the record, I *don't* work too hard. I just have a lot of responsibility. It's not easy K, running the place on my own, with one assistant.'

'So get another one then. I *know* you can afford it. You need to take some time for yourself, Sis. I hardly see you any more.'

'We'll see. The bakery's my baby; I just don't like leaving in the care of anyone else. *You've* got kids, you know how it is.'

'Firstly, my kids are not the same as your bakery; Secondly, the day the youngest of them started attending school was one of the best days of my life. I love both of my children more than life itself, but I'm *more* than happy foisting them off on someone else from time to time! Schools aren't really places of learning Alexa, they're places you leave your kids, so that you can live a semi-normal existence for at least six hours a day. If your bakery *is* truly like a baby, I should think you'd want to get away from it, every now and then.'

'What made *you* so sensible all of a sudden, dear sister of mine?'

'Bringing up three children!'

'You only have two chi… ohh right, I get it.'

'I've always liked Stephen. Seriously, he's not a bad guy. A bit awkward, I'll give you *that*, but let's face it, if he was *too* bloody charming and self-confident he'd be like that last chap of yours. You'd be sharing him with half of the single women in London.'

'Aargh, don't remind me!'

'I'm your sister. It's my *job* to remind you about these things, so you don't repeat your mistakes!'

'He *is* cute, and at least he doesn't live with his mother.'

***

Kenneth arrived at Stephen's apartment just before midday. He looked as though he hadn't slept in days.

'Morning Ken, how's the old salt mine? Have they replaced me with a newer model yet?'

'Hi boss. It's good to see you.'

'You look more tired than usual, Ken.'

'I am, boss. I don't like working in the new department they've shoved me in whilst you're away. Jim says it's good for me to do a bit of a rotation, but it's *bloody awful*.'

'Jim's right. It *is* good for you. Also, it'll make you appreciate me more when I come back.'

'I won't argue with that, boss!'

'Do you have papers for me to sign?'

'Yeah, Denise gave me an envelope. Signing for an early holiday bonus or something?'

'I hardly think so. It's more likely to be something ghastly from the legal department. Stop being such a nosy little bastard.'

'You always tell me that it's my job to know things, boss!'

'Very funny Ken. I hardly think that that includes my personal financial position, but good try.'

'I do miss you boss, honestly; my new supervisor doesn't have a sense of humour.'

'Yeah, I suppose they'd *need* to have a sense of humour to deal with you. Who is it?'

'Jeremy Smith. I don't think he likes me very much.'

'No, he doesn't like *anyone*, Ken. He especially hates *me*, because I got the job he wanted, and I made him look like an idiot last year during one of those investment proposal meetings.'

'Probably served him right.'

'To be fair, I behaved appallingly, but I've never liked the pretentious sod, so I thought I'd put him in his place.'

'What did you do?'

'He was presenting a case for investing in a newly listed tech company, and he hadn't done all of his homework. I knew he was working on a proposal for it, so I did my own research. I found some troubling information regarding the solvency and management structures at the company, and disclosed this information to the board after he'd made his pitch. Needless to say, he looked a right twat, and we never took a position on the stock. I don't think he'll ever forgive me for that.'

'Sounds like he should have done his homework a bit more conscientiously, boss. He only had himself to blame.'

'That's how I felt at the time. But it has recently been pointed out to me that we're supposed to work as a team. I should have brought the information to his attention before he made the proposal, Ken.'

'Wouldn't that have the effect of just covering up his shoddy research, and letting him coast.'

'Again, that's how I felt at the time. But on reflection, I can see that that reasoning has some pretty significant flaws.'

'How so? You saved the directors from making a bad decision on the back of his proposal.'

'Yeah, but it didn't need to come at a cost to Smith. I could have made the same cockup, Kenneth, and I would have been inordinately grateful if one of my colleagues caught me before I fell. I let Smith fall on purpose. It's true that he's always been an insufferable prick, but he's a member of the team, and it does none of us any good sabotaging our colleagues just because we don't like 'em.'

'Okay, I suppose I get it.'

'Good. Anyway, you can see one of the negative effects of my rash behaviour first hand now. I made an enemy of Smith, and now the bastard's taking it out on *you*. That's the ripple effect of poor decisions. They don't necessarily just come back to haunt the person who made them, they also have the potential to cause discomfort to others.'

'This recent incident is changing your outlook a bit, isn't it boss?'

'Yeah. As it should be.'

'Still, it's unfair that Smith's taking his frustration with *you* out on *me*!'

'Life's unfair, my lad. But it shouldn't be for too long, and it'll make you stronger. Think of it like a short prison sentence. It'll toughen you up!'

'You're secretly happy about this, aren't you boss?'

'No Ken, I'm openly happy about it. Jim put you with that twat for a reason, and I agree with him. A little hard time under a tyrant is often a valuable experience. It teaches you to appreciate not having to work under one, but more importantly, it teaches you how awful it is to be mistreated. So hopefully, when *you're* the boss one day, you remember what it was like, and treat *your* subordinates better.'

'Were you ever under any difficult bosses?'

'Loads of the bastards. I only started working under Jim about five years ago.'

'I suppose you handled it like a soldier.'

'God no! I almost had three nervous breakdowns. I ended up drinking heavily to get through it, which was a bloody terrible idea, so don't do *that*; it just makes matters worse.'

'Shit…'

'Thing is, most of the time, the things I thought were bad about my various old bosses weren't actually that bad, on reflection. I learned a lot from them. Of course, that's not necessarily going to be the case with Smith; I'm sure *he's* just an arsehole.'

'Well, that's comforting to know.'

'It's not my job to comfort you, Kenneth, it's to *prepare* you. The reality is that if I get the promotion I'm gunning for, they may not allow you to keep working under me. They may want you to get some time under a more junior colleague of mine. Probably not Smith, but you never know, so you need to toughen up a bit.'

'Bloody hell, boss! I hadn't thought about *that*. Please try and motivate for me to stay on under you when you get that promotion!'

'You sound confident that I'll get it. I may not. In fact, the company may fire me over this problem I'm having with the FCA. Then you'll have no choice but to make the adjustment.'

'Course you'll get it, boss. I'm not just saying that. Your reputation is hardcore at the office, it's no wonder old Smith hates you. I also think you'll get through the FCA thing, it's just a minor setback.'

'Thanks for the vote of confidence Ken. If I end up getting promoted, I'll try swing it so that you stay on under me. If I end up in bloody prison for insider dealing, you'll have to grin and bear it. Just promise to come and visit me from time to time.'

'I appreciate it boss.'

'I've ordered pizza. I thought you could do with a meal; you're looking appropriately undernourished. You can tell Smith I kept you for *'work-related'* stuff. He won't necessarily believe you, but he won't check in with *me* because it'll make him look weak.'

'Brilliant! Thanks!'

***

Stephen's confirmation of the bookings with the EDgE representatives for later that week had triggered their system to complete the reference checks. Jim had received a call from the reference checking personnel at the site that morning, and following his brief chat with them, he decided to find out whether or not they'd also been in contact with Mary.

'Morning Mary, it's Denise. Are you available to speak with Mr Roberts? I have him on the line.'

'Yeah, absolutely Denise, put him on.'

'Thanks, you're going through.'

'Hi Mary, have you got a few minutes? Sorry I didn't pop downstairs to see you in person, but I'm between meetings, as usual.'

'Not at all Mr Roberts, how can I help you?'

'Firstly, stop calling me 'Mr Roberts'. You know I don't like that; I'm not the type. It's *Jim*.'

'Okay Jim, other than that, what can I do for you?'

'Have that *EDgE* crowd contacted you about the personal reference for Stephen?'

'Yes…'

'During your chat with them, did you pick up anything *odd*?'

'Yes…'

'Ah, so it wasn't just *me* then?'

'Oh no, not at all, I went and did a little digging, actually…'

'Me too…'

'Yes, well, then I guess we're both on the same same page.'

'Indeed. Do you think he *knows*?'

'Not a chance, sir.'

'No, didn't think so. I Just wondered if you knew something about him that I *didn't*.'

'No, not likely sir. Should we say anything?'

'No way. He needs to figure these things out for himself. Plus, what harm could it *really do*?'

'Depends on your definition of *"harm"*, I suppose, sir.'

'Quite…'

9

The papers Stephen had to sign for the office were consents for the disclosure of his trading history, employee record and various other items of personal and professional information to the FCA.

They could simply have subpoenaed the information, or obtained it through one of the other enforcement mechanisms tied to his registration with them, but Ian advised him to simply have the company send the documentation to them as a pre-emptive courtesy. After all, as the solicitor pointed out, the sooner they had what they were after, the sooner their investigation would be concluded.

Even though the thought of assisting the investigators at the FCA galled him, Stephen accepted this approach. He had nothing to hide, and it was clearly the most sensible route to follow. Ian had, on his instruction, liaised with the legal department at Ashden, Cole & Roberts in order to secure the necessary information, and to have the relevant consent papers drawn up.

As far as Stephen was aware, they didn't actually need his consent to make these disclosures to the FCA, but there was nothing the in-house lawyers liked more than being overly efficient, and attempting to cover every single conceivable angle. So he signed the papers without comment or complaint, and sent Ian an email indicating that he'd done so.

About a quarter of an hour later he received a call from the solicitor.

'Good afternoon Mr West. This is Amanda from Wright & Hill. I have Mr Wright on the line for you, please hold…'

'Alright, thank you.'

'Afternoon Stephen. I hope you're well.'

'Hi Ian, I'm well, thanks. What can I do for you?'

'Thank you for signing those documents and having that information forwarded on to the FCA. I've also received the relevant information from the company.'

'Ah, great. I asked them to send you copies of everything.'

'Thanks for that.'

'But I take it you need something else from me?'

'Indeed. I've been putting together a short affidavit for you to depose to in respect of your version of events leading up to the Ringmire trade. I believe I have all the salient facts, but obviously there could be some gaps, so I'll be sending you a draft to peruse during the course of the next day or two. In addition to that, I'll need you to have a word with your father.'

'Excuse me?'

'Yes, I thought this would be a bit of a touchy subject. That's why I didn't simply ask you over email.'

'What on earth do you want me to talk to *him* about?'

'On your version, the only reason you knew about the *Davaproxin* drug was because you'd had an argument with your father about it. I'm sure you appreciate the fact that if your father were to sign a statement corroborating the argument in question, it would give a lot of strength to the foundation of your position. We could crack on without it, but to be honest, it would be foolish.'

'Surely it's not that much of a big deal?'

'It could be. If they buy your story as set out in your affidavit and the supporting documentation we're going to give them, then that will be the end of the matter, and you'll be off the hook, so to speak. If they have any doubts whatsoever about the veracity of the statement or the corroborating evidence, they'll take it to the next level. This will inevitably lead to either a judicial or quasi-judicial hearing. At this point in the process, we would have to bring your father in to testify. If *we* didn't they could subpoena him themselves.'

'Oh…'

'So you see, one way or another, he's likely to be involved. This way is by far the least painful.'

'Fuck!'

'I know it's going to be difficult Stephen. Nobody wants to tell their parents that they're under investigation, and it's even worse asking for their assistance. But I can assure you that you'll be thankful if we manage to avoid the messy business of hearings.'

'I understand. But it's going to be bloody difficult.'

'Then my best advice is to get it done immediately, and get it over with. Once you've spoken to him, let me know, and I'll contact him to arrange the logistics of putting a statement together and having him depose to it in the appropriate manner.'

'Thanks Ian. Sorry I'm a bit touchy about it, but I don't get along particularly well with the old man, so it's going to be a bit of a nightmare.'

'It'll be fine. I've never come across a client who couldn't get their parents to help them out with something like this. When the chips are down, its extraordinarily rare for a parent to refuse to offer assistance.'

'That's not what I'm worried about, to be honest. It's the fact that it'll involve me swallowing my pride.'

'I know it may not sound particularly consoling, but in my experience, swallowing a little pride never tastes as bad as you think it will.'

'I hope you're right!'

***

After ending his call with Ian, Stephen just sat on his sofa and stared at the wall.

The last time he'd spoken to his father, which was over Christmas, he'd behaved like a spoilt child. He'd avoided speaking to him ever since. Partly because he realised that he'd made a fool of himself, and partly because he knew that his father would remind him.

Stephen had gone up north to spend Christmas with the family for the first time in three years. He was due to stay between Christmas Eve and New Year's day, but the markets were in turmoil at the time, and he left on Boxing Day so that he could get back to work. This really upset his mother, and his father upbraided him about it. His response to the old man (in front of his mother, brother and sister-in law) was:

"You don't understand because you never had a proper career! Some of us have to make sacrifices, because our jobs carry real responsibility!"

He hated himself for saying what he'd said, almost as soon as he'd said it. But he was far too proud and stubborn to apologise. Now, not only did he have to admit that he was in trouble, but he had to ask for assistance. He felt nauseous.

It occurred to him that although it would make the conversation even more difficult, it was best to have it in person. It would be cowardly to do it over the phone. So he booked a ticket on one of the early trains out of Euston Station the following morning, and made a brief call to his father to ask if he'd be willing to meet him for an early lunch. He agreed, and although he was curious as to why his son wanted the meeting, he realised that it was evidently something Stephen only wanted to discuss when they saw one another, so he didn't probe.

The lunch would have to be a fairly truncated affair, because he needed to get back to London before his six o' clock meeting with Bridgette. But that suited him, because although he would have liked to have seen his mother, he didn't feel like hanging around longer than he absolutely had to. He calculated that if he left Lancaster on a direct train before three, he'd make it back with time to spare.

He wasn't exactly looking forward to seeing Bridgette either, but at least he could report to her that he'd signed up for online dating, and was starting to resume some old hobbies. He'd ordered a box of computer parts and had even gone down to his local art supply shop and bought some decent high gauge paper and graphite pencils. He was going to do some sketching. Charles was right, he was a very talented artist, but he'd allowed himself to drift away from drawing and painting.

He wondered whether or not he should tell Bridgette about the computer gaming thing. Perhaps she'd think it was a bit childish? But she did instruct him to do some of the things he did at University, and she was definitely astute enough to understand that, like most men of his generation, he would undoubtedly have spent a fair amount of time in front of a computer screen.

In fact, when he thought about it carefully, he realised that he spent far more of his late teens and early twenties playing computer games than he did chasing girls, or going to parties. Maybe that was why he was so inept when it came to socialising? Maybe getting back into computer games would actually be counter-productive?

He'd have to come clean with Bridgette and ask for her opinion on the subject. So far, he'd been doing exactly what she'd told him to do, so he gathered that that would make her reasonably well disposed towards him.

He could tell her that he'd even made the ridiculous 'photo appointment' with the people at *EDgE*, for that Friday, and that they were going to do the 'interview' at the same time. After confirming the appointments, he'd gotten an email from them offering him a further discount on those 'date pack' things - so out of sheer curiosity, and in some sort of attempt to convince himself that he wasn't really a miser, he purchased the 'silver edition' for £200.00.

He could also report to Bridgette the fact that he was starting to unwind and think less about work, which he supposed was a fundamental part of the programme. He felt a little bad for poor Kenny, having been assigned to work under Smith. But Jim wouldn't have placed the lad there, if he didn't have a good reason, so he tried to put it out of his mind.

Although he was dreading most of the things he had planned, he was inordinately pleased by the fact that Alexa had sent him a message asking whether or not he had any plans for that the weekend.

He was busy with Kenny when the message came through, and he'd only responded about an hour and a half later, after taking the call from Ian, and making arrangements to go up and see his father. But when he replied to say that he was free, she messaged back almost immediately, and suggested that they meet up at noon on Saturday. She'd arranged to take the afternoon off, and asked him if he would be interested in going to see the bakery and then getting something for lunch.

He was very interested in any activity which involved seeing her, and asked if he could make a reservation for them somewhere in the area. She responded by indicating that that wouldn't be necessary. They could make a decision about where to go once they met up. He was excited, although he was worried that they'd end up without any options. He didn't really like the idea of going anywhere without a pre-arranged plan.

Speaking of plans, Ollie had agreed to come and spend the day with him on Thursday, so that he could take him through the computer game. That would work out marvellously, because at least he would know something about it before he was due to meet up with Alexa, and perhaps his friend could give him a little more information on her.

He would also have to arrange a car to get down to Surrey. He couldn't exactly ask her to collect him at the closest station, and he wasn't sure whether or not he'd be able to find any reliable taxis that far out.

He didn't own a car, because he didn't really need one where he lived. In fact, he wouldn't have had anywhere other than the office to store the thing, and they'd probably charge him for the pleasure. He thought about renting one, but rental cars were conspicuous, and he didn't want Alexa to think that he was trying too hard. He'd have to borrow one. He wondered whether Jim still kept a run-around car at the office. If he did, he would almost certainly let Stephen borrow it, although with Jim, there was no telling what the thing would be. With any luck it would be something small and understated. But he doubted it.

***

The following morning, Stephen caught the eight thirty train out of Euston. It was the direct train, so it arrived in Lancaster just before eleven 'o clock. He'd arranged to meet up with his father at twelve, so he whiled away the time by walking up Castle Hill and ambling around the grounds surrounding the castle walls. There was renovation work being done on and around the structure, but it was still fairly quiet, because much of it was still not open to the public.

Like most other visual art forms, historic architecture always brought Stephen a great deal of comfort. He always felt better after taking in historic buildings or looking at sculptures and paintings.

He'd managed to secure a lunch reservation at a decent local pub that he knew had very private tables. He didn't want to be overheard talking about his case with the FCA, much less having to grovel and apologise to his father. He arrived ten minutes early and ordered a beer. He was going to need it.

'Hi Dad.'

'Hello Stephen, what's wrong?'

'Straight to the point then?'

'Come on son, it's not like you to arrange an impromptu meeting like this without a pretty significant reason. Also, we haven't spoken to one another since Christmas.'

'Fair enough.'

'You're not ill are you?'

'No, I'm not ill.'

'Have you knocked up some bird?'

'No.'

'Because if you have, your mother won't be disappointed, she'll be thrilled.'

'No, it's not that.'

'Well, don't keep me in suspense. What brings the great and powerful Stephen West home to the northern wastes?'

'You don't have to be like that, Dad.'

'Stop pretending we're on good terms my lad. You upset your mother terribly when you were here last time, and although she's doubtless forgiven your behaviour, *I haven't!*'

'Well, that's one of the reasons I'm here.'

'Really?'

'I'm sorry. I behaved like a petulant child and said some things I honestly didn't mean.'

'Okay. That's a good start.'

'But that's not the only reason you're here. I'm not an idiot Stephen. Contrary to what you may think.'

'I don't think you're an idiot, Dad.'

'You think everybody other than you is an idiot, Stephen. I don't take it personally, trust me.'

'I'm trying to make amends, Dad.'

'Oh god Stephen, you aren't on one of those twelve step Alcoholics Anonymous programmes are you?'

'No!'

'Then why the sudden need to make amends? You've never given a shit about who you've hurt before?'

'Well, maybe I'm trying to grow up and be a better person.'

'Huh…'

'Don't you think I'm capable of that sort of thing?'

'Honestly… I don't know Stephen. I think you're capable of anything intellectual, but I'm not too sure how capable you are of empathy.'

'I'm trying to fix that. I know I've been an ungrateful swine, and part of piecing my fairly pathetic life together is going to involve these sorts of conversations.'

'Alright, but what's the other thing. I suppose you need some sort of assistance?'

'Yes, in point of fact, I do.'

'Well?'

'Right… please tell me you remember that little argument we had regarding that diabetes drug, *Davaproxin*.'

'How could I bloody-well forget! Your mother's been on to me about being more conscientious about my eating ever since. Have you come to apologise for not minding your own business in respect of *that* too?'

'No. I won't apologise for trying to keep you alive longer, you miserable old git!'

'It must be really wonderful to be so clever, Stephen. Does it feel good to always be right? I expect it *does*, doesn't it.'

'It's bloody awful, Dad!'

'Then why don't you stop?'

'I can't turn off my brain. I wish I could.'

'You could turn off your mouth though.'

'I'm only starting to figure that out *now*. Maybe I'm not so bright, after all?'

'Maybe not.'

'You know what scares me Dad?'

'Being average?'

'No. I know I'll never be average. That's not me being arrogant. It's just a fact, and it needs to be said, so that you understand where I'm coming from.'

'Alright.'

'I'm scared of complicated things.'

'Stop taking the piss, Stephen. You don't find anything complicated, you never have.'

'I'm serious, Dad. I'm scared of things that don't usually occur to normal people, because I understand statistical probabilities, and if I don't control myself, I obsess over them. I give you a hard time about the diabetes thing, and your eating habits because I'm scared that you may die before I have the chance to give you any grandchildren.'

'I didn't think you wanted kids.'

'I don't know if I do. But I know that if I end up having any, I want them to enjoy a relationship with you and Mum. I know I don't come across as a very sentimental or affectionate person, but I am, I just have no idea how to show it.'

'So this is your long overdue way of telling me you actually care then?'

'Yes. I understand how fragile the human body is. Not in general, basic terms; in significant detail. I never studied medicine, but I probably understand things about science that most people can't get their heads around. I have a photographic memory, and I used to spend all of my free time absorbing information on whatever material I could get my hands on.'

'I thought that was just because you liked to show us 'normal people' how clever you were.'

'It's not that. I used to be a nervous wreck, because I obsessed over how precarious life is. I've tried so hard to turn that part of my brain off, that I've become numb. I know how volatile markets and currencies are; I know how unlikely it is that we can avoid wars and acts of terrorism; I know and understand what needs to be done to stop climate change, but I also know and understand the paradox faced by democratic systems that will, in all likelihood preclude the human race from ever taking the steps necessary to do so.'

'I see. You know, I think your drawing and painting used to help you relax. You were always a far more pleasant individual when you were busy drawing something.'

'I know. I've sort of lost that since I started working. I'm scared that if I stop obsessing over my work and try to live a more balanced life, I'll have the time and the energy to obsess over the things that frighten me again.'

'So what's gone so terribly wrong that you need *my* help?'

'My arrogance has done me an injury, of sorts. I shorted a healthy chunk of Ringmire Pharmaceutical stock before the results of their public *Davaproxin* tests were due to be released. It's a long story, but the reason I looked into the stock in the first place was because I'd had that row with you about the drug.'

'So, what went wrong then?'

'The value of the shares took a nosedive for an unrelated reason, almost immediately following the initial part of the transaction.'

'So you made some money?'

'I made a truckload of money. I didn't know you understood how shorting worked?'

'I know exactly how it works, Stephen. I didn't work in a baked bean factory for a living, my lad. In case you forgot, I also have a degree in finance.'

'Sorry, it's just that very few people know how it works.'

'If I were to guess, I would say that they suspect you had insider knowledge.'

'Yes. They do.'

'And you want me to go on oath and confirm the story that you knew about the drug because of the row we had.'

'Precisely.'

'I can do you one better than that, son.'

'You can?'

'Clearly that photographic memory of yours isn't as infallible as you think it is.'

'I don't remember absolutely *everything* about *everything*, Dad. I don't have hyperthymesia, or anything like that.'

'I don't even know what that is, Stephen.'

'Never mind, sorry, it's irrelevant. You were saying?'

'Well, I tend to remember when you've been even more obnoxious than usual. In this case, that may actually prove useful.'

'How so?'

'After our little argument about the diabetes drug, you sent me a long, patronising email about diabetes research, and the need for me to be more conscientious about my eating and exercise habits.'

'I suppose that may help.'

'It gets better. You also said, in your obnoxious email, that you were so convinced about the fact that the drug was unlikely to cure the condition, that you would keep an eye out for the release of any studies or test results related to the drug, so that you could forward them to me and prove your point.'

'Shit! that *will* be helpful to me.'

'I can't believe you didn't remember it, to be honest.'

'Well, sometimes I feel bad about having been obnoxious, so I try to block out the memories. I often only think about what I've said or done long after the saying or doing.'

'You need to work on that.'

'I know.'

'I'm happy to help in any way I can, Stephen. But I want you to apologise to your mother for your behaviour last year, and make a plan to come and see her more frequently. My help isn't conditional upon you doing that, but I'll be seriously disappointed if you don't. In case it's unclear, I *am* guilting you into making it up to her.'

'I get it. I'll be a better son, I promise.'

10

Stephen managed to get onto a train back to London just before two 'o clock, which gave him ample time to make it to his consultation with Bridgette later that day. He could, technically, have gone home before heading out to Knightsbridge, but it would have been a waste, because it would involve a bit of doubling back, and would only have enabled him to spend around twenty minutes at home before having to set out again.

So instead, he went straight to Knightsbridge, and took a slow walk in Hyde Park to kill the time before his appointment.

He was feeling slightly better about his prospects in the matter with the FCA, but he was now genuinely ashamed of how he'd treated his parents at Christmas. He was also starting to feel particularly lonely. He couldn't remember when last he'd spent so much time alone without being caught up with work. Long train rides and walks in the park never used to feel like this, because he was always either glued to a laptop, a newspaper, or actively trying to solve some sort of work-related puzzle in his head.

It occurred to him, whilst ambling around the park, that he hadn't actually thought about work since the previous Thursday, when he'd stopped himself from reading the news items concerning *Ringmire*. After he left the office the week before, he still spent much of his time obsessing over what was happening in the markets, but for the last five days, he hadn't even bothered to pick up a newspaper, or read any of his work-related emails.

Whilst it was true that he was on gardening leave, and was busy attending gaming conventions, and trying not to drown in rivers, he wasn't precluded from keeping up with market conditions.

He knew it was unlikely that there would be anything else about *Ringmire* or *Davaproxin* lurking in the columns of the financial papers. The lifespan of those sorts of stories was never particularly long-lived, because there was always some new crisis pervading the collective imagination of the business press. The only stories which tended to linger longer than about forty eight hours were those involving wars.

Stephen arrived at Bridgette's offices at exactly six 'o clock, and was immediately ushered through to her office by Susan, who was looking even more attractive than he'd remembered.

Bridgette stood up to greet him, and Susan disappeared without a sound.

'Nice to see you again, Stephen! How have you been getting on with your appointed tasks?'

Stephen wasn't ready to be thrust into the middle of a discussion about what he'd been doing. He was hoping to get settled and exchange some pleasantries first, so that he could order his thoughts a little. He still wasn't quite comfortable with the idea of sharing his personal life with a complete stranger. It was hard enough doing it with his father earlier that day.

'Hi Bridgette. I'd like to think I'm doing rather well with them.'

'That's' a little vague, isn't it? Either you are or you aren't.'

Bridgette had an uncanny knack of making Stephen feel like he wasn't the smartest person in the room. It was a feeling he wasn't remotely used to, and it simultaneously irritated and intrigued him. What was worse, was that she could turn it on and off with such effortless grace, that he was never quite prepared for it.

'Alright then. I'm doing well with the tasks.'

'That's more like it. You need to start being a little more self-assured. I get the impression that you're very self-assured, even cocky, at work.'

'Yeah, that's true.'

'You clearly have difficulties with women though. Is that something you're starting to accept, or are you still in a little bit of denial about that?'

'No, I accept that now. I still wouldn't put it down to "*perceived sexual inadequacy*", but I suppose that that's a matter of semantics now.'

'Not quite. But, I'm willing to forego the formality of labelling it, as long as you agree that you have a problem. It's far easier for me to help you once you've made that concession.'

'Fair enough. I concede.'

'Good. I think I understand part of your problem, and it goes back a little to what we touched on briefly last time we met. Although you're assertive at work, you're not necessarily assertive or forceful outside of work.'

'I am if I'm in the right sort of environment. But I suppose that's a fair point, generally speaking.'

'I assume by 'the right sort of environment', you mean, your comfort zone. That is, speaking to people you know, about topics in respect of which you have a detailed understanding; or at least an interest.'

'Yes.'

'Right. So basically, you like to know enough about your topic and your audience to be able to show off how clever you are.'

'That sounds a bit harsh, I wouldn't necessarily put it that way.'

'How would you put it, then?'

'I would say that I only like being around people I know, and talking about things that I find worthwhile.'

'So if you don't know about them, or aren't interested in them, they aren't worthwhile?'

'Well, now that you put it like that…'

'You see Stephen, you're insecure. That's not a terrible thing, we all have various insecurities. The problem is that *your* insecurities alter your behaviour in ways that aren't conducive to making friends and influencing people.'

'How so?'

'You either become obnoxious, or come across as a bit of a wet blanket. I must admit, the stark juxtaposition of your default responses is rather fascinating. Most people normally fall on one side of that spectrum.'

'Well, at least I'm not boring then.'

'You certainly aren't boring, Mr West.'

'So how do I fix that problem?'

'Unfortunately I can't give you a pill for that. You need to pick out the more dangerous of the two responses and work on that first.'

'I'm assuming that that would be the 'obnoxious' response.'

'Actually, no.'

'Really?'

'I know it sounds a little counterintuitive, but women will deal a little bit better with an obnoxious man than they will with what we call a 'beta male'. You'll recall I brought up the alpha slash beta thing briefly with you last time we spoke.'

'Yes.'

'As I said before; going around behaving like a testosterone fuelled Neanderthal isn't the type of thing I would ever advocate; but behaving like a bit of a weakling and being sickeningly sweet is a turn off for most heterosexual women. You can't be too nice.'

Stephen looked across the table at her with an expression that betrayed the fact that he didn't have the faintest idea what she was on about.

'I can see by your expression that you don't understand me, Stephen. You *genuinely* don't get it, *do you*?'

'No.'

'Okay. Let's get back to basics then.'

'Thanks.'

'You see, Stephen. Although human relationships appear to you to be rather complicated; they *aren't*! I won't go into all of the juicy details right now, but suffice it to say that when it comes to the subject of men and women engaging in romantic relationships, it's important to understand the most basic fundamental principle first. That is: heterosexual women *like* men!'

'I get that, Bridgette. But I don't get how being nice isn't a good thing.'

'I don't think you do get it, to be honest?'

Stephen just stared at her blankly.

'My point is that women who are interested in men, tend to prefer the ones who *behave* like men.'

'So what you're saying is that being polite isn't "*manly*"?!'

'It depends on context, Stephen. But you need to understand something about the laws of nature if you're going to go out into the world and try to find a heterosexual female partner.'

'Alright. I'm listening.'

'Women who have what some might call, a high '*mate value*', are only genuinely interested in men who *also* have a high '*mate value*'. On a primal level, the qualities which give a woman this value are: youth, attractiveness, a child bearing shape, and a motherly disposition. The qualities which give a *man* this value are: confidence, strength of character and economic resourcefulness. It sounds old fashioned and patronising, but most of us can't escape our biology. No matter how evolved we think we are.'

'So how is being "*nice*", not strong or confident?'

'Being '*nice*', is weak in this context, because it's bland, and demonstrates lack of confidence. The word '*nice*' gives it away Stephen; it's an awful word, used to describe things that aren't terrible, but aren't brilliant, either. They're sort of just, '*nice*'; like a good rug, or a tasteful table decoration. Do you think a woman wants a relationship with someone '*nice*', or someone '*amazing*'?'

'I haven't thought about it like that, to be honest.'

'Clearly!'

'I'm not sure many people *do* think about it like that, Bridgette.'

'Maybe not. But you see Stephen, girls don't go searching for men that would make their mothers happy. In my experience, most mothers aren't actually that good when it comes to evaluating the men their daughters bring home. A lot of them like bland men for their daughters, because they're more stable and less likely to run off with someone else.'

'I'm fascinated to find out why that isn't a *good* thing, Bridgette.'

'It isn't a good thing because it ignores a biological imperative. In isolation, that doesn't really present a fundamental difficulty, but when you look at it in the context of a broad set of decision making parameters, it just muddies the waters.'

'I still don't get it.'

'What I'm saying is that if mommy dearest ignores the fact that her precious little girl likes a bit of rough, and is searching for someone with a high mate value, she's either going to end up resenting her mother for pushing her into a relationship with someone she isn't head over heels for, or she's going to act out by running off with the drug addled lead singer of a rock band; or at least someone who closely resembles that sort of character.'

'That sounds like a bit of a cliché to be honest.'

'It is. But that doesn't make it any less accurate. Most women like men who are assertive, even if that makes them a bit rough around the edges. Not in the sense that they're dirty or foulmouthed, but in the sense that they adopt a bit of a cavalier attitude towards conventional social rules and societal norms. So being a little pushy or arrogant isn't always a bad thing, as long as it's in moderation.'

'Are you telling me that women actually think like that, Bridgette?'

'It's a male myth that we're made of sugar, spice and all things nice. We let you think it, because it suits our agenda, but don't be fooled. If women weren't as interested in *men* as men are in *women*, the species wouldn't have survived for this long.'

'So I have to be an arsehole then?'

'Yes, and *no*.'

'Forgive me Bridgette, but that sounds a bit imprecise.'

'I'm curious Stephen, remember you told me when we fist discussed this, that you'd behaved like an *"arsehole"* on the last date you'd been on.'

'Yes, I'm surprised you remembered that.'

'You're not the only person here with an exceptional memory. You claim to have a photographic memory, don't you? Jim told me about that.'

'I do have a photographic memory. Not an eidetic one, in case you were wondering whether or not I'd mixed up the correct terminology.'

'No, I assumed you'd be the type of person to know the difference. But be that as it may, I too have a good memory, and I distinctly recall you saying that you'd been less than pleasant on your last date.'

'Yes. So?'

'So did she ask to see you again?'

'Shit… she did.'

'I rest my case.'

'I'm clearly out of my depth here, aren't I?'

'Yes. But you'll figure it out as long as you're willing to modify your behaviour a little. Like with everything in life, there has to be a balance, Stephen. Unfortunately, it's not something I can script for you. You have to learn the balance yourself, but think of it this way: when you pitch an idea to your board of directors, do you do it directly, or do you behave like a pansy, and engage them in all sorts of idle chitchat before you get down to business.'

'I do it directly, of course. Time is money.'

'The same principle applies to dating, Stephen. Engage actively, not like a wet blanket. Be courteous and polite, like you would be with your board; but not obsequious, or glib.'

'Seriously?'

'Yes. Do you ever phone your male friends, just to talk?'

'No.'

'Of course you don't. It's not male behaviour to engage in idle, aimless chitchat.'

'But surely, talking to a woman is different. I'm sure I've read somewhere that women like a man who listens.'

'That's nonsense Stephen, it's bad pop-psychology. Women like *other women* to listen to them, because most men don't have the necessary attention span, and most of them try and offer solutions to problems that women don't actually want a solution to. We're complicated; at least *that* bit of pop-psychology is true.'

'But…'

'Stephen, when you were in high school, did you ever become very good friends with a girl you were trying to date, only to end up being sidelined by some jerk she picked up at a party?'

'Obviously I did. It happened to most of my mates at some point.'

'And yet, very few of you learnt anything from that experience.'

'Go on.'

'You thought that the more you got to know her; the more you listened; the more you sat on the telephone talking about random trivialities: the more likely she would be to fall for you. So you probably spent months on end behaving like one of her girl friends, the net result of which, was that she started to *see* you as a girl, so the side of her brain that controlled her mating impulses didn't even register you as a viable male option.'

'I feel like a bit of an idiot now.'

'It's not your *fault* Stephen, most men don't figure it out until they're about fifty. They then go through a mid-life crisis, and try to make up for lost time by chasing twenty five year olds.

'Alright, that makes sense, I suppose.'

'I'm a bit difficult with you on purpose, Stephen. It's to teach you how to deal with strong women. You're a successful, bright young man, who is standing at the crossroads of life. You can either shrivel up into obscurity, or you can stand up and take life by the scruff of the neck.'

'That sounds a bit dramatic, Bridgette.'

'Although it's another terrible cliché, it's most often the case, that behind every successful person, is a strong and capable partner. I can't stress enough how important it is for you to secure a relationship with a strong partner. I may be wrong, but I honestly believe that your future success and happiness depend on it.'

'Really?'

'Life is a team sport, Stephen. You're only as good as those you choose to play alongside. Weak women are not good partners for successful men, because although their helplessness is attractive at the outset, and satisfies the man's desire for a certain degree of vulnerability, it gets old quickly. You can't love someone you don't respect.'

'I can understand that.'

'That said, be open minded when it comes to the exercise of dating, and try to figure out who you are. If you're uncomfortable with yourself, you can't expect somebody else to be comfortable with you.'

'It's tricky. I suppose I'm not really normal.'

'What's normal? Everyone thinks their problems are unique and special. They aren't. We don't need to categorise our difficulties and evaluate where they fit, we just need to identify them and crack on.'

'I just wish there was a more clearly defined solution. You know, like some sort of blueprint that I could follow.'

'No you don't. You think you do. But that's not how life works, Stephen; and it's all the richer for it. That's all the dating advice you're going to get from me for now though.'

'Alright, what else would you like to talk about?'

'How is your little difficulty with the financial authorities going?'

'Well, I think it's going as well as can be expected at this point. It's actually forced me to reconnect with my father. I went to see him today.'

'Good. I know we haven't plumbed the depths of your daddy-issues, and I don't really plan to, but I assume the two of you have a complicated relationship. It's important that you square that away, so to speak. I hate the popular notion that all psychological problems can be traced back to unresolved issues with parents; it's never that simple. But I have to concede that it's popular for a litany of compelling reasons.'

'It turns out he may be able to help me, so I'm grateful for that.'

'Good. Make sure you let him know that you're grateful. If you haven't thanked him, pick up the phone and do it.'

'I will.'

'Are you writing in the diary?'

'Yes. It's a bloody awkward exercise though.'

'I can understand that. But I want you to keep doing it.'

'Okay.'

'What hobbies are you resuming?'

'I'm going to start drawing again, and my mate Ollie has convinced me to start playing computer games again. I know it sounds a bit childish, but I did enjoy gaming when I was at university, and you specifically told me to go back to some things I did back then.'

'Absolutely, what are you planning on playing?'

'A thing called *The Other Planet*. My best mate Charlie designed it.'

'You know Charles Taylor?'

Stephen almost fell off his chair. He went dead silent and looked across at Bridgette enquiringly.

'We were at university together.'

'I play *The Other Planet*, Stephen. Your friend 'Charlie' is reasonably famous in gaming circles; I surprised you haven't been playing his game.'

'You're kidding me!'

'No.'

'But...'

'All human beings play games Stephen, there's no difference between golf, chess, snooker and computer games. Do what makes you happy, and stop assuming that playing computer games isn't a valid pastime. That's just an old fashioned perception.'

'I'm still trying to get to grips with that.'

'Embrace it Stephen, there's no use in trying to pretend to be something you're not. Do what you want to do, not what you think society *expects* you to do.'

'You don't think it's counter-productive then?'

'No. It can be, but you're intelligent enough to keep your playing under control. Computer games have an interesting psychological effect. Like many other things, they're useful in moderation. Companies, like the one that your friend Charles works for, employ psychologists to help them capture the necessary components of gaming motivation. It's no wonder that they keep producing hits, and that the gaming community is growing exponentially.'

'So there is an actual psychological component to it?'

'Stephen. There's a psychological component to everything.'

'I suppose that must be true.'

'Computer game companies aim to target these motivations, and most of them manage to capture at least one of the primary ones. Current research suggests that there are three main motivating components to online games, each of which can be broken down further into multiple sub-components. The primary ones are: achievements, social connection, and immersion. Most games get the first component right, but the really serious ones manage all three. Of course, that's just scratching the surface when it comes to the deeper psychological aspects of why gaming is becoming so pervasive, but the simple fact of the matter is that computer games, and most table-top role playing games are more psychologically appealing than any sport could ever hope to be.'

'Really?'

'Yes. Like most basic games, sports tend to get the achievement motivation right. This motivator is rooted in developing skills which can be improved over time; gaining a working knowledge of rules and systems; and competing with others within that framework. The problem is that competition is a far more nuanced psychological concept than most sports can realistically manipulate.'

'Sounds interesting.'

'It's fascinating, actually. You'll have noticed that executives in your field are more likely to play golf than tennis?'

'Yes, I suppose that's true. That's certainly my experience.'

'It's not because tennis is more physically demanding. It *is*, but that isn't the point. The point is that as we get older, most of us tend to opt for games that aren't as competitive between players. In golf, you don't really have to compete against the people in your group of players. You can compete against yourself, and spur one another along. There are obviously those who prefer to compete, but most social players opt out of direct competition, and this makes the game a lot more socially driven.'

'That makes sense.'

'Some personality types can use competition as a form of relaxation, but they're in a fairly small minority. Most people prefer to tackle games co-operatively, and most traditional sports simply can't cater for that proclivity. Sure, you can play a team sport, but the competition aspect is still very direct. Most massively multiplayer online games and tabletop roleplaying games cater for the need for social co-operation directly, and they do it in style. You can compete with other players, but most players find it more satisfying to co-operate with one another against the obstacles generated in the game.'

'Yeah, I can see how that works. It's one of the things I really enjoyed about gaming.'

'Even non-tech companies have started using Dungeons & Dragons, and similar table top roleplaying games for corporate team-building. It's brilliant, because it encourages deep co-operation, and takes account of the fact that, within corporate teams, there's often vast differences between physical capabilities, and insecurities around physical activity. It's seriously unfair to insist that everyone take part in rock climbing, abseiling, or even paintball.'

'Wow. I had no idea the world was changing so much.'

'It is, and it's a good thing. As long as you realise that there's a potential for exploitation, and go in with your eyes wide open, you should play the games that you enjoy.'

'I do feel a lot better about playing games now.'

'I'm glad I've been able to help. I see we're running out of time, let's continue this conversation next week.'

11

The following day, Stephen's computer parts arrived, and he spent most of the day assembling them and installing the necessary software on his new machine.

Once it was up and running, he noticed that Ollie had sent him an email with a glossary of gaming terms for him to learn. He was impressed with his friend's attention to detail, but he wasn't sure it was necessary to spend a great deal of time going through it. He was sure that he'd pick up all the necessary jargon whilst playing the game. It was definitely worth a brief look [1].

After going through the glossary of terms, Stephen closed the mail and had a quiet chuckle to himself. He was grateful for the fact that he had the sort of memory that would retain much of what he'd read, but he knew he'd have to give it another read at some point.

He felt that he ought to have known more of the terms Ollie had described. But on reflection, he realised that when he played digital roleplaying games, they weren't online - at least not the ones *he* used to play. Far from being intimidated by the seeming complexity of the new gaming world, he was excited by it.

***

Ollie arrived just after ten o'clock on Thursday morning, bearing two cappuccinos and a wide grin. He was clearly happy to help Stephen out with his re-introduction to the world of cyber gaming.

Stephen was also more enthusiastic than he'd imagined he'd be when he first made the decision to try it out.

'Morning Ol, ready to teach your old mate about this game?'

'Absolutely. Did you see I sent you an email yesterday, with a glossary of common terms.'

'I did indeed. I've already been through them. I remember some from when I used to play, but a lot has changed, I see.'

'Well there weren't many MMORPG's back then, just RPG's.'

'So we're going to speak in acronyms then, Ol?'

'Stephen, when did you learn the most French? In school? Or when we spent six weeks in that dodgy campsite in Provence during our first long university holiday? Nobody spoke bloody English, so we had to learn, fast.'

'Point taken!'

'Right. So we'll use the lingo as much as possible.'

'Okay, fair enough.'

'The first thing is that you're going to have to learn about the basic game *"lore"* - you know what that is, right?'

'Yeah, I'm not that old, mate!'

'Right, but unless you still have that ridiculously good memory of yours, you may want to make some notes.'

'I think I'll manage, Ol.'

'You'll have to concentrate, because our mate Charlie must have been taking some strong stuff when he came up with the basic idea for this game.'

'I can't wait!'

'So it's like this:

It's the year 2347 (or something like that) you can look on the game's website if you want to get precise. The humans have managed to perfect interstellar travel, and they've been on a pretty ambitious space colonisation mission. They've managed to colonise a few dozen planets, but they've never encountered any extra-terrestrial life, even though the planets they've inhabited actually support life in pretty much the same fashion as Earth does. Sounds a bit too convenient, but whatever… it's not like we aren't invested in the notion of suspending disbelief.

Then, they find *'The Other Planet'*.

They land, and find that the place is like something out of the Lord of the Rings. It's inhabited by elves; and orcs; and goblins; and dwarves; and all *manner* of magical and mythical creature known to fantasy geeks of pretty much every persuasion.

If you thought *that* was strange, wait till you get a load of this: there are also hostile alien forces, and *dinosaurs* on the planet.

But it gets even *more* interesting. They obviously have magic, and swords and things; but they also have modern weapons, like hand-held rail guns, and composite bows that shoot laser guided arrows with depleted uranium tips.

Basically, if you can dream it up, then Charles and his team of fantasy-peddling nerds have probably beaten you to it, and thrown it into the game - they have swords that can cut through tanks, flying machines, pterodactyls you can ride, jet packs, and bullet proof wizard's robes. In any given encounter, you could have a wizard on a magic carpet fighting a T-Rex, alongside a dwarf carrying an axe that has an edge like a lightsaber.

As I say, Charlie must have been taking some sort of recreational drugs when he came up with this stuff. It's mental.

But, it turns out that his ridiculous fantasy world is loved by no less than twenty million subscribers. So either there's something strange in the water, or he's just a genius who managed to tap into the collective consciousness of enough weird people to fill a small country.'

'Oh. My. Word.'

'Yip, I don't really get it either, but it's incredibly well made, and fun to play.'

'It sounds *brilliant*!'

'You see? Something about that combination of ridiculousness just *works*. It's like peanut butter and chilli on toast. It sounds bloody awful, but it's magnificent!'

'I can't actually remember the last time I was this excited.'

'Probably when my sister-in-law agreed to go out on a date with you!'

'How did you know about *that*?'

'Come on Steve. I'm married to her *sister*. I knew before *you* did, my friend!'

'Good point. Got any tips for me?'

'Not a chance. I'm happy to be a casual onlooker. Far safer that way.'

'For *you*, maybe!'

'Why would I care about making anything safe for you, Steve?'

'Nice mate *you* are!'

'My self preservation mechanism is just strong Stephen. Karen would remove my testicles if I said or did anything wrong regarding her sister. You're on your own.'

'Fine! Just teach me all about this crazy game, so I don't look like a fool if it comes up.'

'Fool is not the correct term. It's '*Noob*', remember? Learn the terminology, Steve!'

'For fuck sakes, Oliver! *Really*?'

'Do you want my help, or *don't* you?'

'Okay, okay. I'll remember to use the correct terminology.'

'I should have a special T-Shirt made for you to wear on the date:

"The Other Planet Fanatic, AFK while my spells are on cooldown, and hoping to circumvent any harsh RNG during my date, so I don't get Pwned and she doesn't Ragequit!"

'That's not funny!'

'It's bloody hilarious. She'd love it.'

Oliver spent the rest of the day teaching Steve most of what he needed to know about the game. He was hooked after the first ten minutes, but his enthusiasm grew steadily throughout the process.

Although he did feel a bit like a tadpole that had been dropped into the middle of the ocean. The game was far deeper and more involved than any game he'd experienced before. Charles and his team had created a complex and fully immersive alternate digital world.

Stephen imagined that he probably wouldn't run out of things to do in the game for at least a few years, and that alone made it particularly compelling. On top of that, Ollie explained that they released new expansions every two to three years, and continuously provided snippets of new content to keep those who were up to date with the game interested in between these expansions.

As far as he could tell, the model was about as perfect as you could reasonably expect for any game. As long as they kept updating it and providing new material, it would probably never die. Those who grew tired of it eventually, would end up being replaced by new players and the game world would basically keep itself alive for as long as the company had the will and the resources to maintain it.

Ollie explained that the entire model was Charles' brainchild from inception, and for the first time in his life, Stephen was actually willing to concede that one of his mates was probably smarter than him. Charlie was clearly a genius.

As with all roleplaying games, you had to choose a race and class for your character. This didn't work the way he remembered from when he'd played digital role playing games in his teens. Back then, you got to choose one of no more than about five ready-made characters, all of which had pre-defined genders, appearances and abilities which were similarly cast in stone.

In this game, however, you created your own character from scratch. You would first choose a race and gender; then a class; followed by a specialisation within that class; a political alignment; a primary language; three professions; two crafting skills; and, of course, a fully customisable appearance.

There were a dozen races to choose from, each with its own racial bonuses and abilities; more genders than Stephen knew existed; sixteen classes, each of which had no less than five completely unique specialisations; nine possible political alignments; two dozen languages; eighteen professions; and fourteen crafting skills. The appearance customisation tool was so advanced and detailed that you could basically make an accurate replica of your own face and body - not that you necessarily would. But it was good to know the possibility existed.

Stephen chose a half-elf *'death ranger'* with a random assortment of features that Oliver recommended. He would have to learn how everything worked in the game before he decided to create another character. He wasn't intimidated by the sheer volume of options though - he had the sort of mind that enabled him to find comfort in detail.

There was nothing wrong with the old style of game in which you just ran around killing monsters and picking up gear and gold, but it did tend to get boring eventually. The addition of things like professions and crafting skills was clever, because it encouraged the investment of time and energy to a process which could be repetitive, yet compelling enough to keep you from rushing through the primary game content. It created breathing room for the development team at the same time as providing deeper immersion for the players.

The in-game currency wasn't gold like it would have been in one of the older games. It was 'Crypto Credits' and the the wizards had tablets instead of tomes. Stephen thought that was a bit of a stretch, but he was willing to go with it.

The game had shops and vendors, like most old computer games, but it also had an *"auction house"*, so you could buy and sell equipment, and materials for the various professions from other players, either by bidding on them, or by agreeing with the other player to pay the maximum price allocated for the item.

This was all open-ended, so it was pretty much controlled by normal market forces of supply and demand. The game didn't interfere, and so the players had created their own economy. Stephen was very impressed by how it functioned. A good economist could actually manipulate the market to some extent, if they were so inclined. But apparently there *was* some sort of oversight by the developers to stop really bad behaviour, like some sort of FCA. Stephen smiled wryly to himself when he read up about that part of the in-game economy.

Then there were guilds… These seemed to be pretty much one of the main points of the game. Your character could join a group of other Player Characters, and then go and conquer dungeons together, or do specific scenarios and quests with one another.

Oliver explained that although most guilds were fairly casual, some were serious, and required a lot of time commitment. Some were even *professional*! Apparently, the professional teams competed in various esports leagues, and got paid like professional athletes. These players made a seriously decent living out of the game.

Apparently, even *non-professionals* could make a living playing the game, by having podcasts, websites, apps and YouTube channels which gave guidance to players.

Stephen's mind was blown by the complexity and detail of the world that his friend had created. He knew that he would enjoy playing this game a lot more than he'd enjoyed the games he'd played twenty years ago.

***

Stephen woke up earlier than usual on Friday morning. The people from

EDgE were due to arrive at nine to take photographs and conduct the 'vetting interview', and he wanted to be fully awake and ready in case they showed up earlier than expected. He also wanted to make sure that the apartment was suitably tidy.

After inhaling a double espresso and having a hot shower, he straightened the apartment out and found that he still had about an hour and a half to kill. So he settled down and took out his art supplies. He was actually itching to dive back into *The Other Planet*, but he'd spent the whole of the previous day, and most of the evening playing; so he stopped himself. He remembered what Bridgette had said about keeping his playing under control.

He was a little rusty with the pencil, but after about half an hour, he'd found his rhythm, and was pleased to note that he hadn't lost his ability to draw.

The doorbell rang at precisely nine 'o clock.

'Good morning Mr West. My name's Elizabeth, I'm here for your photo appointment. My colleague, Jason, will be here shortly for your vetting interview.'

'Hello! You're right on time!'

'We don't waste the time of our members, Mr West. Is there anywhere in particular you would like me to set up my equipment?'

Elizabeth looked every inch as severe as she sounded. She was far taller than average, and slightly thinner than she ought to have been. This was highlighted by the pinstripe trouser suit she was wearing, which made her look like a giant praying mantis. She had long dark hair, tied in a French plait, and wore sensible flat shoes that looked like an expensive version of the the sort of thing worn by elderly school teachers. If she'd have been wearing heels, she would have been taller than Stephen, and he wasn't exactly diminutive, at six foot three.

'Yes, of course, come through to the sitting-room area, I'm sure the lighting will be okay in here.'

'Not to worry Mr West, we provide our *own* lighting...'

He should have realised that, because she had a large black kit bag over her right shoulder, and was pulling a massive wheeled suitcase behind her. There was no way she only had a camera and tripod with her.

He closed the door behind her, and ushered her into the sitting room area.

'Would you like help carrying your equipment.'

'No, thank you.'

Ordinarily, Stephen would have been a little perturbed by her curt and direct manner, but he was learning to let that sort of thing wash over him.

The doorbell rang again.

'That must be Jason. Perhaps you should let him in, Mr West…'

'Of course, please call me Stephen.'

'Okay Stephen, as you wish. I'll set up whilst you have a chat with my colleague.'

Stephen smiled as he turned to let Jason in. Elizabeth reminded him a little of Bridgette.

'Hi. Jason I presume?'

'Indeed Mr West, good morning… how are you today?'

Jason was far more personable than his cohort; and about half a foot shorter. He was a lot younger than Stephen had expected, and was dressed in an open-neck shirt and designer jeans. Stephen found it odd that the photographer was dressed like an executive and the 'vetting' chap was dressed for a night on the town, but he was relieved that Jason seemed to be a bit more friendly than Elizabeth.

'I'm well, thank you Jason, please call me Stephen.'

'Thanks Stephen, I'm sure you know why I'm here, but don't worry, my interview is *very* informal… is there somewhere we can sit down?'

'Yeah, let's sit at the table. Would you like a coffee?'

'That would be marvellous. Black, no sugar.'

'Great, same as me. I'll just go and ask your colleague if she'd also like a cup.'

He half expected her to tell him that she'd bought her own, but it would have been rude not to offer.

'Elizabeth, I'm making coffee, would you like a cup?'

'No thank you Stephen, I don't do stimulants. But tap water would be nice.'

Stephen smiled to himself. He couldn't imagine how 'nice' tap water could possibly be, but it reminded him of Bridgette's scathing definition of the word, and forced him to concede that the ever perceptive executive coach had, once again, made an accurate assessment.

He prepared the coffees, along with a 'nice' glass of tap, before taking a seat at the table with his interviewer.

'So Stephen, I've been through your background, and done some checking. You seem to be a very successful individual. I can see by your apartment that you have impeccable taste. Is that *your* work over there?'

Stephen had left his drawing on the table. He'd been busy working on it when they'd arrived.

'Thanks Jason, yes. I'm trying to get back into drawing. It's an old hobby I shelved when I started working.'

'Looks like more than a *hobby*. Artistically talented, *and* successful in business… impressive.'

'I can sense a *'but'* coming.'

'No buts. Just a how? *How* are you still single?'

'All work and no play has clearly made me dull. Hence the dating site. I've been advised that it's about time I put myself 'out there', so to speak.'

'Sounds like good advice. But I have to ask: have you *ever* been involved in a romantic relationship?'

'Yes, I was in a few very brief relationships in my early and mid twenties. But nothing really stuck.'

'We see that a lot with our members. Some of them even *marry* young, but then drift away from their partners. It's quite normal given your proclivities… they don't really suit conventional relationships.'

Stephen was a little taken aback by Jason's comment. What did he mean, '*proclivities*'? It was the wrong word, contextually.

'So I guess that a lot of your clients work long hours, and have demanding careers then?'

'Yes. That *is* often the case.'

Stephen was starting to feel mildly irritated. Jason's response didn't resolve his underlying question, and he could sense that his counterpart actually knew it. He wasn't adept at reading these sorts of things, but for some reason he'd picked this up, and it was bothering him.

Before he could say anything, Jason continued.

'When did you realise that you were, how shall we say, *unique*?'

'How do you mean, *unique*? I know I don't *date* much. But otherwise, I'm pretty *normal*.'

'Oh, don't get me wrong, Stephen. You appear to be *perfectly* normal, but we both know that you *aren't*. You needn't worry though, this is a *safe space*, you can rest assured that our discretion is *absolute*.'

'Jason. I don't mean to sound rude. But what the bloody hell are you talking about?!'

'Stephen, I know that you feel this is something you would like to keep private, but it's hardly appropriate to try and keep up the pretence around us?'

'What bloody *pretence*?!'

Just then, Elizabeth emerged, and broke into the conversation. The fact that it was becoming rather heated, didn't seem to phase her.

'If you don't mind me interrupting gentlemen, I need to get these photographs done. Please change into the outfit in the bag, Stephen. It should all fit, it's completely adjustable.'

She produced a small, black canvass tote bag from within the large wheeled suitcase that had also been home to her assortment of lighting paraphernalia, and held it out for him.

'*What?*'

'The bag Stephen. You needn't be worried, it's all perfectly clean. We just like the outfits to be uniform in our member's gallery.'

He was still irritated by the fact that he hadn't managed to finish his conversation with Jason, so he didn't take the opportunity to question Elizabeth any further on the subject of having to don the required 'uniform'. At this point, he just wanted to get the whole process over with.

'Okay, fine! Give me a minute, will you?'

He stalked off to the bedroom to change. He was actually curious to see what it was that they wanted him to wear. The interaction was becoming stranger by the minute, and he suspected that the required getup for the photo shoot wasn't likely to be anything as mundane as a golf shirt and a pair of sensible trousers.

His suspicions turned out to be correct. Though he wasn't even remotely prepared for what he discovered when he emptied the bag out onto his bed.

He was confronted by an assortment of items that instantly cleared up any misconceptions he may have had regarding the nature and purport of Jason's questions and comments. So although he was suitably horrified, he was relieved that he'd actually been talking to his interviewer at cross purposes.

Strewn out before him was: a leather thong; a blindfold; a netting vest; a pair of handcuffs; a leather collar with spikes; a black rope… and a red ball-gag.

They were the missing pieces of the puzzle regarding the expensive and somewhat mysterious dating site Stephen had managed to sign up for. Once he realised what was going on, he felt like a complete idiot; because, on reflection, all of the necessary signs had been present from the start. He hadn't been paying attention; perhaps Jim was right about him going around with blinkers on.

He wasn't quite sure how he was going to handle the conversation he was about to have with Elizabeth and Jason, but his thoughts on the subject were interrupted by the stark realisation that Jason had probably already spoken to both Mary and Jim.

Although he was reasonably certain that Jason would have handled these discussions with tact, there was a distinct and terrifying possibility that the people at Edge had made the assumption that Stephen's choice of references was made on the basis that the individuals in question were acquainted with his alternative lifestyle. Indeed, this was a perfectly reasonable and pragmatic assumption for them to have made.

Then again, had that been the case, surely one of his two colleagues would have broached the subject with him already. Or would they?

He realised that the only way he was going to put himself out of the misery of frantic speculation on the subject, would be to have the necessary conversation with Jason. So he put the assortment of S&M accoutrements back into their bag, and headed out to face his visitors.

'Stephen, is there some sort of difficulty? Do you need assistance with the outfit? You can leave the blindfold off until we're ready to shoot.'

'Umm, actually. There's been a terrible misunderstanding, Elizabeth.'

'In what respect?'

'In respect of the fact that I had no idea that EDgE was an S&M dating site.'

'Oh, so...'

'So, I honestly thought this was just a standard dating thing. I'm not into S&M. Don't get me wrong, I have no prejudices, it's just not my thing.'

'You thought this was just a normal photoshoot for a normal dating profile?'

'Yes.'

'You honestly had no idea what was going on here?'

'No. That's why I got so hot under the collar with Jason when he was trying to question me about my 'proclivities'; I thought he was alluding to my career.'

Jason was visibly relieved. He'd evidently been a bit worried about the fact that his earlier conversation with Stephen wasn't going particularly well.

'Ah, that makes a lot more sense then. Sorry for the misunderstanding, Stephen.'

'Don't be. It was my fault, I should have realised what was going on when I first signed up. I've been a bit preoccupied, and I'm not really good at this sort of thing to start with. I've never even been on an internet dating site before.'

Jason smiled and shook his head. Even Elizabeth seemed to take pity on Stephen, and gave him an almost motherly look of concern.

'Jason. You didn't happen to contact those references I listed on the intake form did you?'

'I'm afraid I did.'

'Ah... did you... how can I say this? Umm...'

'No, I didn't come straight out and tell either of them about the nature of the site. Although I did assume that you'd listed them because they knew you well enough to understand your… sorry, this is not something I've ever encountered really.'

'No, I get that.'

'Basically, I tried to remain as discreet as possible. We always do; but I'm not sure as to whether or not the nature of my questions gave anything away.'

'Okay.'

'I tell you what, I'll have a word with my team. I'm sure we can arrange a refund of the joining fee, less some minor administrative expenses.'

'I would really appreciate that, Jason. I'm sorry for wasting your time.'

'Not to worry, Stephen. The last thing we want is for people to feel that they've been misled.'

'Thanks. May I at least help with packing up your equipment Elizabeth?'

'No, don't worry about that, I'll manage. I could do with another glass of water though.'

'Sure I can't offer you something more exciting?'

'No.'

'Jason?'

'I'll have another coffee if you're making.'

'Splendid.'

12

After they'd left, Stephen felt a little drained. As he settled down on the sofa, he remembered that he'd ordered that expensive date pack from the site. Then he remembered that he'd specified his office as the delivery address, because they required a signature on delivery and he wasn't sure whether or not he'd be in to accept it. His plan was to have Mary sign for it, although he'd forgotten to say anything to her.

He felt slightly nauseated. Mary had a standing instruction to open all of his mail and parcels for him. He didn't ever have anything to hide, and she ran most of his life for him anyway, so it made no sense to open his own mail. Invariably it would be something she would be filing for him, or reminding him to pay. Even the date box thing wouldn't have been a shock to her, because she knew he was trying to get back into the dating game. In any event, he was planning to tell her not to open it.

There was no way that the contents of that box would be innocuous.

His only hope was to get hold of it himself, before she got her hands on it. It was definitely too late to cancel the order. He'd ordered it on Monday, and it had a three to five day delivery-time estimate, so unless it had already been delivered (which he doubted, because he hadn't heard anything from her), it would either be delivered that day, or Monday at the latest.

He decided to call Kenny. He'd have him intercept the thing, and tell him to leave it sealed.

'Kenny!'

'Hi boss! *How's* the leave going?'

'Shelve the niceties for the moment, Ken. I have a seriously important job for you. There's at least a pizza and a good night out in it for you, if you get it right. Understand?'

'I'm all ears, boss!'

'Good! Also, if you cock it up, I'll have you assigned to Smith *permanently!*'

'Shit boss. That's a bit harsh!'

'I just want you to get a full appreciation for the gravity of the task at hand, young man!'

'Okay boss. What do I have to do?'

'I'm expecting a parcel to be delivered at the office. In fact, the sodding thing may already have been delivered. You're going to have to go and check with Mary.'

'Ummm…'

'Are you still there, Kenneth? It sounds like your brain has escaped you; such as it is…'

'No… I'm here boss… but…'

'No buts Ken, this isn't exactly rocket science. I need you to intercept the bloody thing, and get it to me… *yesterday!*'

Kenny stayed silent on the other end of the line, and Stephen could hear the pace of his breathing increase.

'And by '*yesterday*' - I mean so fucking fast, that if you've somehow managed to figure out how to go back in time - *do it!*'

'It's too late, boss.'

'What the fuck are you *talking* about, Ken?!'

'Boss, the package arrived this morning.'

'So go and get your grubby little hands on it, and get your arse *over* here!'

'You obviously haven't checked your mail…'

'*Excuse me*?!'

'Okay. Listen boss, don't kill the messenger… but there's been a balls up… sort of… *literally*.'

Stephen stayed silent.

'You still there, boss?'

'I'm listening.'

'Thing is… that package was just marked '*West*'.'

'So what?'

'There's another '*West*' here at the office… and since you're currently away…'

'Oh fuck… who is the other '*West*', Kenny?'

'Umm… I don't really know how to tell you this…'

'*Who*?!'

'*Irene We*s*t*, boss…'

'Jesus! Not the same *Irene* who works under Smith?'

'Yes boss, *that* Irene!'

'What the fuck *happened*, Kenneth?!'

'Well boss, it's like *this*: she got the parcel, and assumed it was for her; since it only had the one name on it… so she opened it.'

'Oh for fuck sakes!'

'When she *did*, she immediately realised that the contents were not intended for her.'

Stephen just closed his eyes. His mind was reeling.

'There was some pretty saucy stuff in there, boss… I never knew you were…'

'I'm not! I didn't fucking know what was in the parcel *either*! I still bloody-well don't! But I recently discovered that it isn't likely to be what I intended when I ordered it.'

'Sorry boss… it's just not every day that a parcel containing that sort of thing shows up in the office.'

'What *exactly* was in it, Ken?'

'You sure you want to know, boss?'

'Just bloody tell me, we may as well get it over with.'

'Okay, but again… please don't think I had anything to do with it getting out.'

'Just *tell* me!'

'There was a nice bottle of plonk; a black silk scarf; some Belgian chocolate…'

'That wasn't all, *was it*, Kenneth?'

'No boss…'

'What *else*?'

'Other things boss, sort of eclectic things…'

'Out with it Kenny!'

'Okay fuck it… boss, there was a full-size leather onesie with the crotch cut out of it; a whip; some police-grade handcuffs; a gimp mask… and a very lifelike dildo with balls and *everything*…'

'Oh god! What did she do with it, Ken?'

'Well, you see boss… that's sort of the problem.'

'*What*?!'

'Smith was milling about the office when she opened it. Naturally, he was interested in the contents… and she was properly embarrassed, so she searched around for some sort of evidence that the parcel wasn't *hers*…'

'*And*?!'

'There was a hand-written letter in the box. Addressed to *you*. It was pretty professional too, boss; whoever you ordered the stuff from…'

'Shut up Kenny. I didn't knowingly order *that* shit! I just ordered a bloody '*date box*' off a website… *okay*!'

'Fair *enough,* boss. But it must have been an interesting site. I mean, that sort of stuff is pretty *unique*…'

'I'm well aware of that, Kenneth! The site didn't give it away. Let's just leave it at that, for now. What happened then?'

'You see boss, once Smith figured out it was for you, he sort of went all giddy and *mental*.'

'I'll bet he fucking *did*… the bastard!'

'He took pictures of the contents of the box, along with the letter, and sent an email out to the whole office, asking if anyone knew where you were, so that he could forward your parcel on to you…'

'…'

'If it's any consolation boss, Jim's had him brought up on disciplinary charges for the stunt. He's furious about it, and I think Mary even keyed the side of Smith's *car*…'

'*Fuck*!'

***

Given that the proverbial cat was now well and truly out of its bag, and was evidently strutting around the offices of Ashden, Cole & Roberts like it had just won best in show at the feline equivalent of crufts, Stephen decided that he'd better get hold of Jim and try to do some damage control. He didn't want him to get the wrong idea about his extra-mural activities.

'Hi Jim.'

'Stephen! Good to hear from you! I hope the leave is going well.'

'You mean, exile?'

'Don't be so negative. Take your breaks when you can get 'em. You haven't been mucking about in your emails have you? I need you well rested, my lad. Time off isn't effective if you keep nosing about in work-related things.'

'I know what's happened, Jim.'

'Ah…'

'You have to understand that there was a mixup with that parcel Jim. I know it was addressed to me, but I promise you I didn't have the faintest bloody idea what was *in it*.'

'Stephen! I know it must have been a mix up, and although I don't give a toss what your sexual preferences are, I guessed you weren't into that sort of thing anyway. I assume it was a welcome present from that rather unique dating site you went and subscribed to.'

'Yeah, it sort of *was*…but… how…'

'I have a confession to make, son. I realised exactly what you'd gotten yourself into after receiving that call from the dating agency. So did Mary.'

'Did you think that I joined it on *purpose*?'

'No. Neither did Mary. We both guessed that you hadn't the faintest idea what was going on.'

'So why didn't you bloody-well *tell* me?!'

'I thought you needed to learn about it yourself. Mary and I aren't always going to be there to pick up on these things for you Stephen. You needed a bit of a kick in the pants…'

'Oh yes?'

'It's no good being naïve in respect of what's out there on the internet. You need to check things, you need to follow up and get a solid understanding before jumping into the pond. You seem to do a good enough job of it when you research things for work!'

'It turned out to be more than a simple *'kick in the pants'*… don't you think?'

'To be fair, Stephen, it's not as if I could predict that you'd have a bloody full-on bondage kit delivered to Smith's secretary with a handwritten note in it, addressed to *you*.'

'I get that. But it's been a right cockup *hasn't it*?'

'I wouldn't worry about it lad. By the time you're back, it ought to be long forgotten. I've had the tech people remove it from all of the email accounts, and I've told HR to find some harsh way to deal with Smith. They're sitting with the lawyers *now* and putting something together. That little bastard's days are numbered. Doing what he did wasn't *cricket*; and it hasn't endeared him to the board. I asked them to fire the wanker on the spot, but the lawyers are too scared to do that, as *usual*.'

'It's nothing less than I deserve Jim. What I did to him with that investment proposal last year was just as puerile. This is my comeuppance.'

'Huh. Interesting… Bridgette's doing a good job with you.'

'Yes. I think she is.'

'Anyway, Mary's besides herself, especially since she wanted to tell you in the first place, and *I* stopped her. So don't blame her for not alerting you, please.'

'No, I won't. I'm very fond of Mary, she's always been extremely loyal.'

'Yeah, look after that one Stephen, she's a gem. I had to stop her from coming to blows with both Smith *and* Irene.'

'Well, since it looks like you owe me one, Jim…'

'What?'

'I need to borrow one of your cars tomorrow to go on a date down in Surrey. *Please* tell me you still keep one at the office.'

'Yeah I still keep a car at the office, I'll have Kenny drop it off for you in the morning, just tell him when you want it.'

'Thanks Jim! It's not something ridiculously flash is it? I don't want my date to get the wrong impression.'

'It's the Range Rover we used last week Stephen. You'll fit in down in the country; they *all* drive them down there. It's like a uniform.'

'Why couldn't you just have a normal runabout car, like a small fiat or something, Jim?'

'I like to support British brands Stephen, and I'd be sending the wrong message if I drove about in a mini.'

'You're a snob, Jim.'

'Yeah, but I'm a *generous* snob. Take the Range Rover, at least you won't get stuck if you land up in a field!'

'Alright, thanks.'

'I'll give Kenny the keys before I leave.'

'No, I'll come and get it Jim, don't send Ken. He has enough on his plate.'

'I don't want you coming near the office. Besides, if he wasn't running this errand, I'm sure Smith would think up something far less pleasant for him to do with his time. I'll tell Smith he's busy for me the whole day, so at least he can get some peace after he's delivered the car.'

'On a Saturday?'

'Since when was Saturday not a work day, Stephen?'

'Fair enough.'

'Oh, and Stephen…'

'Yes?'

'Try not to pierce the leather with any of your sharp bondage gear.'

'Very droll. I'm glad at least *one* of us can get a laugh out of my situation.'

'You have to laugh about it son, because crying about it does you no good. Enjoy the date!'

'Thanks.'

Stephen had almost forgotten how much he relied his boss. Jim was by far the most relaxed and generous individual he'd worked for. He'd been taking him for granted lately, and it made him feel a little guilty.

He decided to give Mary a call. He didn't want her to worry needlessly about the incident.

'Hi Mary.'

'Stephen, I…'

'Don't worry M, I know all about the situation there at the office. It's alright, I'm sure I'll live through the shame.'

'I should've told you when I figured out what you'd signed up for. Sorry Stephen.'

'I *know* Jim told you not to, M.'

'Yes, but nevertheless, that was no excuse.'

'Stop being so hard on yourself. Jim was right, I needed to figure that one out on my own. I need to be more aware of things.'

'I suppose I've sort of sheltered you from a lot.'

'You have… and I'm exceedingly grateful for it. But I can't go through life with blinkers on, M. I'm like a bloody adolescent half the time. I just do my job, and let you run the rest of my life. I'm inordinately good at research when it comes to investment stuff, but I tend to ignore everything else.'

'It's what I'm here for, Stephen!'

'I have to be able to stand on my own two feet, or I'm never going to grow up and get an actual life.'

'You're changing, Stephen.'

'It's for the best. Anyway, If you'd like, you *can* do me a small favour.'

'Whatever it is, consider it done!'

'I assume you still have my "*parcel*" there?'

'I do.'

'Please re-seal it and send it back. I'll unsubscribe myself from the site, but it would be fantastic if I could get a refund for the box, it was seriously expensive!'

'I have no doubt about that. It really *is* rather… *well stocked*.'

'I know. Kenny gave me a comprehensive breakdown.'

'He shouldn't have done that!'

'No, I forced it out of the poor little sod. I'm not hiding from it, M.'

'I understand.'

'Oh, one last thing…'

'Yes?'

'I have a *real* date tomorrow in the countryside, and I need some advice.'

'Just try to be yourself. You'll be fine!'

'I was hoping you'd have an idea about what sort of thing I could do with her. She wouldn't let me book anything.'

'You'll figure it out.'

'I hope so.'

***

The following morning Stephen met Kenny for an early breakfast.

Buying his intern a meal and a decent coffee was the least he could do, considering that the poor chap was being dragged out of bed early on a Saturday to deliver a car.

'How's work, Ken?'

'It's not too bad at the minute, thanks boss. Smith's too busy dealing with HR to be bothered about tormenting me.'

'Good. I know I probably deserved his little act of vengeance, but I'm still pleased he's being punished for it… maybe that makes me a bad person.'

'No boss, he was a twat. What if you really *were* into that S&M stuff? I'd be willing to bet that if you were, you wouldn't be looking at it this philosophically. What he did was a serious invasion of privacy. What you did to him was shitty, for sure, but it wasn't deeply personal.'

'Maybe you're right Ken. You're far smarter than you look, you know.'

'Thanks boss.'

'Speaking of which.'

'Yes?'

'You're pretty good with the ladies, aren't you?'

'I've been known to get around a bit.'

'Well, I'm not looking for tips on how to be a man-whore, but I have a date this afternoon, and…'

'I know, Jim told me. That's why I'm dropping his car off.'

'Let me finish.'

'Sorry, I'm just not used to you asking *me* for advice. I'm basking in the glory.'

'I haven't bloody-well asked you yet, you silly sod. You only get to bask once you've delivered some dramatically useful piece of wisdom.'

'Sorry, boss. I'll let you finish.'

'Thank you. This girl I'm going to see told me not to book anything. She says we can figure something out when we meet up.'

'Okay…'

'My question to you is: what would you do? Would you just book something anyway, in case?'

'Maybe she just wants a shag in the car?'

'Unbelievable, Kenneth. I take back what I said about you being smarter than you look.'

'Come on boss, what about my clever insight regarding Smith's conduct?'

'Even broken clocks are right twice a day.'

'Come on boss, I've been on plenty dates where that's actually happened.'

'I'll bet you have. But what the hell makes you think that I'd be into that sort of thing?'

'Sex in the car is actually quite comfortable, if you get into the right position boss. It'll be an absolute doddle in the Rangy, coz it's so big.'

Stephen just stared at his young counterpart across the table. He wasn't sure whether or not he was actually having a laugh.

'Kenneth. I'm going on a first date with a seemingly intelligent and successful woman. I'm not reenacting the opening scene of a mediocre porn film.'

'I was actually just taking the piss, boss. I couldn't help myself. But I wasn't kidding about the car sex thing, it's not as tricky as it looks.'

'I'll take your word for it, Ken.'

'But in all seriousness, I seldom book things when I go on dates. It allows for a certain degree of spontaneity which most women love.'

'Sounds stupid.'

'If you don't have a booking, you can ask her exactly what sort of thing she's in the mood for.'

'If you don't have a booking, that's likely to become academic Ken; because you're unlikely to get a table at lunch time on a Saturday, and you'll end up looking like an idiot.'

'Ah boss, I love the fact that I know more about this sort of thing than you do.'

Stephen was once again rendered mute. He didn't get what Kenneth was on about, but he was willing to accept that his young protégé was knowledgable when it came to this sort of thing. He knew for a fact that the youngster was very popular with women.

'Go on then… enlighten me.'

'You see, boss, if you've agreed with her up front that you won't make a booking, she won't complain if you have to wait for a table somewhere. She's probably counting on the wait.'

'Why?'

'Because it's easier to get to know someone over a drink at the bar, than it is sitting across a dinner-table. There's something less forced and awkward about it.'

'Then why wouldn't you just agree to go for a drink in the first place?'

'It depends on the context, boss. A drink is noncommittal, which is fine if you're just testing the waters, and neither of you are convinced that there's likely to be a spark. Or, if you're both after the once-off car shag thing we discussed earlier.'

'So what you're saying is that, because she agreed to get something to eat, she's a bit more invested?'

'Maybe. Perhaps 'invested' isn't the right term, but it's a sign that she's willing to give you more than the amount of time it takes her to drink a glass of wine.'

'Alright, that sounds plausible.'

'Having a drink and waiting for a table is a perfect opportunity to ease into the date before getting down to the more serious business of sitting at a lunch or dinner table together.'

'Interesting. But what if the place is so full that you don't even get to wait?'

'Yeah, that can happen. Then you can make a decision to go and look elsewhere. If she says 'let's just have a drink then', she's probably having second thoughts about you. But if she's willing to go hunting for another table at another place, you're ahead on points.'

'Sounds a bit risky.'

'He who dares, boss.'

'I suppose that makes sense, in a way.'

'Some of my most successful dates have started off with getting rejected by half a dozen fully booked places, and ended up with takeaway pizza in a park.'

'I think I'd probably end up losing my cool after the third attempt, to be honest.'

'That would be silly, boss. Every rejection brings the two of you closer together.'

'How so?'

'Because it becomes a quest, and you have to work together to find a place. It's like a team building exercise.'

'Wow Kenneth, you've clearly put some thought into this, haven't you?'

'What can I say, boss. I like women… a lot!'

'I still think it sounds a bit stupid, but I'll give it a try.'

'Can I bask in the glory of being the one with the smart ideas now?'

'No. Your hypothesis hasn't been tested yet.'

'You're a hard man, boss.'

'What can I say, Ken. I like results… a lot!'

13

After finishing their breakfast, Kenny went off to enjoy the balance of the first Saturday he'd had off in over six months. Stephen smiled to himself when he realised that the poor chap was probably going home to sleep for the rest of the day. He looked dog tired.

The notion of going on this date with Alexa without a plan frightened Stephen. He was used to planning things, or at least having things planned *for* him by Mary. Plans were a way to avoid chaos and uncertainty, and not having one made him itch.

He needed a plan, in case they couldn't find anywhere to eat. He didn't really buy Kenny's nonsense about the hidden virtues of waiting for tables at restaurants; nor did he put much stock in the more ludicrous sounding suggestion, that getting turned away from half a dozen establishments could somehow engender a feeling of mutual affection in a pair trying to navigate a first date.

After about ten minutes of sitting in the parked car and mulling over the problem, he came up with what he thought was a fairly decent solution.

He was going to get the necessary kit for a picnic. The more he thought about it, the more appealing the notion became. He wouldn't push it on her, but at least it would give him a clear fallback position.

He found the closest M&S and procured a selection of picnic foods, wine and water. He then realised that he would need something to put them in. After a quick internet search, he found a shop in the area that sold insulated picnic bags.

Once he'd got his hands on the picnic bag, which even came with one of those clever rolled up picnic blankets that had a waterproof lining on the bottom, he headed down to Surrey. He'd timed it well, so he expected that he'd be there just in time.

The drive down to Surrey was pleasant. Although he wasn't enamoured with the notion of a long commute to and from work every day, he could understand why people suffered the inconvenience in order to live in greener and more peaceful surroundings. The countryside was spectacular in summer, especially when the sun was shining.

He'd never been to Shere, but he'd heard that it was one of the more picturesque villages in the Surrey hills. When he looked it up on the GPS on his phone, he noted that it sat firmly in the middle of what the map asserted was an "Area of Outstanding Natural Beauty", and the closer he came to his destination, the more convinced he became that the description of the area was accurate.

When he got there he saw that most of the buildings in the village were Tudor, a feature that gave the whole place an almost surreal feeling. It was like a very well designed film set, which blended seamlessly into its almost impossibly green surroundings.

He arrived outside the bakery five minutes early, only to discover that there was no parking. In fact, he realised that even if a parking space were to open up, it would be irrelevant, because the Range Rover was almost wider than the road, so it wouldn't fit. He'd forgotten about this particularly irritating drawback of travelling by car. Parking!

After crawling along the length of the high street, and scanning the area for a gap big enough to berth HMS Roberts, he was forced to concede that he'd have to find a public parking lot - assuming there was such a thing in this area. So he opened up the GPS on his phone to search for one.

Of course, being in rural England was like being in some sort of alternate dimension, in which mobile signal only existed in faint and intermittent whispers. By the time the map had loaded, he was panicking, because he was causing a small traffic jam, and a particularly unfriendly pensioner in an old wreck behind him was leaning on the hooter and making obscene gestures.

In the midst of this panic, he dropped the phone through the gap between his legs, and watched in dismay as it slid under the pedals. There was no way he was going to try and retrieve it at that point, because he didn't feel like having a violent altercation with the difficult old bastard behind him, so he decided to just keep driving and find a parking lot the old fashioned way.

He had that *'hunted'* feeling people tend to get whenever they know that the person in the car behind them is pissed off about something they've done. Because of this, he wasn't concentrating on his surroundings, and he ended up back on the A25 north of the village. By this stage it was already ten past twelve, and although he ought to have pulled over to retrieve his phone, he didn't.

Instead, he decided to speed up and find a way back into the village by following road signs. The idea to follow road signs wasn't a terrible one, the other idea *was*.

Range Rovers are designed to insulate their occupants from the elements. They make going over nasty dirt roads (and even mountainous terrain) an absolute pleasure. But what they *also* do, is insulate their occupants from the sensations of speed and acceleration. Accelerating *to*, and driving *at* a hundred miles an hour in a low-slung sports car, feels exhilarating and dangerous. Doing the same thing in a Range Rover, feels like taking a slow Sunday stroll. The large V8 gains momentum as smoothly as custard flowing over a steamed pudding. Unless its going ridiculously fast, the occupants barely notice any sensation of speed, whatsoever.

When Stephen saw the figure step out into the road in front of him, clad in the familiar high-visibility uniform, he realised that he was going to be very late for his date.

'Afternoon, officer.'

'Good afternoon Sir. Do you have your drivers license on you?'

'Yes, here it is.'

'Mr West... do you know know why I've pulled you over?'

'I can hazard a guess.'

'And what would that guess be then?'

'I suppose you suspect I've been speeding.'

'You a solicitor, Mr West?'

'No. Why?'

'It's usually only solicitors or barristers who refuse to admit that our radar guns give accurate readings.'

'Sorry, it's just a habit I picked up from a friend. Come to think of it, he was a solicitor, so… I suppose you have a point.'

'Do you know how fast you were travelling Mr West?'

'No officer, afraid I don't.'

'You were travelling at a speed of fifty six miles an hour.'

'Alright. I accept that.'

'Do you know what the speed limit is on this road, Mr West?'

'No, but I suppose it isn't sixty?'

'No. It's forty.'

'Ah…'

'Do you know why we impose these limits, Mr West?'

'Yes.'

'Well then, you'll appreciate that…'

The officer was interrupted in mid sentence by the sound of Stephen's phone ringing from the footwell.

Given that it was now approaching half past twelve, Alexa was calling him to find out what was going on. Stephen didn't quite know what to do. If he lunged forward under the dashboard to retrieve the phone, it wouldn't look very good, but if he left it, he had no idea how long it would take before it rang out. Clearly, the policeman wasn't going to continue until the noise died down.

'Are you going to cancel that call, Mr West?'

'I don't suppose you'd be all that pleased if I were to answer it?'

It was a stupid response. A feeble attempt to try and buy some time, in the hope that the caller gave up before he had to try and extricate the phone. The officer just raised an eyebrow and looked at him as though he was daring him to answer it.

Stephen realised that he'd have to take the plunge… literally. So he used the electronic controller to move the seat back, then dived under the steering wheel to retrieve the phone. Once he had it, he sat up, cancelled the call and looked at his counterpart as if nothing had happened.

'Mr West, where was your mobile telephone?'

'In the footwell.'

'Is that where you normally keep it when you're driving?'

'No.'

'Then why was it there?'

'I dropped it.'

'When did you drop it?'

'About ten minutes ago.'

'Whilst driving?'

'No. I was parked. I was looking for directions on the GPS.'

'Do you mean to tell me that this vehicle doesn't have a built in navigation system?'

'No, I'm sure it does.'

'So then why would you be using your phone to find directions?'

'Because I don't know how to work the navigation system.'

'How long have you had the vehicle?'

'It's not mine, officer. I borrowed it this morning from my boss.'

'I see. Does your boss know you've borrowed it, Mr West?'

'What are you trying to imply?'

'I should think that's fairly obvious.'

'Well you can call him if you like, I'll give you his number.'

'What's his name?'

'James Roberts.'

'Do you think he keeps his insurance certificate in the vehicle?'

'I'm sure he does. Would you like me to have a look for it?'

'Yes.'

Stephen leaned across the passenger seat and opened the glovebox. He was praying that Jim actually kept his insurance certificate with his service book. Fortunately, he did.

'Here we go, officer.'

'Thank you.'

'Would you like to call him?'

'No, that won't be necessary.'

The policeman handed the certificate back to Stephen and paused to collect his thoughts.

'You know what I think, Mr West?'

'No.'

'I think that you were using your phone to send text messages whilst you were driving. That's why you weren't paying any attention to your speedometer... When you saw me step out into the road, you dropped your phone, because you panicked and you didn't want me to catch you driving and texting.'

'That's not true officer. I don't ever use my phone whilst driving.'

'Really?'

'Really!'

'Would you mind showing me the phone then?'

'Not at all.'

Stephen handed him the phone through the window.

'Before I look at this device, do you confirm that you're consenting to my doing so? And that this consent is being given freely and voluntarily?'

'Yes officer. I have nothing to hide.'

'Very well then.'

It only took the policeman a few seconds to go through Stephen's most recent messages, and confirm that nothing had been sent or received in hours. He didn't appear convinced that Stephen hadn't been in the process of sending a message whilst driving, but he was forced to concede that, had he genuinely dropped the phone in a panic, it was unlikely that he would have had time to clear what he'd been typing, so he was prepared to give him the benefit of the doubt.

'I don't mean to be impertinent, officer, but I'm really late for a date.'

'Alright Mr West. Far be it from me to get in the way of your social endeavours. I assume that that is why you were flouting the law, and barrelling along at sixteen miles an hour over the speed limit?'

'Yes, I suppose that's fair.'

'Well, Mr West, I'm going to fine you for speeding. You can be grateful that the relevant notice won't be sent to Mr Roberts, given that I've been able to identify you. In future, you would do well to plan your trips more conscientiously, so that you don't have to break the law in order to show up on time.'

'I get it.'

After ten minutes of filling out forms and checking various details, Stephen was released. By this stage, it was just before one o'clock. Mercifully, he managed to find a public parking lot just north of the High Street in the village, but when he tried to call Alexa back to explain the situation, she didn't pick up the phone. He'd have to face the music in person.

***

Alexa's bakery was a small shop in one of the Tudor style buildings just off the High street. It had one of those diminutive doors, and little cottage pane windows that didn't exactly allow a clear view of the interior from the street. If it weren't for the easel chalkboard set up outside the door, advertising the current cakes on offer, you wouldn't know it was a bakery. There was one of those little swing signs above the door, but you could only read it if you were approaching from the side.

Stephen ducked under the ludicrously low lintel, and found himself in a very stylish shopfront. A long, wide, glass display counter dominated the space. It was filled with some of the most well decorated cakes, cupcakes and biscuits he'd ever seen. They looked more like ornaments than baked goods - the pictures he'd seen of Alexa's work on the internet didn't do them justice. She also had a small section with assorted loaves of bread, some croissants, and *pain au chocolate*.

Behind the counter stood a young man who appeared to be no older than sixteen. He was wearing a buttonless short-sleeved version of one of those white chef's jackets you see on cooking shows, and a long navy blue apron with white stripes.

'Afternoon Sir, is there anything I can do for you?'

'Ah, hello. Is Alexa in?'

'Yes, she's in the back. Are you sure there's nothing I can assist you with?'

'No. Thanks. Can you let her know that Stephen's here to see her.'

'Oh… Stephen. Yes, she's been expecting you. Although I think you're a bit late.'

'Yes. I'm painfully aware of that. What did you say your name was again?'

'I didn't. It's Freddy. I'm Alexa's apprentice.'

'Pleased to meet you Freddy. As you can imagine, I have some explaining to do, so would you be so kind as to see if Alexa's willing to see me?'

'Certainly, Stephen. I'll be back in a bit.'

'Thanks.'

Stephen wanted the floor to open up and swallow him. He wasn't expecting his initial interaction with Alexa to be particularly fun, given his tardiness, but he certainly didn't expect to be sneered at by her adolescent flunky.

After a few minutes Alexa appeared out of the door behind the counter. She wasn't dressed in her chef's whites. She was wearing an ocean blue knee-length circle skirt with a floral pattern; a casual white short-sleeved blouse; and flat brown sandals. She looked prettier than Stephen remembered. Freddy was conspicuously absent.

'Stephen, nice of you to show up.'

'I can explain…'

'Go on then. What's kept you so long?'

'Well, I sort of got lost looking for parking… and ended up being pulled over for speeding.'

'You couldn't have been going too fast… given that it's now one 'o clock and we were due to meet at twelve.'

'It's complicated… I was actually here just before twelve. I couldn't find a parking, and it took me about a quarter of an hour to find my way back to the main road… where I got stopped for speeding whilst trying to find my way back into the village.'

'And the business of getting stopped took over half an hour then?'

'Yes, well, I'd dropped my phone in the footwell whilst trying to use the GPS, and when you called I was in the middle of being given a blocking for speeding by the nice policeman who'd pulled me over.'

'Ah…'

'As I'm sure you can imagine, when I had to reach under the dashboard for the phone, the officer didn't form a particularly charitable view of the circumstances. It took me some time to convince him that I hadn't been texting while driving.'

'Oh dear.'

'I'm terribly sorry I'm so late, I honestly got lost, and I really did get pulled over. I can even show you the fine if you'd like.'

'No, don't worry Stephen. I was just a bit put out when you cancelled the call.'

'Sorry, I sort of had to. I did try to call back.'

'I see that.'

'I suppose I ought to have called you when I couldn't find a parking spot.'

'Yes. That would probably have been a good idea. I could at least have directed you to the public car park up above the High Street. I take it you found that now? You haven't gone and parked illegally or anything?'

'No. I found the car park. Thanks.'

There was an awkward silence that neither of them seemed to know how to break. Eventually it was broken for them by Freddy, who came bustling through from the back carrying a new item for the display counter.

Alexa rolled her eyes and looked around at Freddy with the sort of expression you'd give to somebody who'd just done something unbelievably stupid. He got the point, put the item down on the counter, and made a hasty retreat.

'Sorry Stephen, where were we?'

'Do you think we can press reset?'

'What?'

'Can we pretend that I didn't mess up the simple business of arriving on time to meet up with you? I promise you, I'm not that bad once you get to know me.'

'Yes. Let's do that.'

'I really like the front end of your shop, your cakes look better than some of the ones I've seen in magazines.'

'Thanks. Do you often read baking magazines then?'

Stephen felt like he was back in Bridgette's offices, being pulled apart at the seams and made to feel slow and awkward. Oliver was right about his sister in law, she had a prickly disposition. He still liked her though. There was something about her that fascinated him. He couldn't quite figure out what it was, but it was compelling enough for him to want to.

'No. I…'

'Just kidding Steve. I appreciate the compliment.'

'Has anyone ever told you that you have a bit of a mean sense of humour?'

'Yes. Although they tend to put it a little less politely than that.'

'Ah.'

'I think the popular consensus is that I'm a bit haughty; but I prefer to think of myself as direct. I certainly don't mean to come across as superior or disdainful.'

'You don't. You just seem to have a knack for sniffing out weaknesses and exploiting them.'

'So I'm like a dog then?'

'No… I…'

'Sorry Steve, sometimes I just can't help myself. I'm the first to admit that I'm a bit difficult. If you're willing to put up with that sort of thing, and call me out on it when it bothers you, I'm sure we'll get along just fine.'

'I think I can manage.'

'You say that now, but wait till you get to know me…'

'I'd like to get to know you.'

'Alright then, but don't say I didn't warn you.'

'Fair enough. Can I still have a tour of the rest of the bakery?'

'No. Let's leave that for another time. How about we go and get a coffee or something?'

'Yes, of course. I thought we were going to get some lunch?'

'We were. But I'm no longer hungry. So let's do coffee.'

'Alright.'

Stephen was a little crestfallen, but at least he didn't have to worry about finding a place or getting a table. Alexa knew exactly where she wanted to go, and although they happened to have an open table, he suspected that even if they didn't, they would've made some sort of arrangement for her. It was a small, tastefully decorated coffee shop within crawling distance of the bakery.

When they passed the counter, he realised that all of the cakes on display were Alexa's. He had a very good eye for artistic signature - once he'd seen a work of art, he could quite confidently pick out details in other pieces that matched. His photographic memory helped him retain the necessary information almost indefinitely.

They ordered coffee and sat at a small table near the window.

'So Steve, you're a bit of an artist then.'

'I suppose you could say that.'

He'd only just salvaged part of the date, and it still felt as if she was looking for an excuse to find an exit, so he wasn't about to come clean about his occupation. Technically, he *was* a pretty decent artist, so just because he didn't do it for a living, didn't make his statement a bald-faced lie.

'I'd love to see some of your work. It's only fair, given that that you've seen some of mine.'

'You're right. But I had to travel all the way down to the wilds of Surrey to see yours, so you'll have to come up to the city to see mine.'

'Are you already trying to extort a second date out of me Stephen?'

'I saw a gap… can you blame me for trying to take it?'

'I'm flattered. But you'll have to work a bit harder than that.'

Stephen realised that he'd better find a way to change the subject. Discussing his imaginary graphic design job wasn't going to end well.

'So what got you into baking then?'

'I've loved baking since I was a child. My mom was a very good baker, and it fascinated me.'

'It must have been nice knowing exactly what you wanted to do from a young age.'

'Well, I didn't actually. I came back to baking.'

'Really? What did you do before this?'

'I was a chemist.'

'Seriously? What kind of chemist?'

'Not the kind that dispenses medicine at your local pharmacy.'

'No, I gathered that. If you were, you would have called yourself a pharmacist.'

'Yes. Sorry, most people still tend to use the wrong terminology, so I got into the habit of clarifying it. I worked at a large chemical company after I completed my degrees. I've only been baking for just over three years now.'

'Wow, that's quite a change.'

'Yeah, I woke up one day and realised that I didn't enjoy my job as much as I thought I would.'

'Brave move.'

'Brave or stupid… I haven't quite figured out which yet.'

'So is it just you and Freddy?'

'Yeah, the business has just started to keep its head above water, so although I'd like to take on another assistant and give myself a little breathing room, I don't think it's prudent.'

'That sounds sensible.'

'Did you always want to be a graphic designer then, Steve?'

'No. Actually, for as long as I could remember, I just wanted to be real artist... you know, the archetypical ones who produce masterpieces that nobody gives a toss about until they've been dead for a century.'

'I like that kind.'

'Yeah, it's romantic. But I wasn't too keen on living under a cardboard box until I eventually managed to sell something. I don't do too well in the cold.'

'I can understand that.'

'I suppose I'm not as brave as you.'

'Are you saying I live in a cardboard box, Steve?'

'No... I...'

'Just kidding. You're easy to mess with Steve. Try to relax.'

'You're a little intimidating, to be honest.'

'I've heard that before.'

'Are you originally from this area?'

'No. I grew up in Leeds actually. Where are you from originally?'

'Lancashire.'

'Huh, I wouldn't have guessed that. I know you were at uni with my sister up there, but I assumed you were from down south for some reason. You don't have a northern accent.'

'No, I tried hard to lose it.'

'Why?'

'It's complicated.'

'I get it. I don't exactly sound like I'm from Yorkshire anymore.'

'Actually, you sound like you're from somewhere like Cambridge.'

'Well, that's where I went to University... so...'

'Seriously?'

'Yes. And now I run the little bakery in the village. Before you ask... no... my parents are *not* proud.'

'Why not?'

'Would your parents be proud if you did the whole 'artist living in a box' thing?'

'I thought you said that you *didn't* live in a box?'

'I didn't actually say that...'

Stephen was still trying to get used to Alexa's dry sense of humour. He battled to tell when she was joking.

'I honestly don't think that running a bakery is equivalent to living under a box, Alexa.'

'Tell that to the once proud parents of a girl who put herself through a Cambridge education on scholarships, loans, and part time jobs. Contrary to popular belief, Oxbridge graduates don't all have summer homes and titles.'

'I suppose that's true.'

Stephen was starting to see visions of a self-satisfied Bridgette, smiling and pointing out that his assumptions about Oxbridge graduates were childishly naïve.

'They weren't counting on the fact that my education would give me the sort of perspective necessary to understand that working in a laboratory my whole life wasn't going to make me happy.'

'I assume neither of them are chemists then?'

'No. My dad's a history teacher at a private school and my mom's a bookkeeper.'

'Surely they've seen the bakery though, and they understand that you're making a success of it.'

'They refuse to accept my decision. So even though they visit their grandchildren, who live less than ten miles away, they've never even bothered to come and see it. My mom is curious, but not curious enough to abandon her principles.'

'I'm sorry to hear that.'

'Don't be. My sister's successful enough for both of us, and she's even given them grandchildren. I think she secretly relishes the fact that she's now the favourite. It was the other way around when we were growing up, and it got even worse when I went up to Cambridge.'

'I know the feeling.'

'Don't your parents approve of your chosen career?'

'They do. But they're perpetually irritated by the fact that I never make the time to see them.'

'Why don't you?'

'My father and I have a tricky relationship.'

'Sounds pretty standard.'

'So apart from baking, and gaming, what do you do for fun around here?'

'Sleep.'

'Really?'

'To be honest Steve, I work most of the time. I play games when I get a chance, and read the odd book, but…'

'I'm the same, so you're in good company.'

'I haven't decided whether or not you're good company Steve, don't be presumptuous.'

'It was just an expression.'

'What makes you think I don't know that? Didn't you just hear all about my posh education?'

'You were right about being difficult…'

'Told you.'

'You did. Can I change the subject and try a slice of one of your lovely cakes?'

'How do you know they're mine.'

'It's an aesthetic sense, I can pick up patterns in works of art.'

'Stephen, you're making me blush.'

'Well that's a welcome relief.'

'That's the first semi-charming thing you've said to me so far.'

'Sorry. I'm still trying to get over the fact that I was an hour late to meet you.'

'So am I.'

'I did plan to take you on a picnic, you know…'

'Seriously?'

'Yes, I even got one of those fancy picnic blankets with the lining at the bottom.'

'How romantic, Steve.'

'I thought so.'

'Maybe we can use it next time we see one another.'

'Are you telling me you're willing to see me again?'

'No. I haven't decided on that yet. But I haven't ruled it out, so your picnic blanket may yet see some use.'

'It would be a shame if it didn't, really.'

'So you want to see *me* again?'

'I do.'

'Interesting.'

Stephen ordered them each another coffee and some of Alexa's red velvet. She seemed a little more relaxed, especially after he extolled the virtues of her cake, but the conversation stayed relatively superficial. She needed to get back to relieve Freddy and close up the shop, so they didn't stay long. She usually closed at two on Saturdays. They walked back to where he'd parked the car and parted ways in that awkward manner people tend to leave one another, even on wildly successful first dates.

14

As soon as she'd let Freddy go and closed the shop, Alexa phoned Karen.

'We need to talk!'

'Hello to you too, *dear sister*!'

'Hi…'

'How was the date?'

'Mostly shit!'

'I can't believe that, Steve's such a nice guy… what happened?'

'He showed up an *hour* late!'

'That doesn't sound like him at all, did he give you a reason?'

'Apparently, he got lost trying to find a parking spot, and ended up being caught speeding whilst trying to get back into the village…'

'Come on Allie, you can't blame him for *that*.'

'Assuming he was telling the *truth* about it…'

'Why would he lie?'

'Okay, fine… but it kind of set the tone for the afternoon.'

'Where did he take you for lunch?'

'I didn't agree to have lunch with him.'

'I thought that was the plan?'

'I changed it. I was irritated with him.'

'Bloody hell, Alexa. Really?'

'You think I over-reacted?'

'Of course I do.'

'I had to get back to close the shop at two. He was an hour late, so we wouldn't have had time for lunch anyway.'

'I thought you'd taken the whole afternoon off? Do you mean to tell me that Freddy couldn't have locked up for you?'

'Maybe.'

'Aside from showing up late, what was so bad about Stephen? It must have been something, because even you aren't usually *that* full of it.'

'He was a bit awkward.'

'Of course he bloody was. He was late, and I'm willing to bet that you let him know how you felt about that, in no uncertain terms.'

'I did indeed!'

'Alexa, if he wasn't a bit awkward after that, then I'd be worried.'

'Why?'

'Because then he'd be a bloody sociopath.'

'Now look who's overreacting.'

'Alexa. You made your mind up that you didn't like him when he was late. You wanted to hear his explanation, simply because you like watching men squirm, not because you had any intention of giving him the benefit of the doubt. When he did squirm, you judged him for it.'

'Of course I judged him for it. What kind of idiot gets lost in a village that's hardly bigger than a medium sized cricket pitch? He's obviously not very bright.'

'You forget that I actually know Stephen West, Alexa. He's not an idiot. In fact, as far as I'm aware, I've never met anyone with an IQ as high as his. You probably haven't either.'

'Seriously?'

'Don't ever tell anyone I told you this, especially him, but Ollie found out about it from Stephen's father when he went and stayed with them over one of the university holidays. He has an IQ over one sixty, Allie. He's what they classify as *"Exceptionally Gifted"*.'

'You can't be serious?'

'I am, Allie. You've met your match my girl. Stephen West is considerably smarter than you.'

'But he seems so unassuming.'

'Clearly he battles with women. He wouldn't be the first clever guy to have that problem, would he?'

'No, I suppose you're right.'

'But he doesn't *look* that clever?'

'What do very clever people look like Alexa? Come on… enlighten me… you went to that posh university, I'm sure you know loads of them.'

'Don't be like that. You know what I mean.'

'You think that the universe automatically balances these things out? Dumb people are pretty, and very smart people have hunchbacks and goitres?'

'Sort of… yes.'

'Last time I checked, you were the one in our family with all the looks… and the brains. So no; that's not how it works, Sis.'

'You're smarter than me K, and only you have this ridiculous notion that I'm '*the pretty one*', as you always like to say to people. Stop fishing for compliments, you aren't that insecure.'

'If I'm so smart, then listen to me for a change. Don't pre-judge Stephen. You could do a whole lot worse than him.'

'Did you know he drives one of those big flashy Land Rover things?'

'I didn't think he had a car, he lives in the city; it's probably a rental.'

'Then he's a bit of a twat. Who rents something ridiculous like that for a day, just to go on a *date*?'

'A nice chap who didn't want to ask you to pick him up at the station. Most men have complexes about things like that; they don't ever want to come across as anything other than fully self-sufficient. Let's face it, we tend to judge them if they aren't.'

'Yeah maybe, but this thing was obscenely large and ostentatious. If it was true that he was caught speeding, then maybe he's one of those spoiled city types who think it's okay to go and race around the countryside in their overpriced status symbols, like a bunch of petulant *man-children*!'

'You're overthinking it Sis… you're searching for reasons not to like him, despite the fact that you obviously do. If you didn't like him, we wouldn't be having this conversation. Do you think one of those petulant '*man-children*' you've just described would've come across as awkward and apologetic if they were late?'

'No, probably not. Still, he didn't really open up about himself or his work, I got the feeling he was hiding something. He kept diverting the conversation and trying to find out more about *me*, and the bakery.'

'Alexa, the poor guy was probably just trying to sound interested… we're always telling men to be better listeners, and to take notice of who we are and what's important to us… we can't very well get irritated with them when they try to *do so*.'

'Shit… I suppose you have a point there.'

'Give the chap another shot at it, Allie. Let him take you to dinner, or a show or something… better yet, take *him*!'

'You really think I should?'

'I do. Go up to London for a change. Meet him on *his* home turf.'

'You know I bloody hate the city, Karen.'

'Stop being a bitch. You want to be all independent and self-reliant, but you don't want to meet the men half-way. That's hypocritical bullshit, and you're smart enough to know it!'

'Why do you always have to be so *sensible*?!'

'It's my responsibility as a big sister. Anyway, he's *hot*!'

'He is. It's also good to know he's actually clever. I've always liked the clever ones.'

'I know, that's obviously genetic, because I do too. That's why I told you.'

'Okay, I'll *do* it!'

***

Stephen dropped Jim's car off in the basement at Ashden, Cole & Roberts, but kept the keys. He knew Jim didn't want him going into the office, but he had nowhere to park the thing at home, and he didn't want to disturb Kenny. He'd get the keys back to Jim on Monday.

When he got home, he collapsed on the sofa, and spent the evening reading one of the old novels he'd had on his shelves for years but had never found the time to open. He had at least twenty such items of literature in shelves, and on various surfaces around the flat. They weren't supposed to be purely decorative, but that's how they inevitably ended up, after he'd acquired them.

He read extensively as a child, and even more whilst attending university. But ever since he'd started work, it was something he only got around to on holidays. Of course, given that he hadn't had a holiday in over three years, reading something for pleasure felt distinctly different. Not new, but nostalgic - like meeting up with an old friend.

He spent most of Sunday buried in a new drawing. He only stopped to make himself a cheese sandwich, which he rather eccentrically paired with an expensive Bordeaux he'd been given as a gift. He'd been waiting for a special occasion to open the bottle, and he decided that re-discovering his love of putting pencil to paper was special enough; even though he didn't have anything more salubrious than a cheese sandwich to have with it. He couldn't remember the last time he'd felt better.

He woke with a slight headache on Monday morning, but was still suitably refreshed. He had some books at the office he wanted to get his hands on, and he thought that the best way to do that would be to have Mary meet him with them. He could give her Jim's keys at the same time.

They met up for lunch at midday, about a block away from the office.

'Hi Stephen. How are things going?'

'Better than I thought they would, actually. I'm still really worried about this insider dealing thing, but I'm getting back into some old hobbies, and you'll be pleased to hear that I'm not even reading the financial news.'

'Well that's good to hear. I'm impressed. What has you so distracted that you've finally torn yourself away from the state of the markets?'

'I've taken up drawing again. I'm also playing a computer game and reading fiction, but I think the art is what's keeping me distracted.'

'I told you I had you pegged as a creative type! I never knew you were actually an artist though?'

'Well, I can't exactly claim the 'artist' title, but I do like to draw and paint occasionally. I did a lot of that sort of thing in my teens and at uni.'

'You really are a multifaceted individual, Stephen.'

'Thanks M, I'm trying to expand my field of focus. The good doctor has prescribed the exercise, and although it pains me to say it, she's probably right.'

'Ah, Bridgette. You may as well listen to her Stephen, she's certainly being well remunerated for her efforts.'

'Yes, I spose that's true.'

'That reminds me. You remember you have another meeting with her tomorrow?'

'How could I forget?'

'It's in the morning this time, so make sure you put a reminder on your phone.'

'Thank M, I've got it covered.'

'Oh, by the way, I have some bad news for you.'

'Oh yes?'

'There was a problem with the refund on that package. Apparently they won't take it back, because the items in the box are no longer in their original packaging.'

'Bugger!'

'Yeah, I moaned like hell about it, but they've said it's one of their policies. Smith should refund you, because *he* was the one that unwrapped everything! It makes me so bloody *mad*!'

'Don't worry about it M. *School fees*!'

'School what?'

'You know, the payment you end up having to make to learn a lesson…'

'Ah, right. Yeah, I suppose you have to look at it like that.'

'Oh, while I remember, here are Jim's keys. Please give them to Denise when you see her. I think she normally keeps them for him.'

'Yeah, she does. How was the date?'

'Fuck, Mary, I'm bloody useless! I got lost, was almost an hour late, and to add insult to injury, I got a hefty speeding fine and a bollocking from the local constabulary.'

'I'm sure you were a perfect gentleman on the date, that would have made up for being a bit late. As for the fine, I suppose it also constitutes "*school fees*".'

'Yeah, I'm trying to be philosophical about it, at least Jim won't receive the notice because they gave it to me on the spot.'

'Jim wouldn't care.'

'Yeah, I just don't enjoy looking like an idiot in front of him. You know how it is.'

'I get it. So when's the second date then?'

'There *isn't* one; yet'

'Stephen, you need to arrange a second date at the end of the first one! That's important. It tells her that you enjoyed yourself, and that you're interested in pursuing her!'

'I tried M, she told me she'd think about it.'

'Shit!'

'Is that *bad*?'

'Yeah, I'm not going to bullshit you Stephen, it's not *good*.'

'I didn't think so either.'

'Well, let's choose to focus on the fact that she didn't turn you down outright. It's pointless being pessimistic about it.'

'Spose not.'

'Oh, back to your little box of naughty treasures. I'd actually sent it back to them before they informed me that they wouldn't take it, so they've sent it back to your home address.'

'Ah. Well, at least then *Smith* won't get his grabby paws on it again. Maybe I can sell the stuff off online.'

'Well, you can at least eat the chocolates and drink the champagne. I don't normally go in for bubbly, but it looks like an expensive bottle.'

'I don't exactly feel like celebrating at the moment.'

'Stop being mopey Stephen, it doesn't suit you. Besides, you said yourself that the forced leave isn't going as badly as you thought it would. Keep the champagne to celebrate your upcoming promotion.'

'That's assuming I don't get sent to jail for insider dealing.'

'You'll be fine, just follow the programme, and do as the good doctor orders…'

'You're right. Do you have those books for me?'

'Oh shit, sorry, I forgot them on my desk. I'll send Kenny to you with them after work if that's okay?'

'Don't be silly M, I'll come past the office. I promise I'll wait outside, and either you or Ken can bring them down to me.'

'Okay, sorry Stephen. It totally slipped my mind.'

'Not at all M, you have enough on your plate at the moment without running around with books for me. To be honest, I just wanted to have the catch up. The books were an excuse.'

'I'm flattered Stephen. You miss me that much?'

'I do, M. Seriously!'

'Well, I miss you too.'

'Come on then, we can walk back to the office together.'

'Right.'

Stephen and Mary walked back to the office and she left him out on the pavement while she went up to collect his books.

While pacing around outside the building, he bumped into a colleague he was hoping to avoid.

***

'Hello, Smith.'

'West… what are *you* doing here? I thought you were still on gardening leave.'

'Popped in to pick up some personal items.'

'Oh, yes. Your little box of *goodies…*'

'Very funny Smith. For the record, that parcel was procured in error.'

'Bullshit!'

'You believe what you *like*, Smith. Far be it from *me* to ruin your little fantasies. You're welcome to picture me in a gimp suit if it gets your heart-rate up.'

'Nice try, West. Stop pretending it doesn't phase you that your dirty little secret's doing the rounds here at the office.'

'The only thing doing the rounds here now, is your reputation as a complete *tosser*. I hear you've been in a bit of trouble as a result of your childish antics. I'm told that you have to attend six months worth of night courses on appropriate workplace conduct.'

'It was well worth it!'

'Christ Smith, you really *are* a childish prat. You'd subject yourself to half a year of night classes, just to play a crass prank on a work colleague. Clearly you *need* the night classes.'

'Don't tell me you wouldn't have done the same thing to *me*, given half a chance.'

'Of course I bloody-well *wouldn't*! How stupid do you think I *am*?'

'Maybe you just don't have the balls!'

'They should have you undergo some kind of mental assessment Smith. Enjoy the night classes, and remember to try and learn something about being an adult.'

'Piss off, West. It was a perfectly innocent prank, just like we used to do at university… Oh wait, you didn't go to university… did you?'

'There are more than two universities in the country, Smith.'

'Yeah, but the other one's in Scotland, so it doesn't really count.'

'I'm sure your alma mater is exceedingly proud of you, Smith. You really are a shining testament to the hallowed halls of Oxford.'

'At least they don't have to worry about me getting nicked for insider dealing… how's that going for you by the way, West?'

'You know I can't say. Not that I'd ever discuss such a thing with you if I could.'

'That's okay Stephen, I hear Wandsworth prison isn't that bad, as long as you have the right connections. I'm sure you have plenty of those, given your background.'

'What's that supposed to mean?'

'Oh nothing, was just wondering how many of your old Polytechnic classmates were also doing time for securities fraud.'

'Very funny, Smith.'

***

Mary came out of the building carrying Stephen's books. As soon as Smith saw her, he made a hasty retreat. There was absolutely no love lost between the two of them, and she was likely to be even less pleasant to deal with than Stephen.

'What was that all about?'

'Oh, just some friendly banter.'

'Friendly?'

'Well, no, not really. I know I'm supposed to work with that bastard; but I hate his guts, and I can't help behaving like a child whenever we interact with one another. Clearly the feeling is mutual.'

'He's a first rate arsehole, you don't have to sugar coat it with me, Stephen.'

'Jim's right though. He's part of the team. I'm going to have to learn how to deal with him. He just knows exactly which buttons to push to get me riled up.'

'He's jealous that you're more intelligent than him.'

'You wouldn't think it, the way he goes on about the fact that I never went to bloody Oxford or Cambridge.'

'You know that's just a defence mechanism, don't you?'

'I'm starting to learn that. I still have a bit of a chip on my shoulder about not doing my master's there. It's as if the twat knows it.'

'He doesn't, he just treats everyone like that as a reflex, because it's all he has. He's not charming, and he's certainly not good looking.'

'I didn't think you looked at men like that, M.'

'I don't, but I can still appreciate aesthetics.'

'I suppose that makes sense. You didn't really key his car did you?'

'I don't know what you're talking about…'

'Oh no, Mary… you did, didn't you?'

'As I say, I have no idea what you're talking about. Anyway, enough about Smith.'

'Thanks for the books, M.'

'Interesting reads Stephen. I'm beginning to put two and two together now. I wondered why on earth you had books on art history. I thought you were just using them to research something to do with art values, but that's obviously not it. You are actually interested in art history, aren't you?'

'Very.'

'I like this new, multifaceted Stephen West!'

'It's actually the old Stephen West you're getting to know now.'

'Even better!'

***

After Mary had gone back into the building, Stephen ambled across the road and into the small bakery he'd been frequenting for the last few years. He wanted to pick up some decent bread while he was in the area and this particular bakery made the best sourdough he'd ever tasted.

After buying a loaf, and a double espresso to go, he stepped out onto the pavement.

'Steve?!'

'Cindy?! What are you doing on this side of town?'

'Oh, I just had to drop something off for my father. He works in the building across the street. Actually, I think he owns it…'

'He what?!'

'Yeah, I think he's the senior partner of the company that takes up the building. They've been here since before I was born, so I assume they must own it by now. The company's called Ashden, Cole & Roberts. My father is Arthur Ashden.'

'Seriously?'

'Yip. In fact, it's "Sir" Arthur Ashden. He's a bit smart. I haven't really got a clue what they do here though; I think it's some sort of bank.'

Stephen almost fell over into the street. She was right, Arthur Ashden *did* own the building, or at least a third of it.

As far as he was aware, the three partners owned the structure through a separate property development company that they'd set up over twenty years ago. Of course, mulling over the technical details of who owned what, and how that ownership was structured, was completely irrelevant to the conversation and the situation in which he now found himself. But Stephen had a habit of running these sorts of details over in his mind whenever he felt overwhelmed.

'Umm…'

'A bit lost for words there, Steve? Bet you didn't think my daddy was a knight of the realm, eh?'

'Umm… no, I didn't.'

'I don't really like to advertise it. People tend to get the wrong idea about me.'

'I can imagine.'

'By the way, Steve, you owe me another coffee date. Don't think I've forgotten! I was wondering what was taking you so long?'

'Ah, sorry, I've just been a bit tied up.'

'Oh dear, yes, how selfish of me. I can imagine things have been a bit unsettling for you since the pirate incident. Are you managing to find your feet again? In the markets?'

'Yes… I'm getting there, thanks.'

'Now that I think of it, I'm sure daddy could help you if you need any assistance with financing, or something like that. I'll ask him!'

'No! That won't be necessary Cindy… really… thank you so much for the thought, but I like to get things done under my own steam, if you know what I mean…'

'Stephen! You need to take help where you can get it. Don't be so proud!'

'No really, Cindy, I'm finding my feet again nicely. I shan't need any help, I promise!'

'Well, I tell you what Steve; I should have thought of this earlier, but it's never too late. I'll start an awareness campaign on my various social media platforms. I'll see if I can drum up some more business for you, and at the same time, I can reach out to the trading community, and see if anybody else has been negatively affected by the piracy out there in the Solent.'

'Umm… look, Cindy, there's something I need to tell you about that story.'

'Stop being silly, Steve! I have to run. I won't do anything until our next date though, we can discuss it then. How about next Saturday? I'm away this coming weekend. We can do brunch here in London somewhere, how about that? I'll send you a message to confirm.'

'Umm.. Okay.'

'Don't sound so enthusiastic.'

'Sorry, I just have a lot on my mind at the moment.'

'I can see that. Let's have a proper chat when we get together; I'll message with details.'

'Great. I'll see you then...'

15

After a restless night, spent almost entirely on considering the possible ramifications of the stupid story he'd told Cindy, Stephen almost missed his mid-morning meeting with Bridgette.

Fortunately, although he'd cancelled his seven 'o clock alarm, he woke up at nine, so after some extraordinarily quick ablutions and skipping out on his morning espresso, he was able to get to the train in time to make it. He had to run from Knightsbridge station though, so when he arrived at Bridgette's offices, he was a bit out of breath and looked as if he'd been chased there by something dangerous.

Susan evidently noticed this, because she didn't bother to ask him whether or not he'd like coffee, she just asked how he took it.

His response was: *'black, no sugar… and in a pint glass!'*

Bridgette also noticed that he was a bit the worse for wear.

'Good morning Stephen. You look like you just ran here.'

'I did. Sort of.'

'Slept through your alarm then?'

'Indeed. This leave is evidently dulling my senses.'

'Nonsense. The leave's good for you. You were probably just up all night playing computer games.'

'No, I had a bit of a restless night. I battled to sleep.'

'I'm sure your legal affairs are being handled expediently Stephen, you shouldn't worry so much about the situation. From what I hear, this sort of thing happens to a lot of people in your line of work.'

'It's not the FCA case. But thanks for reminding me about that, I haven't spoken to my solicitor in a while, I'll have to give him a call.'

'Well then, what is it that's keeping you up at night?'

'A few things, but the one that's currently on the top of the list has to do with that date I told you about when we first met. You know the one where I was an arsehole and she asked to see me again?'

'Yes.'

'I bumped into her yesterday, and we've set up that second date.'

'That shouldn't be keeping you up at night Stephen. I would have thought you'd outgrown that sort of anxiety.'

'Wait until I tell you the source of the anxiety, before you make any assumptions.'

'Now I'm intrigued.'

'I'm sure I didn't tell you exactly what I did on that first date. I know you like brevity, so to cut a very long story short, I told her that I was a flea market grocery trader who'd been robbed by pirates on the crossing to the Isle of Wight.'

'You can't be serious.'

'Dead serious. I was trying to get rid of her.'

Bridgette smiled, but managed to stifle a laugh. Stephen could see that she was having to work hard to maintain her composure.

'You missed your calling Stephen. You should have been a comedian. That's hilarious.'

'Yeah, I was very pleased with myself at the time.'

'But it backfired, didn't it?'

'More spectacularly than you can possibly imagine.'

'I have a pretty vivid imagination Stephen, but please, don't keep me on tenter hooks.'

'Well, instead of running away, and instead of calling me out on my bullshit, she wanted to hear more about my story. Hence her asking to see me again.'

'Okay. Doesn't sound too catastrophic though.'

'We're getting to the juicy part.'

'You know I'm enjoying this, don't you Stephen? You're playing it out for me to build suspense.'

'Yeah, I spose I am.'

'Go on then. Entertain me.'

'I bumped into her yesterday outside my office.'

'You're not supposed to be near your office are you?'

'Another long story - but far less important.'

'Alright, sorry I interrupted.'

'She wants to help me 'find my feet' again following my imaginary incident. To this end, she plans on raising awareness of my plight through her supposedly massive social media presence. Apparently she's what they call an "*influencer*".

'Oh dear…'

'It gets worse, Bridgette.'

'She's already posted some material?'

'No, thankfully not. But I found out that we share a very important connection… she's Arthur Ashden's daughter!'

'No!? Not 'Sir' Arthur Ashden? The chairman of the company you work for?'

'The very same.'

'Stephen… I'm not usually one to react rashly to these sorts of things, but you need to fix this situation. Quickly!'

'Yeah, I'm obviously going to have to come clean and beg for mercy.'

'Yes. I'm afraid that's the only sensible course of action. It would be far more difficult to grow a beard and leave the country.'

'Quite.'

'I hate to rub it in, but are you now willing to accept that you have a problem with women?'

'I accepted that last time we met.'

'Sorry, you're quite right.'

'I think I'm improving though. Honestly… I went on another date on Saturday, and although it started very badly, it ended reasonably well.'

'So you didn't talk about the pirates or anything silly like that then?'

'No, I didn't. I did show up an hour late, because I got lost and ended up being done for speeding. But I think I recovered from that. Time will tell.'

Bridgette looked as though she felt truly sorry for Stephen. She took on a far more motherly disposition than the one she usually adopted when dealing with him.

'I'm sorry to hear that you've been having these difficulties Stephen. It sounds like you're trying hard to follow the programme. How are all the other things going?'

'I told you about that dating site last time we met, didn't I?'

'You told me that you signed up to one. But we didn't really get the opportunity to traverse the subject in any detail.'

'Well, it turned out to be dedicated to S&M matchmaking. I only figured it out when they showed up with a kitbag full of leather bondage gear, and a photographer, to take photographs of me in costume.'

Bridgett burst out laughing. She tried hard to stop herself, but she couldn't stop the tears running down her cheeks.

'I've never seen you laugh before, Bridgette.'

'I'm sorry Stephen, I honestly don't want to be having a laugh at your expense. It's just rather hilarious and I'm battling to help myself.'

'Well then you're going to love the next part…'

'Oh no… please tell me it doesn't get worse?'

'They sent a large box of bondage paraphernalia to my office… due to some administrative mishap, which I won't go into, the box found its way into the hands of the only individual at the office who has a vendetta against me. The bastard took photographs of the contents and sent them to every bloody staff member on the office mailing list.'

Bridgette closed her eyes and cupped her hands over her mouth. Her amusement had turned to shock and disbelief.

'Oh Stephen! I *am* sorry. I'm glad to see you're being so calm about the whole thing though.'

'Yeah, I'm not actually too bothered about that particular incident. I just feel like I could do with some luck for a change.'

'Here's the thing, Stephen. Up until now, you've been hiding away from life, and burying yourself in your work. When that's the nature of your existence, things don't tend to go wrong that often… but they also don't tend to go *right*. At least, not in any way that makes a genuine difference to your happiness and quality of life… Opening yourself up to the world comes with a host of risks, but I promise you, they're worth the reward.'

'That makes sense.'

'The storm of unfortunate events is all happening at once, because you haven't given yourself the chance to acclimatise properly before diving in. To be fair, that's *my* fault, because I've forced you out of your comfort zone rather abruptly. But we're on a clock, and I sense you have the strength to see the process through.'

'I hope so.'

'You'll be fine. Your attitude is changing for the better. Try to keep it up.'

'I'm not so sure. Yesterday I bumped into that colleague of mine who posted the pictures of my bondage gear, and I wasn't as mature as I wanted to be about the whole thing.'

'Nobody's perfect Stephen. You didn't punch him did you?'

'No.'

'Good. Although he did cross a fairly significant line.'

'I've treated him pretty appallingly in the past, I deserved it.'

'Is this the chap whose investment proposal got sunk after you disclosed his shoddy research to the board?'

'How on earth did you know about that?'

'Jim told me in his personal evaluation of you. One of his biggest concerns about you is the fact that he doesn't consider you to be a team player.'

'Yes, he's told me that, and I've taken it on board quite seriously.'

'Good. But I disagree that what this individual did to you equates to what you did to him.'

'You're the second person who's told me that actually.'

'Who was the other one?'

'My young intern.'

'What was his take on the situation?'

'He says I wouldn't feel as philosophical about the whole thing if I was actually into S&M. He thinks that this chap's conduct was worse than mine because it was so deeply personal.'

'He's right.'

'I did far more damage to *his* reputation than he did to *mine* though.'

'That may be true. But what he did was like simultaneously outing and shaming a homosexual person who wanted to maintain their privacy. Remember, *he* didn't know that the package was obtained in error.'

'I suppose he didn't.'

'How do you think Mary would feel if someone spread her sexual identity around like that?'

'You know about Mary too?'

'I do… and I also know that *you* know, or else I wouldn't have said anything.'

'Jim?'

'Yes. I asked him if you were sleeping with your personal assistant. He didn't know, and being Jim, he just went and asked her directly. She was very forthcoming with him.'

'He tends to have that effect on people.'

'He does indeed. Anyway, she told him that you weren't sleeping together, that she's a lesbian, that you know about it, and that you're both keeping it a secret from the rest of the office. She also told him explicitly to tell me all of that. I think it was her way of sending me a message that you're loyal and protective over her. That's how I interpreted it.'

'To be fair, she only told me just before I was sent off on gardening leave, so I didn't even have the opportunity to break her trust.'

'But you'd take that secret of hers to your grave, wouldn't you?'

'Yes. I would.'

'Well then, Mary and I were both right.'

'About what?'

'That you're a decent man, Mr West. Now *you* just need to believe it.'

'Don't you have a pill for that?'

'You also appear to have a good sense of humour.'

'I need one at the moment.'

'You're doing fine! Now go and get some sleep!'

***

Stephen left Bridgette feeling a little better, and slightly more awake than he had when he'd arrived.

He called Ian for an update on the FCA case, and was assured that it was under control. His father had provided the solicitor with the information he needed for a statement, and both this and Stephen's affidavit would be ready for signature early the following week. Ian told him that his father had volunteered to come down to London to sign the papers, and indicated that he'd confirm a time and a date for this once he sent Stephen his own affidavit in draft format. He said that he'd get that to him over email by Thursday.

With all that had been going on lately, Stephen hadn't really been thinking about the case. He realised that he hadn't actually phoned his Dad to thank him for his assistance yet, so he got hold of him to do so, and to ask if he'd like to have lunch or something when he came up to sign the legal papers. The old man seemed a little surprised by the call, but sounded happy to hear from him.

By this stage, it was almost lunch-time, and Stephen decided to see whether or not Kenny was able to tear himself away from the office for a chat and something to eat. He wanted to find out exactly how it was that Kenny managed to set him up on a date with Arthur Ashden's daughter. It couldn't have been a coincidence. Although he was very fond of his young intern, he was deeply irritated, because he assumed that the little bugger must have known exactly who Cindy was.

As Stephen had anticipated, the offer of a free lunch motivated Kenny to ensure that he had time to spare, and they met up at a small pub about a block away from the office.

'Hello Kenneth.'

'Hi boss… how's the leave going? bored yet?'

'Before we get to the pleasantries, you're in for a bit of a bollocking.'

'What could I possibly have done this time boss? You haven't even been in the office for two weeks.'

'Remember that coffee date you set up for me with *"Cindy"*?'

'Of course boss, I thought *you'd* have forgotten by now though. I was kind of hoping you *had*, to be honest.'

'Well, I was *trying* to Ken. But I bumped into her on the sidewalk outside the offices yesterday.'

'Shit boss, *that's* a crazy coincidence…'

'*Is it?*'

'What do you mean? It has nothing to do with *me* boss, I promise. I haven't been in contact with her again. I didn't want her to try and get hold of you through *me*.'

'Where did you meet her, Kenneth?'

'Funny story actually boss. Another of those weird coincidences. She was at one of the office social events. I think she was mates with one of the secretaries.'

'It wasn't a fucking "*coincidence*" Kenny! She wasn't here because of some bloody connection to one of the secretarial staff.'

'She *wasn't*?'

'No.'

'Sorry boss, I'm battling to follow you… and I'm battling to understand what I'm in *trouble* for.'

'You're in trouble for being an idiot, and not doing your research before setting me up on a date with the woman! You could at least have found out how it was she came to be at that party before playing matchmaker of the year.'

Kenny gave Stephen a quizzical look.

'Did you even manage to find out what her bloody *surname* was before you arranged the date?'

'Umm… no… sorry boss, I just thought she was hot and friendly.'

'Well, at least you had the brains to figure *that* out…'

'Do you want to know what her surname *is*, Kenneth?'

'Not really boss, but I spose you're going to tell me…'

'It's "*Ashden*"…'

'Wow, *that's* an interesting coincidence.'

'*Is it?*'

'Umm…'

'Jesus Kenneth, take your head out of your arse and use your brain! I want you to put this little puzzle together for yourself.'

'Oh, so what you're saying is that she's somehow related to the *big* boss?'

'Congratulations Ken, I thought you were *never* going to get there…'

'Oh, shit…'

'*Oh shit* indeed!'

'But surely you can just ease out of seeing her again boss? Feed her some bullshit story and move on?'

'It's not quite that simple Kenneth… I already *did* feed her a bullshit story… in a fit of abject stupidity, and it's backfired quite horribly.'

'What happened?'

'I got bored during the date, and because I was so wrapped up in my own self-importance, and because I thought I was far more intelligent than I actually *am*, I made up an amusing story about myself that I thought would scare her away. Instead of just being a *gentleman*, and letting the date take its natural course before making a tactful retreat, I behaved like an utter prick, and toyed with the poor woman.'

'So I'm guessing it didn't scare her off then, boss?'

'No. It had the opposite effect.'

'Shit… What did you tell her?'

'That's not important. What *is* important, is the fact that I'm now in world of trouble, because if Ashden senior finds out how I treated his little princess, my prospects at the company are likely to get even bleaker than they already are.'

'How would he find out, boss?'

'How do you think?'

'Surely she doesn't talk to him about her love life?'

'She may well do once she puts the pieces of the puzzle together, Ken. I'm sure you're familiar with the old admonition regarding scorned women.'

'I don't quite know what to say boss…'

'It's alright Ken, you didn't know. But let it be a lesson; don't make assumptions.'

'No, I see what you mean.'

'You and I both made stupid assumptions here. To be fair though, *your* stupidity was completely eclipsed by my *own*. You need to know that I'm not perfect, but you *also* need to know that I'm man enough to admit it. I daresay, that *isn't* a lesson you're likely to learn whilst working under Smith.'

'Definitely not, boss. What are you going to do?'

'I'm going to take the only course of action available to me now. I'm going to come *clean* with Cindy, get down on my fucking knees, apologise profusely, and hope I do such a convincing job of it, that she takes enough pity on me not to tell her father about the incident…'

***

After parting ways with Kenny, Stephen headed home. On the way, his mood was significantly improved by the receipt of a text message from Alexa.

Hi Steve. It's Alexa. How's your week going?

His heart skipped a beat. Either she was about to try and let him down gently, or she wanted to see him again.

Hi Alexa. A bit manic to be honest, but not all bad.

Sorry, have I disturbed you?

No! Not at all

You aren't driving and texting again are you Steve?

No, I've learnt my lesson. I'm behaving myself.

Good. I wouldn't want you locked up.

Does that mean you'd like to see me again?

Maybe…

How do I turn the maybe into a yes?

Agree to show me some of your artwork.

Done. But you've just given me some leverage, because we'd have to meet up for me to do that.

You could always send me a pic… apparently all the kids are doing it now.

How would you know it's genuine?

Good point… okay Steve, let's meet up.

Just tell me where and when… and send a detailed map so I don't get lost!

I'll come up to London. How about Saturday night?

Sounds splendid. Will you allow me to take you to dinner?

Tell you what - I'll take <u>you</u>.

Wow. Okay. I won't say no to that.

Good, but we're going somewhere else first. I'll meet you at five in Trafalgar Square. Try to show up on time!

I'll get a large blanket and sleep there the night before.

Don't do that. With your luck, you'll end up being had up for vagrancy.

Good point. But don't worry, I'll be there.

Stephen couldn't remember the last time he felt so excited about something. He forgot all about his various difficulties and arrived home in a far better state than he was in that morning when he'd left.

He went to bed early and slept considerably better than he had the night before.

The following day, he spent his time working on some sketches in one of the small sketchbooks he had lying around. When he was at University he often carried a sketchbook around with him, but he hadn't done that in years. He did, however, still keep some empty books around, and he thought it would be a fairly easy way to show Alexa his work.

He didn't really like showing people his drawings. He knew they were fairly good, so he had no qualms about how they'd be received. It was just that they were personal to him. They were *his*. He couldn't really explain it any better than that when asked, even though he knew it sounded a bit odd.

But Alexa had asked very nicely, and she was right that it was only fair, given that he'd seen her cakes.

He really liked this woman, and now he had a second chance to make a decent impression. He was still really worried about the fact that he'd lied to her about his occupation though, and this brought him back down to earth every time he got too excited about their upcoming date.

He would have to find the right moment to tell her truth, but there was no need to rush with it. His timing would have to be perfect.

16

Stephen woke up later than usual on Wednesday morning, and was confronted by a screenful of text messages from various people.

He had a message from Charles asking if he was keen on having a drink that evening; a message from his Dad asking about plans for when he was due to meet up in London; a message from Mary asking whether he'd like her to have his mail forwarded, because it was starting to pile up at the office; a missed call from his solicitor (which made his stomach turn a little); a missed call from an unknown number; and a message from Alexa asking whether or not he liked Italian food.

He decided to call Ian back first, because it probably had something to do with the signing of those papers and he wanted to know what was happening with that before he replied to his father.

Ian wasn't available to speak with him, but his secretary indicated that the papers would be ready for signature on Monday. She also indicated that she'd already made an arrangement with his father for that day. He was due to sign his statement in front of a commissioner of oaths at eleven o' clock. She suggested that Stephen make himself available at the same time, and indicated that she'd sent him a draft of his affidavit that morning by email. She suggested that he go through the document and speak with Ian later that day to discuss any changes that would need to be made. She'd provisionally booked a short consultation for three o' clock.

Stephen agreed to meet with Ian, and downloaded the document he'd received so that he could print it out and go through it before then. He really didn't feel like going through the whole *Davaproxin* story again, but he understood that it was necessary and steeled himself for the exercise.

Going through his version of events again felt surreal. It was like looking at the actions of another person through a magnifying glass. Ian was clearly a talented storyteller, because his construction of Stephen's narrative was clear and engaging. It certainly sounded convincing to *him*. Not that that was any indication of its merit as an objectively reasonable piece of evidence.

He started to worry about the case again. He knew he'd done nothing wrong, but still felt apprehensive. He was also reminded of how reckless he'd been. The fact that it had paid off was largely irrelevant. Statistically speaking, his gamble had been foolish, and he ought to have restrained himself. He was worried that he may have actually been losing the plot, and only slightly comforted that he recognised the problem.

He got hold of his father and told him that he'd meet up with him on Monday at Ian's offices, after which they could get lunch in the city.

Last, but not least, he replied to Alexa to tell her that Italian food was his favourite. This wasn't a lie.

***

After being shown into one of the boardrooms at Wright & Hill, Stephen felt a little relieved. Maybe it was Ian's calm and reassuring presence. He certainly had a very good bedside manner for a lawyer. The only other lawyers he knew were the ones at work and they were particularly cold and obnoxious.

Still, when Ian entered the room, Stephen did what most clients with ongoing matters tend to do when meeting their solicitors for follow up consultations; he searched the solicitor for indications that would give away how he was feeling about the case. Of course, good solicitors know that clients do this, and really good ones take on an inscrutable demeanour. Ian was a very good solicitor, so Stephen didn't have the faintest idea of what he was thinking or how he was feeling about the matter.

'Stephen. Good to see you. How are things?'

'Interesting, Ian. That's all I can say.'

'It doesn't sound like you're having a proper break.'

'I am, sort of. Some days are more peaceful and uneventful than others.'

'Well, at the risk of sounding tedious. I encourage you to take it easy and get some rest in.'

'Message received, Ian. I'm grateful for the advice, and I'll try my best to follow it.'

'I take it you've seen that awful article they published in the Financial Times this morning. Did they really try to contact you for comment? Or were they using a little creative license.'

'What article? I have a missed call from an unknown number. But that was from late last night when I was already sleeping.'

'Typical. Sorry, I thought you'd seen the garbage. '

'I assume they've found out about the investigation. Do you have a copy of the thing for me to have a look at?'

'Yes, give me a second and I'll have them bring it through with some coffee. It turns out that you aren't the only one in a bit of hot water with the Financial Conduct Authority over this pharmaceutical company.'

'Thanks. Who else is in the shite?'

'They mentioned two others, *Marvin Jones*, and a chap called *Price*. I can't recall his first name off the top of my head, sorry.'

'Interesting.'

Ian popped out briefly and returned a few seconds later.

'Don't worry about the article, Stephen, its a typical half-researched, overly dramatic attempt at creating a scandal that doesn't quite work. In fact, I'm surprised the editors even let it out onto the page. They're obviously short of decent copy at the moment.'

'I would have thought that the whole *Ringmire* thing would have blown over already?'

'Well, it has, mostly, but they obviously just found out about the investigations at the FCA. Also, that Jones chap is a bit of a serial offender; in the sense that he isn't scared to make waves and behave obnoxiously. So the Journalists tend to look out for stories involving him. You're guilty by association I'm afraid.'

'I know all about Jones. He's an unmitigated narcissist.'

'Well then you can see how this made its way into the papers. It's unfortunate, but it's actually a bit of good news.'

'How so?'

'I'll explain once you've had a look at it.'

Just then, the door swung open and one of Ian's assistants drifted into the boardroom with a silver tray which she placed in the middle of the table, before reaching under her arm and producing a folded copy of that day's Financial Times. She placed it alongside the tray and disappeared.

Ian stood up, picked up a coffee cup by the saucer in one hand, the paper in the other, and placed them both neatly in front of his client.

'Thanks Ian. I could have got that myself.'

'And that would have robbed me of the opportunity to be an attentive host, Stephen.'

Stephen looked across at the solicitor with a smile. He liked him. That sort of comment could easily have sounded smarmy, but it didn't; and his delicate act of placing the paper and the coffee in front of him wasn't an affectation either.

There, staring up at him like a rusty bear-trap was the offending article. He knew from the title that it was likely to be unpleasant.

LIKE VULTURES ON A ROTTING CARCASS

Recent events in the city have once again demonstrated the true nature of the so-called 'financial elite'. No less than three high-flying traders have recently been placed under investigation for making a proverbial 'killing' at the expense of an ailing company.

That company is Ringmire Pharmaceuticals, a previously strong entity with a proven track record, which was recently rocked to its core by the actions of a rogue employee.

Whilst most normal investors, including more than one pension fund, sustained heavy short-term losses which will never be recovered in real terms, at least three of the City's elite traders, including James Price, Marvin Jones and Stephen West, have made significant windfalls by betting against the market, and taking advantage of Ringmire's ill fortune.

The Financial Conduct Authority won't disclose the figures involved, but they must be significant, given that they've triggered the investigations. Indeed, it seems highly unlikely that these vultures didn't have some sort of insider knowledge before short-trading the Ringmire stock. Where there's smoke, there's bound to be fire.

We attempted to contact each of the individuals for comment, but were only able to reach Jones, who told us rather abruptly to speak with his solicitors.

We also attempted to reach out to the companies where these traders work for comment, but aside from making it clear that the trades in question had nothing to do with the companies themselves, they closed ranks like a bunch of common street gangs.

So much for transparency and accountability in the financial sector. We eagerly await the outcome of the relevant investigations, but if the past has taught us anything, it's that the city takes care of its own. **More on page 6...**

'My god Ian, surely that's defamatory?'

'No, unfortunately it isn't. There's a little bit of questionable speculation, but nothing solid enough for us to take them to task for it. Besides, that would only add fuel to the fire, and give them an excuse to do more digging.'

'Let them dig. I have nothing to hide.'

'That doesn't matter, it's still not a good idea to court media attention, trust me.'

'Fair enough. What was that good news you were alluding to earlier?'

'Ah, yes. Assuming Jones and Price *didn't* have inside knowledge, they must have similar stories to yours. I assume you haven't been speaking with either of them?'

'No, I know *of* Jones, but I don't know him personally; and I've never heard of the other chap.'

'Good. That means that you aren't connected to either of them by first degree, and they must have had similar reasons for shorting the stocks.'

'I didn't think any of my colleagues were that reckless.'

'You may still have taken the largest position on the stock, it's just that they may have taken positions above the FCA's threshold. If Jones' reputation is anything to go by though, he'll have been even more reckless than you.'

'That doesn't make me feel much better. But you're probably right.'

'Of course, either or both of them could actually have *had* insider knowledge, which wouldn't necessarily be helpful to you, but let's wait and see what comes out in the wash.'

'What's your feeling on it, Ian?'

'You'll never get a lawyer to give you a straight answer to that sort of question, but I'm willing to say that I'm cautiously optimistic.'

'I'm satisfied with that.'

'Do you need me to make any amendments to the affidavit before I finalise it for signature?'

'No. I was certain I would, and I've been through it twice, but it's spot on.'

'Thanks, I thought it was accurate.'

'Can I take this paper with me?'

'Why on earth would you want to do that?'

'Morbid curiosity. I want to see what they've said on page six.'

'Suit yourself, but it trails off a bit, into a more general dig at the greater finance community. I obviously scrutinised it to see if there was anything blatantly actionable.'

'I thought you said it was best not to court media attention?'

'There's nothing wrong with doing it when you're certain of victory. I may be risk averse, but I'm still a lawyer, Stephen. I wouldn't do myself out of the opportunity to make fees on a winning ticket.'

'And there I was, thinking you did this altruistically…'

'No you weren't.'

'Thanks for the chat Ian, I do feel slightly better.'

'I'm glad! See you on Monday. If the media do contact you now, please don't say anything to them. Blame me if it makes you feel any better. Tell them I've advised you not to comment. You're welcome to give them my details if you like.'

'Will do.'

***

Given that Karen worked in the city, she also kept abreast of the financial news, and she saw the article about Stephen.

That evening, she had a word with her husband about it.

'Oliver…'

'Yes dear.'

'Did you know that Stephen's under investigation for insider dealing?'

'Yes.'

'And when were you going to tell me about it?'

'I wasn't.'

'Excuse me?'

'Karen. I don't mean to come across as impatient or rude, but I have ethical duties which survive the cessation of my legal practice.'

'What do you mean? You haven't been advising him, have you?'

'No, but I referred him to Ian.'

'Then I don't see any ethical dilemmas in telling me about it.'

'Stephen came to me for a referral in my capacity as a solicitor, and he was entitled to expect that I'd exercise the discretion that's expected of members of my profession. Just because I no longer practice, doesn't mean that I'm not bound by that responsibility.'

'Okay, I get it. But still… you've had me keep my mouth shut with Alexa about the fact that he's a trader, and now it looks like he may also be a dodgy one. You can see how this puts me in an invidious position, love.'

'Do you really think Stephen's dodgy?'

'No, not really. I'm rather fond of Stephen. That's why agreed to this little ruse in the first place. But maybe he's changed? We haven't seen him in a really long time.'

'He hasn't changed an inch, love. I'd stake my reputation on it.'

'You're really that sure?'

'I am.'

'Well, your instincts are good enough for me then.'

'Thanks love. I honestly think he had a bit of bad luck. Probably did something that made sense to him, but other people can't quite fathom. You know he thinks on a different level to most of us.'

'Has Ian said anything to you about the case? I know you lawyers still talk to one another about these things, even though you don't share them with anybody else.'

'No. Ian wouldn't speak to me about it, because he knows I'm Stephen's mate. He wouldn't put me in that sort of position. Even if he did say anything to me, you know I wouldn't tell you. By the way, we only talk to other lawyers about these things when we're brainstorming options and debating tactics.'

'That's no fun. Don't you at least gossip about your clients?'

'No. We hear enough crazy stories, it loses its appeal pretty quickly.'

'I'm not sure I'd ever get tired of learning all the dirty secrets of my clients.'

'It's a double edged sword, love. Trust me. But as far as Stephen's concerned, I can't imagine he has any dirty secrets. I get the impression that his life is remarkably boring.'

'Yeah, Alexa seems to have formed that impression. Either way, he'd better come clean to her about what he does. Or I'll tell her.'

'You secretly like the fact that she's going out with someone in finance though, don't you?'

'Yes. You've got me there. I can see her falling for Stephen West. If she does, she'll be forced to reconsider her position regarding those in my line of work.'

'Playing devil's advocate here sweetheart, but is she really wrong?'

'What are you saying Oliver? Choose your next words very carefully, my boy.'

'I'm just saying, most of the finance types I met whilst working were a bit obnoxious. Obviously not everyone, but a pretty hefty sample size.'

'And the lawyers?'

'Oh god K, I know *they* were mostly a bunch of arseholes, that's one of the litany of compelling reasons I left the profession.'

'It does nobody any good to generalise to that extent, Ollie.'

'No. I spose you're right.'

***

Stephen met up with Charles at the same place they'd gone to last time they had drinks. He'd insisted that it wasn't necessary to go somewhere in his neighbourhood, but Charles was adamant about it, and indicated that the choice of venue had nothing to do with his friend's convenience. Although he suspected otherwise, Stephen wasn't going to challenge him on it. The little speak-easy really was a great place.

This time it was Stephen who arrived early. He ordered Charles a whisky, and himself a beer; he wasn't going to risk another cocktail hangover, and he knew Charles seldom drank anything other than whisky. He remembered that his friend favoured peaty malts, so he ordered him an Ardbeg.

'Stevie!'

'Hey Charlie, good to see you again, mate.'

'I enjoyed our last drink, and realised we should do it more often. You still on leave?'

'Yeah.'

'Found yourself yet?'

'Getting there. It's a process.'

'It's a lifelong process mate, but I'm glad you're on your way. How's the love life? Got any dates yet?'

'I had a date with Alexa the other day. Cocked it up a little bit, but she seems to be a sucker for punishment, because we've got a second coming up this weekend.'

'Don't be so hard on yourself. You couldn't have done that badly if you're seeing her again.'

'No. Maybe not. I really like her though, so I'm a bit stressed out about it.'

'Yeah, I know that feeling.'

'I didn't think you suffered from the same insecurities that plagued the rest of the male population, Charles.'

'Don't let appearances deceive you, I'm just good at hiding it.'

'It's comforting to know that even you have some weaknesses.'

'I'm a giant weakness Steve, I have a weakness for pretty women, so I date two; I have a weakness for silly games, so I design them; and I have a weakness for my mother, so I don't tell her about the fact that she's unlikely to get any grandchildren.'

'Your game is awesome by the way.'

'You really like it?'

'Don't pretend to be surprised Charlie, you know it's good.'

'I'm like all creative types Stevie, I still want to hear it. Even a bestselling author who's sold over a million copies of his book, wants his friends to tell him they think it's good. Aren't you that way with your art?'

'Other than my parents, only you and Oliver have really seen my art work. I don't like to show it to people.'

'You should Steve, it's good. I'm still a bit pissed off by the fact that you're super bright *and* talented at drawing. It sort of serves you right that you're no good with the birds.'

'Who said I was no good with the birds.'

'You... incessantly.'

'Fair enough.'

'I'll give you a bit of solid advice though mate. Show 'em your artwork and you can probably dispense with the necessity of having any personality.'

'You think I don't have a personality?'

'Of course I don't think that, you know what I mean. That came out wrong. I meant you wouldn't have to try as hard to impress them if they knew you were a talented artist. Most women I know love that sort of thing.'

'Yeah, I get it. I just don't like the idea of going around and blowing my own trumpet, that's all.'

'That's not it Steve. I know you well enough to know that you enjoy a bit of trumpeting. It's clearly a bit more complicated than that. Don't try to kid a kidder, mate.'

'Shit Charlie, that's a bit harsh.'

'It's said with all the love in the world, Stevie. If you're going to lie to yourself, then enabling you by buying into your delusions is wildly counter-productive. I don't really care about the deep-seated psychological reasons, leave that for your therapist, I'm just saying… use the art thing, don't waste it.'

'Why do you always make me feel like an idiot, Charles?'

'Because somebody has to bring you down to earth now and then, mate.'

'Alright, I spose that's fair. I've just been having some appalling luck recently. I'm feeling particularly 'down to earth' right now.'

'You still in trouble at work?'

'Yeah, in a sense. But to be honest, I care less about it every day. I know that sounds pretty bad, but I'm growing a bit apathetic about work.'

'Huh, that *is* interesting.'

'How so?'

'You've always been so tied up in that job of yours. It's odd that you're becoming apathetic about it, even though you *are* trying to take a break and find yourself. Have you ever considered the notion that you're actually over it?'

'My career?'

'Yeah. It happens you know.'

'No way. Not me, I'm good at what I do, and I enjoy it.'

'Do you really enjoy '*it*'? Or do you just enjoy the fact that you're good at it.'

'That's an odd way to put it, but you may have a point. I'm not sure whether it really matters though.'

'Of course it does.'

'Yeah, maybe it does, but that's likely to take a lot more soul searching than I have time for right now. It may sound silly, but I'm more concerned about the fact that I need to find a way of breaking the news to Alexa that I'm not a bloody graphic designer.'

'You haven't told her yet?'

'No.'

'Shit Steve, I thought that's why you had a bit of a rubbish first date. You're treading on thin ice now, mate.'

'I'm aware of that. It's what's currently nagging at me. To make matter's worse, she's not the only woman I've lied to recently, and that's also backfired quite drastically.'

'Bloody hell Steve, I never took you for the lying type.'

'You know I'm not. I just haven't really been myself lately. The other one I lied to was also a date, but I did it for the opposite reason; I was trying to chase her away.'

'So you only lie to women you're dating then?'

'Yes… I mean… no… ah fuck, I don't know Charlie. Let's just say I'm working on my various issues. Obviously my boss was right when he told my *"executive coach"* about my difficulties with women.'

'You really *are* rubbish with women, aren't you Stephen?'

'I'm sure there are *some* chaps who are worse than me. But they're probably either in prison or suffering from hideous deformities.'

Charles didn't respond to Stephen's comment. He just looked across at him and smiled sardonically.

Stephen was a little perturbed, because it seemed as though his friend was actually trying to work out whether or not his ability to charm the opposite sex exceeded that of the incarcerated, or the deformed. Alternatively, Charles had seen through his attempt at fishing for sympathy and he wasn't taking the bait. Either way, the awkward silence didn't fill him with joy and optimism.

'I have the perfect solution to your problem Stephen. It's pretty drastic, but it'll work.'

'Tell me. I'll do anything.'

'Be careful about making those sorts of comments Stevie, I told you it's pretty drastic.'

'I've got a fairly vivid imagination Charles, and I can't think of anything that's drastic enough to give me a shock.'

'Wait till you hear it.'

'Okay, hit me.'

'Quit your job and come work for me.'

'What?'

'It's quite simple really: one, I need a good new artist; two, you *are* a good artist; three, working as an artist for a gaming company is basically the same as being a 'graphic designer', any differences are purely semantic; four, you're pretending to yourself that you're going to be a stockbroker your whole life, when it clearly doesn't engage you as much as it used to.'

The awkward silence was back. Stephen just stared across the table at his friend in disbelief. Clearly, he was wrong about the fact that Charles couldn't shock him. His mind usually ran through things at such a pace that he didn't need to draw breath before considering the implications of what he was hearing… this was different. There was a simple and elegant logic to it that made him feel uncomfortable.

'My god, Charles. I love how your mind works, but that's insane.'

'I've done more outrageous things to impress girls.'

'No Charlie, I don't believe that. You're suggesting I give up my entire career to impress a girl.'

'No. Not really, I'm just suggesting that you give it up earlier than you otherwise would. The city isn't the hill you want to die on, Stephen. You know it as well as I do; you're just not willing to admit it to yourself yet.'

'You're mad, Charles.'

'Yes. But I'm usually right.'

'Why do you need a new artist anyway?'

'I'm having a standup fight with my art director over the next expansion for *The Other Planet*, and I'm running out of time and options.'

'Creative differences?'

'Indeed. It's common knowledge on the forums now that we're going to be introducing dragons into the game in the new expansion next year, so it's not something I can't discuss with you.'

'Wow. I don't really look at the forums. That sounds cool though…'

'Yeah, I think it's going to be bloody spectacular. But the design of the dragons is leading to all out warfare in the office…'

'Why?'

'I want *traditional style* dragons. Like the ones in Dungeons & Dragons. That's not fucking hard, *is it*?'

'No.'

'The art director, and his team of two dozen snivelling young artists can't… or rather, *won't*, give me what I want. He says that his people don't want to do anything *"derivative"*, because it insults their *"creative integrity"*… whatever *that* is?!'

'I'll admit that's a bit mental.'

'Yeah, I'm properly sore about it… I mean, since when do artists get to bite the hand that feeds them like this? I'm pretty sure that throughout history, artists have painted and sculpted things the way their patrons have bloody-well *wanted* them to do it… not *this* lot!'

'No, you're *wrong* mate, artists have always been a difficult bunch. It depends how good they think they are… the insecure ones are likely to go along with your instructions, but only until they gain the confidence to tell you to piss off.'

'You can't be *serious*?'

'It's true, Charlie boy. Even the most impoverished artist on earth will be difficult about that sort of thing… a lot of the bastards would rather starve to death, than compromise their *"creative integrity"*…'

'Christ…'

'Yeah. Speaking *of*… even *Michelangelo* couldn't help himself when he painted the Sistine Chapel. He didn't like his patron, Pope Julius II (not many people *did*, to be fair), so even though he painted his face on the body of one of the prophets, he painted a rude gesture on one of the cherubs, aimed at the likeness of the Pope. Luckily for *him*, it was obscured by a soot buildup, and was too high up to be noticed at the time.'

'*Seriously?*'

'Seriously… and that particular Pope was known for having a violent temper, so it wouldn't have gone particularly well for the artist if it was discovered. Still, Michelangelo didn't give a toss…'

'Bloody hell.'

'So if your team don't want to do a traditional dragon, you won't make the bastards do it, you're right that you'll have to hire someone *else*. You can threaten to fire them, but they'll just laugh in your face.'

'Fuck sakes!'

'Yeah, it's shitty. You just have to find someone who likes the idea of painting traditional dragons. It shouldn't be *too* hard.'

'So you'll do it then? Come draw dragons with your best mate… you know you want to.'

'I've never seen you like this Charlie.'

'Like what?'

'Irritated and flustered by something. I'm just enjoying the moment and trying to take it all in.'

'You have some strange ideas about me mate, I get just as flustered as anyone, just not necessarily by the same things.'

'Still, it's comforting to know that you do.'

'You haven't answered my question, Stephen… and I know why.'

'Enlighten me, uncle Charlie.'

'Because even though you have an IQ that's as high as a respectable cricket score, that clever brain of yours can't come up with a single compelling reason not to take me up on my offer.'

'No, it's because your proposal is so bloody outrageous that it's left me speechless.'

'Crap. You've never been speechless.'

'Clearly you've never seen me on a date.'

'Thank fuck for that, but seriously, are you actually saying no.'

'No.'

'So you're not saying 'no' then?'

'I just did.'

'No you didn't.'

'You're being obtuse, Charles.'

'You're being obdurate, Stephen. Do you, or do you *not* want to come and draw pretty pictures for me?'

'I don't.'

'Liar!'

'If you're so convinced that I do, then why even push me for an answer?'

'Because admitting it is the first step.'

'To what?'

'Self-discovery and personal fulfilment.'

'Okay Yoda, but seriously… I'm not giving up my career to draw dragons for you… as fun as that sounds.'

'You don't think it would be fun?'

'I wasn't being sarcastic, I know it would be loads of fun, but it's unrealistic.'

'I'm not giving up on you Steve, the offer will stay open as long as I work at the company.'

'Thanks Charles, I may be sacked anyway, so you could actually get your wish. If I do get given the heave ho, I won't be able to work in the industry again.'

'Well here's to that! A toast. To my mate's possible sacking!'

Stephen couldn't help but have a laugh. He'd forgotten how much he'd missed Charles Taylor. He was definitely a challenge at times, but he needed to be challenged more often by those close to him, and he knew it.

'I tell you what, Charlie; if you want me to vet some artwork for you, I will. Your art director doesn't sound too enthusiastic about normal dragons. I'm old fashioned, so I love 'em, and I know enough about the artistic process to tell you which of your candidates are any good.'

'Thanks Steve. I'll take you up on that. It will be like a sort of phasing in project, while you come to terms with your impending career change.'

'Don't get your hopes up. I'm only doing it because I like the game now, and I'd be seriously pissed off if you introduced rubbish dragons in the next expansion.'

17

Stephen spent most of the following two days playing *The Other Planet*. He'd started off doing some sketches, but his rhythm kept being broken by phone calls from inquisitive journalists. It seemed that once you found yourself in the papers for something controversial, the entire media establishment descended upon you for 'comment', as they liked to call it. Clearly *he* wasn't the only 'vulture' around.

He wondered how many of his friends and colleagues had read the article. It made him feel a little nauseated when he realised that every one of his colleagues was likely to have read it. Smith had probably framed it, and had it hung in his office like a certificate. At least his Dad already knew the story. Even though he was now retired, the old man still read the financial papers. Fortunately, his mother had better things to read.

He'd become tolerably good at fobbing them off. Some were more resilient than others, but by and large, they seemed to back off as soon as he mentioned his solicitor. Only the young ones asked him who this solicitor was, and he was happy to divulge the information because he liked the idea of them wasting their time trying to get anything out of Ian. It only later occurred to him that he'd be charged for each of the calls fielded by Wright & Hill.

The parcel of S&M paraphernalia arrived on Friday, having been re-posted by *EDgE*. He'd actually forgotten about it. M was right about the Champagne and chocolates; they looked expensive. He took them out and re-sealed the box. He didn't feel like taking an inventory of the other contents just yet.

He spent most of the day on Saturday trying to distract himself, because he was filled with nervous energy. Reading was pointless, because his mind kept wandering. The same happened when he tried to play on the computer, and drawing was out of the question. He'd also had far too many cups of coffee, and almost nothing to eat. He was irritated with himself, because he thought he'd grown out of this sort of thing. It felt like he was sixteen again.

The nerves kicked in after he received a message from Alexa just before lunchtime. But once they were there, they stuck around.

Morning Steve… are we still on for tonight? You haven't forgotten, have you?

Of course I haven't forgotten… Even though it's summer, it's still cold sleeping on those concrete benches in the Square.

How sweet Steve, I hope you at least found a way to have a shower before I arrive.

I brought soap. I'll have a bath in one of the fountains.

You'd better make it a quick one… they don't take kindly to that sort of thing.

Yeah, I'll be quick.

But also try to be thorough, Steve. See you later x

I look forward to it.

After rearranging his bookshelves, tidying up, doing his dishes, and having a long shower, Stephen couldn't contain himself in the flat any longer; so he got ready and headed for Trafalgar Square. He arrived two hours before he was due to meet up with Alexa. He toyed with the idea of taking a walk around the National Gallery, but it occurred to him that that may well be what Alexa had planned to do with him before dinner, so he got as comfortable as was possible on one of the concrete benches running along the eastern wall of the Square.

He'd taken his sketchbook with him, because he'd promised to show Alexa some of his work, and he wasn't presumptuous enough to assume he'd get her back to his flat after a second date. He felt a bit spare at the notion of showing off his drawings, but he remembered what Charles had said about women loving that sort of thing, and it wasn't as if it was unsolicited.

He decided to do some sketches of the Square to wile away the time. It had been ages since he'd sat down and taken the time to soak up the beauty and majesty of the monuments in and around the Square. Nelson's Column and the lions were on his left, the eastern fountain was directly in front of him, and the Gallery was up on the right, behind the imperious statue of King George IV, riding his horse. There was no lack of material to draw from.

The weather was also perfect. There wasn't a cloud in the sky, and he could feel a very faint spray from the fountain every now and then, as the breeze caught some of the mist created by the cascading water. It certainly wasn't a bad day to be out with a sketchbook.

At roughly a quarter to five, he received a message from Alexa.

Hi Steve. Are you still on your bench? Or have you been locked up for vagrancy?

Still on my bench. The long arm of the law hasn't reached me yet!

Seriously? You're on a bench in the square?

Yip. I'm under the trees in front of South Africa House.

I'll meet you there.

After a few minutes, he saw Alexa descend the stairs into the Square. She was wearing a similar outfit to the one she'd worn on their first date, although she now wore closed shoes and an oxblood coloured skirt with a matching leather handbag. The colour really suited her, although Stephen couldn't really imagine any colour that wouldn't.

He stood up to greet her and noticed that she was slightly taller than he'd remembered, then realised she was wearing high heels.

'You're on time Steve!'

'Yes. How about that?'

'I'm impressed! So you obviously found a parking in that great big tank of yours. Must have been a bit tricky around here.'

'I don't own that ridiculous thing. I borrowed it from my boss. I use public transport here in London.'

'That's far more sensible. I hope your boss didn't get a copy of that speeding fine.'

'Me too.'

'Well, enough about your criminal history Steve. I thought that since you're an artist, of sorts, you'd appreciate taking in a little art at the National Gallery before we get something to eat.'

'I'd love that.'

'You're not just saying that to be polite are you? It occurred to me on the way here, that if you're surrounded by art all day, you may get a bit tired of it.'

'Not at all. I used to come to the National Gallery at least once a month for the first few years after I moved to London, and I haven't been back in over five years.'

'So you sure you haven't had enough of it?'

'Not at all, I've been meaning to come back for ages. Are you interested in art though?'

'I'm obsessed with art and architecture.'

'Well then, that's something we definitely have in common.'

She looked down at the book Stephen was holding in his left hand, and smiled.

'Is that a sketchbook you have there with you?'

'It is indeed.'

'I'm impressed. You remembered our little deal.'

'A deal's a deal.'

'Go on then, show me!'

'No way. This is my insurance. If I say or do something stupid, you may still be willing to stick around out of curiosity. The longer I have this on me and unopened, the longer I can use it as leverage.'

Alexa burst out laughing.

'You're funnier than you look, Steve.'

'I suppose it's better than looking funnier than I am. I'll take that as a compliment.'

***

They headed up to the gallery and made their way through the grand entrance. For Stephen, walking into an art gallery, specifically this one, was like wrapping himself in a warm blanket in the middle of winter. It was comforting. This was his version of what some people called a 'happy place'. It was one of the only places in which he was ever able to switch off his mind and relax, much like when he sat in front of a sketchpad or an easel.

'So Alexa, where would you like to start?'

'Not too sure, I also haven't been here in years.'

'Well, what's your favourite style of art?'

'I favour the impressionists.'

'Ah, I also like most of the impressionist works. They have some really special ones here.'

Stephen made an immediate turn right and led them through the Wohl Galleries to the impressionist room at the eastern corner of the building. Unless you planned on spending an entire day browsing the various exhibits, it made sense to concentrate on a limited selection. Stephen was an expert at finding his way around.

'Ah, this is it. You really do know your way around here, Steve.'

Stephen smiled, 'I'm just glad they haven't moved things around too much.'

'I love the impressionists.'

'Is there anything specific about them that stands out for you?'

'Not really, no. I just find them peaceful and captivating.'

'I can understand that. I like most of Renoir's work.'

'Me too. I like almost all of the popular impressionists, to be honest.'

They walked around the various impressionist works in the room in silence. Stephen did like the impressionist work, but it wasn't his favourite. He preferred the more classic style of painting with more defined lines. He always felt that the impressionists were a bit rushed. This was true of course, given that they adopted John Constable's practise of painting on the spot. Some felt, as Constable did, that this gave the work a more realistic quality, (especially when it came to capturing fleeting changes in light and shadow), but Stephen wasn't a member of this camp.

After a few minutes, he broke the silence.

'If you had to choose one though? Who would be your favourite?'

'Monet. Without a doubt.'

'Yeah, I suppose you can't really do better than the founder of the movement, can you?'

'Absolutely not.'

The room fell silent again, and they each wandered around at their own pace, as people naturally tend to do in galleries and museums. Although Stephen was careful not to stray too far. He wanted to keep their conversation going. He never spent any time around art enthusiasts, so he was genuinely curious about her views on the subject.

'Of all the work here, which one of his is your favourite?'

'I'd have to say *'The Petit Bras of the Seine at Argenteuil'*. It's timeless.'

'Yes, that's an interesting one. He preferred painting the other side of the river where the sailboats were, so it was a bit of a departure from the norm.'

'You obviously know your impressionists quite well, Steve.'

'I know a bit about them, although my interests tend to vary quite wildly, so my knowledge is most often anecdotal. I wish I'd studied art history formally.'

'Oh, I though you would have done.'

'No, regrettably not. So I don't know as much as I'd like to.'

'I think you're probably just being modest, Steve.'

Stephen was getting dangerously close to having to disclose what he *actually* studied at university. If she asked him a straight question now, he wouldn't be able to lie to her, so he was decidedly worried about the prospect. His only hope was to try and steer the course of the conversation slightly. He had every intention of telling Alexa the truth, but timing was important, and he sensed that this wasn't the right time.

'Are there any impressionists that you *don't* like?'

'I'm not the biggest fan of Manet to be honest.'

'Yeah, his work isn't really at the top of my list either.'

By this stage they'd explored most of the room, and were drifting up towards the Constables and the Turners.

'What's *your* favourite style, Steve?'

'Call me old fashioned, but I always go back to the Dutch realists.'

'Well let's go look at some of those then. I take it you know where to find them.'

Stephen smiled and nodded. He took her hand and led her through to the opposite corner of the building, stopping briefly every now and then to admire notable pieces on the way. She only let go once they'd reached their destination. Stephen took them straight to the Rembrandt room.

'So, I suppose he's your favourite then?'

'He is indeed.'

'Why Rembrandt?'

'He understood something about realism that very few other artists bothered to appreciate, or would even deign to accept.'

'Well there we go Steve; that's an artist that didn't live in a cardboard box.'

'He almost did, eventually.'

'Did he? I thought he was one the ones who was actually wealthy during his lifetime.'

Stephen was impressed. Alexa clearly had more than a fleeting interest in art history.

'He came from a reasonably affluent family, and there's no doubt he made decent money selling his work, but his wife was the wealthy one. He married well.'

'Oh yes, I remember reading a bit about that somewhere.'

'Problem was, he was profligate. He probably bought more art than he ever produced; and he was prolific.'

'So you don't think he married for love then, Steve?'

'Call me a cynic, but no. I think he liked shiny things. That said, the historians tend to agree that his marriage to Saskia was a happy and faithful one. By all accounts, he only started messing around with affairs after she died.'

'Oh yes, didn't he marry the nanny or something?'

'No. He couldn't, because Saskia had a clause in her will that disinherited him in the event of remarriage. I can't remember the exact mechanics, I think it had something to do with the use of their son's inheritance or something, but that was the net effect.'

'Ouch.'

'Yeah, although we shouldn't feel too sorry for him. He had the nanny locked up after she took him to court for breach of promise. She claimed he promised to marry her, and he later claimed that she'd stolen and pawned some of Saskia's jewellery. By this stage, he was romantically involved with the next nanny. If it was true that poor old Geertge Dircx stole that stuff and sold it off, you couldn't really blame her.'

'So you think he was the one telling fibs?'

'Absolutely. There's little doubt that he was the sort of chap who would've sold his dearly departed's personal effects. The bastard even sold her grave when he eventually ran out of cash.'

'That *is* pretty vile behaviour.'

'Yeah, although admittedly, his exploits were still pretty tame compared to a lot of artists, especially the one who seems to have indirectly influenced most of his work with shadows and lighting.'

'You must be talking about Caravaggio?'

'You *also* know your artists.'

'Were you testing me, Stephen?'

'A little.'

'That's not fair. You know more about this stuff than I do.'

'Not necessarily. You probably know a lot more about impressionists than I do, this is just my main area of interest.'

'Well, I know that Caravaggio was a complete nutter.'

'Maybe he was just misunderstood?'

Alexa burst out laughing, then caught herself when she saw that one of the other visitors in the room was giving her a disapproving look.

'You're joking, right?'

Stephen chuckled.

'Yeah, I am. He was a lunatic. A talented one though. I honestly think I'd put him second on my list of favourites; even though he wasn't one of the Dutch realists.'

'So basically then, your two favourite artists were a spendthrift who loved to paint pictures of himself; and a crazy murderer who spent the last few years of his life on the run.'

'Pretty much. Sounds a bit creepy when you put it like that.'

'Why those two? Is it just the realism thing?'

'Yeah, I suppose it's the realism. Caravaggio liked to paint real people, and he wasn't scared of choosing ugly models either. In fact, he seemed to prefer it. With Rembrandt it's something deeper though. It probably sounds a bit trite, but he had a way of catching the essence of the people he painted, even when he painted himself, which I'll admit, was probably a bit too often.'

'Why does that interest you so much?'

Stephen stopped and considered the question carefully before responding.

'To be completely honest, Alexa, I've always battled to understand people. I envy Rembrandt, because he must have had a deep and abiding understanding of the people he painted. That's why I don't normally draw or paint *people*, I don't think I can do them justice unless I have an idea of what they're thinking.'

'I get that.'

'I used to come here often and stare at the portraits on display, willing myself to develop a better sense of perspective. I wanted to understand what the artists saw in their subjects, and how they saw it.'

The room fell silent again. Stephen wondered whether or not he'd overshared. He'd never told anyone about that before, but it sort of just came out. It wasn't a conscious decision. There was nothing Alexa could really say, but she smiled at him and moved a bit closer.

She took his hand, and they headed back down through the Italian rooms, chatting briefly about some of the more famous pieces, before exiting out onto the Square.

'So Steve. I've booked for us to go and have something to eat at a small Italian place I've heard is particularly good. There are two ways to get there, the more direct route, or the scenic route. Which would you prefer?'

'Let's take the scenic route.'

'I thought you'd say that.'

They were still holding hands. She steered them along the route, past South Africa House, and the stairs going down to Charring Cross station; crossing the road and ending up on Northumberland Avenue. They headed slowly east down the Avenue, past Great Scotland Yard on the left, and turned under the railway just before the bridge at Embankment Place.

'You know your way around here by the looks of things Alexa?'

'I do. Just because I avoid it now, doesn't mean I don't have a fairly comprehensive knowledge of the place. The head offices of the company I used to work for were around here, so I spent my fair share of time getting to know the place.'

'Ah, that makes sense. Don't you miss the buzz of the city a little bit?'

'Not really, although I love the history and the architecture. I'd forgotten that Great Scotland Yard was actually a road. There are so many little things that tend to go unnoticed while people bustle around the streets getting to where they're going.'

They headed straight into the Victoria Embankment Gardens and Stephen noticed the giant chess board painted onto the ground near the entrance.

'Nice place for a game of chess. Do you play?'

'Not really, to be honest. I got sick of losing to Karen when we were growing up. She was always more patient than me, and she loved winning so much that she ended up taking the game a lot more seriously than I did. What about you?'

'I played a bit with my Dad, but by the time I was nine I was beating him fairly convincingly, so he gave up. My brother wasn't remotely interested. I played a bit in clubs at high school, but never seriously.'

'Sounds like you were good.'

'I wasn't really. I was better than average, but nothing special.'

'Are you trying to be modest again, Steve?'

'No, not at all. Chess is a weird game. Raw intellect gets you to a certain point, but then you end up playing people who've memorised openings, closings, old matches and mid-game theory. It's hard work. Unless you're really passionate about it, it becomes a bit oppressive. Basically, I got to the point at which I knew how much I didn't know, and that scared me off. I wasn't interested enough to do the required learning.'

'I never realised the game was that involved.'

'Most people don't. It's fun when you find someone with vaguely similar ability, but otherwise it can get demoralising pretty quickly.'

They walked through the gardens admiring the various memorials, stopping to have a closer look at the larger ones. They didn't branch off in separate directions to look at the plaques though; that would've meant letting go, and Stephen had no intention of doing that. Neither did Alexa.

'I used to come and sit here often during lunchtimes, especially in the summer.'

'I've never actually walked through the main part of the Gardens before. It's really quite peaceful.'

'Yeah, It's one of my favourite spots. The statues are also very good.'

'I like the one we just passed of old Rabbie Burns.'

'Yes, that's one of Sir John Steell's. Quite the artist, Steell. He did another one of Burns that's in Westminster Abbey. Apparently there's another in Dundee and one in New Zealand.'

'Yeah, I know of Steell. His work is all over the world. His brother was a fairly good painter, actually; but he wasn't really prolific like his elder sibling.'

'You really do have an impressive knowledge of art and artists, Steve.'

'I just have a good memory, and I love art.'

They continued to walk through the gardens, until they reached the statue of Robert Raikes just before the rear entrance of the Savoy.

'There's another exceedingly famous sculptor for you, Steve. I believe that one was done by none other than Sir Thomas Brock.'

'I actually didn't know that. I thought Brock only did statues of Queen Victoria.'

'No you didn't!'

'No. But you must admit that he did a lot of statues of her Majesty. This must have been one of his earliest works?'

'It definitely was. Before his Queen phase.'

'I don't know the subject though… who was Raikes.'

'You're slipping, Steve.'

'Should I know who he is?'

She laughed.

'We probably all should, but I'll be honest; I only found out myself after reading the plaque on the statue. He's probably known in some particularly knowledgeable religious circles.'

'Was he some sort of famous priest or something.'

'No, he owned and edited a newspaper. But he also invented Sunday School, and by necessary implication, the English State school system.'

'Wow, that's quite a legacy.'

'It is indeed. Come on then, this is our exit.'

Alexa led Stephen around the statue and through the gate behind it into carting lane.

'So you're taking me to the savoy then?'

'You should be so lucky, Steve.'

He laughed.

'I'm actually not the fine dining type. Give me a piece of cheese, a baguette and some wine, and I'm sorted.'

'That sounds amazing to me too. Although I do like the odd fine dining experience from time to time.'

'I'll remember that.'

'Think you'll get another date, Steve?'

'I fancy my odds.'

'Cocky. I like that! Come on then, let's go and find you some bread and wine.'

She took him up the steep lane and the stairs which ran alongside the loading entrance of a pub. They crossed Strand and ended up at a cosy little Italian restaurant on the other side of the road.

They were seated at a small table near the back. Alexa ordered a bottle of wine and some water. She was in charge, and Stephen was surprised to find that he was comfortable with that.

'So when did you start being fascinated by art and art history, Steve?'

'In my early teens I suppose. I was always a bookish type, and I ended up reading whatever I could get my hands on. My mom was an art enthusiast, so she collected books on art and art history. After running out of things to read one holiday, I picked up some of these books and immediately got hooked. It helped that I was already interested in drawing.'

'That reminds me… aren't you going to let me have a look at those drawings of yours yet?'

'I don't know, maybe I still need some leverage to keep you here until we've had something to eat.'

'You haven't said or done anything stupid so far Steve, I think you're safe.'

'What if I order spaghetti and eat it like a five year old?'

'Do you normally eat spaghetti like a five year old Steve?'

'No, it was just the only example I could think of.'

She laughed and smiled across the table at him.

'I think you're just shy about your work.'

'I'm not actually, I just never usually show it to anybody. In any event, I've already accepted the fact that it'll be a little anticlimactic after what we've just seen at the gallery.'

'Stop pretending to be modest, show me your work Stephen. Don't be a tease.'

He laughed and handed her the sketchpad. He knew his work was decent. It wasn't his best, because he was still getting back into the flow of things; but it was good enough to impress most people, even himself.

Alexa *was* impressed. She didn't need to say so, because her body language and expression gave it away almost immediately. She went silent and just stared at the first picture for what felt to Stephen like ten minutes. It was, in fact, about two minutes; but two minutes feels like a very long time when you're sitting studying someone, trying to determine what they're thinking.

She paged slowly through the book, there were only six sketches in it, but she spent enough time on each one to make it seem as though she was reading a page in a densely printed novel.

When she'd finished, she closed it and slid it back across the table to him. She didn't smile, she just looked at him curiously.

'You know you're talented, don't you Stephen?'

'I get by in a crowd.'

'Stop being ridiculous, your work is beautiful.'

'Thanks. I really appreciate the compliment.'

He didn't quite know what to say next, but mercifully, the waiter arrived to check on the wine, and to try and cajole them into considering the day's specials. He didn't need to try very hard. Both of his guests seemed visibly relieved by the interruption, and made the most of it by asking various questions about the dishes on offer. The waiter needed no further encouragement, and spent a great deal of time going through each item on offer, and extolling the virtues of the new wines they had stocked for summer.

Alexa ordered a mushroom risotto, and Stephen a carbonara.

After ordering food, and more wine, the conversation moved on to more general topics. Alexa was surprised to find out that although Stephen had spent time in France and Germany, he hadn't ever been to Italy. She'd toured most of Italy, Greece and Spain. Italy was her favourite though. They spoke about art, a little about computer games, and even about their families. Stephen wanted to find a way to come clean about his job, but he was having a fantastic time, and he didn't want to ruin the evening.

When their food arrived, Alexa insisted that he try her risotto, and she tried his carbonara. They ordered another bottle of wine, and ended up sharing a tiramisu.

They stayed far later than they'd expected, and only decided to call it a night at around eleven o'clock. Alexa wanted to catch the train back to Guildford before midnight, because it was a relatively long journey back home.

They left the restaurant and headed down Strand, back towards Trafalgar Square. It was now dark, but the streets were still a hive of activity. Alexa was done holding his hand by this stage, and had opted instead, for holding onto his entire arm with both of hers. This made him grin so widely that he was worried she'd think he was a lunatic, but he wasn't capable of stopping himself, so he just went with it.

They made their way to Charing Cross station, and he accompanied her on the tube to Waterloo. It was only once they got into the large arrival and departure hall at the terminal building that she let go of him, to check that she had her ticket.

'You know, Alexa, I'm not sure how safe these trains are at this time of night.'

'Are you worried I may get attacked by a drunken criminal on the way,

Steve?'

'You can't be too careful these days… maybe I should come with you, just in case.'

She laughed and smiled at him.

'Don't worry, Steve, I'm sure I'll be alright.'

'But what about me?'

She hugged his arm again and laughed.

'I'll send you a text when I arrive, so you'll only have to worry for about an hour.'

He looked down at her and grinned.

'It was worth a shot.'

'Yes. It was. But I'm not that easy Mr West. You know what they say comes to those who wait?'

'I thought you said you were impatient?'

'Not when it comes to this sort of thing, Steve.'

'Fair enough. I'm not going to stop thinking about you though.'

'I know. I also intend to make it even harder for you.'

'How so?'

She let go of his arm, turned to face him, grabbed the lapels of his jacket and kissed him. It wasn't one of those polite, and slightly dismissive kisses people give after a date when they aren't sure whether or not there are any long term prospects. It was the sort of kiss that's vaguely inappropriate in a public place, but that neither of the participants are willing to tone down for the benefit of the witnesses.

She pressed up against him and he could feel every curve of her body. He could also feel her heartbeat and smell her perfume. His knees almost buckled, and he realised that she could feel the effect she was having on him, because as his jeans tightened, she pulled him even closer.

When she eventually stopped kissing him, she whispered in his ear.

'I hope I've given you something to look forward to.'

He smiled and whispered back.

'That's not fair.'

She grinned playfully, kissed him on the cheek, and dashed through the turnstile onto the platform, only turning to look back once she was through. She smiled and blew him a kiss before boarding the train.

Stephen felt like he needed to sit down, but he forced himself to regain some semblance of composure, and left the station feeling like a teenager who'd just had his first real kiss.

18

Alexa had taken Sunday off. Although it pained her to hand the reins over to Freddy for a day, she'd anticipated that she'd be back from London late enough to make waking up at four in the morning to bake bread impossible. That was the problem with the bread and croissant baking side of the business. It was a good source of everyday income - especially from the local restaurants - but the hours she needed to keep in order to do it were an absolute nightmare; especially on the weekends, when the demand for fresh loaves early in the morning was at its peak.

She took advantage of the fact that she didn't need to be up before dawn, and arranged to have brunch with her sister.

They met up at a very fashionable little cafe near to Karen in Godalming.

'I'm genuinely shocked that you dragged yourself away from the bakery this morning Allie.'

'You see… I'm getting better. I'm giving Freddy more responsibility.'

'I'm impressed. You look good, by the way. Having a break on a Sunday obviously suits you.'

'I had a good evening.'

'Oh yes?'

Alexa smiled across the table at her sister.

'I took your advice… I went to London.'

'To see Stephen?'

'Indeed!'

'And?!'

'I told you. I had a good time.'

'That's hardly enough information Alexa. I'm your sister! I want to know everything!'

'I took him to the National Gallery, and then we went to a little Italian place down the road.'

'That must have gone over well. He loves art.'

'So do I.'

'I know that, but this isn't about *you*, Sister dearest. I want to know more about what happened.'

'We have similar tastes in art, and he clearly knows a fair bit about it. I got the feeling he was sharing about a tenth of his knowledge on any particular subject. He was definitely in his comfort zone.'

'Yeah, apparently he has a photographic memory. At least that's what Ollie tells me.'

'Is that really even a thing?'

'I don't know. I heard somewhere that nobody really knows, because it can't be tested. We have to take the word of people who claim to have it. Or we don't, depending on whether or not we believe them. With Stephen, I'm inclined to believe it though.'

'Me too. He does seem rather bright.'

'You really like him, don't you?'

'Yes. I really do.'

'I told you you would. You owe me one! You'll have to name your first girl child after me.'

Alexa laughed and almost chocked on the tea she was drinking.

'It's only been two dates now, Sis… and I'm not really inclined to count the first one. So don't get ahead of yourself.'

'Did you give him a good night kiss, then?'

'Stop trying to make me blush!'

'It worked… you're as red as a post box. You're going to get married and have five children.'

'Don't be ridiculous, Karen!'

'Sorry, I'm just enjoying myself. I know you. You're too prudish to go handing out kisses to random blokes. You only do that sort of thing if you're really serious.'

'Some would simply call that 'sensible', not 'prudish'. I'm just not a slag… you should be pleased about that!'

'Sorry. I just sometimes wish I was more of a slag when I was younger. I've only been in a serious relationship with one man my whole life. I love Ol, and I couldn't imagine myself with anyone else, but you know how it is. A girl can wonder.'

'As long as it's wondering with an 'o', I spose.'

'Obviously. As I say, I'm very happily married. In fact, we're far happier now that he's no longer swimming around in the shark pool.'

'Was his job really that bad?'

'It was awful. It eroded his sense of humour.'

'Stephen's actually quite funny.'

'He is, but only when he's at ease. He tends to live in his head quite a bit.'

'Yeah, I got that impression from some of the things he said. He was reasonably open about himself, although he never really talks about his work.'

'I thought you didn't really care what people did for a living?'

'I don't. Unless they're bankers or other types of degenerates working in finance and posing as polite members of society.'

'You forget that I'm a banker Alexa. Where does that leave me?'

'You're not like the rest of them.'

'You have a chip on your shoulder. You need to think very hard about your position when it comes to people in the city. Those sorts of generalisations are poisonous.'

'Maybe you're right. But still…'

'Let's not argue about it now though. I'm glad you had such a good time with Stephen. He's a great chap. Ollie will also be pleased that the two of you are getting along so well.'

'As long as he doesn't try to warn him off.'

'Why on earth would he do that?!'

'Ollie has known me long enough to know how temperamental I can be. I get the sense he's quite close to Steve.'

'Ollie's very fond of you Allie, I can't imagine that he'd be anything other than encouraging.'

'I'm glad.'

'So when's the next date?'

'I'm seeing him again on Friday. We're going to Guildford, there's apparently going to be a cheese market set up in the High Street.'

'Ah yes. I heard about that. Well, have fun!'

'I've no doubt we will. We're both into that sort of thing.'

***

Stephen spent that Sunday drawing pictures of dragons for Charlie. After their conversation on Thursday, he'd been in touch to ask Stephen to draw him some dragons that he could use to show his art director what sort of thing he was looking for.

It was absolute nonsense, of course. Charles could have downloaded a million pictures from the internet if he needed to demonstrate what he was after. He just wanted a pretext to sell Stephen's work to the company.

Albeit that this was patently obvious, Stephen played along, because he was bored and he thought it would be fun to draw dragons. Also, he didn't think it could hurt to get some pictures together for a portfolio of sorts. Maybe he *was* going to need to reconsider his career options. If he ended up getting the sack from Ashden Cole & Roberts, he didn't know whether or not he could face starting somewhere else. That was assuming he managed to escape the hot water he was in with the FCA. If he *didn't*, then he'd definitely need to find something else to do, and he had no idea what else he was qualified for.

He was having fun, until he received a message from Cindy, containing a link to a mockup website she'd designed for her little awareness campaign. She'd bought the domain:'*www.savethevictimsofthesolentpirates.com*' and written a rather touching piece in the '*about*' section, describing '*the gallant survivors of the pirate attacks*', and the need for the British people to come together to support them.

Stephen nearly had a heart attack. He only calmed down slightly when he realised that she hadn't actually published the site yet. He pleaded with her not to, and she promised that she wouldn't do anything until after their meeting the following Saturday. He tried to get the meeting moved up to earlier in the week, but she insisted that she'd be out of the country until Friday.

Needless to say, he didn't sleep particularly well that night, and his mood wasn't improved the following morning, when Oliver called him to tell him that Karen was getting increasingly uncomfortable keeping his little secret from Alexa. His friend tried to cheer him up by pointing out that she wouldn't be as phased by the whole thing if she didn't think that Alexa was serious about him. That only made him feel worse.

He was due to meet up with his father at Ian's offices just before lunch, to sign those papers, and it wasn't as if that was likely to be a pleasant experience, because the solicitor would most likely insist that he re-read them before signature. He didn't want to re-read them, because he didn't feel like re-living the whole episode again. He also didn't want to discuss it with his father again, and they were due to go for lunch afterwards. He was starting to feel claustrophobic.

After having showered and had his first double espresso, he was hit with another potential source of discomfort… Jim was calling.

'Hi Jim.'

'Morning my boy, how's the leave going?'

'Bloody awful at the minute, Jim.'

'You must have read that stupid article then. I told you to stay away from the papers!'

'No you didn't.'

'I told you to stay away from work, so it was implied.'

'Fair enough. I haven't actually been reading the papers though, my solicitor told me about it.'

'Ah. Good. Are you suing the bastards?'

'No, he says it's not worth it. He doesn't think it crossed any significant lines.'

'Bloody lawyers. Still, I spose they end up saving us from ourselves sometimes. Speaking of which, didn't you borrow my car the weekend before last?'

'I did, I thought Mary gave you the keys back.'

'Oh, yeah, I got the keys alright. But I just got some sort of traffic violation notice. It's a confirmation of receipt of payment for a fine of some description. What the hell were you doing down there in Surrey, son? Drag racing or something?'

'I wasn't going *that* fast Jim. Sorry, I did get done for speeding, but I thought since they gave me the notice, you wouldn't receive anything.'

'Unfortunately the public sector is a lot more efficient than people give them credit for. Don't worry about it though, I was just having a laugh. I was actually just looking for an excuse to give you a ring and find out how you're doing. You can't be that torn up about the pointless little article in the newspaper?'

'No. It's not that, I've just had a succession of minor stresses that are adding up. It's the sum of the parts that's got me a bit miserable.'

'Then why don't you bugger off somewhere for a few days and recharge?'

'I have a meeting with Bridgette tomorrow and a pretty important date on Friday. I don't think I could fit it in.'

'Reschedule with Bridgette, that'll give you three clear days. It's not the longest sojourn, but you'll find that it's amazing what three days can do.'

'Where would I go?'

'Anywhere you want. It's summer. Go to the South of France. You like wine and decent grub don't you?'

'I do.'

'Well then, I tell you what. I have a small place in Nice that's currently empty. I'm having the kitchen renovated at the moment; so for once, none of my supposedly 'poverty-stricken' friends or relatives have been interested in using it. Mary tells me you aren't much of a chef, so you can do without a kitchen, and use the place.'

'Wow Jim, are you sure you don't mind?'

'Of course not. In fact, it would suit me to have a pair of eyes on the builders. It'll keep them on their toes. The place is a bit *'rough and ready'* at the moment, because we're still in the process of kitting it out properly, but it's in a bloody convenient location.'

'That would be amazing, Jim.'

'I'll give the keys to Kenny, and you can arrange to get them from him later. Fly out tonight, so that you can make the most of the time. I'll text you the address.'

'Thanks Jim. You're far too good to me.'

'I know, it's one of my many vices. How's your French?'

'Tolerable.'

'Good. Mine's awful. I want you to explain a few things to the builders for me when you see 'em. I'll put the details in a separate text message to you. The wife's been trying to get me to do it now for a few days, and I keep putting it off. Dealing with that lot is difficult enough face to face, it's bloody murder over the phone.'

'It's the least I can do, Jim. Although don't blame me if they still cock it up. My French is mostly good for ordering food and getting directions.'

'It can only be better than mine. Just give it a shot.'

'Will do!'

Stephen felt considerably better. Jim was right, he just needed some distance to give him perspective.

He called Susan to postpone his meeting with Bridgette for the following week, booked an early evening flight to Nice, and packed a suitcase before heading out to meet up with his Dad and Ian. It made no sense coming back home after seeing his father off.

He put the dragon pictures he'd drawn for Charlie in a large envelope that he had lying around, but he didn't have any stamps, so he'd have to ask

Kenny to post it for him when he collected the keys. He contemplated the idea of sending photos of the work instead, but photos seldom captured drawings properly, and he was a bit old fashioned when it came to his artwork. He got the feeling that if he didn't send the pictures to Charles, he'd get no peace from the man during his trip.

Stephen knew that this was the sort of trip that he needed to take alone. But he wanted to take Alexa. He also knew that it was a bit too soon to ask her to go on an impromptu overseas trip. That sort of thing was quite a big step, and it may scare her off if he came on too strong at this point. He spent the entire trip to Ian's offices agonising over whether or not to ask her. He was no closer to a rational decision when he got there, but he decided that asking her wouldn't hurt, so he sent her a message.

Morning beautiful. I hope you slept well last night.

Morning handsome. I did sleep well, thanks. You?

I don't sleep anymore, I've become an elf. I just meditate for four hours every night. How can I sleep when I can't stop thinking about this impossibly gorgeous woman that kissed me at the station the other night?

She sounds amazing, are you sure she's even real?

I hope so. Although she does have this faintly magical aura.

That's soooo cheesy, but it's cute.

I'm going away for three days. Come with me!

I can't. It's my busiest time of year. Wedding season!

But if it wasn't wedding season? Would you have considered it?

Depends…

On what?

Where are you going?

Nice.

Shit Steve. Yes, that would definitely make it harder to say no.

Are you sure you can't leave Freddy in charge? It's only three days.

I can't. Sorry. But thanks for asking. You get points for that!

I thought it may come across as a little forward.

No. We're past that.

I promise I'll take you once you're able to take some time off. I'll treat this like a reconnaissance mission.

I can't wait. Enjoy your trip. xxx

***

Signing the relevant paperwork for the case wasn't as bad as Stephen expected it would be. But then, he was looking forward to his trip, so that probably helped matters.

His father seemed pleased to see him, and he got on rather well with Ian, which was helpful, because the solicitor clearly put his mind at ease regarding the case. The old man couldn't help being a little concerned about the situation, and even though Stephen tried to ignore this, he was grateful for the sentiment.

After finishing up at Wright & Hill, they went to a nearby pub for a beer and something to eat.

'What's with the suitcase, son? Ian told me he thinks the case is likely to go reasonably well. I don't think you have to skip the country just yet.'

'I'm getting out of town for a few days. I just need some space to think. A change of scenery is likely to do me good.'

'Where you going then, the *Côte d'Azur*, or somewhere posh like that?'

'Yes, actually. I'm going to Nice.'

'Sounds about right.'

'Don't be like that, Dad. My boss has offered to let me use his flat there for a few days. I'll be back by the end of the week.'

'Oh, swipe me. How nice to be one of the rich and famous.'

'More like poor and infamous at the moment.'

'You're the furthest thing from poor I've seen in years, Stephen. You're right, you do need to get some perspective.'

Stephen was irritated. He was trying to be civil with his father, and now the old man was having a dig without any provocation.

'I thought you'd got past being jealous of my success, Dad.'

'Is that what you think? You think I'm jealous of you?'

'Yes.'

'I thought you were a genius. Clearly you're not.'

This is how their fights always started. His father would be overly critical of something Stephen had said or done, then Stephen would respond in kind by behaving like a precocious teenager.

'It depends on your definition of genius. I don't consider myself a genius, by the way. The term's overused. Are you trying to tell me you're *not* jealous of what I've achieved in life so far?'

'I'm not immune to jealousy. Hell, I'm jealous of your brother. But in your case, there's nothing to be jealous of.'

Stephen almost dropped his drink into his lap. He realised this, and put it down on the table carefully before continuing.

'Hold on a minute… Will's a fucking high school rugby coach, Dad. You're just trying to be provocative.'

'I'm not. Will's the happiest little bastard I've ever met. He makes bugger all money, but he wakes up every day and gets out of bed as if he's five years old and it's Christmas morning. I don't get it, to be honest, but *he* does, and that's all that matters.'

'I don't mean to sound like a petulant child here Dad; but I'm thirty eight years old, and I'm a bloody multi-millionaire with a highly lucrative career, and a future so bright you need sunglasses to stop going blind when you try to take a look at it.'

'Aside from the fact that your '*achievements*' have clearly gone to your head; why are you still so miserable then?'

'I'm not.'

'Then why are you running off to hide away in your boss's villa, like some sort of spoilt brat on an American reality show?'

'It's complicated.'

'No it's not. It's as simple as basic arithmetic.'

'Go on then, enlighten me!'

'You don't really believe all that bullshit about how bright your future is, and you're scared shitless, because now that you've had the opportunity to pull your head out of your arse, you're starting to see your shining career for what it really is.'

'And what is that, then?'

'A glamorous, yet somehow dirtier, version of digging coal.'

'You've gone mad.'

'Have I?'

'Clearly!'

'Do you know why your boss is really sending you to the French Riviera, my lad? Have you used that vast intellect of yours to figure *that* out? Or are you happy to live in denial about it.'

'Oh here we go…'

'Come on Stephen. Be as patronising as you like, but tell me why it is you think he's letting you go and partake of his hospitality.'

'Because we're close, and he sees me as a surrogate son. You may not like that, and I think it's a little cras saying it. But you wanted raw honesty, so there you have it.'

'You're flattering yourself again Stephen. That's not why. You're so blinded by your inflated ego, that you can't interpret what you're seeing, my lad. Your mother ruined you, and I let it happen, so I'm certainly not free of blame on that score.'

'Oh yes?'

'I'd bet my admittedly flimsy little pension on the following: James Roberts has no doubt had you to multiple suppers at his mansion in Chelsea; taken you around half of the fancy golf courses in the country; taken you to dozens of fancy luncheons; allowed you to drive around in at least one of his Chelsea tractors; he's probably even taken you fishing or shooting.'

'So? What of it?'

'He has… hasn't he?'

'How do you know he lives in Chelsea?'

'Good guess. Where else would someone like him choose to live? It seemed to fit.'

'Your point?'

'He's not filling the gaps that your inadequate father left in your terribly prosaic upbringing; nor is he living out the dream of having a son. He's shoring up his investment, like a good economist.'

'That's a little bit cynical. Even for you, Dad.'

'No it aint. It's straightforward. Roberts is getting you used to the good things in life, so that you're motivated to stick it out and look after his company once he's retired. He knows you're incredibly intelligent and capable; but he also knows you're about as street smart as a toddler, so he can manipulate you.'

'Then why is he encouraging me to go off and *find* myself then? How does that fit into this alleged plan?'

'Because he's shitting himself a little, since you stepped out of line and gambled your life savings on a flimsy bit of speculation. He's wondering whether or not you can be trusted with the future of his biggest asset. He's already invested quite a bit in you, but if he has to ditch you now, he won't consider it anything other than a sunk cost.'

'You're wrong.'

'I wish I were, son. But I've been around the block a few times, and I know a stitch up when I see one. It's true that I don't move in the same exalted circles as your dear boss and his partners, but interestingly, I come from the same place that they came from. I've done my research. My background isn't actually that distinct from his.'

'So what. He just made something of himself.'

'Oh, I know that. You just have to ask yourself what he had to do to get there in one working lifetime. I'm not saying he's definitely crooked, I just think it's worth asking yourself the question; and taking the time to consider the whole situation dispassionately.'

'You can believe what you like, Dad. I trust Jim Roberts.'

'I'm not asking you not to. I'm just asking you to consider the possibility that he may not be who you think he is, and his motives may not line up with what you interpret them to be.'

'You're full of shit, Dad.'

'Maybe I am, but I want you to consider these points while you're sunning yourself on the beach in France: how much help did Roberts offer you when you first got into trouble with the FCA? How much distance has he put between you and the company since it happened? How does the timing of packing you off to the continent map on to the consideration of your position by the FCA's investigative team?'

Stephen had to stop and think about those questions. They were difficult enough that he couldn't just answer them off the cuff. After an uncomfortable minute of silence he was able to martial his thoughts sufficiently to venture a response.

'Jim found himself conflicted when it happened, so he obviously couldn't step in and give me any direct assistance. He isn't in control of company policy in situations like this. Distancing me from the company is not only good business, it's legally sound; and frankly, I don't follow that last little point of consideration.'

'Well, let's put it this way: You've only just signed your affidavit, and it'll likely be submitted for consideration later this afternoon. Practically speaking, it'll only land up in the hands of the right people tomorrow. Roberts will know this, because the company's lawyers have a legitimate right to know it, and they'll be harassing somebody at the FCA so that they can stay up to date with what's happening.'

'So?'

'If they find your explanation wanting, and decide to conduct a full hearing, you'll be far enough away for the company to close ranks in your absence. The physical distance may seem abstract to you, but you'll be surprised how important it is from a psychological point of view. If the FCA buy your story and drop the case, you can return the conquering hero. Roberts will be waiting for you at the airport with a cigar and bottle of Veuve Clicquot. He'll also likely offer you a promotion. You'll be ever so grateful for the Riviera holiday, the fancy plonk, and the bonhomie engendered by the warm welcome, that he'll end up owning you.'

'I thought *I* was the one with the vivid imagination. You forget that Jim is the one who has me seeing a bloody psychologist so that I can figure out what I want, and he's been encouraging me to consider my career carefully.'

'Let me guess; he also want's you to start dating?'

'What on earth does that have to do with it?'

'Probably more than all of the rest of that stuff put together. If you get serious with somebody, you'll become even more malleable, because your partner will quickly become used to the lifestyle and you'll instantly become more invested in a secure and lucrative future. Not to mention the fact that both you and your partner will remain tied up in your professional identity.'

'I don't see how that's a bad thing.'

'It isn't a bad thing, unless it comes at the cost of your happiness. For once in your life, take a lesson from your brother, Stephen. He *is* a rugby coach, he doesn't just do it to pay the bills. It doesn't even always *pay* the sodding bills. But he doesn't give a toss, he just makes a plan.'

'Sounds marvellous.'

'My greatest ambition for you is that you end up like that one day.'

'For fuck sakes, Dad. You're lucky I'm well off. I'm probably going to have to put you in one of those mental care homes soon.'

'You'll pay for it then? Last time I checked you were as mean as the grave.'

'I'm happy to pay for things that are necessary.'

'Touché.'

Although his Dad's position on Jim was controversial, Stephen had to concede (internally) that it was, at the very least, superficially plausible. Being emotionally invested in his own narrative regarding Jim was one thing, but he couldn't be intellectually dishonest about the situation; so he grudgingly agreed to consider the old man's questions carefully during his impending trip. He'd already forced himself to engage in the entire debate, which was something he'd never actually done before - he usually stormed out after about two or three minutes - so he was resolved see the rest of the exercise through.

His father could see that he'd managed to plant a seed in Stephen's mind, so he left it at that. They finished their lunch, engaged in some small talk, and parted ways on a reasonably amicable basis.

Stephen went to meet Kenny so that he could pick up the keys to Jim's flat and give him the envelope to send on the way to the airport; and his Dad headed for Euston station.

19

Stephen's plane departed Heathrow at exactly five o' clock that evening, and landed in Nice at five minutes past Nine. It was only a two hour flight, but the difference in time zones lost him an hour. Fortunately, he'd carried his small suitcase on with him, so he didn't have to wait to reclaim any baggage. He hadn't eaten anything on the plane, and he was starving.

Jim's flat was right in the hub of the fashionable Carre D'Or Terrace, so it was fairly easy to get to. It was a ten minute bus trip up the coast from the airport, and the busses ran frequently. He could have taken a taxi, but the cost was exorbitant, and he was still reeling from his father's suggestion that he was living the lifestyle of the rich and famous. So as if to prove some sort of point to himself, he took the bus.

It dropped him off on Rue Rossini, two blocks above his destination, and almost directly opposite a very good looking Bistro on Rue Alphonse Karr. It was just after half past nine. He realised that if he went to drop off his suitcase before heading out to look for something to eat, he ran the risk that he wouldn't find a place with an open kitchen; so tried his luck and was able to get a table across the road.

He was fortunate to get in, because the place was packed, and he suspected that it was the sort of establishment where you'd ordinarily have to book quite far in advance in order to get a table. It helped that he wasn't part of a larger party of covers.

France was one of the few places he'd been to, where it was easy to find a table for one; and eating alone at a restaurant didn't make him feel awkward. It was probably because the French considered eating out to be as common as picking up a takeaway coffee.

He ordered grilled sole, pre-ordered a Grand Marnier soufflé for dessert, and opted for a bottle of Chateau Saint-Maur rosé.

Another interesting thing about eating out in France, was that ordering a bottle of wine for yourself wasn't considered remotely odd or excessive, even if you did it at lunchtime.

After the first glass of wine, and half a baguette, he felt himself beginning to unwind. By the time he'd finished his meal, he felt almost relaxed.

Jim's flat was just less than ten minute's walk away from the restaurant, so Stephen didn't bother trying to get a taxi. The weather was sublime, and walking through the streets of Nice was far from unpleasant. It was in a block that occupied the southwest corner of Rue de la Buffa and Rue Maccarani. You couldn't really get more central and convenient than that. He estimated that it was probably less than a five minute walk from the beachfront, and there were dozens of shops and restaurants in the immediate vicinity.

The flat itself was immaculate, and beautifully appointed. Jim's wife must have been in charge of the interior decoration, because there was no way that his old boss would have had the time or inclination to pay the sort of attention to detail necessary to create something that well executed.

The floors were solid engineered walnut, polished to the extent that you could almost see your reflection in them; the walls were white, and were adorned by a collection of colourful Fauvist prints, mostly including the works of Matisse and Derain. Stephen got the impression that the theme would continue throughout the flat, and smiled to himself when he considered this. People who themed the artwork in their homes this strictly were most often the same as those who filled their shelves with old books that they had no intention of reading.

The entrance to the long, narrow kitchen was only a few feet from the front door, so the builders hadn't managed to make too much of a mess getting to and from their workspace.

Stephen was surprised that they were renovating the kitchen, given how well-finished and stylish it was; but he could see that they were obviously trying to install an additional eye-level oven, and remove the existing under-counter one. They evidently did a fair deal of entertaining in the flat, but it seemed a little excessive. Jim had given him the list of further instructions to pass on to the builders, which included various amendments to the shelving arrangements inside certain of the cupboards, and replacement of various small fittings throughout the room. Looking at the kitchen in its current state made him realise just how pedantic the proposed changes were.

The passage from the front door opened up into a combined sitting room and dining area, the latter of which held a stylish glass eight seater dining room table, and the former, two uncomfortable looking blue sofas which seemed as if they'd been made specifically to fit the space.

There were three bedrooms, one of which had an exquisitely designed en suite bathroom; a small utility room; and a large guest bathroom with a vastly oversized shower.

Although it didn't have a television, a microwave, or Wi-Fi; it wasn't remotely *'rough and ready'*, as Jim had described it.

He felt dirty from his trip, so he had a shower before turning in for the night. He was exceedingly grateful for the use of the place, although his father had half-ruined the experience for him by suggesting that his employer's motives weren't as charitable as they purported to be. Fortunately, he was tired enough that his thoughts on the subject didn't keep him up for long.

***

Stephen woke the following morning to the sound of two builders clattering about in the kitchen. Jim had evidently had the presence of mind to inform them that they'd be working around a houseguest, so when he shuffled through to the kitchen, he was happy to discover that they weren't surprised to see him.

After a brief introduction, he offered to try and find some coffee, which gesture instantly endeared him to his new acquaintances.

Fortunately, he was able to follow through, because Jim had a sealed bag of beans, conveniently stored above his coffee machine. Even more fortunately, the machine was similar enough to the one Stephen had at home, to make it easy for him to operate. It had a built in grinder so he didn't have to do anything more onerous than filling it with water and coffee beans, and pressing a button. This was a relief, not only because he was dying for a coffee, but also because he got the feeling that the French kitchen fitters would probably have gone on strike if he'd offered them instant coffee.

The sun was already up, and it looked as though the weather was going to be spectacular. If Jim *was* trying to butter him up by sending him to this little piece of French paradise, it was working. The flat was on the third floor of the building, and although it had a balcony, it didn't have a sea view. But the view from the east facing windows was outstanding; you could even see the outline of the Mont Boron hills over the rooftops in the distance.

He got dressed, grabbed his sketchbook and some pencils, and headed out to explore his surroundings.

He'd never spent any time in Nice. He'd only passed through once, during a backpacking holiday he'd taken in the South of France with Oliver and Charlie when they were still students. They'd spent some time looking at girls on the beach, and drinking at a bar in one of the less salubrious parts of town, but they hadn't really bothered taking in any of the sights.

It wasn't going to be hard finding somewhere to sit and enjoy a leisurely croissant and a few espressos; but he didn't stop at the first place he came across. He headed down the Rue de la Liberté until he found the tram tracks to the east, and managed to find his way down to the tram stop at Masséna. He boarded the tram and it took him down to the edge of the old city, which was considerably closer than he'd imagined it would be.

It was mid-morning, and the place was already buzzing. He wandered through the narrow streets until he got to the old Cathedral, and was lucky enough to get a table at one of the many little cafe's surrounding the small courtyard outside the building.

He ordered a double espresso, and a croissant, and settled in like one of the locals. He didn't plan on extending himself too much, and he spent a couple of hours sketching the Cathedral and the colourful buildings around the courtyard.

He considered it a bit of a waste that he was only sketching these buildings, because their unique yellow, pink and orange colouring was what made them interesting. Some of them looked like glasses of diluted cordial that had been left out long enough for the colour to drain away from the top and deepen at the bottom. Even the green shutters were irregularly weathered.

He felt like he was sitting in the middle of an oil painting. It was no wander so many artists used to frequent the area.

At around midday, he decided to head north towards Cimiez, because he wanted to go and see the Marc Chagall and Matisse museums, and both of them were in this area. He stayed on foot and found that it was actually far easier getting around this way than figuring out the various bus routes. In any event, nothing was particularly far away from anything else, and it only took him just under an hour to walk back to Le Carré d'Or from the Matisse museum.

He hadn't bothered eating anything for lunch, and decided to have an early supper at a decent restaurant close to the flat. After running some searches and phoning around a bit, he managed to find the sort of place he was looking for, and treated himself to another exceptional meal, and another decent bottle of wine.

This was precisely what he considered to be the ultimate holiday, and he he was slightly annoyed with himself for not having done it sooner. Although he *did* wish that Alexa was with him.

He spent the following two days in much the same fashion as he'd done on the first. Waking up late; wandering around the more interesting areas; taking in the various cathedrals, squares and art museums that gave the place its cultural charm; drawing some of the more interesting monuments he visited; and enjoying ridiculously good food and wine at some of the best restaurants in town.

He didn't really spend any time on the Promenade des Anglais, or the beach - they weren't really his thing - but the sea air was a welcome feature, even though it seemed to make him more sleepy than usual (although he suspected that could also have had something to do with the fact that he'd been ordering wine by the bottle).

He wasn't ready to go home at the end of the week, and was specifically unimpressed with the notion of flying out on one of the earliest flights of the day on Friday. But he was motivated by the fact that he had another date with Alexa that afternoon, the prospect of which excited him even more than the prospect of another day in paradise.

***

Stephen's plane landed at eight thirty on Friday morning. He'd regained the hour he'd lost when he left earlier in the week. On landing and adjusting the time on his watch, he realised that he probably could have gotten away with taking a slightly later flight. But he hadn't wanted to risk any delays which could have caused him to be late for Alexa that afternoon. They were due to meet in Guildford at two o' clock.

He took the tube from the airport into the city so that he could meet with Kenneth to return Jim's keys. He didn't have any intention of going near the office, and he didn't want to bother Kenny again over the weekend.

They met at a small artisan coffee shop a few blocks away from the office.

'Hi Ken!'

'Hi boss, how was the trip?'

'Too short.'

'I hear you. Still, what was *'casa del Roberts'* like? Is it as grand as I imagine?'

'It's like the inside of a fancy interior design shop, if that's what you mean.'

'So a bit soulless then. That's a pity.'

'You aren't taken in by that sort of thing then, Ken?'

'Naa. I like the idea of a holiday place with a bit of character. You know, rustic but comfortable furniture on concrete floors, with faded old Persian rugs and mismatched crockery. Not the staged kind though, the kind that grows into itself over years of subtle neglect. I don't know, I just thought that Jim would be the sort of chap who'd live like that on holiday.'

Stephen smiled across at his young protégé. The more he got to know him, the more he liked him. He felt exactly the same way about what a perfect Mediterranean holiday home should be. Although he hadn't considered it in nearly as much detail as Kenny had.

'I don't know so much, I think he lets Mrs Roberts just do as she pleases. Clearly she's not enamoured with the notion of mismatching crockery or worn sofas. Who really knows what Jim's into? He might be the same.'

Kenny gave Stephen a curious look. There was something in his boss's tone that he'd never picked up before when Stephen spoke of Roberts.

'Can I ask you something personal, boss?'

'Of course you can, Ken.'

'You won't get pissed off with me?'

'That's a chance you'll have to take. I can't promise that sort of thing blindly.'

Kenny went silent and looked at him thoughtfully before speaking. Stephen could tell that the young man was choosing his words with care.

'Are you starting to suspect that Jim isn't the person you think he is?'

'What makes you say that?'

'I'm a perceptive individual, boss. I sensed a bit of bitterness in your tone there, and the context led me the rest of the way.'

'Bloody hell, Kenneth.'

'Am I wrong though?'

'No. Although I don't think it's appropriate for us to discuss that sort of thing.'

'Why not?'

'Because I'm your boss, and Jim's mine.'

Kenny laughed.

'In life?'

'What do you mean?'

'Is Jim your boss in *life*? As in, outside of the office?'

'No. Obviously not.'

'Didn't think so. But you act like it sometimes. I get that it's a respect thing. It's why I always call you '*boss*', even when neither of us are working. I do it because I respect you, and I look up to you, like you look up to Jim.'

'So, what's your point then?'

'I respect you, because I know you respect me. But to be perfectly candid boss, Jim patronises you, and you let him get away with it. I've been trying to summon the courage to point it out to you for a while now.'

Stephen went quiet. He didn't quite know what to say. Part of him was furious with Ken for being so familiar, but when he thought about it a bit more, the feeling was replaced with curiosity.

'You're treading dangerously close to the line here Ken, but *because* I respect you, I'm going to ask you to elaborate a bit.'

'Alright, to be perfectly honest, you shovel shit for James Roberts, and all he does is pat you on the back from time to time, and string you along with promises of promotions and large bonuses. He drags you around golf courses so that he can chat you up and try to convince you that he has your best interests at heart. By the way, he knows you don't like golf. So do I. It's obvious. He makes you play, because he *can*. It's a power thing.'

'That's how the world works Ken. You eat shit until you get to the point at which you no longer have to.'

'You're wrong, boss. You *always* eat shit! The volume doesn't even diminish over time; you just get used to the taste.'

'That's incredibly cynical for someone your age, Kenny.'

'It's just realistic, boss. I'm not bitter about it.'

'Why not? In fact, why don't you hate *me*? I send you on stupid personal errands like my old bosses used to do with me; drag you around to lunches, and do other ridiculous things like that.'

'The main thing is that you've never patronised me, boss. You do the other things, because you've been conditioned by Jim, and those of his ilk, to consider it standard operating procedure. I like hanging out with you, and I like doing things for you, because I respect you and you're an incredible teacher. You're considerably smarter than Roberts and his cronies, and you know it, but they've been taking advantage of your good nature for years.'

'I don't agree with you there, Ken. I've done very well with the help of the company, and Jim's even been encouraging me to find meaning in things other than money recently. That doesn't seem like the sort of thing he would do if he were simply using me.'

'Let me guess… the whole, *'happiness is more important than money'* thing, and *'money is just a means to an end'* thing?'

'Those *'things'* are true, Ken.'

'Oh, no doubt. But they're so true that they've become trite. The problem is that you only ever hear them from obscenely rich bastards, who've only had the relevant epiphanies after they've made enough money to retire to their gaudy flats on the Riviera.'

'Now you're the one who sounds bitter.'

'I'm not remotely bitter, boss. Trust me. It just fascinates me that nobody else seems to notice the bullshit. There seems to be an inverse relationship between aptitude and self-respect in our line of work.'

'Then why do you stick it out?'

'I'm lucky. I don't have to. Not for long, anyway.'

'What do you mean? Is this your elaborate way of quitting?'

'No. I'll probably stay at Ashden, Cole & Roberts longer than you, boss.'

'And how long do you think that'll be, then?'

'At least another five years. I'm not done learning.'

'So you think I'll get the sack then?'

'No, I think they'll promote you when you're cleared by the FCA.'

'Are you being sarcastic, because I'm not in the mood. I've just come from a very pleasant holiday, and you're ruining what's left of the afterglow.'

'Sorry boss. I'm just angry, because I can see what they're doing to you, and I don't like it. You have to understand that I never wanted to have this conversation with you. But I know that the FCA thing is likely to be finalised soon, and I wanted to explain my views on the whole situation before anything else happened.'

'Alright then, why do you think I'll leave? Notwithstanding your generous prediction regarding my supposed promotion?'

'I think you'll leave within the next five years, because you're intelligent and you're not devoid of self-respect.'

'And you? Why stick it out? What do you plan to do with your life?'

'I'll probably travel for a bit before I decide.'

'And do what? Wait tables?'

'No. I'm one of those nasty little trust fund brats. If all goes according to plan, my assets will be released to me after I turn twenty nine. By the way, I'm far wealthier than James Roberts.'

'But...'

'You're wondering why I've been running around as a slightly overqualified errand boy.'

'Yes.'

'My dear old Dad cut me off when I left home.'

'Seriously?'

'I say '*cut me off*', but that's a bit of an unfair exaggeration. He bought me an old car, and rented me a shitty apartment with no furniture in it other than a bed and a kettle. Then he made me get a student loan, and suggested that I study finance, because he felt that I should understand how to manage my own money when I eventually got my hands on it. I agreed, because I couldn't think of anything else that interested me, and I was mature enough to appreciate the wisdom of it.'

'You're kidding me.'

'Nope. I had to get random odd jobs while studying, so that I could afford to pay for food, petrol and utilities. Once I finished my degree, the old man took the car back from me, and had the lease signed over into my name, so that I no longer relied on him for anything other than the odd Sunday lunch.'

'Shit.'

'Yeah, it's not what you think it ought to be like for people with my background. But once I got over the initial shock, I came to appreciate the fact that my Dad knew exactly what he was doing.'

'It sounds a bit harsh, to be honest. So what conditions do you need to meet to release your Trust assets?'

'That's one of the more brilliant aspects of my Dad's plan. The Trust is structured in such a way that the assets can't be accessed until I can demonstrate that I have a genuine qualification, and that I've managed to pay it off myself. So I have to pay off the student loan before I get anything. That way, the trustees can be reasonably certain that I've figured out how to manage money, and look after myself. Getting the finance degree on its own would never do that.'

'Interesting. Except that it seldom makes financial sense to accelerate payments on a student loan in this country. People normally pay undergraduate loans off over more than twenty years. Most of the time it works out cheaper from a gearing perspective.'

Kenny laughed again, and gave his boss a pitying look. One of the most curious things about Stephen was the fact that his raw intelligence seldom overruled his pedantry when it came to managing basic spending, and Kenny had grown to learn this.

'You're right. But let's face it; that sort of thing doesn't really apply, in my situation, does it?'

'No. I suppose it doesn't.'

'What the Trust mechanism *has* done, is teach me the value of money; because it's bloody hard paying off that kind of cash in an accelerated time period. The lawyers structured the Trust deed so well, that I don't really have any way of cheating it. The only way I can pay the loan off is by living well beneath my means, and making intelligent investments with every single pound I can spare.'

'You're not joking. In fact, it seems almost impossible in your estimated timeframe, given what you've been earning and what you can reasonably expect to earn within the next five years.'

'That's true, but now you've taught me about short trading, I could probably do it in half that time.'

'Don't go down that road Ken, look where it's just got *me*.'

'Somehow, I don't think the size of my potential investments will come up on the FCA's radar, boss.'

'Fine, just don't make any trades before letting me have a look at them.'

'Thanks, boss. Anyway, I understand that I won't be able to simply short-trade my way to riches. I've learnt a hell of a lot from you, and I'm growing my little portfolio quite steadily.'

'I'm happy to hear that.'

'I didn't want you to find out about my plans this way, to be honest. I've always felt a little guilty that I haven't been straightforward with you, but I didn't ever want you to perceive me as a spoilt brat. I know you have a bit of an issue with the private school crowd.'

'You needn't worry about that, Ken. I respect the fact that you haven't just been given a handout upfront, and I admire your resilience.'

'Do you agree with my assessment regarding Jim though, boss?'

'No. I don't. But I'm grateful for your candour; it couldn't have been easy to tell me what was on your mind. You're not the first person who's addressed those concerns with me recently either. I do take them seriously, and I plan on making my own assessment of the situation; in time.'

20

Stephen's chat with Kenny took longer than expected, and he barely had enough time to go home and change before catching the train to Guildford.

Fortunately though, he made it with about a quarter of an hour to spare, and he met Alexa outside the small station on the other end.

She was wearing a short, green summer dress, and a smile that gave away her enthusiasm for seeing him. He instantly forgot about the difficult conversation he'd had with Kenny that morning, and greeted her with a hug and a kiss that rivalled the last one they'd had. She seemed pleased by the fact that he was clearly just as happy to see her, as she was to see him.

'I missed you this week.'

'Don't be so needy, Steve.'

'Are you saying you haven't missed *me*?'

'Oh, I have, I just wasn't going to *say* it. I can't have that sort of thing going to your head.'

'Well, now it's out there, you can't take it back.'

They both laughed as she grabbed his hand and led him down towards the town centre. They went over the bridge, crossed Onslow Street, and walked through the gauntlet of chain restaurants on Friary Street to get to the bottom of the High Street.

'So what's the story with this cheese market then?'

'I'm not too sure to be honest, it's not a standing thing, like the rather large *'chilli and cheese festival'* that they had at Shalford park a few weeks ago. That's apparently quite an event. Maybe this market is just all the leftover cheese from *that*.'

'Sounds good.'

'Are you being sarcastic Stephen?'

'No, I love cheese.'

'Good. Me too!'

They headed up to the security boom which cordoned off the bottom of the High street. There were stall tents running all the way up the steep, brick-paved street on both sides, and despite the fact that it looked like it was likely to rain, the locals were out in force.

'It's fairly busy for a Friday.'

'Not really… there's a fruit and veg market on the road that runs parallel to this every Friday, and it's always as busy as this, even early in the morning. I often come to buy berries for my cakes, when they're in season.'

'I've never been to Guildford before. It looks like a nice place. I love the bricked street.'

'Yeah, so do I. But you probably guessed that. I do live in a village that looks like it comes out of a Beatrix Potter book.'

'You do indeed. How was your week?'

'Murderous. I'm glad I've taken the afternoon off. I'm actually closing on Sunday, because Freddy and I are both shattered. How was your week, Steve?'

'I want to lie and tell you it was also arduous.'

'Lucky sod!'

She laughed and shook her head.

'Nice must have been amazing. I'm jealous!'

'I'm taking you next time. You've already agreed, remember?'

'You're trying to bribe me to keep you around.'

'Absolutely. I figure my looks and charm can only go so far.'

'They certainly don't go as far as the south of France. Your game is improving, Steve.'

'What can I say? You're keeping me on my toes.'

They made their way through the various stalls slowly, and sampled a myriad of different cheeses. Stephen bought far more cheese than he'd bargained for, and only realised it when they got to the top of the hill, and he found himself carrying two shopping bags full.

Alexa also noticed his haul at this point, and laughed at him.

'You planning a cheese party, Steve?'

'I wasn't, actually. I just got carried away there. You distracted me.'

'I never knew I had the power to make men buy loads of cheese.'

'Use your gift wisely, Alexa. You know what they say about power and responsibility.'

'The other people on the train home are going to love you.'

'Oh god, I'm about to become a public transport pariah.'

'It's my way of chasing other women away from you, Steve.'

'Well, then I'll run with it!'

'Good! Come on, let's go and see if we can get a coffee.'

She led him a short distance back down the High street and ducked through a small, arched corridor that opened up into a mini square, which held an assortment of small tables and chairs under umbrellas. They found an open spot, and Steve went to order coffees. When he got back to the table, he saw something which made his heart sink. Between him, and the table where Alexa was sitting, was somebody else he knew, holding a takeaway coffee and peering around for an open seat.

He contemplated running down the other side of the corridor, and then around the block, so that he could come back in from the other side. But he'd ordered coffee to stay, so he couldn't very well run off with the tray and cups. Even if he could have done, he wasn't handy enough with drinks trays to manage that sort of thing without spilling everything on the way. All of this ran through his mind before he decided to forge ahead and hope he wasn't noticed.

He made it all the way to the table before he was recognised.

'Steve?'

'Oh, hi Cindy. Fancy seeing you here. I thought you'd gone away for the week.'

She laughed and smiled at him.

'You're a bad listener Steve, I told you I was coming home today, remember?'

'Oh right, yes.'

'Actually, I've been thinking about you all week. I wanted to give you a call, but I've been a bit tied up.'

'Ah…'

Alexa was now looking at them curiously. Cindy was, as ever, looking like something out of a modelling catalogue; and she seemed to be somewhat more than a casual acquaintance.

'Steve, are you going to introduce me to your friend?'

At this point, Stephen could feel his heartbeat in his ears. He went silent and almost dropped the tray he was holding.

'Umm…'

'Hi, I'm Cindy.'

'Alexa.'

'Pleased to meet you Alexa.'

'And you. How do you know Steve?'

'Oh, we met a few weeks ago. On a blind date.'

Stephen felt like he was about to vomit, but he somehow managed to put the tray down on the table in front of Alexa. He wanted to say something but the words just didn't present themselves.

'Really?'

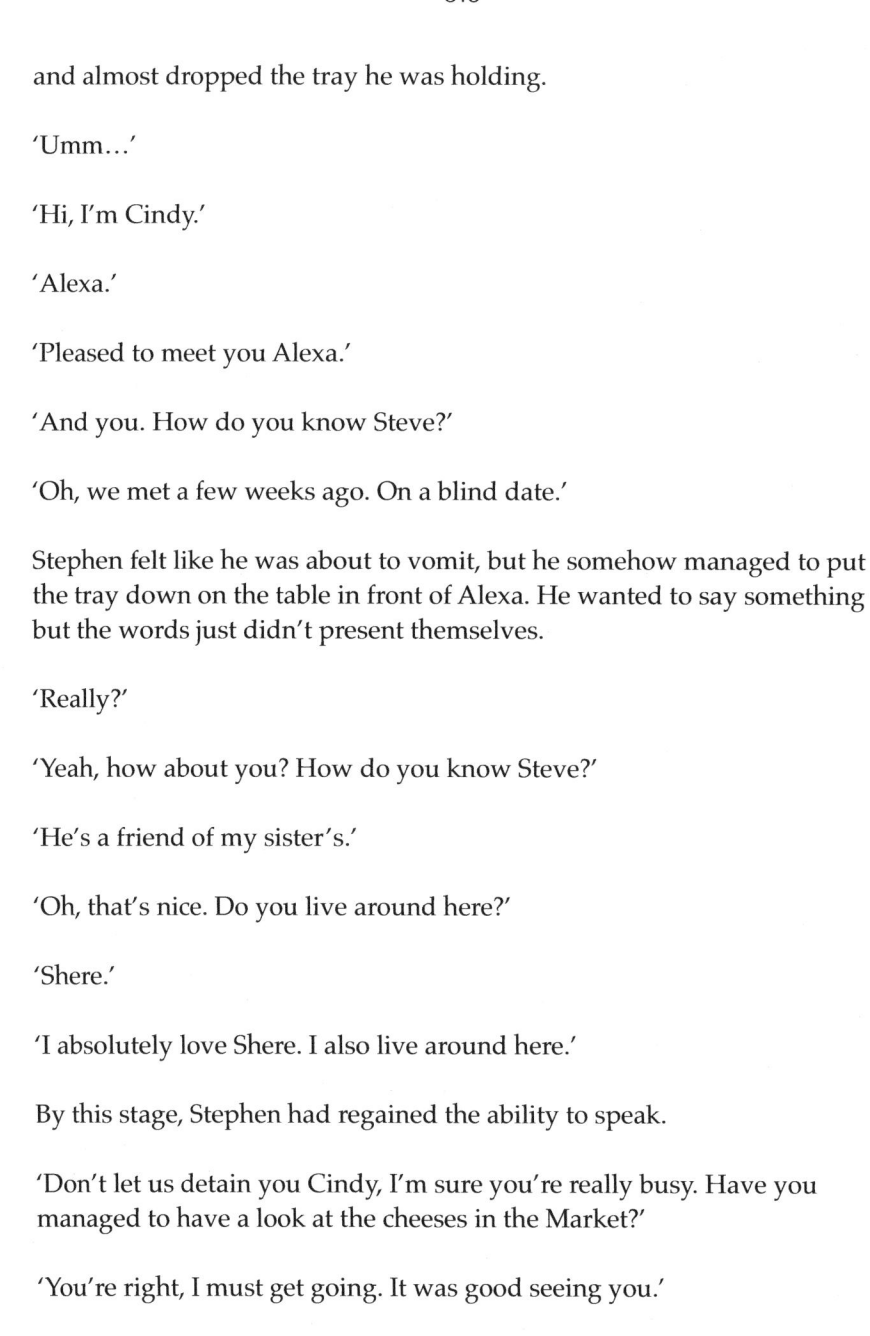

'Yeah, how about you? How do you know Steve?'

'He's a friend of my sister's.'

'Oh, that's nice. Do you live around here?'

'Shere.'

'I absolutely love Shere. I also live around here.'

By this stage, Stephen had regained the ability to speak.

'Don't let us detain you Cindy, I'm sure you're really busy. Have you managed to have a look at the cheeses in the Market?'

'You're right, I must get going. It was good seeing you.'

'You too.'

'I'm sure I'll see you around, Alexa.'

'Nice meeting you, Cindy.'

'Oh Steve, don't forget our brunch tomorrow! I'll text you the details.'

She smiled and walked off towards the market. Stephen sat down and tried to smile, but his expression looked more like a grimace.

'So Steve. Fancy that... you really get around, don't you?'

'I can explain.'

'I hope so.'

'I'm most definitely *not* seeing Cindy.'

'Sound's like you're seeing quite a lot of her. Sounds like you even have another date planned for tomorrow.'

'It's not a date. I promise you.'

'Does *she* know that?'

'Well...'

'Wow, Stephen. Are you hedging your bets here?'

'Of course not. She's just one of those people who don't ever take no for an answer, so I sort of agreed to see her, and I was going to use the opportunity to extricate myself.'

She sat back, tilted her head, and looked at him as if he was a dog who'd been caught shitting on the carpet.

'It seems to me like you *have* been hedging your bets. She's clearly interested in you, and you're clearly powerless in her presence. So what's your plan? Are you going to just go on seeing both of us until one of us falls out of the picture?'

'No. I'm not seeing Cindy. I only agreed to see her again so that I could get rid of her.'

'Stephen. You don't need to see someone in order to get rid of them. Is there something you're not telling me?'

Stephen went quiet. The last thing he wanted to do was explain the full situation with Cindy to Alexa, but he realised that he'd just run out of options.

'Yes.'

'Marvellous…'

'Alright. Let me get us some more coffee before I tell you. It's embarrassing, that's why I've been so cagey about it.'

'No. You don't get to run off and buy yourself time to come up with a story. Tell me now, or you can find your way back to London and delete me from your list of contacts.'

He breathed out deeply, took a sip of his tepid coffee, and looked up at her weakly.

'She has leverage on me, and I've been trying to come up with a way of dealing with it.'

'My god, Stephen. Leverage?'

'Well, it's not even leverage… yet. But it will be.'

She just looked at him.

'Right, so I did go on a date with her a few weeks back. We got set up on a blind date by a chap who works for me. This was before I met you.'

'Okay.'

'The date was rubbish. I was in a bad mental space, and I didn't like her. Instead of behaving like a normal decent human being and getting out of the situation politely, I decided to have a little fun at her expense and I concocted a stupid story about what I did for a living, thinking it would chase her off.'

'Right. I still don't get it.'

'Wait till you hear the rest.'

'I'm fascinated.'

'I told her that I was a produce market trader, and that I lost all of my goods and equipment at sea.'

'What?'

'To be a bit more precise, I told her that I was attacked by Somali pirates on the ferry on the way to the Isle of Wight, and that I was thrown overboard and had to swim to shore.'

'You're joking?'

'I wish I was.'

'Surely she didn't believe that bullshit.'

'She's not a bright girl, Alexa. That's part of why I'm such an arsehole. I took advantage of her credulity. I thought she'd bugger off once she thought that I was penniless.'

'But she didn't. Clearly.'

'Quite the opposite, in fact. Turns out she's actually a decent person, which, rather poetically, turned the situation against me.'

'She wanted to help you?'

'Yes. She wants to launch some sort of social media campaign to raise funds and awareness for my plight, and the plight of the other *victims* of the pirates. She's even designed a website. I can show you.'

'Oh shit!'

'She hasn't published the site yet, because I've managed to hold her off until we've spoken again. That's why I agreed to see her tomorrow.'

'Why didn't you just come clean when she proposed it?'

'Because it gets even more interesting.'

'How so?'

'Because just before she revealed her plan with the website, I discovered that she's actually the daughter of the chairman of the company I work for.'

'So let me get this straight… you had no idea who she was?'

'Blind date…'

'But…'

'Remember I told you the date was set up by one of my subordinates. He met her at an office party and just thought she was friends with one of the secretaries.'

'Oh my word.'

'So now you understand my predicament. If I don't see her tomorrow and figure out a way to diffuse the situation tactfully, I'll probably lose my job, or at least my future prospects at the company I work for.'

'Wow, Steve. You really know how to get yourself into trouble.'

'It seems that way. Please don't hate me.'

'I don't hate you, Steve. I just have some trust issues. But I don't think you could have made that story up on the fly, so why don't you go and get us another coffee and we can try to pretend that it never happened.'

'Thank you. I promise, it's the truth.'

'I suppose it could have been worse. At least you aren't boring Steve. I could have ended up with one of those obnoxious tools in the finance industry.'

She gave him a pitying look and then smiled, before gesturing for him to go and replace their drinks. When he returned, she looked at him thoughtfully. This time she wasn't smiling.

'Be careful with Cindy, Steve. I don't think she's stupid. She's a predator, and she likes you.'

'You think so?'

'I do. You're pretty bad at picking up signals, aren't you Steve?'

'Appalling.'

'You're lucky I think that's cute.'

'I wasn't going for *cute*, but I'll take it. I'll also take the advice regarding Cindy.'

'Good, because you're mine now. I'm not sharing you with some hot little blonde with a saviour complex.'

Stephen smiled. I didn't take any time at all for her comment to sink in.

The rest of the date went well, and Alexa agreed to see him again on Sunday. In fact, she agreed to go to London and have lunch with him at his flat. He admitted that he couldn't cook, but he now had enough cheese to feed about a dozen people, so they decided that it would be cheese and biscuits.

He was't looking forward to his meeting with Cindy the next morning, but the thought of seeing Alexa again so soon was exciting enough to make up for it.

Charlie had wanted to meet up with him earlier in the week, and even threatened to gate crash his holiday at one point, so he was forced to agree to see his mate that evening, even though he was dead tired. He had absolutely no intention of going out though, so he invited Charlie to have a takeaway pizza with him at home.

Fortunately, he got no resistance to this suggestion, and Charlie even volunteered to pick up the food for them, instead of having it delivered.

He arrived at eight thirty, about an hour after Stephen got home, brandishing two very large pizza boxes and a bottle of wine.

***

'Hey Charlie! Thanks for bringing food, I'm starving!'

'It's a pleasure. Although it feels like I'm bloody courting you.'

'I get the feeling you *are*. Clearly you got the dragon pictures I sent.'

'Yeah. They were outstanding.'

The two of them sat down at Steven's small dining room table and opened both pizza boxes. They didn't bother with plates.

'They were fun to do, to be honest.'

'Even my art director was forced to admit that he liked them.'

Stephen smiled at his friend, and sighed deeply.

'I'm not quitting my job to come and draw pictures of dragons, Charles. Even though the thought is mildly appealing.'

'Come on Stevie, why the hell not?'

'Because I'm a successful trader.'

'Are you really?'

'Was that an unsubtle dig at my career, mate?'

'I thought it was pretty subtle. But whatever. Admit it Steve, the stuff you do for a living isn't exciting you any more. Maybe it did at one stage, but I can tell that now you're marking time.'

'Marking time?'

'Yeah. You're going through the motions. You're waiting to be promoted, so that you get a bit more status, a bit more money, and a set of golden handcuffs that would be almost impossible to get free of, once you're used to wearing them.'

'I'm almost at the top of the greasy pole Charles. I can just about taste victory. It'd be daft to throw all of the hard work I've done away now.'

'You think the pole doesn't just get higher as soon as you reach a new level?'

'If I can get through the shit I'm currently in, and jump through a few more hoops, they'll make me a director, Charlie. It's what I've always wanted.'

'Always? Since you were a kid?'

Stephen was growing impatient with Charles, he was sick of being interrogated about his career. His father's little outburst was bad enough, then Kenny, and now even Charles was jumping on the bandwagon.

'Of course not. It's a figure of speech.'

'I'm a director, it's not special mate, it's just a title. In fact, it's one I don't even use. I prefer *'lead game designer'*. You know why?'

'Why?'

'Because I *am* a lead game designer. Nobody really *is* a 'director'.'

'I get it. But you know what I mean.'

'I do know what you mean, but I still think you're being intellectually dishonest.'

Stephen shook his head and laughed sardonically.

'You're not being impartial here Charles, you have an agenda. A pretty fucking weak one at that; because it isn't particularly hard to find people capable of drawing dragons. You could open a competition on your website and have half a million candidates to choose from, at least a thousand of whom will be as good, and probably better, than me.'

'So?'

'So why *me*, Charles?'

'Because a little nepotism never hurts.'

'Can you hear yourself, mate?'

'With clarity, Steve. We don't hire people just because they can do what we want them to do. You're right by the way; there are many thousands of people in the world who can do what we want. We hire those of them who we can trust, and who bring more to the table than raw ability.'

'I'm not getting into this with you Charlie, it's mental.'

'My game is mental. But it works, and it's currently the number one MMORPG in the world… by a margin.'

'You're also mental, Charles.'

'Of course I am. But I'm your best mate, and I can see you're dying in that shitty job of yours. The same way I would be dying, if I was working out insurance statistics for a living. If I was killing myself like that, I would expect you to sit me down and tell me I was full of shit.'

'That's a bit dramatic Charlie. I'm just taking a timeout and re-evaluating things.'

'You've already re-evaluated. I can see it in your eyes. You just haven't come to terms with the answer you've arrived at.'

'And you think the answer lies in a cave, guarding treasure and breathing fire.'

'I think the answer is simply something completely different to what you're currently doing. But since you're probably no good at cooking or flower arranging, art isn't a bad option.'

Stephen was now visibly angry. Charles noticed, so he tried to lighten the mood by offering his friend a glass of wine.

'Yes please Charlie, I would love a bloody glass of wine. Open the bottle and I'll get some glasses.'

'Good. Maybe you're just tired, Steve. A drink will calm you down a bit.'

'No it won't, mate. It'll just make it easier for me to tell you to fuck off.'

'That's a bit harsh.'

Stephen found two wine glasses and placed them down firmly in front of his guest. Once Charles had filled them up, he took one by the stem and motioned to his counterpart in the way people do when they're offering to say cheers. Charles reciprocated. They clinked glasses, said 'cheers' and each took a sip before gingerly placing their glasses down on the table.

'Charles. With all the love in the world… fuck off!'

'You don't mean that.'

'Look mate. I've been on this sodding *"journey of self discovery"* for a month now. I'm sick to bloody death of everyone around me telling me who I am, how I'm supposed to feel, how I *do* feel, what I should be doing with my life, and how I've cocked things up. Can you appreciate that?'

'Sure. I get that.'

'My boss told me I needed to find myself; the executive coach he appointed to assess me mirrored the sentiment; and you agreed wholeheartedly with both of them. My father has subsequently told me that he thinks my boss has ulterior motives, a view shared and impertinently expressed by my intern.'

'Ah.'

'Both of these individuals have cast aspersions on my career, and sought to convince me that I've been wasting my life, as if I've been flipping burgers at music festivals for two decades. Now my best mate is lining up to tell me how I'm supposed to live my life. What ever happened to the *"self"* in *"self discovery"*?'

Charlie just stared across at Stephen and gave him a pitying smile.

'Sorry mate. I got carried away. You're right. I shouldn't be pushing you. It's just hard to shut up when those you love seem unhappy. You've seemed unhappy ever since we reconnected with one another, and I formed the opinion that it was the job. I've rather patronisingly foist this opinion on you. It came from a good place though.'

Stephen sighed and grimaced.

'It may be the job, Charlie. But I have to figure it out on my own. It's not that I don't appreciate the advice. It's just that it's muddying the waters, instead of clarifying things for me.'

'I hear you.'

'My boss may be a conniving prick; or my dad may be bitter and jaded by the fact that Jim's muscled in on his territory. My intern is very cocksure, and he's blindly loyal to me for some reason; so his views on the subject may be the result of an overactive imagination and a misguided desire to look out for me. It wouldn't be the first time a subordinate's done something like that.'

'You may have given the poor kid Stockholm syndrome.'

'The though had occurred to me. I also wondered whether or not Jim may have done the same to *me*… but I don't think it works like that.'

'No. Probably not.'

'Jim is what he is. I just need to decide if I can live with that.'

'If you don't get sacked…'

'Yes. Thanks for reminding me.'

'Right now I see it as my only shot at getting you to come and work with me. I know it's selfish, but here's another thought for you to add to the mix Stevie…'

'Go on then…'

'I forgot how much I missed you, and I just want to get to spend more time together. Granted, I've taken it to a bit of an extreme. But I've also realised something about myself recently.'

'What's that?'

'I don't want to make any new friends.'

'Seriously?'

'Think about it Steve. When was the last time you got excited about meeting new people and building personal relationships. I'm not talking about romantic partners; that's different.'

'I can't quite remember, to be honest.'

'That's my point. As you grow older, your circle of friends is far more likely to decrease than it is to expand. I've found that as my circle of friends gets smaller, I'm anxious for the quality of those friendships to improve. By that, I just mean that I want to spend more time with my mates, and get to know them even better than I do. I want to get to know their partners better. If they have kids, I want to know the kids, and I want them to know me.'

'I didn't know you were sentimental about things like that, Charlie.'

'I think we all are, to a certain degree. It just hits us at different times. Do you even know Ollie's kids?'

'No.'

'Me neither. It's unacceptable, mate.'

'You're right about that. I also want to see you and Ol more. I don't know Jen and Amy at all, and I haven't spent any time with Karen since university.'

'That's the thing. It sounds insular and a bit selfish, but I'm not interested in making new friends. I'm happy with the ones I've got, and I want them all to myself.'

Stephen smiled across at his friend and laughed.

'So just tell me you want to spend more time with me Charlie. I share your views on the friendship thing. But we don't have to work together in order to see more of one another. It would probably be counter-productive anyway. You'd get sick of me in about a fortnight.'

'I disagree, but I'm not arguing about the job thing anymore. You've made your point, and I respect that.'

'Good! Let's just eat pizza and talk about something else, until I fall asleep and you have to let yourself out. I've been up since five this morning.'

21

Stephen woke up fairly early the following morning. Charles hadn't stayed very long, so he'd managed to turn in well before midnight. He was actually woken up by a message from Alexa, wishing him luck for his meeting with Cindy. She took the opportunity to warn him again about the fact that she thought Cindy had an agenda, and he got the impression that she was feeling a little insecure.

He replied to her message, assuring her that he was going to follow through with his plan to come clean to Cindy and get rid of her as gently and tactfully as possible. This seemed to placate her, although she insisted that he call her to tell her all about it as soon as it was done.

Mercifully, Cindy had chosen a place relatively close to where he lived, so it would only take him about twenty minutes to get there on the tube. They were meeting at trendy brunch place on St Pancras Square at eleven.

Stephen was slightly early, and managed to find an out of the way table. Cindy hadn't made a booking, because apparently they didn't take them in the mornings.

After his first double espresso, she arrived. He was thankful that he was sitting down, because if he'd been standing, he would probably have fallen over when he saw her. She was wearing tight blue jeans and a short black t-shirt. She looked gorgeous as usual, but that had absolutely nothing to do with Stephen's reaction. The t-shirt had a steampunk skull and crossbones on the front, with a large caption below it that read *"STOP THE SOLENT PIRATES!"*.

'Hi *Steve*! Do you like the T-shirt I designed?'

Stephen was lost for words, he actually thought he may have been dreaming.

'Come on Steve, you don't have to be so shy. I made you one *too*!'

He closed his eyes. He thought that maybe if he *was* dreaming, he could will himself awake.

'Stephen?! Why are your eyes closed.'

'Sorry, I'm just tired.'

'Have some coffee and wake up! Look at the T-shirt! Here's your one, I hope I got your size right.'

She pulled a folded t-shirt out of her large handbag and opened it up to show him. She had an almost child-like grin on her face. She was clearly excited.

'Umm…'

'Don't you like it?'

'Oh fuck… Cindy… listen, before we even go any further. I have something to tell you…'

'You don't *like it*? Everyone *else* seems to like it. I showed my dad, and even *he* thinks it's marvellous. He can't wait to meet you, by the way!'

'Oh god, no! It's not that. It's something else.'

'Well? What *is* it then?'

'Look, I'm not going to beat around the bush on this, and I apologise in advance for being such an unmitigated arsehole. But I lied about the whole pirate thing, Cindy. I was just talking crap the whole time!'

'What?'

'I'm so sorry, you have every right to be mad at me, and even to tell your *dad*, if you feel you have to. I behaved like a complete bastard on our coffee date, and I feel terrible about it.'

'Why would I tell my *father* about something like that?'

'Because he's my boss! I don't sell things at a *street market*, I trade on the *stock market*. I'm a stockbroker, and I work for your dad's company.'

'Anything else? While you're at it, Steve?'

'No. Just that I'm sorry. Really sorry. I don't know what came over me.'

'Well at least you've come clean. It took you long enough…'

She sat down and smiled mirthfully at him across the table. Her reaction didn't seem to fit.

'I know. Again, I'm sorry.'

'I have a confession to make too, Stephen West.'

'What?!'

'I know *exactly* who you are. I always *did*, ever since that intern of yours set us up on the coffee date.'

'But…'

'So here's *my* side of our convoluted little story, Stephen…'

'Please, go on.'

'I first saw you at one of the office parties I attended a few months ago. I don't really enjoy those godawful events, but my father likes me to attend them, because *he* thinks they're fun, and he can't imagine why I wouldn't share his enthusiasm. I think it's his way of proving to me that he does fun things… which is incredibly lame, but I don't have the heart to tell him so.'

'Okay.'

'After fending off the typical neanderthals who try their luck with me, I usually end up drinking on my own and feeling stupid, because I don't really *get* the whole finance thing.'

'Right, so?'

'Your young friend came on to me, and I told him that I only dated men a lot older, and a lot better looking than him. I suppose that last quip was a bit cruel and inaccurate, because he's actually quite attractive, but I'd already had to get rid of about five others by that stage, and I was mildly irritated.'

'I suppose I can understand that.'

'So he pointed *you* out in the crowd, told me that you were his boss, and asked if I'd like him to set us up on a coffee date. I thought you were cute, so I agreed.'

'I then found out that you worked directly under Jim Roberts, who *I* know simply as "*uncle Jim*". He's my godfather, and we're very close.'

'Oh god.'

'Oh god indeed, Stephen. Jim had told me before that you were an absolute genius, and that you were also a good chap. So I was excited to meet you.'

'Shit.'

'We then met up for that coffee, and I *also* behaved a little foolishly, I'll admit. I pretended to be a bit dull and vacuous, because in my experience, the men in your industry tend to *prefer* women like that. I could see that you were a bit bored and preoccupied, and I probably should have dropped the act at that point, but I was slightly put out by the fact that you seemed completely disinterested. So I laid it on a bit thick to try and get under your collar.'

'Well, that worked.'

'Let's not pretend that *my* little indiscretions were worse than *yours* though, Stephen. When you lied to me about what you did, I thought you were just trying to make sure I couldn't track you down again, but when you told me the pirate story, I wanted to fall over laughing (it was bloody hard to keep a straight face). That's when I actually started to *like* you.'

'Ah.'

'I realised that although you were a bit of a prick, you weren't nearly as boring as any of the other chaps I've met from the company. I played along a bit, so as to get some revenge, and also get to know you a bit better. I knew you were shocked that I wanted to see you again, and I revelled in your discomfort.'

'So you're *not* a social media influencer?'

'Fuck no! I have a bloody first class degree in *Greats* from Oxford, you *twat*!'

'Oh...'

'Yeah, go figure. Apparently little blonde girls can *also* go to good universities and get proper degrees in classics and philosophy.'

'I see.'

'But basically, what I'm trying to tell you, Mr West, is that I'm not just a stupid rich bimbo that runs around all day in yoga pants, and thinks that black holes are the things in the road closed off by manhole covers.'

'I'm starting to get that. Although it makes me feel even more of a bloody idiot.'

'It *should*.'

'Honestly, the only reason I made up that story was because I *genuinely* thought that you were one of those dumb barbie dolls that most of my colleagues love to date. I know that's not a valid excuse, I concede that my behaviour was terrible.'

'Good. Because I'm not done with you, Stephen. You are now in my debt, because I *haven't* told my daddy about your ludicrous behaviour, nor have I mentioned anything to uncle Jim!'

'I'm listening.'

'I need you to help me win a bet I've made with daddy dearest.'

'Okay?'

'My father knows I'm bright, but it still baffles him that I've taken no interest in his business. Sometimes I think he wished he had a child who was interested in taking over the company one day.'

'I can understand that. Weren't you ever interested?'

'No bloody way. Besides, I consider it to be menial and boring.'

'Thanks for the compliment.'

'Don't be offended Steve, you're in good company.'

'So what's the story with this bet, then?'

'After a protracted argument with my father about his antipathy for my chosen career, I told him what he does is so easy I could do it in my sleep.'

'Ah. Do you really think that?'

'Of course I bloody don't. But you know how it is in the middle of these arguments. You tend to say stupid things you don't really mean.'

'I know *that* feeling all too well.'

'So I bet him that I could beat him at his own game.'

'How?'

'We've agreed that we will each take a set amount of money - nothing huge, because although I'm a bit of a princess, the mean old sod keeps me on a relatively short leash - and grow it over a period of one year. Whoever has the most money to show for their trading endeavours after the period is the winner, and will keep all the money earned by both parties.'

'I see. So when did the bet start?'

'About two months ago.'

'How's it going?'

'It's a bit of a whitewash at the moment. He's schooling me.'

'What did you expect? Just because he has people like me doing that sort of thing for him nowadays, doesn't mean he's not one of the best in the business. You're mad.'

'That's where you come in, Steve. Help me beat the smug old swine.'

'That's cheating!'

'That's how I'm going to afford a fancy holiday next summer.'

'What if he finds out?'

'How would that happen? He set me up with my own trading account, you can just advise me on the side.'

'I'm not even allowed to do that currently. I'd be breaking the law.'

'Oh, yes, that's right. I heard all about your little indiscretion from daddy. A few days after our first date, I asked him about you casually. I told him I'd met you at the office party.'

'What did he say?'

'I can tell you word for word if you'd like. But perhaps I shouldn't.'

'Please do.'

"Don't talk to me about that smart arse West bastard! He's gone and got himself in hot water with the FCA, and it's making us all look like a bunch of thieving scoundrels. If he wasn't so bloody good at his job, I'd have sacked him already. Not that your sodding godfather would have let me."

'Well, I can't say he wasn't being completely honest. I *was* a smart arse, and I did make the company look bad.'

'I know, I saw the article on you in the financial paper. I don't usually read that sort of thing, but daddy showed me, as if to prove his point about you.'

'Bloody hell.'

'Yeah, you're not in his good books right now. To be honest, it made me more interested in you.'

'Really?'

'Yeah, I know it's a bit of a cliché, but…'

Stephen felt a little too satisfied with the notion that Cindy was interested in him, and he caught himself wondering how differently things might have gone if both of them had been a little more honest on their first date. He liked the intelligent Cindy, even if she was a bit of a spoilt princess.

Although he liked Alexa more, and he saw a future with her. He wasn't about to throw that away, no matter how well he thought he'd end up getting along with Cindy Ashden.

'So you understand that I can't help you, until and unless I manage to get through this investigation.'

'That's okay, I think you'll come out of it okay. Here's the deal: if you *do*, then you can help me win my little bet; if you *don't*, I won't bother you anymore, I'll consider us even.'

'I suppose that's fairly reasonable. Although I still don't feel right about the idea of assisting you to cheat my boss.'

'Don't be a wet, Stephen.'

'Okay, I'll do it.'

'Thanks!'

She smiled at him in a way that made him feel deeply uncomfortable. It was an intimate smile. One that made him feel like he was cheating on Alexa simply by having brought it about.

Somewhat mercifully, the feeling was interrupted by a waiter who'd come to take their breakfast order. After a quick look at the menu, both of them chose something and sent him on his way.

'So, for interest sake, how badly are you doing?'

'Extrapolated over a year, I'm sitting at around ten percent. I've heard that's average. Daddy dearest is doubling that apparently.'

'No. It's not actually average, it's pretty good for a short term investment. That average is based on long term earnings, so it doesn't take account of violent swings in the market. You actually aren't doing too badly. Your Dad's obviously trading very aggressively, so his fortunes may turn.'

'Stop sounding so surprised when you pick up that I have more than three brain cells, Steve. I really convinced you that I was vapid, *didn't I*?'

'You could've been an actress, Cindy.'

'I'll take that as a compliment. Will you at least look at what I've invested in so far and let me know what you think?'

'I shouldn't.'

'But you want to.'

'I can't say I'm not curious.'

'Give me your e-mail address and I'll send over a breakdown.'

'No. Don't do that. The FCA will be monitoring my emails. They'll think I'm trading while under suspension.'

'Even your personal mail?'

'They aren't stupid, Cindy.'

'Okay, I'll print it out. Send me your address so I can post it to you.'

'Alright. But I'll just have a brief look. I can't advise you on it yet.'

'Understood.'

She smiled in the self-satisfied way people tend to do when they've gotten their way after an argument.

'So what career have you chosen that pisses your dad off so much? *Is* it acting?'

'No, he'd *love* that. I'm training to be a *police officer*.'

'A what?!'

Cindy sat back, sighed deeply, and rolled her eyes.

'That's pretty much what *he* said. You're all the bloody same, you money people. If it doesn't fit into what you consider to be a *lucrative* career path, you accord it no value. It's no wonder most of your male colleagues date such shallow women Stephen, it's a reflection of how poorly you assess real value!'

'I never thought of it that way.'

'Stephen. If you're as bright as Jim thinks you are, you probably have a fair notion of what my family's worth.'

'Yes. It's somewhat obscene.'

'Indeed. So as you may well imagine, it's highly unlikely that even my grandchildren would ever have to work a day in their lives in order to get by.'

'That's being *conservative*. But I get it, you can do whatever you want to do.'

'Correct.'

'So why the police?'

'Because I just think that I may as well do something responsible and worthwhile with my time. In *any event*, with my dad's connections and *my* education, I would probably rise up in the ranks fairly quickly. I may end up having to study law at some point, but I can get my head around that. It's not like I would end up spending my life on the beat. But even if I *did*, what's so wrong with *that*?'

Stephen was impressed with Cindy's resolve. He smiled at her and shook his head.

'Nothing, I suppose.'

'That's another reason I want to win this silly bet with my father. He needs to learn to respect me, and my decisions.'

'You think that that would work?'

'I think there's a chance it would. Maybe not a significant chance, but I have to try.'

'You'd still be cheating though.'

'Whatever, I'd learn to live with that.'

'Even though you'd effectively be fleecing the old man?'

'That depends. You sound confident that I'll win.'

'No. I'm confident that *I'll* win.'

'That's *if* you manage to get out of trouble with the FCA and help me.'

'Yes. I'm trying to be optimistic about that.'

They both laughed. He was becoming more and more comfortable with Cindy, although he was making a conscious effort not to get too comfortable. The waiter, as if sensing the lull in their conversation, magically appeared with their food. This gave Stephen the opportunity to catch his breath.

'Anyway, Steve. I'm sure that after you've taught me the basics, I'll be able to do most of the work myself. You strike me as someone who'd be good at teaching.'

'I'm not too bad at it.'

'As long as you can keep yourself from staring down my top while you're looking over my shoulder.'

'Oh shit! Sorry, I haven't been staring at you inappropriately have I?'

'Actually, you *haven't*. That's what pissed me off in the first place! Girls notice these things Steve. We say we don't like it, but if you *don't* stare, we get all self-conscious and wonder what's wrong with us. We're complicated.'

'About that…'

'That girl I saw you with, Alexa. You're seeing her, aren't you?'

'Yes.'

'Pity. I was beginning to like you. But I get it. Maybe it wasn't a good idea for me to be looking too close to home.'

'It's not that I don't like you. In fact, I'm now kicking myself, because you seem like exactly the type of person that I would be interested in dating. But I'm serious about Alexa.'

'I'm happy for you Steve. I think we could be mates though. I like your sense of humour.'

'I think so too. For the record, you have no need to be self-conscious, you're gorgeous!'

'Thanks, Steve!'

They finished their brunch, and had a good laugh about various things. He told her about his experience with the S&M dating site and Smith, and about almost drowning in the river whilst fishing with Jim.

He also told her about his trip to Nice, and she agreed that her godfather's flat was a bit over the top. She confirmed his suspicions about Jim's wife being behind the interior decorating. She told him that her dad teased him about it often, but that he didn't exactly have much of a leg to stand on, because her own mother hired an interior decorator to furnish their houses, and their designs weren't that far removed from the Roberts' holiday pad.

Stephen teased her about the fact that she'd said 'houses' in a way that implied it was normal to have more than one, and she admitted that they had three.

After they'd parted company, Stephen went home and called Alexa. He was in a bit of a bind, because he didn't want to tell her about his job yet, and explaining the whole scenario with Cindy would obviously give it away.

So he resolved to explain the situation once he'd had the chance to come clean about what he did for a living. He wasn't inclined to do that over the phone, so he planned to do it when he saw her the next day. He simply told Alexa that he'd confessed to Cindy, and she'd taken it reasonably well.

Alexa wasn't stupid or naïve, so she asked him whether or not he'd mentioned to Cindy that he was in a relationship. He was relieved to be able to confirm that he had. Fortunately, she left it at that.

He spent the rest of the afternoon cleaning his flat, and generally preparing to have her over the following day. Although he was excited at the prospect of seeing her again so soon, he was apprehensive about the conversation he'd have to have with her regarding his job.

It had also occurred to him that it would be difficult to explain the fact that he'd agreed to see more of Cindy, regardless of the context in which he'd be seeing her. His feelings on this particular issue were at least partly attributable to the fact that he actually quite liked her.

***

Stephen woke up far earlier than he'd wanted to on Sunday morning. In fact, he was up, showered and dressed by seven, and was sitting on the edge of the sofa trying to read a novel as if he were waiting at a station platform, worried that he may miss his train. It felt the same, because he couldn't quite get into the story. His mind kept wandering off; not to anything in particular, he was just generally distracted.

He pulled out his journal, and spent half an hour recounting recent events and posing questions to himself about his thoughts on various issues. The journal was starting to evolve into a list of questions and speculative answers, and he was finding it rather useful in this form.

Alexa was only due to come over at around one, and although he'd planned to go and buy some bread and sundry supplies that morning, the shops weren't going to be open before ten, so he had to find a way of amusing himself until he could go out.

He forced himself to keep reading, even though it involved re-reading the odd page or two whenever he caught himself wandering off. He considered playing the computer game, and even drawing something, but his ennui wouldn't permit it. He was itching to get out to the shops, and left just before ten, so that he could arrive just as they opened. This enthusiasm didn't help matters in the long-run though, because his excursion was far shorter than he'd bargained for, and he was back on the edge of his sofa in just under an hour.

He found himself wondering why he'd never bothered to get a TV. That would be a perfect distraction, because it wouldn't involve any concentration. He wasn't '*anti*' television, he just seldom spent enough time in his flat to do anything other than sleep, so he couldn't justify the expense. Besides, he had a slightly scaled down print of Chardin's '*The Attributes of Exploration*' where a TV would logically have gone, and he didn't think it was worth moving it.

He decided to move the coffee table, and lay his recently acquired picnic blanket on the floor over the large red Shiraz that occupied the space. They could have an indoor picnic. Setting it up was something to do, and he thought Alexa would like the idea.

Somewhat mercifully, she arrived earlier than he'd expected. Although their previous date had been a little strained, she seemed very happy to see him. She was wearing another one of those short summer dresses, this time, a grey one that almost mirrored the colour of her eyes. Stephen loved the way she looked in that style of dress, although he was slightly preoccupied with thoughts of getting rid of the thing altogether.

'Wow, Steve. I like your flat. I was worried it would be like one of those slightly grubby places that men tend to inhabit when left to their own devices.'

Stephen laughed.

'How do you know I didn't go and put this all together quickly, just to impress you?'

'Because although you tidied it up quite nicely, you still didn't bother to dust the surfaces or the picture frames.'

'Shit.'

She chuckled.

'Don't be upset, Steve, your lack of attention to detail has worked out quite well for you in the circumstances. I really do love the way you've decorated. Especially the rugs.'

'I have a thing for Persian rugs.'

'I see you've gone and covered one up with that picnic blanket… are we having an indoor picnic?'

'I thought it was quite a good idea.'

She laughed and smiled at him.

'You see, I told you we'd get some use out of it. I love the idea of an indoor picnic.'

'I'm glad. I was hoping you wouldn't find it a bit too cheesy.'

'I told you I find the cheesy stuff cute…'

'Thank heavens for that.'

'You're far more charming and smooth than you think you are Stephen… that's also cute.'

'You mean, it's manly and rugged.'

'Why do men hate being described as *cute* so much?'

'No idea, to be honest. It's probably just a male ego thing.'

She sighed and looked around. Stephen could tell she was assessing his decorating choices again.

'This is going to sound a little bit insulting, but I'm too curious not to ask…'

'Go on.'

'Do graphic designers normally make the sort of money that enables them to furnish their places like this? Karen said you weren't a trust fund kid.'

Stephen laughed nervously. He had no idea what the average graphic designer earned. He assumed that there were some wealthy ones, but the industry was largely unknown to him. Perhaps it was time to come clean.

'Yeah, well… about that… I'm not exactly a graphic designer…'

'You know what Steve, sorry, I'm actually not that sort of girl. I don't want to know. Frankly, I don't care how much money you have or don't have. I'm just happy you aren't one of those awful banking types.'

'You know your sister's a banker, right? They can't all be that bad, surely?'

'I know. Just the male ones. Liars and cheats, the lot of 'em.'

'That's a bit harsh, isn't it?'

'I dated one of them once. For quite a while, actually. About two years. It turned out that he was under the impression we were in what people call an "*open*" relationship. It clearly wasn't that "*open*", because he failed to tell me about the fact that he was seeing two other women at the same time.'

'What an arsehole.'

'Yeah, he was one of those stock brokers. Loads of money, and a bad attitude to match.'

'Ah well… the thing is…'

'Let's not talk about it anymore, Steve. You don't need to be submerged in all of my baggage. Not yet, anyway. I need a glass of wine, and a kiss.'

Stephen was happy to oblige on both fronts. He'd set aside a Beaujolais he'd picked up at the airport on the way out of Nice. After pouring them each a glass, both of which he left on the counter, he turned around and pulled her into his arms.

'You've forgotten the wine, Steve.'

'It has to breath.'

'So do I…'

'You sure about that?'

'No.'

By this stage, neither of them were remotely interested in the wine, or in Stephen's little picnic on the sitting room floor. He was holding her as though she was in danger of being swept away, and neither of them could take their eyes off the other.

'I haven't shown you around yet, have I?'

'No.'

He smiled down at her and brushed his hand through her hair.

'How rude of me.'

She grinned up at him and grabbed hold of his belt buckle with her right hand.

'Go on then… show me!'

She didn't need any help navigating though. She'd figured out exactly where she wanted to go, and dragged him along by his belt until they got there. She pushed him over onto the bed and climbed on top of him, furiously unbuttoning his shirt as she went. He wanted to get her dress off, but he realised that he wasn't running the proceedings… at least not yet. She obviously sensed his anticipation, so once she'd managed to get rid of his shirt and un-buckle his belt, she leant back pulled the dress off in one swift and uninterrupted motion.

He stared up at her, fixated on how beautiful she was. She smiled, and blushed a little. He didn't need to say anything; his eyes conveyed the compliment. She also didn't need to offer any further guidance or encouragement for him to take the lead.

They only left the bedroom that afternoon to fetch the wine, and a few bottles of still water. They never made it to their picnic.

He begged her to stay the night, but she had to get back to open the bakery early the next morning. She had a large order to fulfil and Freddy couldn't manage it on his own. She did stay until around eight that evening though, and neither of them really wanted to part company. They agreed that he would go to her place next, and that they weren't going to wait an entire week, but they didn't make any concrete arrangements past that.

22

The following morning, Alexa received a message from Karen.

Hey Sis, how was the date?

Amazing!

I want to hear all about it.

You seem even more curious than usual.

You know I like the idea of you and S being together.

You're a hopeless romantic K.

Come for supper! The kids are away at their grandparents again, and I can get Ollie to give us some space.

Okay, will you then leave me in peace for the rest of the day.

Yes! I'll get Ol to make us pasta or something.

Sounds fantastic! x

***

Stephen received a call from Ian's secretary.

'Good morning Mr West. This is Amanda, from Wright & Hill.'

'Morning Amanda, I take it Ian wants a word?'

Stephen didn't understand why lawyers made a habit of getting their secretaries to place calls for them. He always found it vaguely insulting when one of these secretaries phoned him, and asked him to hold the line for the person who was trying to contact him. It was unnatural. If they wanted to talk, why not just pick up the phone and dial it themselves?

'No, not right now Mr West. He'd like you to pop in and see him. How is your morning looking tomorrow?'

'It *was* looking restful Amanda, but I get the feeling I'll be making my way to see your charming boss, instead of sunning myself in Hyde Park.'

'He'd appreciate it if you could make it for nine. Does that suit you, Mr West?'

'Yes, that suits me. Has he given you any indication in respect of what the meeting may be about?'

'No, sorry Mr West, he hasn't, and I'm not permitted to speculate. He did say that he wanted to see you today, but he's been called away to court on an urgent matter, and he isn't sure whether or not he'll be done before close of business.'

'Thanks Amanda, I'll have to wait then.'

Stephen knew exactly what it was about. The Financial Conduct Authority had evidently reached a decision in respect of whether or not they wished to proceed with a formal hearing. In his admittedly limited experience, lawyers liked to give important news to their clients in person, especially when the news was bad.

He would have to exercise a little patience and wait for the solicitor, although he battled to stop himself from speculating about the various possibilities.

He noticed that while he was on the line with Amanda, somebody had tried to contact him from the offices of Ashden, Cole & Roberts. He assumed it must have been Mary, so he called her back.

'Hi Mary.'

'Oh hello Stephen, It's good to hear from you. How was your trip.'

'Splendid thanks, M. Were you trying to call me this morning? I have a missed call from the office number.'

'No. It may have been Jim, or Kenneth. I think he's having withdrawal symptoms.'

'Do you think I've given the poor little bugger Stockholm syndrome, M?'

'No. What prompted that question? Has he been stalking you or something?'

'No, I'm just a bit worried about him, that's all.'

Mary sighed.

'Are *you* okay, Stephen? You don't sound yourself.'

'I think the FCA have reached a decision on how to proceed with that case they're conducting against me. My lawyer's asked me to go in to see him tomorrow.'

'Oh… try not to assume the worst.'

'Easier said than done, M.'

'Actually, speaking of which, did you remember you're seeing Bridgette this afternoon?'

'I did. Are you honestly still keeping track of my diary, Mary?'

'I miss you Stephen, it's my way of staying in the picture.'

'I appreciate the sentiment, but you really don't have to. Also, what if I get sacked? or I give it all up to become a window washer? You'll need to get used to living without me.'

'I can't see you getting sacked.'

'What about the other thing?'

'I don't know you well enough to make a call on that one. You've changed, Stephen. So have I, to be honest.'

'Really? How have *you* changed?'

'I've realised I don't really like working here without you. If you *do* end up canning the whole thing, I'll seriously consider moving on.'

'To do what?'

'I haven't the foggiest.'

'Well that's a sobering thought, M.'

'Not really. I have a fairly broad skillset. I'll find my way.'

'What does your partner do?'

'She's a chef.'

Stephen laughed.

'What's so funny?'

'My new girlfriend's a baker. I just thought it was an interesting coincidence.'

'Yeah, I don't think either of us are cut out to work with our partners. I know you can barely make toast, and I'm not much better, to be honest.'

'Hey. I've learnt a lot while I've been on leave. I can now make a mean plate of bacon and eggs. And I'm becoming very good at working the microwave.'

It was Mary's turn to laugh.

'Stephen, my cats can basically use a microwave… that's not a skill.'

'That's a bit of an exaggeration. But I take your point.'

'Do you need me to do anything for you before your meeting with the lawyer?'

'No, thanks M. You could find out who's trying to contact me though. I'm not in the mood to chat to Jim, unless I absolutely have to.'

'That's new. Am I sensing some latent tension there?'

'Yes.'

'Alright, I'll let you know.'

'Thanks, M.'

Stephen didn't really know how he felt about Jim at that moment. He was skeptical about his Dad's position on the man, and even more skeptical about that of young Kenneth. But the sum of the parts was nagging at him, and he realised he'd have to have a candid word with Jim at some point. It occurred to him that he hadn't bothered to thank him for the use of his flat after he'd returned from Nice three days ago, and this made him feel rather guilty.

That said, it was almost certainly true that Jim would know what was happening at the FCA, and he didn't want to find out from him before having spoken to Ian, so he put off calling him until the next day.

Seeing Bridgette that afternoon would be a handy distraction. He no longer dreaded his meetings with her, even though he considered her to form part of the cabal that was trying to tell him how to live his life.

***

Stephen arrived at Bridgette's offices early, and decided not to bother distracting himself by walking through the park, or browsing local bookstores. He went straight up, and got comfortable on her well-worn Chesterfield.

Susan told him that Bridgette was still busy with a client, and offered him coffee. She didn't need to ask how he took it this time, although she obviously sensed that he wasn't as desperate for strength and quantity as he was on his previous visit, because it was considerably milder and served in a teacup, instead of a large mug.

He was on his second one, when the client Bridgette had been seeing shuffled out of her office. She was a tall woman, about his age, wearing a charcoal pin-stripe slack suit, and carrying a large square briefcase. Stephen knew Bridgette saw both men and women in her professional capacity, but for some reason, he just expected to see a man leaving her office. He guessed that the client must have been a lawyer, because only lawyers and airline pilots tended to carry those ridiculously large briefcases, and she was wearing the customary uniform and countenance of the former.

It was still roughly ten minutes before the time scheduled for the meeting, but Susan went in to tell her that Stephen was already there. She made him wait the full ten minutes, though.

'Stephen. Good to see you. How was your trip?'

'Hi Bridgette. It was very good, thanks. A bit short, but worthwhile.'

'I'm glad. It wasn't a bad idea getting away for a bit.'

'To be fair, it was Jim's idea.'

'Ah. Have you been seeing much of Jim lately?'

'No. Actually I haven't. I get the feeling he's been putting some distance between us.'

She tilted her head and looked at him thoughtfully.

'How do you feel about that?'

'I'm not sure, to be honest. On the one hand, I understand the commercial necessity of keeping me away during the investigation…'

'And on the other?'

'I feel a little bit ostracised.'

'I can understand that.'

'To be completely fair though, he still took me fishing, lent me his car, and even his flat in France.'

'So you think that's his way of assuaging his guilt over the fact that he's had to prevent himself from being seen with you in and around the city?'

'No, actually. That hadn't occurred to me.'

She smiled across at Stephen as if she'd just made an interesting connection. Although she wasn't intent on giving it away.

'But something else *has*, hasn't it?'

'My father thinks that Jim's deliberately buttering me up and priming me to take over the company one day. He's of the view that Jim's motives aren't altruistic, and he's trying to trap me.'

'It's a possibility. What do *you* think though?'

'Well that's just it. I don't know, Bridgette. My intern, who I've allowed to become a bit too familiar, but whose judgment about people isn't terrible, has similar misgivings regarding Jim.'

'So now you're conflicted, because their arguments are logical on the face of it, but you're very fond of Jim and you can't bring yourself to consider the possibility that your bond may be laid on a precarious foundation.'

'Pretty much.'

'I see.'

'You must understand that I'm not very good at assessing the feelings of others Bridgette. We haven't really discussed that issue; aside from how it relates to my well-established difficulty with the fairer sex.'

'I do understand, Stephen. I realised it before having met you. You aren't a stereotypical example of someone with your IQ, but you do exhibit various personality traits that we tend to associate with people like you.'

'I'm worried that I may be labouring under a massive misapprehension, Bridgette, and I don't think I have the tools to figure it out, because it isn't a purely intellectual exercise.'

Bridgette gave Stephen a reassuring smile.

'You'll develop the tools.'

'How do you know?'

'Because a month ago, you didn't consider the notion that there *were* any exercises other than intellectual ones. The fact that you're beginning to acknowledge the true nature of your difficulties, and express them, means that you'll be able to work on them.'

'You think so?'

'I know so. The nice thing about emotional intelligence is that it can be improved over time. You aren't stuck with what you're born with.'

'That's slightly reassuring.'

'It should be. I know you want an answer to the question right now, because you'd like to use it in order to help yourself make a decision about your career path, but the answer won't magically appear, and nobody else can give it to you. You're going to have to be patient and work through the problem.'

'I'm used to working out problems very quickly.'

'Not these sorts of problems.'

'I hear you. But it just seems like a good time to choose a direction.'

'It *is* a good time.'

'But then how do I do it? If I still can't figure out the true nature of my relationship with Jim?'

'Stephen. What do you think I had for breakfast this morning?'

'Some poor unfortunate client.'

'I love your sense of humour, but let's be serious.'

'I have no idea.'

'I didn't think you would. But the answer to that question is no more relevant to your decision than is the answer to the question of whether or not Jim truly is who you think he is.'

'I disagree.'

'Stephen, if you're only working as a trader because of your relationship with James Roberts, you're insane. Bear in mind, I'm a psychologist, so I don't say that sort of thing lightly.'

'No, that's not it. I suppose it's just a consideration. I may want to leave Ashden, Cole & Roberts, but stay in the industry.'

Bridgette sighed and looked at Stephen impatiently while gathering her thoughts. He wondered whether or not he ought to have elaborated on his point, but he got the sense that it wasn't a good idea to interrupt her.

'Let's assume for a minute that Jim's stringing you along. I'm not saying he is, because I don't know, and I'm ethically bound to refrain from commenting on it, one way or another. But let's say he *is*, for the sake of argument, what's the problem?'

'The problem is that he's stringing me along. It's immoral.'

'That's a silly argument Stephen.'

'How so?'

'You have to ask yourself a more fundamental question. If James Roberts is stringing you along, why? To what end?'

'To buy my loyalty, so I look after his interests when he retires.'

'Does he *need* your loyalty for that? Or would that simply be the logical conclusion of your progression through the company?'

'Umm…'

'And how would it be different anywhere else?'

'I suppose it wouldn't.'

'You hadn't thought of that, had you?'

'No…'

Bridgette smiled. He considered the smile to be annoyingly patronising, but he was starting to realise that his irritation had more to do with the fact that he'd missed a trick than it had to do with Bridgette's demeanour.

'That's faintly amusing to me actually, Stephen.'

'Why?'

'Because it's the sort of thing someone like you would ordinarily have considered in the very first instance. You're extraordinarily good at cutting Gordian knots, because you have the intellectual ability to formulate the right questions, and find the answers with alacrity.'

'I get that.'

'But you can't bring yourself to do that when it comes to your relationship with Jim, because you feel that to do so would be a betrayal of the man you consider to be your friend and mentor.'

'I'm still human, Bridgette.'

'That's why I think you have the ability to improve your emotional intelligence. But in this instance, don't you think it's worth looking at your situation in the cold light of day, and taking Jim out of the equation?'

'Yes. You're right.'

'So? Removing Jim from the equation, do you still want to be a trader?'

'I don't know.'

'Okay, let's go one step further and assume you're promoted to the board. Do you really want to have more of a hand in managing the affairs of the company. I don't know all of the internal workings of the industry, but I assume that a board appointment comes with at least a slight change in daily responsibilities. I assume that you'd end up doing less trading and more administration.'

'Yes. That's a fair assumption.'

'So? How do you feel about that?'

'I haven't given it much thought, to be honest.'

'Again, that's something I would expect someone like you to have considered. You've been so keen on getting promoted, that you haven't considered the implications. You're becoming more human by the minute, Stephen.'

'It's not like I haven't been relatively preoccupied recently, Bridgette.'

'You know that's a weak argument in the circumstances, Stephen. But you should also know that I intended that last comment to be a compliment.'

'It didn't sound like it.'

'Well it was. The whole point of our little exercise was for you to be a little more in tune with who you are, and that requires you to think and behave a little more like a normal human being. You're doing inordinately well with that, because for once, you aren't looking at your problems from a purely intellectual point of view.'

'Still, it doesn't seem very productive.'

'That's why you need to use both perspectives. Your scale has just become a little unbalanced.'

'Fair enough. But what do you think? Assuming I'm not sacked or incarcerated, do you think my current career objectives are worth pursuing?'

'You know what I'm going to say, don't you?'

'I have a fair idea.'

'Then pretend you're me. What am I going to say?'

'That you can't tell me what'll make me happy in the long run, that's something only I can do.'

'Spot on. I know it's not the answer anybody wants to hear, because it sounds wishy washy and pointless; especially since there's an implicit expectation that I should produce something of more immediate practical utility.'

'No. I'm starting to get the point of the exercise. I just wondered if you'd care to venture an opinion on the subject.'

'I'm impressed, Stephen. I'll give you something else to think about. It may make maters more difficult, but it may help, so it's worth considering. I have a theory about you, but I'm not sure whether or not it's valid.'

'Go on...'

'Let's say you simply gave up on your current career. What would you do for a living?'

'I'd probably go into something artistic.'

'That was quick. I've never had a client give me such a fast and direct answer to that question. Has it been on your mind?'

'Yes. Charles wants me to come and draw dragons for *The Other Planet*.'

'Seriously?'

'Yeah, seriously.'

'Are you *that* good?'

'You sound surprised, Bridgette.'

'I'm not that surprised, to be honest. You're quite mathematically minded, and there's a misconception that that isn't related to artistic talent. It *is* in many instances. I remember you expressing that you had a talent, but we didn't discuss the point at any length, because we couldn't agree on the validity of art as a career choice.'

'Yes, I remember our brief conversation on the subject. I *am* a good artist, but I maintain my view that drawing things for a living isn't entirely realistic.'

'Then why have you been thinking about it?'

'Because I'm genuinely concerned that I may get booted out of the finance profession, and I think it's the only thing I could do in those circumstances.'

'Well that's a load of nonsense.'

'Sorry?'

'You heard me, Stephen. With your skills and qualifications you could occupy most positions in a non-finance company. You know this. You'd probably even get headhunted for something lucrative after the dust settled.'

'What's your point.'

'You *want* to draw dragons for a living, but you're being cowardly, because you won't admit it to yourself. I assume you told poor Charles where to get off?'

'I did.'

'You think that getting booted out of the city will give you an excuse to curl up and become re-absorbed in your art.'

'Maybe I do. What of it?'

'Why do you need an excuse? Why does it need to be negative? I'll tell you one thing for free, Stephen, if you only go into art for that reason, you'll end up resenting it. That would be tragic.'

'So you think I should forget the stock market, and take up drawing and painting for a living?'

'No. I'm neutral on the subject, but if you do end up doing something like that, I want it to be out of a genuine desire to do so, not as a fallback position. It's like rebound dating.'

'I suppose that's sensible. But what if I *do* get sacked?'

'Don't go and take Charles up on his offer. Do something else until you're sure of your own motivations.'

'Thanks Bridgette. I can't disagree with your logic on that. But for interest sake, what was that theory on me you alluded to earlier?'

Bridgette stopped him and ordered them both a coffee before continuing. They were running out of time, but she didn't have any more appointments that day, so she was happy to extend their session.

'Have you ever heard of '*Default Mode Network*', Stephen?'

'No.'

'Basically, its a network of systems in the brain that lights up whenever we aren't focussing on what's going on around us. Like when we daydream, or engage in any kind of reflective thought or introspection.'

'Okay…'

'It's a very interesting field of study, because not too much is known about it, and it has some powerful effects on the way we think and behave. Part of what makes it fascinating, is the fact that it has the capacity to either be constructive or destructive, depending on context, and one's ability to manage emotional responses.'

'It certainly sounds interesting.'

'It occurred to me from your history, and from assessing our early interactions, that you probably battle to switch off. Is that right?'

'Yes.'

'Is it fair to say that whenever you aren't thinking about work or solving some sort of problem, you worry and get depressed.'

'That's exactly right.'

'It makes sense. Your *Default Mode Network* can either calm you down, or thrust you into anxiety by getting caught up in worrying and negative speculation about various things that concern you. If you're busy or distracted, your DMN doesn't kick in, so you don't worry as much. But, you then sacrifice the benefits of it kicking in to relax you.'

'Wow… I understand that feeling very acutely.'

'I'm sure you do. Studies have also shown that lonely people tend to show more DMN activity, so the fact that you're single and living away from family has probably exacerbated the problem.'

'Okay… but how do I deal with it.'

'You *are* dealing with it. How worried and anxious have you really been recently?'

'Not very, to be honest.'

'But by rights, you should be. You don't have work to distract you, you're still living alone, and you're facing some pretty oppressive legal and work-related difficulties.'

'That's true.'

'But you're happier today than you were when we first met, even though the legal problem hasn't been resolved, and you haven't been able to drown yourself in your work.'

'Do you have any idea why that's the case, Bridgette?'

'As I said, I have a theory. That's all it is to be honest, but I'm quite certain I'm right.'

'Go on then, what is it.'

'Studies have also shown that aesthetics can have a very pronounced influence on how our brains respond while our DMN is engaged. My theory is that looking at, and producing art allows you to use your DMN constructively. You will therefore likely be calmed around art and things that appeal to your sense of the aesthetic.'

'Oh shit…'

'I'm right, aren't I?'

'Yes.'

'As I say, it's just a theory, and I'm not making a concrete psychological diagnosis on the back of it. That's not my place. If you want to explore it in any more detail I can refer you on. But I think that's why the art has drawn you in. I'm also not saying that the art is any better at relaxing you than your work was. That's something only you will be able to figure out. But now that you have a very rudimentary idea of the concept, you can work on it.'

'Wow Bridgette, I'm not sure what to say.'

'I told you I was going to add to your load a bit. But I think it was necessary to bring it up.'

'It absolutely was.'

'Again, I don't think you ought to run off and quit your job just yet, but I think you're better placed to think about your future now. One way or another, I don't think you should ignore your art. Obviously, the old admonition about too much of a good thing still applies, but you clearly need to engage your creative side more often. Playing computer games is a healthy release some of the time, but it probably won't do what the art can for your peace of mind.'

'Yeah, I've already figured that much out.'

'Good. I also don't think you need to see me again any time soon. I'd like to keep you on as a private client, but that's ultimately up to you. Think on it.'

'I will.'

'Are you still keeping that diary.'

'I am. Although I've taken to writing in it about once a week; and it isn't a straightforward narrative of events or experiences any more. It's sort of evolved into a record of my thoughts on particular issues I've been struggling with. It still feels awkward writing it, but I'm getting used to the practice.'

'Keep doing it if you want, but you don't have to. My suggestion would be to write down your thoughts or experiences whenever you feel overwhelmed by something. It's almost like sleep, it will help re-order your thoughts and calm you down. Studies have shown that writing is particularly effective for that sort of thing; more so than any other form of expression, even art.'

'That's interesting. I'll try to keep doing it.'

'I've already prepared my assessment on you for the company. I need to add some points, but I'll send it in the morning.'

'Thank you Bridgette. I really appreciate the help you've given me so far.'

'You're most welcome, Stephen. Stay in touch. If you want to discuss the contents of the report once you've seen it, let me know. I'll be happy to go through it with you.'

'Thanks!'

***

Alexa went straight to her sister's after work. She finished a bit later than usual, so she didn't have time to go home and change. She knew Karen wouldn't care that she was wearing her chef's whites, although she changed into a spare set she had with her at the bakery, because she'd been working with chocolate all day, and she looked like a five year old after one of those birthday parties that involved a chocolate fountain. She even had chocolate in her hair.

By the time she arrived, Ollie had already made himself scarce. He'd cooked them a very nice supper, and although Karen had invited him to stick around to eat with them, he was far happier being out of the way. Even though they'd probably leave the juicy details for after he'd absented himself, he knew that his mate was likely to come up in the conversation, and wasn't remotely interested in hearing about the whole thing, one way or another.

After pouring them each a large glass of wine, Karen was ready to be immersed in the details.

'Go on then! I need to know about the date! Where did you go?'

'To his place in London.'

'Really?!'

Alexa laughed.

'Why does that surprise you so much K?'

'You know why! The whole home date thing is rather…'

'Intimate?'

'Yes. It is!'

Karen couldn't help giggling like a teenage schoolgirl.

'I knew you looked different!'

'What's that supposed to mean?'

'You know what I mean, stop being coy with me… I want to know everything!'

Alexa couldn't help but smile. She was also blushing more than a little.

'I think I'm in love, K...'

'Oh you're *definitely* in love, Alexa!'

'What makes you say that?'

'I can see it written all over you. I'm glad we decided to have supper, instead of just chatting over the phone. I haven't seen you looking like this in *years*!'

'Well...'

Alexa burst out laughing.

'I *do* feel good... I'm not even embarrassed to admit it!'

'Well, clearly you know a bit more about Stephen now... and?'

'He's amazing. He planned a little indoor picnic. We had all that leftover cheese from the festival on the weekend, so he got some wine and bread and set up a picnic on his living-room floor.'

'Romantic!'

'It really *was*.'

'And... go on...'

'His apartment is beautiful. He obviously has really great taste, and he clearly makes a lot of money... not that I really think that's *too* important. But it's nice to know he's secure. Although, he sort of hinted that he wasn't *exactly* a graphic designer, which was a bit of a surprise... I assume it's something related to graphic design, but I sort of took us off topic. He seemed a bit guilty about not explaining it to me, I hope he isn't involved in anything *sketchy*.'

'I hope not.'

'Anyway, I thought he would be a bit awkward, because I get the impression he hasn't dated in a while. But he seemed to just do everything *right*, if that makes any sense... little things, like the fact that he still dressed really well, even though we were only sticking around in the apartment; he was comfortable and self-assured. It just all worked out so... *well*.'

'Did you think that he'd somehow *devolve* when he got to entertain you in his own space?'

'No. But you *know* how men are sometimes, when they're at home. They get all sloppy.'

'Tell me about it...'

'He *didn't*, and he also didn't get all nervous and fidgety when things got a bit more... you know...'

'Good! There's nothing worse than a chap who becomes a wet blanket as soon as he gets your kit off.'

'He was the opposite of that. But in a *good* way!'

'No wonder you're in such a good mood, sounds like old Steve's a bit of a star in the bedroom!'

'He definitely got it right. It sounds a bit silly, but I didn't expect him to be *that* good.'

'To be honest Allie, I think part of it was the fact that you really like him. It *does* make a difference you know...'

'Does it?'

'Absolutely. If he's the best you've had, it probably means that you just *like* him more than you did any of the others. I don't want to burst your bubble, Al, but in *my* experience, men are only as talented in bed as you *let* them be, and when you really *like* them, you help them to reach their full potential. Still, the net result is the same, so well done to *both* of you!'

Alexa laughed.

'Thanks Sis. I don't really care why he's so good. I just know I want more.'

'Good. I think that's the way it's supposed to be. There needs to be a reason we put up with men.'

'I'm sure there are plenty of other reasons, K.'

'I don't know so much, maybe I'm just jaded because I'm surrounded by so many difficult men at work all day.'

'Ollie can't be that bad, *surely*?'

'No, *he's* fine. He's actually *brilliant*. It's the others that give me grey hairs. It's useful having a trained lawyer around though, he can read people and situations like you and I can read nursery rhymes. It's unnerving sometimes.'

'I'm not too sure what Steve's good at. Other than drawing… and sex.'

'That's probably enough for now, Allie…'

'I'm not going to argue with that.'

23

Stephen had another restless night. He thought he could shelve the pervasive speculation he was wrestling with regarding the outcome of the case with the Financial Conduct Authority, but he couldn't. Moreover, Bridgette's theory regarding the *Default Mode Network* thing, along with his father's misgivings about Jim were buzzing around in his thoughts like mosquitoes.

He went through to the city early and grabbed a light breakfast at one of the coffee shops close to Ian's offices.

When he arrived, the receptionist showed him straight through to one of boardrooms and offered him a coffee. Somewhat uncharacteristically, he declined the offer.

After a few minutes, Ian arrived. The solicitor wasn't giving anything away, and this simultaneously impressed and irritated his client. Stephen had only managed to get about an hour of sleep, and he was desperate to find out what was going on.

'Morning Stephen.'

'Hi Ian. Please tell me you have some news.'

'I do indeed.'

'And? Is it good or bad.'

'It's interesting.'

'Good interesting? Or bad interesting.'

'I'd go as far as to say that it's good interesting. You can calm down to a mild panic.'

'Thanks.'

'So here's the story: As I predicted, the role of the other players in the game has been somewhat helpful.'

'You mean, Jones and Price?'

'Yes. It turns out that Jones *did* take a larger position on the stock than you did, but he wasn't being reckless.'

'How do you figure that?'

'He had inside knowledge.'

'You're joking?'

'Nope. Apparently it was blatantly obvious. They're throwing the book at the obnoxious bastard, and rightly so.'

'How does that effect me though?'

'It doesn't really. Not directly, anyway. It simply means that the FCA's appetite for finding a suitable candidate to make an example of has been sated, to a certain extent.'

'Well that's at least something.'

'Yes, it's had its utility. Although I assume that the whole escapade with Jones is one of the reasons it's taken them so long to come to a decision as to how to proceed with your matter. So on the one hand it's been indirectly helpful, but on the other it's probably prolonged the limbo you've found yourself having to endure.'

'So I assume they've made some sort of decision about me then?'

'Yes, and no. That's the interesting bit.'

'It turns out that Price's story is remarkably similar to yours.'

'I'm assuming that's been helpful.'

'Yes. Because they've obviously tried manfully to make a connection between the two of you, and they can't. On the face of it then, and based on the fact that they evidently unearthed sweet bugger all from your emails and phone records connecting you to anyone else involved with *Ringmire*, they're hard pressed to make out a convincing enough case to press on with a hearing.'

'This is sounding encouraging.'

'It is. They've also clearly identified the fact that your browser history and travel movements line up with the story you put forward in your affidavit. So they've decided not to proceed with a hearing. They're also lifting the suspension, and releasing your assets.'

'So that's it then?'

'No. Not entirely. That's what's interesting. They've indicated that they intend to continue investigating in the background. Should any further information come to light that implicates you in any way, they'll re-initiate the process, and go straight to a hearing.'

'That is interesting. But don't they automatically have that right in any event?'

'Yes. Technically. Although they really ought to draw a line under it at some point. They certainly aren't in the habit of continuing investigations after having lifted a suspension.'

'So this is a little uncommon, then?'

'Yes, it is. It's also a little unfair, because you have to live with a sword of Damocles over your head for a while. That said, I suspect that they won't be doing any more actual *'investigating'*. Not in the ordinary and direct sense of the term, anyway.'

'Why?'

'It's a little speculative, but I have a theory. I think that the case against Jones is so good that they intend to throw everything they possibly can at him. That means they'll go for a criminal prosecution, in addition to the other administrative sanctions available to them. They expect that whilst he's giving evidence at a criminal trial, he may implicate either you or Price, or both of you, in some way. In fact, they may be counting on him doing so in order to secure some sort of a plea deal.'

'Ah. So they want to keep their options open.'

'Yes. I would do the same if I were them.'

'Then why don't they just extend the investigation, and let Price and I sweat it out?'

'Because it's a hefty gamble. If they're wrong, and they've prevented you from earning a living while they dicker about bringing Jones to trial, you'd potentially have a hefty damages claim against them for loss of income. Bear in mind, Jones's lawyers will keep them at it for as long as they possibly can.'

'My gardening leave is on full pay though, I assume Price's is too?'

'Yes, but you earn more than your basic salary when you're in the office; what with commissions and bonuses etcetera; and I assume those aren't insignificant? Also, you haven't been trading with your frozen assets, so although they've still been accruing interest, they haven't been earning at their full potential.'

'No. You're dead right actually. I've probably already lost a healthy sum over the past month. Can I sue the buggers for it?'

'No. Because they had a legitimate reason to investigate. But if they kept the investigation active and upheld the suspension any longer, given the facts currently at their disposal, they would almost certainly open themselves up to such a cause of action.'

'So what you're saying is that they've found a clever way to have their cake and eat it.'

'Yes. Pretty much. But to be fair, if you haven't been in cahoots with Jones, then you don't really have anything to worry about.'

'I haven't.'

'Well then, Mr West. It looks like you're more or less in the clear!'

'Wow… Thanks Ian, I'm not sure what else to say.'

'You're most welcome Stephen. It's always nice being able to give good clients good news.'

'Don't take this the wrong way Ian, but I hope I never have to see you again in this context.'

'Me too, Stephen. Please send my kindest regards to Oliver if you see him. I don't get many opportunities to chat with him anymore.'

'I shall do. I'll also tell him how well you handled my matter.'

'Thank you. I really appreciate that.'

They said their goodbyes and Ian gave Stephen the written confirmation from the FCA in respect of their position on the matter.

***

As he was leaving, he got a call from Ashden, Cole & Roberts. It was Denise, she wanted to know if he'd be able to meet up with Jim. Clearly his boss knew what was going on, and it was pointless putting off seeing him anymore, so he agreed to meet at the office within the hour.

It felt good walking into the building without most of the cloud that had been hanging over him for the past five weeks. Some of it was still there, but still, he felt vindicated. The fact that Jim wanted to see him at the office meant that the company no longer felt it necessary to prolong his exile, which also felt good. Although not nearly as good as he thought it would.

Mary had obviously found out via the grapevine that he would be in to see Jim, because she was the one who appeared at the reception counter to greet him and hand him back his access card to the building. She also accompanied him to the boardroom on the fifth floor that had been allocated for the meeting. Once in the boardroom, she gave him a massive hug.

'Is it over? Are you back?'

'I don't know M. Looks like it. I don't think Jim would've asked you to give me back my access card if he was planning on sacking me.'

'I gathered that much. But I still feel like I'm in the dark here. What happened with the investigation? If you don't mind my asking.'

'Of course not. They've lifted the suspension and released my assets. But it seems they're still investigating in the background. They've indicated that if they find anything remotely questionable in their ongoing investigation, they'll attack me like a pack of hunting dogs.'

'You'll be fine. As you say, it looks as if the Company's comfortable with the notion of having you back in the fold.'

'We'll see about that. I'm not willing to engage in too much speculation at this point.'

She smiled and gave him another large hug.

'Well, whatever happens, I'm just happy you aren't in trouble anymore.'

'Thanks, M.'

'I'll leave you to your meeting with Jim. Good luck.'

Stephen smiled and watched her leave. He missed Mary. After about five minutes, Jim walked in, with Denise in tow.

'Stephen! Welcome back my boy!'

The old man gave Stephen a firm handshake and gripped his shoulder tightly with his free hand.

'Hi Jim! Hi Denise!'

Denise was evidently there for the sole purpose of taking Stephen's coffee order. Once she had, and once Jim had indicated that he'd have a cup of tea, she glided out of the boardroom to procure the necessary.

'You've heard then?'

'Course I bloody have. I got drunk on champagne last night celebrating. Why didn't you take my call?'

'Sorry Jim. I was a bit tied up, and I actually only found out myself about an hour ago.'

'Oh, really. That lawyer of yours didn't bother to tell you yesterday?'

'He was busy, and I spose he didn't want to tell me over the phone.'

'Bloody lawyers…'

Stephen laughed. Jim's world view was refreshingly simple, albeit rather selfish. As far as Jim was concerned, the entire planet revolved around him and his particular wants, needs and desires. Oddly though, this proclivity didn't seem to come across as obnoxious to most of those floating around in his orbit. He was generally so charming and generous, that almost all of the people who worked for or with him, found it quirky and endearing. Stephen imagined that this wasn't always the case though. He got the distinct impression that Jim had as many enemies as he had friends in the City.

'So am I expected back at work tomorrow?'

'Yes, absolutely! Unless you want to extend the leave a bit. Although I'll admit that we could do with you at your desk. Your absence hasn't gone unnoticed from an earnings point of view.'

'I'm flattered.'

'Yes well, facts are facts.'

'By the way, thanks again for the use of your place in France Jim, I really had a good time there.'

'You're most welcome. My wife sends her thanks to *you*! Your French must have been up to scratch, because those kitchen builders followed the new instructions you gave them to the letter.'

'Ah, I'm glad.'

'Next time she'll probably have me *paying you* to go and instruct them.'

'The place looks pretty sorted Jim, I don't think you'll need any further additions.'

'You haven't got to know my wife well enough, Stephen. That was only phase one of the revised interior design plan.'

Stephen raised an eyebrow and shook his head.

'Really?'

Jim burst out laughing.

'You don't like the place, do you?'

'I do… it's just a bit…'

'Naff?'

'I don't know if I would say *that*.'

'No, you can be honest. I fucking hate the place. But since I can't come up with anything better, I let Victoria just do as she pleases. The poor bird's got no taste. But neither do I, if I'm being completely honest. So I'm a fine one to talk.'

Stephen laughed. He had to admit that he missed Jim's abrasive candour.

'Speaking of which, I hear you're quite the artist. Well, at least I hear you're interested in the art thing. I assume you're good at it, because you aren't the type of chap who'd keep doing it if you weren't.'

'I'm fairly good at it. Where did you hear about my artistic leanings?'

'It's in Bridgette's report. I also received that this morning.'

'And?'

'And what?'

'Did she say I was a complete nutcase?'

'You know she didn't.'

'How would I know that? She never showed me the thing.'

'Yes, but surely you're insightful enough to know you're vaguely stable.'

'Crazy people don't know they're crazy, Jim.'

'Good point. But no, apparently you aren't a raving lunatic. Bridgette seems to have warmed to you more than I thought she would.'

Stephen smiled. Denise re-appeared with their drinks, and they sat down across from one another at the boardroom table. She asked Jim if he needed anything else from her and he just shook his head and waved her away.

'I'm glad… does this mean you'll promote me.'

'No.'

'Hold on a minute, Jim. Wasn't that the primary reason behind the exercise?'

'Nope. It was to see whether or not you were a risk to the company.'

'You gave me the impression that once I was cleared, and had a favourable report from Bridgette, I'd get the promotion.'

'No I didn't. I thought you had one of those fancy photographic memories?'

'I do.'

'Then you'll remember that I said I would recommend the promotion to my colleagues on the board, once you were cleared by the FCA. I also told you that you'd have to grovel a little bit. It's not up to me. You know that!'

'Will you make the recommendation though?'

'No. I've changed my mind about that.'

'Why?'

'Because we still can't trust you. You may be sane, and Bridgette may think that the sun shines out of your arse; but you have to learn to play nice with the team… even that Smith bastard.'

'That's a bit of a slap in the face, Jim.'

'And your conduct last month wasn't a slap in the face to the company, then?'

'I hardly think you can call it that…'

'The world doesn't revolve around Stephen West, my lad. It doesn't even revolve around *me*; in spite of the fact that I spend almost every waking hour I have, trying to make it so.'

'I just feel like I've been strung along a bit, Jim.'

'Oh, you *have* been, and you'll continue to be, until such time as we deem it appropriate to promote you! So what?'

'I don't get it Jim. It's corporate bullshit.'

'It is indeed. You have to pay your dues in this business, son. If you don't like the taste of the shit we shovel down your throat, then go an see if it tastes any better elsewhere.'

'Are you serious?'

'I didn't like the taste myself, so I started my own company when I was considerably younger than you. Do you have any idea what *that* tasted like?'

'No.'

'Ten times worse. You've had it easy, son. It's never pleasant answering to bosses, and putting up with miles of corporate red tape. But when you run the place, you realise that you eat even more shit, because you're answering to clients. And you can't tell them to sod off, because they pay your bills. You don't just get to quit and move on. You have to swallow hard and try not to vomit.'

'I get that.'

'You don't really, but it's pointless arguing the point, Stephen.'

Stephen felt a little betrayed, but he had to concede that Jim had a point. Strangely, the old man seemed to be enjoying the altercation. He wasn't angry at all. In fact, he was smiling in way that seemed almost benevolent.

'You know I'm your highest earner, Jim?'

'Absolutely. That's why I want you back at your desk as soon as possible. How am I going to tell the wife I can't afford another bloody remodel of the holiday flat, without you bringing in the cash?'

Jim laughed, and Stephen couldn't help a small chuckle, even though he was severely irritated. He felt like a child who'd been caught out whinging about something that was so trivial that he couldn't force himself to maintain his anger.

'Come on Jim. Be straight with me here.'

'Alright. I know there's something else on your mind Stephen, it's not the promotion thing, is it? I'm not that daft.'

'Why do you invest so much of your time in me? Don't tell me it's just because you enjoy my company.'

'You know exactly why. Or at least, you *should*. You tell me.'

'Because you're priming me to take over and safeguard your investment in the company. Maybe even your legacy.'

'Yes.'

'Okay, so then why don't you just promote me and get on with it?'

'Three reasons: one, you're worth more to the company at the moment as a trader; two, you aren't enough of a team player to be able to occupy a leadership role at the company yet; and three, I'm not certain you're fully committed to a future in the industry.'

Stephen was slightly stunned. He sat and stared across at Jim, as if he was searching the older man's face for some sort of indication that he may have been joking.

'I understand your first two points. The last one has me at a bit of a loss, Jim. Does it have something to do with what Bridgette said in her report?'

'Yes and no. You're welcome to a copy of it if you'd like. I'll have Denise send it to you.'

'No thanks, Jim. I have no need to see it. Although I'm curious to understand what she said that may have made you question my ambitions in the industry?'

'Nothing I didn't already suspect before I sent you to her. But I wasn't going to screw with your career trajectory without a second opinion. Especially since my colleagues on the board have various misgivings about your attitude.'

'They don't seem to have any misgivings about my earning potential.'

'No, they don't. Business is business, Stephen. If you want loyalty, get a dog. I've never been anything other than candid with you, my lad.'

'I'm not so sure about that.'

'There's no *'thin skull'* rule here, Stephen.'

'What does that mean?'

'Just because you're not as adept as most people at discerning the reasons behind how I've chosen to mentor you, and the precise nature of my various motivations, doesn't mean I'm fully liable for the fallout.'

'So what you're saying is that you don't have to account for the fact that I thought we shared a unique and meaningful relationship.'

'We *do* share a unique and meaningful relationship, Stephen. But it's not my fault that you were naïve about why I initiated the process of getting us there.'

'But you knew I was.'

'Yes. I'm guilty in that respect, and I'm sorry about that.'

'Okay. Let's say I can accept that. Then why would you callously suggest that I move on if I don't like the situation here? And why do you question my intention to stay in the industry?'

'The answer to the first question has everything to do with the second, Stephen. I obviously don't want you going anywhere else, but I know you wouldn't. Not unless you ran off to do something completely different.'

'And what would you think of me if I *did* run off and do something else?'

'I'd be disappointed. But not in *you*.'

'Really?'

'Yes. I'd be inordinately proud of you, in fact.'

'Why?'

'Because it would take real balls to do something like that.'

'You don't think it would be a reckless mistake?'

'No. I think it would be a courageous decision, and I don't think you'd even consider it unless you had a deep personal reason to do so. In those circumstances, how could it possibly be a mistake?'

'Do you honestly believe that?'

'I do. So does Bridgette.'

'What did she say about that in the report? Specifically.'

'She said that you were clearly wrestling with the notion of a career change, and that once you'd made your decision, you'd follow through with it, full-heartedly.'

'So that's what got you worried about my commitment to a future in the industry?'

'Obviously it has.'

'What if she's wrong?'

'Is she?'

Stephen smiled and went a little red in the face.

'It was sort of a rhetorical question, Jim.'

The old man smiled at him and shook his head.

'You're done. Aren't you Steve?'

'Yes.'

'Please tell me you weren't just waiting for my permission to give it up all this time?'

'No. I only just gave it up about two minutes ago.'

'Good. But you're wrong, you know.'

'How so?'

'You gave it up when you initiated that short trade six weeks ago. You just needed time to come to terms with that. I knew it then, but I wasn't sure. I got the feeling Bridgette would help you figure it out.'

'You're probably right about that. Sorry Jim. I know you invested a lot in me.'

'It wasn't wasted, my lad. We *do* have a special relationship, and I only want it to grow stronger. Although I do have two personal questions for you.'

'Ask away.'

'What are you going to do for a living?'

'Draw dragons for my mate's computer game company. In fact, I'll probably freelance as an artist to various game companies, or book publishers. I may even try my hand at drawing for some comic book publishers.'

'Is there any money in that?'

'I've no idea. Maybe. But I don't really care. Didn't you hear? My assets have been released… If I liquidate some of my non-cash assets and add the proceeds to my existing portfolio, I'll be worth about three million quid. I'll get by.'

'Yes. You certainly will. Especially since you have the skills to grow it.'

Stephen laughed and shrugged his shoulders.

'Anyway, if I ever feel that I'm short a few bob, I'll knock on your door and charge you an exorbitant hourly fee to help train some of your junior traders.'

'You assume the board would approve that sort of thing?'

'It's a safe bet, Jim. At least it *will* be, as soon as they've forgiven me, and started to notice the dent in their numbers. Business is business, right?'

'Absolutely. I'm proud of you Stephen. Honestly.'

'Thanks, Jim. What was the other personal question you had for me?'

The old man's smile subsided slightly.

'Are you sleeping with my god-daughter?'

'Shit, Jim! What makes you think that?'

'She keeps bloody asking about you. She told me the two of you met a while ago, and went on a few dates.'

'No. We're just mates. I've met someone else.'

'Does *she* know that?'

'Well, I've told her. So I assume so.'

'There's a double standard at play here Stephen. The thin skull rule *does* apply when it comes to Cindy. I love you like a son, but if you break that girl's heart, you're fully liable for the consequences, even if she ought to have known better…'

'Understood!'

'Good. Now can we please go out for lunch and celebrate your freedom?'

'Absolutely!'

Stephen ended up having a lengthy lunch with Jim. They discussed various work-related things, but avoided discussing anything too technical. Stephen had been out of the loop, so he didn't have much to say about the prevailing conditions in the market.

He ended up telling Jim exactly what had happened with Cindy, even though he suspected that it may have hit a few raw nerves. Fortunately, it didn't. It appeared that Jim was well aware of his goddaughter's proclivities, and he intimated that he actually felt more sorry for Stephen than he did for *her*. She'd let him in on the fact that she'd asked Stephen to help her win her little bet with Sir Arthur, and Jim thought it was fantastic.

Stephen was a bit nonplussed by the fact that Jim was on board with the ruse, but the old man pointed out that the whole thing was loaded in Ashden senior's favour to start with, so a balancing of the scale was not only fair, but highly appropriate. Jim's loyalty to Cindy outweighed his loyalty to her father, which he felt was equally appropriate, given that he was her godfather. He also heartily approved of her career choice, which he knew irritated her father no end, but which he also felt duty bound to support.

Stephen got the distinct impression that Jim was a little crestfallen on account of the fact that he and Cindy were no more than friends, and the necessary implications of this gave him a particularly warm feeling.

Jim told him that he'd already given Cindy the good news about the result of the FCA investigation.

He indicated that the company would want Stephen to commit to at least two months notice, given his seniority, and Stephen wasn't at all concerned about that. It would also mean that he would qualify for an annual bonus, which wouldn't be insubstantial. He agreed that he would start working his notice in the following week though.

By the time they parted ways, Stephen felt considerably lighter. He hadn't spoken to Alexa since first thing in the morning, so he checked in on her to find out how her day was going. He desperately wanted to share his good news with her, but that would obviously be a reasonably complicated exercise. She seemed happy to hear from him, so that was all that mattered, for now.

He phoned his father and gave him the good news, although he didn't tell him about his sudden career change, because he felt that that was the sort of discussion that was best had in person, and he also wanted his mother to be included.

He then gave Charles a call, and asked if he was in London. He was, and they agreed to meet up for a drink that evening. Charles sounded a little distracted, but he was eager to meet up. Stephen insisted on finding somewhere closer to Charles's office this time, and he got no resistance from his friend in that regard.

24

By the time Stephen got to the little pub they'd selected, Charles was already there, and had found them a small table in the corner. He was having what appeared to be a double scotch, and had taken the liberty of ordering the same for his mate.

'Stevie!'

'Hey Charlie!'

'Thanks for suggesting the drink, mate. I need one today.'

'You look like you do. What's up? Is work still so hectic?'

'Work's under control. Thankfully. The home life's a bit tense.'

'Shit Charles. Sorry to hear that. What's wrong?'

'Nothing too disastrous. I'm just having to deal with some things I've been avoiding. I'm sure it'll work itself out, but I'm a little out of my comfort zone, so I need to clear my head.'

'I know all about that, mate.'

'Yeah. You look like the opposite of how I feel. You must be doing something right, Steve.'

'I have no idea whether or not I am, but I won't go into that right now. What's stressing you out at home? If you don't mind my asking.'

'I can't very well pretend like I haven't been pushing all sorts of advice down *your* throat recently, so you may as well have a shot at giving *me* some.'

'Yeah, I can try. Although given that it's an 'home' issue, I'm not sure I'm that well qualified to weigh in.'

'Jen and Amy want to get married and start a family.'

'Oh Fuck!'

'Yes. That's what I said. Apparently, it wasn't the right response.'

'Umm…'

'I also found my way to 'umm'. Apparently, that was equally inappropriate.'

The two men looked at each other and laughed.

'What on earth are you going to do about that, Charlie?'

'No idea. Feel free to weigh in, Steve.'

'Charles. As you know, I'm not the best when it comes to these sorts of things in *normal* circumstances.'

'No. I get that, but my circumstances are so *un*-normal, that I'll take any advice I can get at this point.'

'Can you legally be married to two women in this country, Charlie?'

'No. It's bloody complicated to be honest, Steve. It's not even like polygamy. That's legal in certain countries. This is polyamory. I don't know for sure, but I don't think it's legal *anywhere*.'

'When you say *'legal'*, I assume you simply mean that you can't have it legally recognised?'

'Yeah. We don't live in the dark ages, Steve. The authorities don't care how you manage your romantic relationships. They just don't have provision for it to be legally recognised as a marriage, and it's a criminal offence to try and be '*legally*' married to more than one person.'

'Yeah, I thought so.'

'Bear in mind, we'd *all* be married to one another. It wouldn't just be one of us, married to the other two. Even the lawyers haven't yet managed to figure out how that would work. I suppose that's why there isn't any provision for it.'

'So then the '*marriage*' would only really be symbolic, in other words.'

'Precisely. That's why I didn't think it was worth bothering. Although Jen and Amy clearly don't see it that way.'

'To be fair, Charlie, in practical terms, all marriages are primarily symbolic. I mean, the legal consequences are only a small part of it.'

'That's true. But so what? Nothing would change in our relationship, one way or another.'

'Then why are you so perturbed by the whole thing, mate?'

'I don't know, actually. It just makes me nervous.'

'Because *legal* commitment or not, it's still a more serious *moral* commitment than what you've currently got.'

'Look at you… making sensible points about relationships, Stevie. Fucking hell.'

'I'm right though, aren't I?'

'Yes. I suppose you are.'

'Do you love them?'

'Yes. Of course I do.'

'Both of them?'

'Of course. What kind of bloody question is that?'

'Sorry. I'm only just getting used to a regular relationship. I don't really understand the dynamic in your situation. Forgive me if I end up sounding offensive.'

'No. That's okay. I'm not offended. I sometimes forget that people don't understand the situation. It's basically identical to a normal relationship, there are just more of us. It shouldn't really complicate the situation, and it *doesn't*… usually.'

'Really?'

'Really.'

'Again. Sorry for sounding dumb and insensitive, but is it really that simple?'

'Yes. I love both of them equally, and I operate on the assumption that they each feel the same way about one another, and me.'

'The assumption?'

'It's the same as a normal relationship in that respect, Steve. You assume your partner feels the same way you do about them, and you go with it. There are no guarantees in either scenario.'

'But aren't there more pressure points in a situation like yours.'

'What do you mean?'

'You know. More potential points of contention. Like jealousy.'

Charles looked across at him thoughtfully and sighed.

'No. I think there's a lot of misconception about that sort of thing, when it comes to how people perceive a throuple. It's true that it's something I need to be aware of; but what you lose on the swings you often gain on the roundabouts.'

'How so?'

'I've been working incredibly long hours for almost six months now. I don't have a lonely girlfriend at home. They keep each other company, so I don't feel guilty about the fact that I've been absent, and they're considerably more understanding of my need to put in the hours, because the loneliness doesn't act as an emotional impediment to that understanding.'

'That's very interesting.'

'Yeah, also, for some reason I can't quite explain, they seem to be more secure than any of the girlfriends I've had in the past. In the sense that they aren't remotely worried about me running off with anyone else. They seem to understand that I'm fully committed, and I never get any indication from either of them that they suspect otherwise. I used to think that it was because they had one another, so if I fell out of the picture, they'd still be okay. But I don't think that any more. Our relationship is very solid.'

'So if that's the case Charlie, why not get symbolically *'married'*, and start a family?'

'You seem to think it's fairly straightforward.'

'It is. Come on Charles, you don't need someone as emotionally challenged as *me* to tell you that. You love Jen and Amy, you're convinced that they love you back, and that they feel the same way about one another, you've been together for what? Half a decade?'

'Seven years now.'

'You're an arsehole.'

'What?'

'If you'd been dating one woman for that long, by now you'd probably have married her. These two poor women have been inordinately patient with you.'

'Marriage isn't everything, Steve. You don't need to be *'married'*, legally or otherwise, to have a perfectly strong commitment. Stop being so old fashioned.'

'I'm not. You're prevaricating, and it's not fair on your partners. They clearly *do* want a more formal sort of commitment; both to you, and to one another.'

'It's different in our sort of relationship. It's like I told you; it wouldn't be me taking multiple wives, but I'm worried that it would look and feel like that was the case. The marriage thing always feels a little patriarchal and possessive when there's more than one partner involved. It looks like one man has taken two women as brides, as if they were some sort of chattels.'

'Yes, I understand that that may well be the perception. But since when did you care about what other people thought?'

'You're right. But still, it's tricky.'

'It's not. You've just built it up in your head. Probably because you're scared to tell your mother.'

'Okay. Maybe. But what *do* I tell my mother?'

'That she's getting her wish.'

'How so?'

'You're settling down, and giving her grandchildren. She can hardly complain, can she?'

Charles was forced to laugh.

'I never thought I'd be getting advice from *you* on this, Stephen. Much less, *good* advice!'

'I'm full of surprises Charlie. More than you think, actually.'

'Really? What else is lurking there beneath the surface, Mr West.'

'I quit my job today! I'll come and draw your bloody dragons… if you'll still have me.'

'Holy shit! Seriously?!'

'Seriously. Although I plan to freelance it. I don't think I'm going to take up formal employment again.'

'Good for you! We'll keep you on retainer!'

'I was hoping you'd say that.'

'It suits us. Less legal obligations, and less ongoing expense commitments. We love that sort of arrangement. We do it with most of our content writers.'

'Well, then I suppose we have a deal!'

'Bloody hell, Stevie. I'm ecstatic!'

'You should be more excited at the prospect of starting a family, Charles!'

'To be honest, I am. But I'm quietly shitting myself about it as well. I hope *that's* normal.'

'Come on then, finish your drink.'

'Why?'

'I'm taking you to look at engagement rings. You'll need two of the bloody things, so we best get cracking. I hope you have a fairly substantial budget.'

'Oh crap. I wonder if they give bulk discounts on things like that?'

'Not a bloody chance, Charlie.'

***

Stephen and Charles spent most of the evening looking at various jewellery shops around the more fashionable shopping areas of London, because that was where the shops stayed open late.

They had a bit of a laugh at some of the shops, because the proprietors clearly formed the impression that they were buying the rings for one another, and they deliberately avoided dispelling the notion. They were pretty certain that most gay couples opted for masculine wedding bands, over dainty diamond rings, but it was fun seeing how the presumptuous jewellers tried to navigate the encounters tactfully.

It didn't help that Charles wanted to try all of the rings on himself. Apparently, Jen had pretty large fingers, and he was convinced that he could use *his* ring finger as a model for hers. In the end though, once he'd settled on the shop, and the designs he was after, he agreed with the jeweller, that it would be prudent to go and check some of their existing jewellery at home, and call in the measurements before taking delivery. The jeweller clearly didn't believe that his new customer was going to be getting married to two women at once, but he wasn't about to complain about the fact that he was shifting two very expensive pieces of jewellery in one transaction. It was clearly the first time he'd sold two engagement rings to the same customer, at the same time.

The two men ended up having late night burgers in Covent Garden, before heading off in separate directions. They'd both had an extremely enjoyable evening. Not because either of them were particularly interested in jewellery, but because of what it signified. Stephen was looking forward to getting to know Jen and Amy, and he got to tell Charles all about Alexa.

***

The following day Stephen woke up far later than usual. It was the best night of sleep he'd had in ages. It didn't hurt that he was absolutely shattered from the day before, but he assumed that at least part of the reason he'd slept so well, was the fact that he'd effectively said goodbye to Ashden, Cole & Roberts.

He had an early message from Alexa, asking how he was and what his plans were for the rest of the week, and a message from Kenny asking when he was coming back to the office. Clearly word had gotten around about his imminent return.

He made himself coffee and replied to Alexa first.

Morning gorgeous. Sorry for the late reply. Don't blame me, blame your favourite game designer. I have no plans for the rest of the week. How about you?

Hey handsome. No fair. Were you out on the town with Charles Taylor last night?

In a manner of speaking…

> *What were the two of you doing?*

Looking at engagement rings.

> *What?!*

Don't worry, I'm not going to spring that sort of thing on you. Not yet.

> *Phew… although I like the 'yet' part. x*

Obviously, this is between the two of us, but Charlie's getting married. Well, at least he's going to ask the question.

> *Doesn't he have two girlfriends?*

Yeah… it was an expensive night out for poor Charlie. I thought he'd need some moral support.

> *Hahaha, that's so funny. The jeweller must have been chuffed to bits.*

He was, although we reckon he didn't believe that Charles was getting married twice at once.

> *What did he think then?*

We weren't sure, but he shut up and took enough money from Charles to rent a large villa in Spain for about six months.

> *Hahahaha.*

It's an expensive business this marriage thing.

> *If you ever propose to me Stephen, bear in mind that I'd rather have the Villa in Spain for six months than an exorbitantly expensive piece of Jewellery.*

I'll bear that in mind.

> *Not that I don't like shiny things… xxxx*

Message received. xxxx

> *You're quite charming when you want to be, Mr West.*

When can I come and visit you?

> *Why don't you come and spend the weekend?*

Done!

> *You aren't off galavanting with celebrities again tonight are you?*

Are we calling my best mate a celebrity now?

> *He's quite famous in the gaming world, Steve… You seem to ignore that.*

Because we've been mates for twenty years Allie, it kind of skews the perspective a bit.

> *That's a good point I suppose, I still can't believe I'm dating Charles Taylor's best mate.*

I'm glad you find that exciting, although…

> *You know what I mean, Steve. xxxx*

I miss you.

> *I miss you too. Now bugger off. I'm busy working!*

After having a shower and getting dressed, Stephen decided to go and have a coffee with Kenneth, and then meet up with Mary. They both needed to know what was going on, and he didn't want either of them to hear the news from anyone else.

He decided to start with Kenneth, because that was likely to be a shorter conversation. They met in one of the coffee shops on the same block as the office. Stephen offered to go into the office for coffee, but Kenny obviously wanted to get out a bit.

'You were right, Ken.'

'About what?'

'That you'd end up being at Ashden, Cole & Roberts longer than me.'

'They didn't give you the sack did they boss? The bastards!'

Stephen laughed and shook his head.

'No. I quit.'

'Really?'

'How can you possibly be surprised by that Ken? You predicted it.'

'Yeah, but I thought you'd hang on for a bit, boss. I was kind of hoping you would.'

'Sorry Ken, but you contributed to the decision, so what can I say?'

'No. It was a great decision, boss. I'm happy for you. Out of curiosity though… did they offer to promote you?'

'No.'

'That's surprising.'

'Jim's not as daft as you think Ken, nor as underhanded. He's a shrewd businessman, for sure, and I've no doubt that he looks after number one. But that's his prerogative, given the road he's taken to get to where he is.'

'I suppose that's fair.'

'He's a good man, Ken. You could do a lot worse than working under him. He's agreed to take you under his wing after I've worked out my notice. So give him your best effort, and try not to be so cynical. He knows your history. Not from me, he knew it because he knows your father… quite well, in fact.'

'Yeah, my Dad's a client of Jim's. I expect that's how I got the job in the first place, to be honest boss.'

'That makes sense. It doesn't phase me though. You're a clever chap, and you deserve the job.'

'Thanks boss. I'm really going to miss you.'

'You don't have to end up missing me, Ken. Stay in touch after I leave. I'm not going anywhere… I may move to Surrey, but no further.'

'Why Surrey?'

'Remember that date I went on?'

'Yeah, I do…'

'It ended up working out rather well.'

'Nice!'

'Anyway, if all goes according to plan, I'll buy a house down there, and you can come and visit.'

'That sounds splendid, boss.'

'Good!'

'What are you going to do though?'

'You mean, for a living?'

'Yeah.'

'I'm going to draw dragons for a massive gaming company. Ever heard of

The Other Planet?'

'Shit, boss. Of course. Who hasn't?'

'Most people over the age of thirty five, Ken.'

'That game is legendary, boss. The company that owns it has the best game design team in the world. Have you heard of Charles Taylor?'

Stephen laughed so hard, he started coughing. Clearly, Charlie *was* quite famous.

'Charlie's my best mate. You aren't the only one here who's managed to get a job through a bit of quiet nepotism, Ken.'

'Boss. I can't believe it. That's one of the coolest career changes I've ever heard of.'

'I can't say I'm not excited about it.'

'Will you introduce me to Charles?'

'Of course I will, Ken.'

They finished their coffees and walked back to the office together. Stephen was going to see Mary, and he'd agreed to meet her at the office instead of dragging her out. He wasn't sure how she'd receive the news, so he thought it would be best to speak with her in private. Ken wished him luck and they went their separate ways at the lifts.

Mary was waiting with a bottle of champagne in Stephen's office when he got there, and he felt slightly guilty that he hadn't given her some warning about what was happening. He didn't want to disappoint her, especially since she seemed to be in the mood for a celebration.

'Welcome home, Stephen!'

'Thanks Mary, but I'm only officially back next week. Did Jim tell you?'

'Yes. He did. But I'm glad you decided to come in and see me today. I can catch you up on some things if you'd like?'

'No thanks M. Just here to chat.'

'That's even better.'

'I have some news, M.'

'Did you get the promotion?'

'No.'

She fell silent. She'd clearly assumed that that was what he'd wanted to talk about.

'What is it? Are you ill or something?'

Stephen wanted to laugh, but he realised that it would be insensitive, given what he was about to tell her.

'I'm out, M. I'm done.'

'But Jim said you'd be back next week…'

'To commence working in two months' notice.'

Mary, sat down on the edge of the desk and started crying. Stephen was still standing in the doorway. He wanted to go and put his arms around her, but he wasn't sure whether or not it would be appropriate, so he hesitated.

'I can't do it anymore, M. I have to get out. I've had enough.'

She stood up, tried to wipe the tears away and forced a smile.

'I understand. I just thought we'd leave together one day.'

'To do what, M?'

'I don't know… set up a consultancy or something.'

'How much do you know about the art world, M?'

'Bugger all. Why?'

'I'm going to become a freelance artist.'

'You're joking?'

'No. I'm not.'

'Would you consider taking me on to help you?'

'No.'

'Why not?'

'Two reasons M: one, I couldn't afford to pay you anything remotely reasonable, at least not for a very long time; and two, I need to do this on my own. It's time for me to grow up and run my own life. We both know that if you came with me, I'd revert to my old habits.'

'You're right… but I also want to leave this place. The stuff I do here is somehow simultaneously boring *and* stressful. I didn't think it was possible for that to happen. You tend to associate '*boring*' with more peaceful occupations.'

Stephen chuckled. It was a strange observation, but he understood what she meant.

'When I told you I'd leave if you did, I wasn't kidding, Stephen.'

'M, I have a proposal for you. It's not a job offer though. I'm serious about the fact that I need to go it on my own.'

'What's the proposal then?'

'I'll pay for you to go and see Bridgette. Let her help you figure out what you really want to do.'

'You'd do that for me?'

'Of course I would. I would also like for us to stay friends, M. I still want you to be part of my life.'

'I don't know what to say…'

'You don't need to say anything. Just take me up on the offer.'

'Of course I will.'

**

Stephen left the office and headed home. It was mid-afternoon by the time he got back, and he felt like it was considerably later, because the morning's activities had drained him.

He didn't like upsetting Mary, and he'd fought hard to stop himself from making her a job offer. He knew that if he did, she'd have taken it; even if he'd offered her considerably less than what she made at the company. That wouldn't have been fair to her. He was also certain that if she stayed on working for him, he'd fall back into his habit of allowing her to run his life.

He spent the latter half of the afternoon cleaning up the flat. He'd almost forgotten about the box of S&M kit he'd hidden in his cupboard before Alexa came to visit, and he decided to take it out and put it on the coffee table, so that he'd remember to try and sell off the various parts online. He considered just binning everything, but his abhorrence for wasting money stopped him.

By around seven o' clock he started to get hungry, so he ordered a takeaway pizza. He was surprised when his doorbell rang about ten minutes later. There was no way that his order could have been completed and delivered in that time.

He was right. It *wasn't* his pizza. It was Cindy, and she was wearing considerably less clothing than even the most scantily clad pizza delivery driver he'd seen in the cheap pornographic films he'd watched with his mates at university.

She was wearing a black mini-skirt, high heels, stockings, and a corset which was immodestly hidden under a short coat, that was only closed with one button just above the waist. In her right hand was a bottle of

Moët & Chandon; and in her left, two long-stemmed champagne glasses.

'Cindy. Hi, what are you doing here?'

'I hear a celebration's in order. I was going to send you this bottle, but I decided that since I was in the city today, I'd come past myself to congratulate you.'

'Wow... umm... thanks.'

Stephen was having difficulty finding somewhere appropriate to look. Cindy was clearly not only aware of this, she was revelling in it.

'You're wondering why I'm dressed like a porno barbie, Steve?'

'Umm...'

His mouth went dry. He didn't quite know how to handle this situation. He had no intention whatsoever of cheating on Alexa, but he felt like he was cheating on her just by being in the same room as Cindy when she was dressed like she was.

'I dressed like this because I'm too naughty for my own good, and I couldn't help myself.'

'But...'

'But, you told me you were serious about that girl I saw you with the other day. Alexa? was it?'

'Yes.'

'I know, and I'd love to tell you that I respect that, but I'm battling with the notion to be honest, and I had to make sure.'

'Bloody hell, Cindy.'

'Am I a bit out of line here, Steve?'

'Yes.'

'Shit. Sorry.'

'Look… Cindy, I'm not going to lie and tell you that you don't look like the highlights package of every sexual fantasy I've ever had. I'm still a man… but I am committed to Alexa. So…'

'You're making this even harder for me Steve, by being such a gentleman. I hope that woman knows what she's got.'

'I hope so too. It's not like you're making things any easier for me, Ms Ashden. My god!'

They both laughed.

'Well, congratulations on clearing your name Mr West. Will you still help me with my bet?'

'Yes.'

She giggled and went a bit red.

'Sorry Steve. Honestly, I'm just not used to being told '*no*'.'

'Don't be too hard on yourself, you've flattered me half to death, Cindy. I won't drink that Champagne with you, because I don't trust myself *that* much, but you're welcome to stay and share a pizza with me.'

'That would be nice.'

Steve's Pizza arrived a few minutes later, and they shared it and discussed Cindy's investment strategy briefly. She noticed the open box of bondage gear on the coffee table, and couldn't help having a laugh.

'Is that the infamous package from the S&M dating site, Steve?'

'It is indeed.'

'Can I have a look?'

'As long as you promise not to try anything on.'

'I think I can contain myself.'

'Have at it then. I don't know how I'm going to get rid off the contents now that their packaging's been removed. The EDgE people won't take it back.'

'I think I'll be able to help you with that, Steve.'

'Are you…'

She laughed.

'No, I've never tried it. Not sure it's my thing. I'm fairly open minded, but…'

'Then how could you help?'

'My best mate, Daisy, runs an S&M club in Chelsea.'

'You're kidding.'

'Nope. I've even been to visit. It's very smart. She does it in a mansion that was left to her by her grandfather. The poor old bugger would probably be turning in his grave, if he knew what she was doing with the place.'

'Oh shit… that's incredible.'

'Yeah. She's a professional dominatrix. She must be fairly good at it too, because she makes an absolute fortune. Not that she needs the money. It's obviously her passion.'

'Wow…'

'Yeah, it's an interesting choice. I'll admit.'

'Do her parents know.'

'Her mom does.'

'Shit.'

'Yeah, I don't think her dad would be overly impressed if he found out. But what he doesn't know won't hurt him.'

'So you think she'd take the stuff off my hands?'

'Yeah, it looks like high quality stuff. I'm sure she's always on the lookout for inventory. I'll take it and show her for you.'

'Thanks.'

After saying their goodbyes, she left with the box of paraphernalia.

Stephen was dead tired, but it was still a little early to turn in, so he picked up the book he'd been reading, and settled in on the sofa. He was asleep within fifteen minutes.

25

At about a quarter to one in the morning, Stephen was woken up by a phone call that he first assumed was an alarm. He only realised that it wasn't, when he couldn't find the cancellation button on the screen.

The name scrolling across the top of the screen was '*Karen Short*'. Stephen woke up instantly in a panic. Nobody called this late unless something was wrong, and his mind immediately jumped to Alexa.

'Hi Karen… *what's up*? Why the late call? I haven't heard from Alexa this evening. There's nothing wrong with her is there?!'

'No, she's alive and healthy. But if you don't have some bloody good answers for me… *you* won't be!'

On hearing that there was nothing wrong with Alexa, he breathed a deep sigh of relief. But he was still a bit shaken up, and the balance of Karen's statement didn't exactly put him at ease.

'Shit, Karen! If this is about the bloody job thing, I promise you I've been trying to tell her, she just keeps changing the subject, and I end up losing the resolve to do it. I know that's no excuse, but I promise I will tell her as soon as I see her.'

'*If* you ever see her again, Stephen.'

'What?!'

He had a litany of questions for Karen, but he was still a bit dazed and confused. Clearly, Alexa had found out about the fact that he'd been lying, and clearly, she'd confronted her sister about the whole thing.

He felt slightly sickened by the fact that his cowardice had not only pissed Alexa off to the extent that she wasn't willing to talk to him, but he'd obviously landed Karen in it as well.

'Is she there with you, Karen?'

'No she *isn't*. She's not inclined to speak with you right now, and frankly, I don't blame her.'

Stephen's anxiety had turned to frustration. He'd had time to wake up a bit, and he was actually slightly irritated with Karen for sticking her nose into his business.

'What is it that I'm supposed to have done Karen? I'm getting too old for games!'

'Don't take that tone with me, Stephen. My poor little sister is fucking heartbroken… and I vouched for you, you wanker!'

'Is it about the job thing?'

'Not really… no!'

'Alexa went to surprise you this evening, at your flat.'

'And?'

'Well… you tell *me*! Did she ever arrive?'

'No, she didn't.'

'That's because when she got there, she saw you inviting a pretty young girl inside. Apparently, the said girl was dressed like a prostitute, and was carrying a bottle of bubbly.'

'Oh, fuck!'

'Oh fuck indeed, Stephen!'

'But…'

'Then she sat outside for just over an hour, whilst you were doing whatever it was that you were doing with this girl.'

'I can explain…'

'We'll get to that part just now, Stephen. But let me finish. Because it gets *worse*!'

'She saw your guest leave, carrying a large box with an odd logo on the side of it. So she went online to see what sort of things the company sold.'

'Oh god…'

'EDgE, Stephen? An S&M dating site? Really?'

'I'll explain if you'll let me get a word in here, Karen.'

'No. Not yet, let me finish.'

'Fine, go on then.'

'So, quite reasonably, my little sister assumes that you are cheating on her with the young blonde dominatrix… not that the S&M thing is the *nasty* part. It just adds a certain *flavour* to the story… don't you *think*?'

'You don't understand, Karen.'

'By the way, Stephen. She then went and did some digging on you, and found out where you *actually* work. Moreover, the first thing that pops up when your name is put into a search engine is that lovely little article that was published in the Financial Times recently… You know the one I'm talking about, don't you?'

'Fuck!'

Stephen's irritation had turned back to anxiety, and he felt like he was about to be sick.

'Oliver seems to think you aren't a cheating bastard, and to be perfectly honest, I never pegged you for the type *myself*. That's the only reason I agreed to have this chat with you. It was *his* idea. Alexa doesn't know we're having it, and I'd thank you to keep it that way.'

'Of course.'

'So now I've said my piece Stephen. My sister is livid with me as well, because I was forced to admit that I knew exactly what you did for a living, and even that I'd read that ghastly newspaper article about you. That's actually why I called you so late. I'm exceedingly pissed off because you've dragged me into your bloody mess.'

'I'm sorry Karen. I can explain everything if you'll let me.'

'Go on then.'

'The girl Alexa saw is called Cindy.'

'I know that. Alexa's even met the cow, and she knows that she has a thing for you.'

'That's true.'

'This isn't sounding any better for you, Stephen.'

Stephen closed his eyes, breathed deeply, and gathered his thoughts before going on.

'She's the daughter of the chairman of the company I work for. You've obviously heard of Arthur Ashden?'

'I have.'

'You can check it out and see that he has a daughter called Cindy.'

'*Whatever*. Get to the point!'

'Cindy and I went out on a date a few months ago, and I behaved like a serious arsehole. I lied about my identity and made up a stupid story to try and chase her off. Alexa knows this, by the way.'

'*Really?*'

'Yes, really. It's a long and slightly convoluted story, but suffice it to say, I didn't know who Cindy was until after I'd made an arse of myself, and I ended up having to grovel a bit, so that she didn't shop me to her Dad.'

'What is wrong with you, Stephen?'

'I don't know, Karen, I'm busy trying to figure that out. It's a process.'

'Clearly.'

'I went out with Cindy again last week, with Alexa's full knowledge and consent, so that I could make amends and try to convince her not to wreck my career.'

'Okay, so?'

'So it turns out that Cindy knew who I was all along, and she was toying with me. She turned out to be rather nice, and I agreed to help her with an investment project she's been working on, once my trading suspension was lifted.'

'Bullshit.'

'Seriously, Karen. I now see the stupidity of agreeing to spend time with her.'

'So what the fuck was she doing at your apartment in stockings and corsets this evening?'

'Honestly Karen, she was trying to seduce me.'

'Well that's bloody obvious. So why did you let her in?'

'Because I'm a fucking idiot.'

'I'm going to need a bit more than that piece of obvious information, Stephen.'

'My matter with the FCA has been resolved, at least for now. My suspension has been lifted, my assets have been released, and I've been allowed to go back to work. Cindy knows this, because she's been keeping abreast of developments through my boss, Jim Roberts. He's her godfather.'

'Shit Stephen, you really know how to land yourself in it, don't you.'

'Yes, I do. Cindy showed up at my place under the pretext of wanting to celebrate the lifting of my suspension; and took the opportunity to try and tempt me into bed with her. I'm not saying I wasn't flattered Karen, and I'm not saying it wasn't incredibly difficult not to take the bait; but I told her I was taken, shared a pizza I'd ordered with her, and sent her on her merry way.'

'With a box of something or other from an S&M dating site?'

'It was a box of bondage paraphernalia Karen. Yes!'

'What the fuck?'

'I'll admit that looks bad.'

'I'm dying to hear an explanation for that one, Stephen.'

At this point, Stephen's anxiety had turned to a mild form of mania, probably brought on by a combination of exhaustion and frustration. He couldn't help but laugh.

'Because I fucking mistakenly ordered the bloody things online, thinking that the "*date box*" I was buying was filled with chocolates, condoms and expensive wine… *okay*?! Cindy offered to sell them to a mate of hers on my behalf…'

'How the bloody hell could you buy something like *that* by '*mistake*', Stephen? I know it's more common now, but it isn't exactly '*mainstream*'. I know it's probably none of my business, but I may as well ask. What kind of *websites* are you frequenting? You're not buying date boxes from strange porn sites are you?'

'No! I'm just bad at doing normal things, because I've been leading a sheltered existence, Karen. I've no idea how to filter things like that properly online, because all I do is *work*, and my personal assistant runs my fucking life in the background. I *know* what that sounds like, but it's just a bloody fact, and I'm working to try and fix it.'

Karen sighed.

'Really, Stephen?'

'I know it sounds stupid and unbelievable, Karen. I know I'm an idiot, but it's all true. I *promise you*! I *love* your sister, Karen. I would do absolutely anything for her, I don't care about anything else. You have to believe me.'

'I do Stephen.'

'What time does she normally go into the bakery?'

'Five. But she's likely to be there early, because she bakes when she's upset.'

'Alright.'

***

The question of how to get out to Surrey at this hour was now at the forefront of his mind. A car was the only option.

Fortunately, he now had his access card, and could get back into the office. If he was lucky, Jim's keys would be in Denise's top drawer, and he could borrow the old man's car again. He considered giving Jim a call to ask, but he got the idea that he'd be more upset at being woken up this late than he'd be as a result of Stephen borrowing the vehicle without asking. So he took a taxi to the office.

The office stayed open around the clock, and it wasn't even remotely strange to the night staff at reception to see him running through the turnstiles at that hour. In fact, he shared the lift up to Jim's offices with two junior colleagues, both of whom looked like they were just starting work for the day. He wasn't surprised to find Jim's keys exactly where he'd expected them to be - his boss was a creature of habit - but he was still relieved when he did.

He took the lift down to the basement, found the car in its usual spot, and jumped in. This time, he wasn't going to muck about with his phone GPS, so he copied the address off the front of his journal into the inbuilt system in the vehicle, and after some fiddling, managed to get it to work.

By the time he got to Shere, it was just before three a.m. He parked on the street outside the bakery, got out, and started pacing up and down on the pavement. He got the feeling that if he stayed in the car, he'd be asleep within minutes.

He wasn't expecting to be accosted by a member of the local police force, and he was so tired and uptight, that his attitude towards the officer in question wasn't particularly helpful.

'Good morning Sir.'

'Officer.'

'Might I ask what it is you're doing hanging around outside the bakery at this time of the morning?'

'Minding my own business officer. I'd thank you to do the same!'

'Sir, there's no need to get short with me. Vagrancy isn't tolerated in this village, and I'll thank *you* for moving along.'

'*Excuse me?*'

'Sir… it's a quarter to four in the morning, and you're loitering outside a bakery. I'm giving you the benefit of the doubt by allowing you to move along quietly.'

'I know the owner of this bakery officer, I'm waiting for her to arrive.'

'A bit *early*… even for a *baker*, isn't it?'

'Look, I'm sure you have better things to do with your time. I'm not a bloody vagrant. That's my vehicle parked across the street. How many vagrants do you know who drive Range Rovers?'

'So wait in the vehicle then Sir, but I can't have you hanging around in the street. It's unseemly, and it makes it look as if I'm not doing my job.'

'Fine!'

'Before you go though, what's your name?

'Charles F Chaplin.'

'Sir. You *are* aware that it is an offence to give false information to the police?'

'I am indeed.'

'Very well Sir. Kindly make your way back to your vehicle.'

Stephen stormed off to the car and climbed inside, slamming the door shut behind him.

***

The police constable was justifiably irritated, and he wasn't inclined to let the matter go just yet. He'd been inordinately polite and patient with this snotty individual, and he'd had it thrown back at him with unnecessary bile. He radioed in to the station.

'Evening Paul, hope I haven't disturbed your four a.m. cuppa, but I need you to run a plate for me.'

'No problem mate, what's the story?'

'I have some smug bastard loitering around the bakery down in the village. I don't think he's a vagrant, but there's definitely something strange about him, he's been pacing up and down nervously for the last hour. He's driving a black Range Rover with registration number LF19 7GHO. Can you tell me who he is?'

'Yeah, hold on.'

'Thanks!'

'That Range Rover's registered to a James Roberts, in Chelsea.'

'Well, he's pretty far from home for *this* time of the morning, *isn't he*?'

'Maybe he's visiting someone?'

'Hmmm, maybe. But I don't like it. He definitely gave me a false name as well. Do you have a contact number for Mr Roberts?'

'Yeah.'

'Give him a call, would you? Ask him where he thinks his vehicle is. Also, ask him if he knows a Mr. *Chaplin*.'

'Is that what the sod told you his name was?'

'Yeah. *Charles Chaplin*, no less. See what I *mean*?'

'Yeah, alright, I'll call the number and see if anybody answers.'

***

'Gary. You *there*?'

'Yeah, did you manage to get hold of Mr Roberts?'

'I did. A right bloody *handful* he was 'n all…'

'And?'

'Sounded like I dragged him out of bed. He isn't in Shere, and he says as far as he's aware, his Range Rover is securely stored at his office in the middle of London. When I asked him whether or not he knew anyone by the name of Charles Chaplin, the old bugger lost his temper with me. He thought I was playing some sort of prank on him. Thankfully I managed to calm him down… he'll thank me tomorrow when he gets his car back though.'

'Thanks Paul. I'm going to enjoy nicking this one!'

26

The constable made his way over to Stephen, who was trying to stay awake by playing a game on his phone. When he heard a knock on the window he got such a fright that he dropped the phone.

'Sir. Please get out of the vehicle.'

'Now what? aren't I allowed to *park* here?'

'Sir, just step out of the vehicle.'

'Fine!'

'Sir, I'm arresting you on suspicion of theft. We have reason to believe that this vehicle does not belong to you, and that you have appropriated it without the permission of its registered owner…You do not have to say anything. But, it may harm your defence if you do not mention when questioned, something which you later rely on in court. Anything you do say may be given in evidence.'

'Oh come on! Officer, this is a misunderstanding. The car belongs to my boss, and I borrow it from time to time.'

'You told me it was yours when we spoke earlier.'

'I misspoke, sorry. It's an expression. I didn't mean that I actually owned the vehicle.'

'This car is registered to a gentleman by the name of Roberts. One of my colleagues has telephoned Mr Roberts, and he insists that the vehicle ought to be at his offices in London. He also insists that he doesn't know any living person by the name of Charles Chaplin.'

'That's *not* my name! You bloody-well *knew* that all along!'

'Sir, are you admitting to me that you provided a police officer with a false name?'

'Yes. I'm sorry.'

'Sir, that is *also* an offence.'

'I know. Look, my name is *Stephen West*. I work for Mr Roberts, please call him back. I can assure you that he'll confirm it, and that he'll tell you everything's alright.'

'We'll certainly do that, but at a more reasonable hour. We're not in the habit of burdening vehicle owners any more than we have to, with such calls. We've already disturbed Mr Roberts enough, so we'll resume contact with him during business hours. In the meantime, you're under arrest, Mr West.'

'Fine. Do what you want.'

'Before we go though. What is your relationship with the owner of this bakery?'

'She's my girlfriend.'

'Alright. What's her name?'

'Alexa Harding.'

'Thank you. We'll look into that information.'

'Please don't tell her I've been arrested.'

He placed Stephen in handcuffs and ushered him into the back seat of his police car. But instead of getting in and taking his prisoner off to the station, he got back onto the radio.

'Hi Paul, do me a favour. Send a car to pick up this lout.'

'Alright Gary, but I need a reason, for the record.'

'He says he's the boyfriend of the nice young lady who runs the bakery. I want to stick around until she gets here. On the *one hand*, he may be telling the truth; but on the *other*, he may be a stalker, and I don't want her to be unaware of this incident. It wouldn't be right.'

'Yeah, sounds sensible to me, Gary. I'll have him picked up.'

'By the way, he says his name's *West*. He claims that that Roberts chap is his *boss*. Give him a buzz at the end of your shift and find out, *will you*?'

'Yeah, I'll make a note of it. What's his first name?'

'Stephen. Apparently.'

***

Alexa arrived at the bakery about five minutes after Stephen was picked up and taken off to the station by two young officers who'd volunteered to collect him. They didn't see much action out in the country, and the opportunity to transport a prisoner was the highlight of an otherwise mind numbingly boring shift.

Constable Bridge, who expected her to show up fairly early, was waiting outside the bakery.

'Good morning Madam. Constable Gary Bridge. I wonder if I might have a quiet word with you, I'm sure it's nothing to be alarmed about.'

'Of course, constable.'

'We picked up a gentleman who was loitering around the front of your shop, just under an hour ago. He claims to know you...'

'Oh no. His name's not Stephen West, *is it*?'

'He claims it is. You haven't had any difficulties with this individual have you?'

'Apart from the fact that he has a lot of explaining to do, no. He's my boyfriend…or at least he *was* until fairly recently.'

'He was waiting for me officer, he *wasn't* loitering.'

'Very well. But we also suspect that the car he was driving didn't belong to him. That black Range Rover over there. Have you seen it before?'

'Yes. Apparently it belongs to his boss, he borrows it from time to time.'

'Do you know his boss' name by any chance?'

'No. I'm afraid I don't.'

'We intend to hold him until we can verify his story.'

'I suppose that's fair.'

'Odd chap this West, are you sure he's exactly who he *says* he is?'

'I'm fairly sure he's not a car thief, if *that's* what you mean, constable. As for the rest; I'm still deciding.'

'You're a wise young lady, if you don't mind me saying.'

'Thank you.'

'That said, I'm going to have his details run through our system. You can't be too careful these days, can you.'

'No, I suppose not, constable.'

'If anything out of the ordinary comes up, I'll let you know.'

'Thank you. As I say, I'm fairly certain he didn't steal the car.'

'Very well, Madam.'

***

After he'd arrived at the station and been processed, Stephen managed to convince the duty sergeant to call Jim back, and hand him the phone. He was informed that, contrary to popular belief, he wasn't automatically entitled to a phone call, but the Sergeant was in a mildly sympathetic mood, and he wasn't averse to waking James Roberts up again so early, because the nasty old bugger had been particularly obnoxious to him earlier on.

'Morning Jim…'

'For fuck's sake, Stephen! Do you know what time it is? I already got woken up by some prick pretending to be a policeman at *four*… What the fuck can be so important that you'd call me at *this hour*?'

'He *was* a real copper, Jim.'

'*What*?!'

'I borrowed your car again. Sorry.'

'What the bloody hell is *wrong* with you Stephen? Are you on *drugs*?'

'My new girlfriend thought I was cheating on her, so I had to get out to Surrey to try and convince her it wasn't true. I didn't want to wake you… I know I'm a bloody idiot, but please tell the local constabulary I'm not a car thief.'

'But you *are* a car thief, son.'

Stephen wasn't expecting that sort of response. Maybe he'd pushed Jim too far this time. His mouth went dry, and he felt his heartbeat speed up.

'Jim, I…'

Before he could continue though, he heard Jim start to howl with laughter on the other end of the line. It was so loud that even the Sergeant heard it and couldn't help cracking a grin.

'Just kidding, you deserved that though!'

Stephen couldn't laugh. He was too overwrought. But he breathed in deeply and forced a weak smile.

'I know I did. Sorry Jim.'

'I suppose I should be happy that you managed to get a girlfriend in the first place. Although it wasn't smart to fucking cheat on her, *was it?*'

'I didn't cheat on her, Jim!'

'Then why on earth did she think you did?'

'Because she saw a very pretty young girl enter my apartment and come out an hour later carrying a box of sex toys.'

Jim started laughing again with renewed vigour. The Sergeant, who was now listening intently to Stephen's side of the conversation, was trying very hard not to laugh, but it wasn't working.

'What the fuck?! It sounds like her impression was well founded my lad, if you were being had up for it at the Old Bailey, you'd have a bloody hard time convincing a jury of your peers that you weren't the guiltiest little bastard in history.'

'Yes. I get that.'

'So what happened? Did you celebrate your new found freedom by ordering an escort or something? Then lose your bottle in the middle of the transaction?'

'No. I said I didn't cheat.'

'I didn't say you did, I said you tried and failed.'

'No. It was your god-daughter Jim!'

By this stage, the Sergeant was crying with laughter. It was getting more interesting by the second.

'Cindy?'

'The very same...'

'What the fuck was *she* doing there, Stephen?'

'She popped over unannounced with a bottle of Moët and two glasses. Ostensibly, to celebrate the lifting of my suspension… that *you'd* told her about!'

'Shit! She obviously likes you then.'

'Well, yes. That seems to be the case.'

'You didn't hurt her bloody feelings did you, Stephen?'

'No. We had a pizza and talked for a bit. Then she left and took that box of bloody S&M gear to sell to one of her mates for me.'

'Oh yeah, her mate Daisy runs one of those bondage dungeons down the road from me. Apparently it's quite popular. Never tried it myself, but it looks interesting…'

'My god, Jim.'

'Stop being old fashioned, Stephen.'

'So your new missus saw all of that then? I mean the coming and going, etcetera.'

'Yeah.'

'Shite! You've got a fair bit of explaining to do.'

'Yes. So please tell the kind Sergeant that I'm not a thief, so that I can get after her.'

'Of course. But you owe me one. Next time you decide to borrow the car, at least send me a bloody message.'

'I owe you many, Jim. Add it to the tab.'

'Go on then, hand me over to the good Sergeant. I also have to apologise to him for being an obnoxious tool when he phoned me earlier.'

'Thanks Jim.'

The Sergeant accepted Jim's apology with grace, and after writing up a brief account of the incident, let Stephen go. He also had one of his junior officers return him to the bakery.

***

The door was open, and he could see that the lights had been turned on inside the shop. So he ducked through the opening. Alexa was leaning against the display counter with her arms folded. Her eyes betrayed the fact that she'd been crying, and all Stephen wanted to do was hold her, but he knew that it wasn't the right thing to do in that moment, so he restrained himself.

'Hi Alexa.'

'Stephen. You look terrible!'

He did. Even though he hadn't spent any time in the cells at the police station, anyone would be forgiven for assuming that he'd been locked up for at least a whole evening. He was unshaven; his shirt was so crumpled that it looked as if he'd taken it off and used it as a drying rag; and he was so tired that he could barely stand up straight.

'I *feel* terrible… and not because of the fact that I've barely slept. I *lied* to you, and I'm sorry.'

She nodded and wiped her eyes with the sleeve of her long chef's jacket.

'Let's start at the beginning. Why did you tell me you were a graphic designer?'

'Because I liked you, and Ollie told me you hated people in finance. It was properly stupid, I *know*, but once it was out there, I was too embarrassed to come clean about it. It got even more difficult to broach the subject as we got closer. I tried to tell you, but I just never found the right opportunity.'

She nodded again, and stared at him thoughtfully.

'I get it. The truth is that Ollie was *right*, I've been labelling people and making unfair assumptions about them based on what they do for a living. So I guess *that* one was partly *my* fault. Karen actually told me that part of the story last night, she admitted that she knew you hadn't told me the truth, and she explained why. I just wanted to hear it from *you*.'

'Sorry Allie. I should have told you at the outset.'

She seemed to accept this, because she sighed and gave him another nod.

'Are you really being had up for securities fraud?'

'I was. I think it's over now, though. They've lifted my suspension, and released my assets. That's another story entirely, but as I say, I think it's over. I didn't do anything wrong, I just took a massive gamble that paid off, and the powers that be suspected I'd been involved in some dodgy conduct, because my gamble was unrealistically successful.'

'So you're going back to work now?'

'Yes and no.'

'What does that mean?'

'I quit.'

'Seriously? Why?'

'I'm done with the city, Al. I'm not saying you're right about all of the terrible bankers and stockbrokers, that wouldn't be fair, but I've realised over the past five weeks that it's not for me anymore. I've lost my passion for it.'

'What will you do now?'

'I'm going to go and work for Charles. Well, sort of... I'm going to freelance. But he's retaining me to design and draw dragons for the new expansion of the game.'

'Wow. That's incredible... So now you actually *are* a graphic designer... of sorts.'

'Yeah, I suppose I will be.'

'It wasn't just because of me, was it?'

'I'm not going to lie and tell you that you didn't play a role. Charlie planted the seed when I told him that I was finding it difficult getting the opportunity to tell you the truth.'

'Seriously?'

'It shouldn't come as much of a surprise to you that Charlie thinks outside of the box. His proposed solution wasn't for me to just come clean and tell you, it was to change careers, so that I wouldn't have to.'

Alexa was forced to laugh, despite the fact that it seemed inappropriate in the circumstances.

'Sorry, Steve. It's just that that is one of the craziest things I've ever heard.'

'It's true.'

'Oh, I believe you. It's still mad though.'

'It certainly is. But I ended up doing it.'

'But not for that reason, I hope?'

'No. Honestly, it wasn't that.'

'Okay, I accept that. But I really want to know what happened with Cindy, Steve. You must understand how that looked?'

'Of course I do Allie. I've been an unmitigated fool with that woman from start to finish.'

'Why was she there with you last night? Please explain.'

'So remember I went to speak with her after we bumped into her at the cheese thing?'

'Yes. I also remember telling you to be careful because she clearly had a thing for you.'

'Yes. You did. But I didn't take proper notice. Sorry.'

'You agreed to see her again?'

'Yes and no.'

'Explain.'

'So it's true that she's the daughter of the chairman of the company I work for. It's just that it's an investment firm, as you now know. Cindy asked me to help her win a bet she'd made with her father, by helping her with an investment strategy. It sounds ridiculous, because it is. But I agreed to help her on the condition that my trading suspension was lifted by the FCA.'

'Okay. But that doesn't really complete the picture for me, Steve.'

'No. I get that… She found out from my boss, who happens to be her godfather, that I was all but cleared by the FCA, and she came to congratulate me.'

'Well, that was clearly a ruse.'

'Yes. I see that now. She got tarted up and came over to '*celebrate*', unannounced. Partly because she was pleased that I could now help her with the bet, but primarily because she wanted to try her luck with me. I must admit that.'

'How did she know where you lived?'

'I gave her my address when I agreed to help her; so she could post me a breakdown of her investments. I didn't want her emailing me, because I was sure my emails were being monitored, and I didn't want the FCA getting the idea that I was trading whilst under suspension.'

'So you bloody let her in?'

'Well I didn't want to leave her out in the corridor, did I?'

'Really, Steve?'

'I don't know why I let her in Allie, but I honestly had no intention of doing anything with her. When I told her that, she was obviously upset, and I let her stay and share the pizza I'd ordered. We didn't even have anything to drink. We chatted briefly about her investment strategy and she left. I promise you.'

'Why was she carrying a box from an S&M dating site when she left.'

'Yeah, well that *is* an interesting story.'

'You can see how I find it disconcerting though, Stephen?'

'When I first got sent off on leave, my boss sent me to an executive coach for some help *'finding myself'*, as they like to say. She encouraged me to start dating, so I went online and signed up at the highest rated site I could find. It turned out that the site catered for a fairly niche clientele. I didn't know this at the time. Nor did I know that the *'date box'* I ordered contained over five hundred pounds worth of bondage gear.'

'Shit Stephen, seriously?'

'Yes. Sorry Allie, I'm not as smart as you may think I am.'

'But why give it to Cindy? Why not just send it back?'

'They wouldn't accept the return because the items in the package had been unwrapped.'

'Were you trying it on, Steve?'

'No.'

'But then…'

'The stuff was opened by one of my colleagues, because the package was delivered to my office and wasn't labelled correctly. Apparently 'West' is a fairly common surname.'

'Oh god.'

'Yes. So it was opened, and photographed for posterity. The photographs were also carefully distributed amongst the entire staff contingent of the firm; lest anyone should miss out on the opportunity to have a laugh at my expense.'

'No!'

'Yes. So Cindy offered to take the kit off my hands, because her best mate is a professional dominatrix, and she thought that she'd be inclined to buy the stuff from me.'

'But…'

'I had the box of stuff out on the coffee table, so that I'd remember to get around to trying to sell it off.'

Alexa sighed deeply, and forced a smile. Although she was tearing up a little, and Stephen couldn't quite determine whether it was because she felt sorry for him, or because she was still upset.

'I have my own confession to make.'

'Well whatever it is, I'm sure it won't be worse than mine.'

'I know you're telling the truth Stephen.'

'How?'

'After speaking with the policeman outside the bakery this morning, I noticed that the door of your boss's car hadn't been closed properly, so I went to close it for you. I saw your phone lying under the pedals. You don't just drive around with your phone in the footwell all the time now, do you?'

Stephen couldn't help but chuckle, even though he wasn't really in the mood for jokes.

'No. I try not to.'

'I took the phone. I don't know why.'

'And?'

'You had a message from Cindy. Sorry, I didn't even want to see it, but it popped up on your lock screen, and I couldn't help reading it.'

She handed him the phone, and he opened the message.

'*Steve,*

Sorry for trying it on with you last night. I know you have a girlfriend, and I know I was way out of line. I feel absolutely terrible. Thank you for being a gentleman and not taking advantage of the situation. I promise I won't try anything again. Please don't think I'm a terrible person, I just had a moment of madness.'

He closed the phone and looked across at Alexa.

'Sorry Allie, I shouldn't have let her in. I can't blame you for the impression you got. Can we pretend it didn't happen?'

She burst out crying. But this time he could tell that they weren't tears of anger, or sadness.

'I love you, Alexa Harding.'

'I love you too, Mr West…'

Epilogue

In the months that followed, Stephen bought a beautiful cottage on the outskirts of Shere, bordering on one of the forests surrounding the area. It had a relatively large garden flat that he turned into an office and studio, and ample space to accommodate any friends and family who wanted to visit. It also had a state of the art kitchen that was large enough, and well equipped enough, for Alexa to be able to test some of her bakes at home, so she was suitably pleased with the arrangement.

She hadn't planned to move in with him so quickly, but by the time the transfer of the property went through, neither of them were willing to spend any evenings apart from one another, so it made sense for her to cancel her lease. Stephen even produced a spreadsheet, detailing the savings she'd make if she moved in with him, and despite the fact that she teased him mercilessly for trying to use a spreadsheet to entice her to live with him; it was far more romantic than it looked on paper, and she couldn't help being a little blown away by the gesture.

They invited Stephen's family to spend Christmas with them, and he used the opportunity to mend fences with both of his parents. He also took the time to get to know his niece and nephew a little better, which went over well with his brother and sister-in-law, and didn't escape Alexa's notice.

Given that both of his friends now lived within a few miles of one another, and despite his general antipathy for straying too far from the capital, Charlie bought a house in Guildford. He resigned himself to the fact that commuting to and from work every day was a price worth paying for being close to Stephen and Oliver.

More fundamentally, though, Jen and Amy wanted to live there, on account of the fact that they'd heard good reports about schools in the area. After getting engaged, they persisted with their plan to start a family, and both Karen and Alexa were nothing but encouraging in this regard. Jen was a software engineer, but she worked remotely, so she had no need to worry about a commute into the city. Amy was an accountant, and once they made the move, she left her position in London to start her own accounting practice closer to home.

Oliver ended up becoming a fantasy writer, and he commissioned Stephen to do the artwork on the cover of his first novel. Stephen refused to charge him for the pleasure, and told him that all he wanted was a signed copy of the first published edition. He managed to secure a contract with a small publishing house, and is hoping that the work takes off to the extent that he's able to make a modest living off of fantasy writing. Karen's convinced he'll become wildly successful. She secured yet another promotion, and is on track to take an even more senior position at the bank.

Alexa eventually forgave Cindy, and she allowed Stephen to help her try and win the bet she'd made with her father. Stephen helped her, but they still lost pretty convincingly. He insisted that this was due to the two month head start Sir Ashden had had, but was gracious in defeat. In any event, it was Cindy who had to forgo her planned sojourn in order to pay for the loss. That said, they'd done well enough that Ashden senior was impressed, and he stopped giving her a hard time about her career choice.

In a somewhat strange twist of fate, she ended up taking a liking to young Kenny, and they started seeing one another, casually. Nobody knew where it would end up going, but Kenny wasn't about to ask any questions, for fear he may put his foot in it, and scare her off.

Stephen got the distinct impression that the young man was convinced it wasn't really happening. Every time Stephen saw them together, it was as if Kenneth was willing himself not to wake up. Kenny was actually a very good looking young chap, and he was almost disconcertingly charming. Cindy was flattered, and he treated her like a princess, so he didn't really have anything to worry about.

Stephen stayed in touch with Jim, and followed through on his promise to help train some of the younger traders on various aggressive market strategies and practical approaches to some of the more complex trading scenarios. He also followed through on his threat to charge outlandish consulting fees for the pleasure.

He ended up making a lot more than he'd expected from his art. He wasn't likely to make anywhere near what he would have, had he continued climbing the ranks at Ashden, Cole & Roberts, but he didn't need to, and he didn't care.

In addition to drawing for Charles' company, he worked on various interesting projects and even started selling large works through a high-end art and antique dealing contact he'd made whilst working in the city.

Mary took Stephen up on his offer, and went to see Bridgette. She determined that she *did* love administration, but she just wasn't interested in the sort of administration she did at Ashden, Cole & Roberts, and she wanted more responsibility.

She ended up going to work for Charles, after the other board members at his company insisted that he take on an experienced personal assistant. He'd previously refused to hire anybody, and his administrative work was in such a state of disrepair, that even Mary battled to get it straightened out. Once she'd sorted it though, she quickly became bored, because it was far too easy for her.

Her boredom was short lived, because the company recognised her potential. They found a more junior assistant for Charles, and promoted Mary. They placed her in charge of managing the young esports stars that made up their various sponsored teams. It turned out that she had a gift for handling the affairs of these players, who were all between the ages of fifteen and twenty three, and all relatively hopeless at doing anything other than playing games. Mary was in her element, and it seemed that she was starting to become recognised as a valuable resource by the professional gaming fraternity. Far from being a simple baby-sitter, she was starting to forge a serious career as a manager.

Alexa was commissioned by Jen and Amy to make the biggest wedding cake she could imagine, and she was overjoyed by the fact that they allowed Charles to have his way, and go with a gaming theme. With Stephen's artistic input, she made an incredible dragon-themed cake, paying homage to the new expansion of the game. Charles and his design team were so impressed with it, that they posted pictures and videos of it all over the company's various social media platforms, and Alexa's little bakery became famous amongst the gaming fraternity almost instantly.

Shortly after the wedding, Stephen went back to Charlie's favourite jeweller in London and made his own exorbitantly priced purchase. He also hired a small flat in Nice for three weeks the following summer, and he was quietly optimistic about the prospect of being able to redistribute the asset while he was there.

-ENDNOTE-

1. Hi mate,

I thought it would be worth sending you a short glossary of common gaming terms to learn, so that you understand what's going on when people try to chat to you in the game using the text chat function. Making new friends is obviously part of the fun, and you need to have a basic understanding of these terms or people will think you're a noob (look up the meaning of that term below).

This doesn't include 'tactical terms' - I'll send those in a separate email. You'll notice that it's still rather long, although I've tried my best to stick to the absolute basics.

Just keep it on your tablet. I toyed with the idea of putting it in alphabetical order so that you could use it as a quick reference guide, but it ended up requiring too much cross-referencing that way. Besides, as far as I can recall, you're a very quick study.

I have, however, broken it down into groupings. First: the mostly non-game related things people will say to you for basic communication purposes while chatting; and second: references to game specific things.

The general terms that aren't necessarily game related

Irl or IRL - In real life (i.e. not in the game world). In case you're confused about the context of the conversation. Some players don't really acknowledge the existence of 'RL', so it's best to be sure.

AFK - Away From Keyboard. This is polite cover-all to tell the people you're chatting to that you aren't going to be looking at your screen for a while. That way, they won't think you're being rude when they send you a message to which you don't respond, and it's easier and less invasive than having to tell them that you're off to the loo. If you find it necessary to share your bowel movements though, you could use the term 'Bio break' (the 'bio' part standing for biological), so that the recipient of your message knows more or less exactly what you're up to.

BBL - Be back later. Because, apparently, sometimes AFK isn't specific enough.

BRB - Be right back. Again, because AFK doesn't really give an indication regarding the duration of your absence.

WB - Welcome back. When your friend returns from being AFK.

TY - Thank you - often the response to WB.

OMW - On my way! Not to be confused with 'Oh My Word' - I got this wrong for ages. I kept wondering why people always said Oh My Word whenever I asked them to meet up with my character for a quest or something. I started to get a complex about it until someone showed pity on me and explained what was going on.

IMHO - in my humble opinion. You'll notice that this seldom prefaces any remotely humble opinion. I don't think most gamers have humble opinions. They are more like passionate unchallengeable beliefs.

K or KK - because typing okay is clearly too difficult, and for some reason 'OK' isn't acceptable.

GG - Good Game. Basically - well done!

RNG - Random Number Generation. This is an algorithmic function that determines certain outcomes linked to random actions in games. The term is most often used to describe a situation which players deem unlucky, and not a result of player error or fault. It's usually accompanied by the prefix 'harsh', to lend a sympathetic tone.

Noob or N00B - a new or inexperienced player. The jury is still out on whether or not the term is truly derogatory. It probably is.

Guild - your 'in-game' family, as it were. Once you've been playing for a while, you can get invited to join a guild, which is basically a large group of players who share common interests. But most specifically, members of guilds tend to have common game-related goals. Some guilds are social, and some are serious. The social ones just form parties to run quests and dungeons in a casual and non-competitive manner. The serious ones are not like that… at all.

LFG - Looking for Group. This one's pretty self-explanatory. If you put it out there in the general chat channel that you're LFG, you may get an 'Inv' (invite). It's very satisfying when you get an inv, but more than a little heartbreaking when you don't. That's why it's best to be in a guild, because your fellow guild members will normally agree to join you on your quest, if only out of politeness. Indeed, they're also likely to have suffered the indignity of having their LFG request ignored at some point, so they know how it can feel.

Loc - Location. The exact coordinates of your character's position on the map in the game. Not your location IRL! If someone wants to know that, they'll probably say

'WYF' (where you from?), and it's probably best not to give them your real-life Loc, at least initially.

Pwn / Pwned (pronounced "Pone" or "Poned" as the context requires) - derived from the term 'own' or 'owned', probably due to the fact that the 'p' is so close to the 'o' on the keyboard that people kept pressing the wrong letter. It means destroyed or dominated in a way that was so impressive that the thing being 'pwned' didn't stand a chance.

<u>The Strictly Game-Related Stuff</u>

PC - Player controlled character. Not to be confused with the machine you are using to play the game. Again, nobody will explain this to you and you'll end up very confused if you keep assigning this meaning to it.

NPC - Non-Player Character. Any characters in the game that are controlled by the computer, but are not mobs. Normally, they give quests and/or sell things.

Mob - monster/bad guy. Technically (in programming terms) it means 'mobile object block' and refers to a computer controlled entity in the game. It just stuck, because it's easy to write.

Boss - a massive mob that takes many PC's to defeat. In the gaming world, you don't do as the bosses tell you... you just kill the bosses and take their stuff!

Elite - A mob who is more powerful than the usual mobs in the game. Like IRL, Elites like to spend time around bosses.

Dungeon or Instance - a specific closed environment in the game that can normally only be completed in groups. They will normally be populated by Elites, and will have multiple Bosses. IRL, like an executive corporate retreat - the difference being that you get to crash this one with your mates and kill all the bosses. If you go in on your own, the bosses and their lackeys will quickly overwhelm you.

PVE - Player vs Environment. Most common form of play in these sorts of games. It means you're playing against the computer and killing Mobs, as opposed to killing (or attempting to kill) other PC's.

PVP - Player vs Player. In most predominately PVE games, you can still elect to play against other players, either in specific areas of the game (which is a bit more civilised), or you can run around attacking other players in PVE areas that don't restrict it. Like the deadly digital equivalent of paintball.

Party - small group of PC's doing quests or running through dungeons together.

PUG - Pickup Group. For those times when you want to join a party that isn't made up of guild members. It's okay, it's not considered to be cheating on your guild... unless you enjoyed it more than playing in a guild group.

Solo - used as a verb to describe the act of playing the game by yourself (i.e. not in a party). This is also referred to as 'soloing'. It's perfectly acceptable to solo. Although if you solo too much, people may start to talk.

Grief - running around and killing other PC's just to cause them 'grief'. Don't do it. If you get known for that sort of behaviour (i.e. being a 'Griefer'), you won't end up being popular. At least not with the type of people you'd want to be popular with.

Cooldown - the time it takes for spells and abilities to become useable again after casting. Your character can't just keep casting spells and using abilities willy-nilly. These things take time, and require planning, and constant attention. Gone are the days of frantically clicking buttons repetitively without thought (also known as 'spamming'). It doesn't refer to someone cooling down after they've lost their cool in the game. Oddly, there isn't a term for that - but that's probably because it seldom happens (the cooling down, not the initial loss of the cool).

Level - reach a new experience level (i.e. level up). It's used as a verb - the noun is expressed simply as 'lvl'. There are no "game levels" in MMORPG's, like there were in old electronic games from the eighties and early nineties. Lvl is the numerically assigned level of your character, and 'level' refers to the process of 'levelling' (I.e. increasing your characters experience to attain higher power and status). I know it's difficult, but you'll get used to the fact that words don't necessarily carry the same meaning as they do IRL.

Exp or Xp - Experience points. This is an old one. You know it from old role playing computer games and Dungeons & Dragons. When you kill things and complete quests you get Exp and use it to level.

Leech - Stealing experience. Yes, apparently it's a thing. Some people follow others (or groups of others) and let them do the work, so that they can complete the quest quickly without having to do much. Since the point of the game is to do "the work" (I.e. play the game), I don't see how this is an issue. But what do I know?

Ding - the sound effect of gaining a lvl . Because your sound effect doesn't play on other players' computers, you need to announce the fact that you levelled by saying 'Ding' in the chat window. If you levelled and nobody heard about it... did it really happen? Perhaps not!

Grats - because typing congratulations is a pain. When someone you're playing with earns an achievement, or announces that they have 'Dinged', it's polite to say 'Grats'. If you get super lazy, you could just type Gz. If you ignore the achievement, the person who obtained it will spend the rest of the day obsessing over why that is the case, often becoming miserable and harbouring feelings of inadequacy.

Gear - the clothes and equipment that your character uses in the game. You get the gear by killing mobs, completing quests, or purchasing it from NPC's or other PC's. Basically, you play the game in order to get gear, so that you can defeat bigger bosses, which then give you better gear with which to defeat even bigger bosses. This happens until you've defeated the biggest boss, at which stage the new expansion of the game is released, with even bigger bosses. It sounds stupid on paper, but it's somehow addictive, and we prefer not to speak of it.

Farming - playing for the specific purpose of acquiring specific game items (normally used to craft gear). A lot like farming IRL really, but considerably more repetitive and mind-numbingly boring. Sometimes you have to do what you have to do, so to speak. The wolfskin cloak your character's after isn't *going to magically appear… well, it will… but only once you've killed enough wolf mobs in the game to get sufficient material for its creation. For some reason, it takes an unrealistically large number of wolves to create a relatively small cloak. IRL it would probably only take one or two, but in the game world, it's likely to take around one or two hundred!*

Grinding - Killing mobs for experience, or to gather resources, without being on a quest. Like farming, this can be painful - but it's sometimes necessary. Clearly, playing games is not always "all fun and games", as they say.

Alt - Alternative Character. Most players have a 'Main' which is their primary character in the game. Any other characters they have are referred to as 'Alts'. This is in case anyone thinks that you're a noob just because you're running around on a level five character with no gear (see below) - you can just tell everyone it's an Alt, and all will be forgiven.

Spawn - come into existence in a particular Loc. Mobs will spawn in pre-designated Locs on the map. When you kill them, they will 're-spawn' in the same Loc after a few minutes so that others can also kill them. This is a bit sad for the mob, but its the circle of life.

Res - to be 'resurrected' after your character gets killed by a mob, or after you accidentally (or purposefully) kill your character by allowing them to fall off a cliff; or a tall building; or out of a flying thing; or if you accidentally fall in lava, or trigger a deadly trap... you get the picture. For some sadistic reason, you need to take your character's ghost back from the nearest graveyard to the scene of your gruesome end in order to res. This presents an interesting difficulty if you fell off a cliff, because you'll have to let your ghost do the same, and when you come back to life you'll have to figure out how to get back up the mountain again. So watch out, this exercise is not fun. If you die in a fight, you can ask one of your team members to 'res' you (if they have the spell), so you don't have to go all the way back to the graveyard.

Ragequit - when something happens in a dungeon that you aren't happy with (normally as a result of an innocent mistake made by another party member), so you behave like a spoilt child and leave the party. It is not normally the player who is allegedly at fault that leaves, it's the spoiled brat who is supposedly aggrieved by the waste of time occasioned by the mistake.

Wipe - when your whole party or raid group dies during an encounter (normally in a dungeon). In social (or casual) guilds this is something to laugh about. It is not good form to try and assign blame to any specific party members. In some dysfunctional guilds, but most often in PUGS, it's a shit-show of recrimination and vicious insults, often followed by ragequits.

So those are most of the basic terms. I'm sure many more will crop up while you're playing, but I think that what I've outlined above is more than enough to be getting on with.

Acknowledgement

Before traversing the business of thanking those who deserve acknowledgement for their invaluable assistance with this book, I would like to thank my readers for taking the plunge and buying a title by a new author who was brazen enough to publish something without representation, and without a traditional publishing deal. Although I believe in the story and the way in which I tell it, I have no objective way of knowing whether or not this belief is remotely well founded.

Your support and willingness to take a chance on reading what I worked on so assiduously, fills me with warmth and gratitude. Any success I enjoy as a result of my endeavours is attributable to those who read and appreciate my work.

On to the business of thanking those more directly involved in the process of bringing this story to life. I feel as though I'm only a small cog in the wheel that carried the book from a figment of my overactive imagination to a fully developed novel.

Many storytellers are in the habit of leaving mention of the most important of their contributors until the bitter end of their acknowledgements, presumably on account of their proclivity to build tension.

But I'm a little different, so I would like to begin by thanking my incredible wife, Sharon Small, without whom this book would not have happened. She not only supported me financially and emotionally for the entire time it took me to produce the novel, but she took on the arduous job of being both a copy and proof editor from day one. She consequently had to put up with me being irrationally defensive about the very important changes she suggested from time to time, and had to endure hours of debate and frustration over parts of the story on which we didn't automatically agree. I won't pretend that I was a pleasure to deal with, although in my defence, she'll have to concede that I followed her direction in almost every instance. I'm exceedingly glad that I did. Insofar as this book was a team effort, she was by far my most influential and valuable teammate.

I'm inordinately grateful to the incredibly incisive and accomplished Anastasia Parkes, who, pursuant to her mandate from the immensely talented team at Jericho Writers in Oxford, assessed the very first iteration of the completed story, and tore it to shreds in the most diplomatic and pleasant fashion I could have imagined. Following her guidance and terrifyingly astute observations about its various shortcomings, I ended up rewriting it from the ground up and doubling it in length, whilst attempting to retain the elements she considered to be worth saving. Although she didn't have sight of the revised product before publication, I sincerely hope that she approves.

When it comes to thanking my impossibly talented cousin, Brittany Small, who illustrated the cover art for the book, I'm at a loss for words (well… almost). After some dodgy experiments with poorly chosen stock cover art, which were received by my sister-in-law, sister, and brother-in-law, Kyle, with what could only be described as unbridled hostility, Brittany very kindly offered to step in and design the thing herself. It was fascinating for me to learn how a real professional artist goes about designing book covers, and I soon realised that I'd struck gold. Brittany instantly understood what I was thinking, without me having to put it into words for her - which was incredibly handy in the circumstances - because despite the fact that I try to make a living by expressing ideas, I didn't quite know how to express my idea for an appropriate cover. All I can say is 'wow'.

Although I spent many years in practice as a lawyer, and fancied myself as somebody who understood the various ins and outs of the financial world, I was being unduly optimistic. Fortunately though, I have some good friends who really *do* know what they're talking about. I have to extend a heartfelt thanks to Jonathan Van Rooyen, who very kindly went over my initial treatment of the fundamentals of short trading, and gave me such strong and meaningful advice, that I was able to bring far more of my protagonist's story to life than I'd originally anticipated. Any mistakes or inconsistencies which may crop up in the final text regarding the trading or legal aspects of the story are attributable to the creative license I took with them, and are solely my own.

Given that I couldn't expect my long-suffering wife to read the story a fifth time, I ended up foisting the penultimate manuscript on her sister, Debby Szilagyi. My wonderfully frank and open-minded sister-in-law was an obvious choice for this job, because she reads extensively in the genre and she's incapable of not speaking her mind. She suggested some significant structural changes that worried me at first glance, but that ended up adding value to the pace and presentation of the story. I'm incredibly grateful for her input in this respect.

My own sister, Claire, had her part to play in a different and somewhat surprising way. Whilst it's almost certainly true that, in objective terms, writers benefit more from critics than they do from irrationally biased fans during the writing process, it's these fans that help up gather the courage to take our stories all the way to publication. Albeit that Claire was perhaps my harshest critic whilst we were growing up, she's become the biggest fan of my writing, and that fills me with the sort of joy that's difficult to describe. Giving her anything of mine to read (even the odd email), inevitably results in a barrage of effusive compliments that never fail to make me feel that my efforts are worthwhile, and pick me up when I'm suffering from the sort of lonely despair that plagues most writers from time to time.

Last, but by no means least, I would like to thank my daughter, Katherine. I imagine it must have been almost intolerably difficult for someone of her age to accept that although I was physically present whilst working on this project, I was perpetually unavailable, and became increasingly agitated whenever she attempted to divert my attention. To make matters worse, she was forced to accept that the content of the story I was writing wasn't age appropriate for her - so I know she felt particularly left out. I can only thank her for a exercising a level of patience exceeding that which any parent could reasonably expect in the circumstances, and promise to finish off the two manuscripts of the children's books she inspired me to write.

About the Author

Jonathan is a qualified lawyer with both bachelor's and master's degrees in law. After running a successful legal practice for many years, he decided to leave the legal profession and follow his passion for writing on a full-time basis. He likes writing across many genres, and is specifically interested in stories containing liberal doses of humour. He lives on a farm in the Surrey Hills with his wife and young daughter… and their two cats.

You can access his website at: **www.jonathansmallauthor.com** to find out more about his upcoming titles and join his mailing list.

Printed in Poland
by Amazon Fulfillment
Poland Sp. z o.o., Wrocław
07 June 2022

4b020007-a66a-4a0d-911e-6cfa9c3ab77cR01